About the Authors

Robyn Grady has sold millions of books worldwide, and features regularly on bestsellers lists and at award ceremonies, including The National Readers Choice, The Booksellers Best and Australia's prestigious Romantic Book of the Year. When she's not tapping out her next story, she enjoys the challenge of raising three very different daughters as well as dreaming about shooting the breeze with Stephen King during a month-long Mediterranean cruise. Contact her at www.robyngrady.com

Since her first venture into novel writing in the mid-nineties, **Kristi Gold** has greatly enjoyed weaving stories of love and commitment. She's an avid fan of baseball, beaches and bridal reality shows. During her career, Kristi has been a National Readers Choice winner, Romantic Times award winner, and a three-time Romance Writers of America RITA finalist. She resides in Central Texas and can be reached through her website at http://kristigold.com

A typical Piscean, award winning *USA Today!* bestselling author, **Yvonne Lindsay**, has always preferred the stories in her head to the real world. Which makes sense since she was born in Middle Earth. Married to her blind date sweetheart and with two adult children, she spends her days crafting the stories of her heart and in her spare time she can be found with her nose firmly in someone else's book.

Dynasties

Dynasties:
The Lassiters

ROBYN GRADY

KRISTI GOLD

YVONNE LINDSAY

MILLS & BOON

First Published in Great Britain 2020
By Mills & Boon, an imprint of HarperCollins*Publishers*
1 London Bridge Street, London, SE1 9GF

DYNASTIES: THE LASSITERS © 2020 Harlequin Books S.A.

Taming the Takeover Tycoon © 2014 by Harlequin Books S.A.
From Single Mum to Secret Heiress © 2014 by Harlequin Books S.A.
Expecting the CEO's Child © 2014 by Harlequin Books S.A.

Special thanks and acknowledgement are given to Robyn Grady, Kristi Gold and Yvonne Lindsay for their contribution to the *Dynasties: The Lassiters* series.

ISBN: 978-0-263-28139-2

MIX
Paper from
responsible sources
FSC™ C007454

This book is produced from independently certified FSC™ paper to ensure responsible forest management.

For more information visit: www.harpercollins.co.uk/green

Printed and bound in Spain
by CPI, Barcelona

TAMING THE
TAKEOVER TYCOON

ROBYN GRADY

One

The Robin Hoods of this world were Becca's heroes. As she watched Jack Reed strike a noble pose then draw back and release an arrow that hit dead center of his target, the irony wasn't lost on her.

Jack Reed was no Robin Hood. He was anathema to everything she stood for. To every living, breathing thing she believed in. Beyond all else, people ought to give back—even sacrifice—to support others who need help. Some mistook that level of compassion for weakness, but Becca was far from easy prey.

Looking *GQ*-hot in jeans and a white button-down, cuffs folded back on strong forearms, Reed lowered the bow and focused on his guest. The slant of his mouth was so subtle and self-assured, Becca's palm itched to slap the smirk off his face. She might have done it, too, if she thought it'd shake him up some. But it was said displays of true emotion only amused him.

Jack Reed owned a property in his hometown of Cheyenne, Wyoming, as well as two residences here in L.A.: an ultramodern penthouse apartment in a downtown high-rise building that he'd purchased as well as this spectacular Beverly Hills estate. With a quiver slung across his broad back, he sauntered over the manicured lawn to meet her. Although he was expecting her visit, Becca doubted he would welcome what she had to say.

She introduced herself. "Becca Stevens, director of the Lassiter Charity Foundation." She nodded at the target. "A perfect bull's-eye. Well done."

"I took up archery in college," he said in a voice so deep and darkly honeyed, the tone was almost hypnotic. "I try to squeeze some practice in every week."

"Difficult with your schedule, I imagine." All that dismantling of companies and banking the proceeds had to take up oodles of time. "I appreciate you seeing me."

His smile, designed to disarm, got bigger. "Any friend of J.D.'s is a friend of mine."

"If J. D. Lassiter were alive, he might not count *you* as a friend at the moment."

The smile widened more. "Straight for the jugular, Ms. Stevens?"

Given Jack Reed was a highly successful corporate raider, he ought to be used to the approach. "I thought you'd appreciate it."

"I only want to help Angelica Lassiter reclaim what she rightly deserves."

Becca let out a humorless laugh and then sighed. "Ah, sorry. Just the idea of someone like you being in any way self-sacrificing…"

His gaze sharpened. "Angelica was J.D.'s only child."

"You're forgetting Sage and Dylan."

"They are Ellie Lassiter's orphaned nephews, adopted after J.D. and Ellie had been told by doctors—"

"I know the background, Jack."

"Then you'll also know that Angelica, J.D.'s own flesh and blood, was his favorite—that he'd entrusted her with the running of Lassiter Media those crucial months before his death. It makes no sense that his will should insult her with a paltry ten percent while controlling voting interest of J.D.'s multibillion-dollar company goes to Angelica's ex-fiancé—" Jack paused for effect "—even if J.D. had handpicked Evan McCain for his daughter."

"J.D. might have liked Evan for a son-in-law. No one would argue he has remarkable business sense." Becca joined Jack as he headed off toward his target. "But Angelica trusted Evan. They fell in love."

"Betrayed by the man she was ready to marry. Tragic, wouldn't you say?"

Oh, please. "Evan had nothing to do with J.D.'s will."

"Maybe. Maybe not. But nothing stops him from re-instating to Angelica what should be hers now. He could do the decent thing by the woman he professes to love." Jack's lips twitched. "I don't know how he sleeps at night."

An image flashed into Becca's mind—Jack Reed lying butt naked on a rumpled sheet, fingers thatched behind his head, an unmistakable thirst reflecting in the depths of his glittering onyx eyes. Nerve endings ignited and flashed over her skin. The tingle raced through to her core, all the way down to her toes.

Reed was an attractive man; she would go so far as to say he was exceptional. If half of what the tabloids published was true, hoards of women had surrendered to the drugging heat she felt radiating off him now. The effect was gripping—beguiling—and, in Becca's case, about as welcome as boiling water on a third-degree burn.

As they continued to walk, she tried to stay focused.

"I'm here to implore you, in J.D.'s memory, to show some human decency. Walk away from this. After her father's death, Angelica's in no shape to link arms with the likes of you."

"Don't underestimate Angelica." His classically chiseled profile hardened as his chin lifted a notch. "She's stronger than you think."

"Right now, she's desperate."

He laughed, a somehow soothing and yet cynical sound. "You don't beat around the bush, do you, Becca?"

No time. "You own an interest in Lassiter Media and rumors are rife. People are bracing for a hostile takeover bid. The charity's donations are down. Regular beneficiaries are actually looking at other options. Want to guess why?"

"I'm sure you'll tell me."

Damn right she would. "The name Jack Reed means trouble—the kind of trouble clear-minded people run a mile to avoid."

He blinked slowly and grinned as if the description was something to savor. "As long as Angelica wants my help, I'll give it."

"You sought her out," she reminded him, "not the other way around."

"Your point?"

Her heart was pounding in her ears. No one wanted to make an enemy of this man, but Becca had a principle to defend. A fight to win. Hell, she'd faced worse situations than this and survived.

"I know what you're up to," she said as they neared the target, "even if Angelica can't or won't face the truth. After you've used her to gain majority control over Lassiter Media interests, you'll aim the next arrow at her back. You'll sell off Lassiter assets like you have with every other company you've acquired."

"Got it. I wear the black hat."

"Simple, isn't it?"

"If only."

Lord above, how she wanted to shake this man. "Seriously, how much money does one person need? Is this worth betraying your friend's memory? J.D.'s family?"

"This is not about money."

"With you, it's always about money."

His jaw flexed as he stopped in front of the target and freed the arrow.

"I understand your desire to help, but Angelica and I have this covered. And make no mistake." His uncompromising gaze pierced hers. "We intend to win."

Becca's focus shifted from the steely message in his eyes to the arrow's bright red feathers, the shaft's long straight line and finally the weapon's potentially lethal head. Then she thought of this man's lack of empathy—his obsession with self-enrichment. How could this superb body harbor such a depraved soul? How could Jack Reed live with himself?

Becca took the arrow from his hand, broke the shaft over a knee and, shaking inside, strode away.

Jack watched Becca Stevens's spectacular behind as she marched off in a fiery temper and had to smile.

When Becca had contacted his office hoping to meet, instinct had said to shake her off. If ever Jack set his sights on a target, he committed to that goal two hundred percent. No one and nothing would sway him. In certain circles, the term pathological was used to describe his drive.

No offense taken.

The same circles might suggest that his reasons for meeting Becca today had been selfish. That it was probable to very likely he would take advantage of his position in this Lassiter standoff for personal gain. And where Becca was concerned, Jack did mean personal.

As she disappeared over the rise, he smiled again.

What a woman.

His cell phone rang. Jack checked out the caller I.D. and, toeing Ms. Stevens's broken arrow aside, connected. "Logan. What've you got?"

"Just making sure we're still on track."

Coming from humble beginnings, Logan Whittaker had worked hard to build a successful career. As a partner at Drake, Alcott and Whittaker Attorneys based in downtown Cheyenne, Wyoming, Logan had looked after J. D. Lassiter's affairs, including the execution of J.D.'s last will and testament. The document had cast some challenges Logan's way. Some unanticipated rewards, as well. Through work associated with settling the will's terms, he had found his future wife.

"I've spoken with Angelica Lassiter again this morning," Jack said. "She's still going forward."

"You're sure about that? I've told Angelica more than once the will is airtight. J.D. was in his right mind when he drafted the terms. With majority voting interest, Evan McCain will remain chairman and CEO of Lassiter Media no matter how many punches she wants to throw. I thought she was finally coming around, listening to reason."

Jack headed back toward the shooting line. "Sure, she has reservations. Her father was a huge influence on her life. Even with him gone, it goes against the grain to disappoint him and battle that will. But her heart and soul are in that company, Logan. She has J.D.'s stubborn streak as well as his keen bent for business."

"How hard will you push her?"

"This isn't my first rodeo." When the attorney audibly exhaled, Jack wasn't fazed. "You're acting under strict instruction here."

"I'm aware of my obligations, damn it. This still leaves a god-awful taste in my mouth."

That all came with the territory…with being obligated, no matter what.

"No one said you had to like it," Jack said.

Logan huffed. "You're one hard-nosed son of a bitch, you know that?"

"That from a corporate lawyer." *Funny.*

As Jack reached back to draw an arrow from his quiver, Logan asked, "How did your meeting with Becca Stevens play out?"

Logan was aware of Becca's phone call and today's arrangements.

"She might run Lassiter Charity Foundation," Jack said, "but Becca is no Mother Teresa. She put on her boxing gloves and told me to back the hell away."

"Did you toss her off your property?"

Remembering the fire blazing in those beautiful green eyes, Jack held the phone between his ear and shoulder as he slotted the arrow's notch against his bow's string. "I would've asked her to stay for lunch if I thought she wouldn't try to run a butter knife through my heart."

"Will she be a problem?"

"Lord, I hope so."

Logan groaned. "For God's sakes, Jack. Tell me you plan to keep your pants on here."

"After the way you mixed Lassiter business up with pleasure, you're in no position to lecture."

When J.D. had bequeathed five million big ones to a mystery woman who didn't want to be found, Logan had not only tracked her down, damned if he hadn't taken her to bed, and more than once. Talk about calling the kettle black.

"I won't deny certain lines got blurred," Logan admitted. "But I fell in love with Hannah Armstrong and married her. I'll hand my resignation in to the bar the day anything approaching marriage enters your head."

Jack laughed. What an idea.

After the men disconnected, Jack resumed his stand behind the shooting line. He drew back the arrow and, enjoying the tension of the bowstring as he took aim, thought of Becca Stevens—the undisguised malice in her eyes, the sweeping conviction of her words. Then he imagined how darn good she would feel folded in his arms...how sweet her smooth, scented skin would taste beneath his lips. In his mind, Jack heard her whimper his name and then cry out as he sank into her again and again.

Jack released his shot and then shaded his brow to measure the result. When was the last time he'd missed a target's center gold ring? This arrow had sailed clean over the top.

Felicity Sinclair's blue eyes sparkled as she shifted her chair closer to the café table and lowered her voice. "Becca, I have something I need to ask."

"About Lassiter Media?"

As Lassiter Media's recently promoted vice president of public relations, Fee was always brimming with ideas. Since Becca's appointment with the Lassiter Charity Foundation two years ago, the women had worked closely. More than that—they'd become good friends, the kind who shared everything, during good times as well as bad.

Winding golden-blond hair behind a dainty ear, Fee explained, "My question has to do with Chance Lassiter."

"That would be your *fiancé* Chance Lassiter," Becca teased.

As Fee reached over to grip her friend's hand, the magnificent diamond on her third finger threw back light slanting in through the window.

"You were there when I needed to vent about that mess last month," she said. "I have to say, it feels a little strange calling Cheyenne home. I love L.A...."

"Well, you're here now. You'll simply have to visit often." Becca squeezed her hand. "Promise?"

"And you promise to drop in on us at the Big Blue."

"I'll bring my Stetson."

Chance Lassiter was J.D.'s nephew, the son of the billionaire's deceased younger brother, Charles. Chance had managed his uncle's world-famous cattle ranch—the Big Blue—and while he'd been rocked by J.D.'s unexpected death, he'd gladly accepted, via his uncle's will, controlling interest in the ranch he loved more than anything...although now, of course, his vivacious wife-to-be had taken pride of place in the charming cowboy's heart.

Fee sat back. "I can hardly wait for the wedding. Which brings me back to that question. Becca, would you be a bridesmaid?"

Emotion prickled behind Becca's eyes. Fee would make a *stunning* bride and, given her talent for organizing grand occasions, the ceremony was bound to be nothing short of amazing. Becca was even a little envious.

Marriage and starting a family were nowhere near a priority, but one day Becca hoped to find Mr. Right—a kindred spirit who got off on giving back and paying forward. This minute, however, all her energies were centered on helping the foundation survive the storm J.D.'s unexpected death and will had left behind.

Of course, there was *always* room for the wonderful women in her life and their very special requests.

Becca hugged her friend. "Fee, I would be honored to be a bridesmaid at your wedding."

The women discussed styles for dresses as well as flowers for bouquets before the conversation turned to a far less pleasant topic.

As coffees arrived, Fee asked, "Have you spoken with Jack Reed yet?"

Suddenly feeling queasy, Becca nodded. Fee knew that she had hoped to get in Jack's ear.

"The backyard of his Beverly Hills mansion houses an Olympic-standard archery field."

Fee's lip curled. "Your regular Robin Hood."

"The joke of the decade, right?" Becca pulled her decaf closer. "I let him know how his association with Angelica is weighing on Lassiter Media, not least of all the foundation. A lot of the funding comes from Lassiter accounts, but other benefactors are shutting doors in our face. While the notorious Jack Reed has a chance of pulling off a takeover bid and then tearing everything apart, we might as well have leprosy."

Fee flinched. "Jack does have a reputation."

Huge understatement. "He's the most ruthless corporate raider this country has given breath to. I hate to think of how quickly he'd chop up the company and sell off the pieces if he had a chance. He doesn't give a flying fig where or how the foundation ends up." Becca held her stomach when it churned again. "He's a scourge on mankind."

"You have to admit though..." Fee lifted her cup to her lips. "He is charismatic."

"If you can call a snake charismatic."

"And incredibly good-looking."

Becca huffed—and then gave it up. "Sure. The guy is hot, in a Jay Gatsby kind of way."

"Gatsby was gorgeous."

"Gatsby was a crook."

"Sweetie, let's face it. Jack Reed is *smoking.*"

Becca's stomach pitched again. "I was taught that power should be used for good. If you have brains and position, for God's sake, help those less fortunate—even a *little* bit."

"Good luck convincing Jack Reed of that."

"Greed." Becca shuddered. "It's a disease." When the waitress delivered their coffees, she pointed to an item on the menu. "Can I have a caramel fudge brownie, please?"

As the waitress made a note and walked away, Fee studied her friend curiously. "Since when do you have a sweet tooth?"

"In school I was always the chubby kid who tried to get out of gym. If ever I felt anxious—upset—I'd reach for cake or candy."

Then she'd joined the Peace Corps and all that had changed. Her life had taken its sharpest turn yet.

Fee set her cup down. "Well, you're the poster girl for svelte now."

"That craving for sweet stuff doesn't win too often anymore. Don't worry," Becca said as the waitress delivered the brownie. "I'll fit into my bridesmaid's dress."

"I wouldn't care if you were a size two or a twenty." Fee had an awesome athletic build but she didn't judge any book by its cover. "I just hate to see you this rattled."

Becca bit into the brownie. As chocolate crumbs fell apart on her tongue, she almost sighed. She tried not to indulge; so many in this world did without. But, dear God, this was good.

"I believe in the foundation," she said, sucking caramel off a thumb. "I believe in the work it does. Do you know how much we've helped with homeless services, with youth camps, with disaster relief?"

When she slid over the plate to share, Fee broke off a corner of the brownie.

"Your team does an incredible job," Fee said and popped it in her mouth.

"And everyone on my staff wants to keep doing our job—raising funds, making a difference—one person and family at a time."

Fee's mouth twisted. "Unfortunately, it's not your company."

At the moment Lassiter Media was at the center of a tug-of-war primarily between Evan and Angelica, two people who ought to be working, and living, together, not pulling each other apart.

"J.D. couldn't have wanted this dissention within the family when he drew up his will."

"Given their connection," Fee added, "how hard she worked in the company the months before her father's death, I don't get how he left Angelica so little. It doesn't make sense."

Becca broke off more brownie and mulled as she chewed. "John Douglas Lassiter was a smart man," she reflected. "A good man with a big heart. The foundation was way more than a tax dodge to J.D. I *have* to believe he had a good reason for the way his will was arranged."

"He must have known Angelica would fight."

"Even her brothers are against her now." At first, Angelica's siblings had supported her attempts to find ways to challenge the will. No longer. "No one is left on her side."

"No one except Jack the Slasher Reed."

"For everyone's sakes, I hope she gives it up soon, before any more damage is done." To the family as well as the company, including the foundation.

"With Jack Reed egging her on, don't hold your breath."

An image formed in Becca's mind…Jack Reed with a quiver slung over his back. He looked so arrogant. So flat-out sexy and self-serving. Becca growled. "It all comes back to Jack."

"You're not finished with him, are you?"

"I can't give up." Becca pushed the plate aside. "I'm not made that way."

Fee sighed. "Problem is Jack Reed's not made that way, either."

Two

Jack waited until the end of the week and then buckled.

Dusting off a tux, he organized a ticket for the Lassiter Charity Foundation gala ball. By the time he'd finished at the office and then showered and drove over, he was unfashionably late. The keynote speaker had long since finished entertaining and educating the glittering crowd. Desserts had been served and suitable music wafted around the ballroom, coaxing couples onto a dance floor that sprawled beneath prisms of light cast by a spectacular Swarovski chandelier.

As he headed toward the VIP tables, Becca Stevens noticed him. Mild surprise registered on her face before she turned in her chair to gauge his approach. Loose, salon-tousled curls mantled her shoulders. Her ears and throat were free of jewels. Sitting proud and erect in a white strapless gown that accentuated her curves and teased the imagination, she gave an impression that lay somewhere between temptress and saint. When Jack stopped before her, she looked up at all six-plus feet of him and arched a brow.

"Did you notice?" she asked.

"That you look exquisite tonight?"

Her narrowing gaze sent a warning. *Don't flirt.*

"When you walked into the room," she explained, "people stopped talking. I think a lot stopped breathing. They don't expect to see you at a charity night. Although in this case they might—given it's a Lassiter Media event."

"Because I'm the big bad wolf here to gobble up everything I can sink my fangs into and then spit out the bones."

She shrugged a bare shoulder. "Not to put too fine of a point on it."

"Would it surprise you to know that I give to charity?"

"The Jack Reed Foundation for Chronic Self-Indulgence?"

He rubbed a corner of his grin. "You're cute, you know that?"

"Wait till I get started."

The only other couple left at the table was engrossed in a private conversation. If the room had indeed been distracted by his appearance, the socialites and Fortune 500 reps were back to mingling as far as Jack could tell.

He took the vacant seat next to Becca's. "When I donate, I do it anonymously."

Becca brought a glass of water to her lips. "How convenient."

"It's your job to blow this foundation's bugle. How much you give away, how much you help the disadvantaged. Publicity equals exposure, equals a greater chance of raising even more funds and getting the money to those who need it."

As the music swelled and lights dimmed more, he leaned closer and caught the scent of her perfume—a hint of red apple, feminine. Way too sexy for her own good—at least where he was concerned.

"But tell me," he went on, "if you had as much personal wealth as I do, would you need to go around bleating to everyone how generous you were?"

"I will never have that much personal wealth. Don't want it. Don't need it. I'm nothing like you. Not in any way, shape or form." When his gaze dropped to skim her lips, she frowned slightly before pushing to her feet. "Don't even think about going there."

No denying he was attracted to Becca Stevens. He had wanted to tip closer, sample those lips, invite her to help fuel the spark. If he wasn't mistaken—and Jack was rarely wrong—there was a part of Becca that wanted that, too.

"Am I that obvious?" he asked, getting to his feet.

"You're ridiculously easy to read."

"In certain things."

"I'll give you a list. Tell me what I'm missing."

As waiters served coffee, Jack crossed his arms. "Go ahead."

"You have an insatiable thirst for money. Correction. For *power*. You like expensive toys. Jets and yachts and prestige cars. You enjoy beautiful women hanging off your arm, the more the merrier. Above all else, you love calling the shots. Being the king of your cancerous castle."

Jack frowned.

Ouch.

"I like being the boss," he said. "So do all CEOs. So did J.D."

"You're missing my point. And, sorry, but you're not in J.D.'s league."

"He might argue with you on that."

Her look was almost pitying. "Modesty is so not your strong suit."

"Perhaps you'd care to find out what is."

"You know, for a smart guy, you just don't get it."

When she breezed out of the room, Jack followed her onto the terrace. He found her standing by a railing, facing a twinkling downtown view. A breeze caught a layer of her gown's skirt; gossamer-thin fabric billowed out, ruffling behind her like filmy wings.

As he headed over, she tossed him an annoyed glance before gripping the railing like she wanted to wring someone's neck. "You can't take a hint, can you?"

"Let's not play that kind of game," he drawled. "You wanted me to follow. You're just not sure how to handle things now that I have."

She faced him. "I'm passionate about my work at the foundation. More passionate than I've felt about anything before in my life, and that's saying something."

"It's how a person uses her passion that counts."

"How about for good rather than evil?"

Most people thought of Jack Reed that way. Evil incarnate. Difference was that Becca wasn't afraid to tell him point-blank.

Hell, she was right. Everyone was. If he could get his paws on Lassiter Media, if he could truly sink his teeth into a vein, he wouldn't let go until he'd drained it all. That was his profession. What he did best.

But with Becca Stevens looking at him as if malevolence might be contagious, for just a second Jack almost hoped he wouldn't get the chance. A part of him actually wanted to let this colossal Lassiter Media opportunity slide off into the water.

Of course, that wasn't possible. Wasn't—*sane.* Neither was continuing to annoy poor Ms. Stevens. It wasn't her fault she was caught up in this fight, any more than Jack could help the part he had to play.

"It's time my black cape and I flapped away before the

first hint of dawn turns us into dust." He affected a bow. "Good night, Becca."

She caught up with him at the entrance back into the ballroom, slotting herself between his chest and the door. Jack didn't know whether to smile and relax or frisk her for a wooden stake.

"What if I show you how serious I am?" she said. "I'll prove to you how much good this foundation does. Have you ever visited homeless shelters, soup kitchens? If you see firsthand, you'd have to understand. You can't be *that* big of a monster...can you?"

"You mean it's possible I might have human emotions after all?"

When she allowed a small smile, Jack grinned, too. "Give me a month," she said, "and I'll change your mind."

"Change my mind about what?"

"About dismantling Lassiter Media's assets."

Interesting. "You think Angelica and I can win?"

Becca lifted her chin. "Four weeks."

"One day."

"One week."

"On one condition."

"Name it."

What the hell. "I'd rather show you."

He slid a hand around her waist and drew her in as his mouth dropped over hers.

She went stiff against him. Hands balled into fists against his chest. He waited for her to tear away and call him every name under the sun. Short of her scratching his eyes out, Jack figured it was worth it.

Instead, her fists melted and palms slowly spread before her fingers knotted, winding into his jacket lapels. Then, making a strangled sound in her throat, she pressed in plumb against him. Jack relaxed into it, too.

As his palm on her back tugged her closer, his other

hand slipped beneath the curls at the warm base of her neck. Gradually her lips parted under his. Kneading her nape, he tilted his head at more of an angle at the same time the tip of his tongue slid by her teeth.

She stiffened again and this time broke away. Short of breath, eyes wild, she wiped her mouth on her arm. Then she called him a name Jack had been called more than once but never by a lady.

"What was *that* supposed to be?"

Jack ran a hand back through his hair. "You tell me."

She siphoned down air, half composed herself. "Fine," she said. "I will. That was a mistake. A big fat *never again*."

"Unless you decide you want to."

She stabbed a finger at his nose. "You repulse me."

"Do you want to hear my condition or not?"

Puzzled, she blinked twice. "Condition?"

"To give you one week to change my mind."

Her throat bobbed as she swallowed and pushed curls back from her brow. "Oh. Right."

"My condition is that we are civil toward each other."

She muttered, "Figures that would be your idea of civil."

It wasn't the time to mention that she had kissed him right back.

"Do we have an agreement?" Jack hesitated and then ribbed her anyway. "Or are you afraid you might find my dark charm irresistible?"

Her slim nostrils flared. "I'd sooner sell my soul to the devil."

"Be careful what you wish for." Jack pulled open the door and noise from the ballroom seeped out. "I'll collect you from your office Monday, ten a.m. sharp."

"I'll arrange my own transport. I'll meet you—"

"Uh-uh. I make the rules. The challenge for you now is to change the game."

"Using any means available?"

Jack smiled into her spirited green gaze. "What an appealing thought."

Three

Early Monday, as Jack finished up his first call of the working week, the vice president of Reed Incorporated crossed over to his desk. A financial dynamo with a killer background in trading, Sylvia Morse set her hands on her hips.

"What exactly are you doing?"

Sylvia had been standing inside his office door for the past few minutes, so, trick question?

"What do you mean what am I doing?" Jack asked.

"I want the lowdown. No B.S. Not to me. You just got off the phone from Angelica Lassiter—*again*. You've moved mountains to acquire every Lassiter Media share you can lay your hands on. You'd do anything to get a hold of hers."

Sylvia's brunette razor-cut looked somehow spikier today, and her normally light gray gaze was definitely darker. He almost asked whether her caffeine addiction had escalated to substances that caused memory loss or confusion, but then Jack remembered her brother was in rehab again and went with the direct approach instead.

He set down his pen. "What the hell is up with you this morning?"

"You're in bed with Angelica Lassiter," Sylvia went on, "to help her regain control of J.D.'s company."

"Metaphorically speaking, absolutely."

"And?"

"Sylvia, you've been my right hand here for five years. Nothing's changed."

"So, you intend to buy up, buy in and then put into play the most efficient, financially rewarding way to sell off the various pieces of Lassiter Media. Except that isn't Angelica Lassiter's plan."

Jack slumped. *Et tu, Sylvia?* "I thought our moral compasses were in sync."

"This is different."

"It's never different." He picked up the pen, put his head down. "Trust me."

"God knows I want to, but something's missing. Unless you're more ruthless than even I thought, and I know you pretty well."

"Better than anyone."

"I'm on your side, Jackie-boy. Always. But, while you'd never admit it publicly, even you must have limits. J. D. Lassiter was a friend. You'd call in on each other's homes in Cheyenne. I thought that kind of relationship would put a spin on things."

"You thought wrong."

"So, feelings never get in the way of business."

Jack got to his feet. "Feelings don't get in the way of anything. Period."

He moved to a nearby credenza. Last week, he'd been sorting through a spread of figures on a boat company he was keen to acquire. Easy money—or it would be in a few months after he'd taken over and maximized the various resources.

"I value your work," Jack told Sylvia, thumbing through the top pages of Baldwin Boats' annual financials. "I value *you*. But if ever you decide you want to, you know—move on—I'd only ever wish you well."

"Where in blazes would you ever find another me?"

Jack returned her mocking grin. "Wouldn't be easy." Then it clicked. "Oh, okay. Sure. I get what this is about."

Her face opened up. "You do?"

"You've been working day and night on the Lassiter deal. Crazy hours. Follows you want a bigger cut when the demolition ball starts swinging."

The intensity in her gaze deepened again before her expression eased and a crooked smile appeared. "Guess you are as big a hard-ass as they say." She crossed over, scanned a spreadsheet. "Baldwin Boats."

Pushing the prickly issue of Lassiter Media aside, Jack nodded. "I'm ready to move on it."

"I spoke with David Baldwin late Friday. He wants you to meet with him. He asked if you'd like a tour of the factory."

Jack had already seen the factory. Damn it, he knew all he needed to know.

He hung his head and winced. "I hate this part."

"You mean the part where a struggling businessman who's put his entire life into a company thinks there might be a chance of talking you into injecting some much-needed capital and becoming partners?"

"Yeah, Sylvia. That part. I've told him we'll put together a good offer. The best he'll get before his company is forced into bankruptcy. I'm not interested in having a beer with the boys out back."

David Baldwin had recently made an appointment to discuss his situation. His company, while not huge, had ongoing contracts and sizeable assets. Baldwin Boats was also in financial strife with no easy way out. Same story. Bad economy, rising costs and taxes. Jack had said he thought they could do business. *His* kind of business, not Baldwin's. On that, he'd been clear.

Baldwin made beautiful boats but Jack wasn't in the manufacturing trade. To his way of thinking, Baldwin could either come out of this with something via Reed Incorporated's offer, or he could walk away with nothing due to bankruptcy. Despite popular opinion, Jack wasn't completely heartless, even where Lassiter Media was concerned. He hoped David Baldwin grabbed the buoy he had tossed rather than clinging to blind hope and going under.

"Just let him know," Jack said, "that we'll have a firm offer to him by end of the month."

When Sylvia turned to leave, he called after her.

"Just a heads-up. Becca Stevens paid me a visit."

"The director of Lassiter Media's Charity Foundation, right?"

"She threw out a challenge. If I gave her some time, she would change my mind about going after the company."

"You're joking."

"She wants to show me where the money goes."

"And you said go jump."

"I gave her a week."

Sylvia's jaw dropped. It took her time to recover. "You schedule your days down to the minute."

"If I play my cards right, I might be able to glean some valuable inside information."

Sylvia was shaking her head. "I've run checks on everyone of any note at the company. Becca Stevens is former foster care and post-grad Peace Corps. She might look delectable on the outside but that woman is no cream puff. If you're planning to ensnare Becca with your charms, tread carefully. She's smart and she's tough and she'll do anything to win."

Jack ran a finger and thumb down his tie. "We should get on like two peas in a pod." Catching the time on his watch, he moved to grab his jacket. "I'm meeting with Joe Rivers to discuss the logistics on that opportunity in China, and then I'm off to meet Ms. Stevens."

"Off to *seduce* Ms. Stevens, you mean." Sylvia angled her head. "Unless she's a step ahead of you."

"How so?" He shrugged into his jacket.

"Maybe she plans to do the seducing."

"To work her way into my heart and save her foundation?"

"I'm not kidding. My information says she's extremely resourceful."

He winked and swung open the door for them both. "Lord, I hope so."

As Jack Reed's luxury black sedan swerved off Sunset and into the Lassiter Media Building's forecourt, Becca strode over and swung open the passenger-side door. She settled into the soft leather seat while, hands locked on the wheel, Jack assessed her quizzically.

At the gala ball, he'd caught her off guard. In a designer tuxedo he'd been born to wear, every aspect of his star quality had been amplified tenfold. The white slash of his smile had almost knocked Becca off her chair. By the time he'd stopped at the table, her heart was thudding in her throat, in her ears. She thought she'd hid his effect on her pretty well.

Until that kiss.

Their head-spinning, utterly unforgivable kiss.

Today Becca was prepared. Alert and armed and ready for anything.

"Nice ride," she said, buckling up. "Smells new." And

while she would never admit it out loud, Jack smelled good, too. Fresh and woodsy and one hundred percent male.

"I know when we agreed to do this I said *my rules,* but I didn't expect you to wait outside for me. I'd have come up to collect you."

"Time is money."

"Well, that's…considerate of you."

"I was talking about the foundation's time and money."

The uncertain look on his face cleared and his dark eyes gleamed as he grinned. "Of course you were."

When he flicked a questioning glance at her legs, Becca secretly quivered. The look wasn't meant to be intimate, but her body didn't seem to know the difference. Warmth washed through her veins, the same shot of heat that had made rubber bands of her ligaments when Jack had kissed her that night.

Becca's hands bunched in her lap.

Don't think about that now.

"Do you wear jeans to the office often?" he asked, steering onto the road.

"Depends what I have planned for the day."

She sounded cool and collected despite her nails digging into her palms. His nearest arm and thigh were too close. Even in the air-conditioning, his body heat was tangible, enough to make her upper lip and hairline sweat.

"Where are we headed?" he asked, changing up gears.

"A high school." Nodding at the stoplights, Becca set her mind to the task. "Next right here."

"A school, huh? Someone need a new gym?"

She studied his profile, the hawkish nose, that confident air. "You really have no idea, do you?"

"I thought that's what this week was about. Giving me a clue."

She planned to do a truckload more than that.

"How well do you remember your teenage years?"

she asked. "You'd have done well in sport. Football's my guess." He only smiled. "You got good grades, too, right? I bet you didn't have to try."

"Chemistry was tricky."

"But you knew what you liked. What resonated. And your parents could afford an Ivy League school."

"I worked hard when I got there."

"What kind of car did you drive?"

He named a luxury German make.

"Fresh off the assembly line?" she asked.

His laugh was warm and deep. "You think you can guilt me out, Becca?"

"I hope I can open your eyes."

He looked across at her again and this time when he took in her jeans, Becca sensed he was labeling her, slotting her into another compartment in his head. The very idea set her teeth on edge.

"You didn't come from money," he said.

He didn't need to know the whole story—or not at this early stage in the game.

"My parents own a bakery."

He threw her a surprised look and held it before concentrating again on the traffic.

"I'm one of four," she went on. "We kids were taught that we needed to take responsibility for others in society who were less fortunate. Giving back and being community-minded are the secret not only to a happy life but also a happier world. During my senior year, I volunteered at hospitals and nursing homes...."

Attention on the road, his gaze had gone glassy. Becca cleared her throat.

"Am I boring you, Jack?"

"You could never bore me." He rubbed his freshly shaven jaw, which still had the shadow of persistent stubble. "It's just that I've traveled a few miles since school."

She appealed to Jack Reed's ego. "I can't imagine how much you've learned since then. How much you could pass on."

"Is that what we're doing? You want me to give a talk to schoolkids about aiming for the stars?"

"A fair percentage of the kids we'll see today have battled depression and suicidal thoughts and some have even attempted to end their own lives."

From the way a pulse had suddenly begun to pop in his cheek, finally she had his attention.

She indicated a driveway. "In there."

The public secondary high school had around three thousand students, grades nine through twelve. Its multistory red-brick buildings, landscaped with soaring palm trees, had been used as filming locations for several movies and TV shows. After parking the car, they headed for an area by the front chain-link fence where a mass of students had gathered. The kids were cheering as a stream of riders on bicycles flew past in a blur of Lycra color and spinning wheels. A couple of students waved a big sign: *Ride for U.S.*

"Do you ride a bike, Jack?" Becca asked over the hoots and applause from the excited mob jostling around them.

"Not one with pedals. Not for a while."

"These people are riding from coast to coast to bring awareness and help to teenagers who can't see a light at the end of their tunnel. Whose parents might be alcoholics, prostitutes, drug addicts or dealers. A lot of those kids bring themselves up. They might be taught to fetch drugs or another bottle of booze from the cabinet."

As the last of the bikes shot past, Jack gazed on, looking strangely indifferent. Detached.

She tried again. "The Lassiter Foundation donates to this cause every year, and we help decide where and how funds raised ought to be spent."

He took out a pair of shades from his inside breast pocket and perched them on his nose. "A big job."

"Not compared to the effort this bunch puts in."

Some students were fooling around with a football. When a toss went off track, Jack reached and effortlessly caught the ball before hurling it back to the boys. Then, impassive again, he straightened his shades.

"You don't have any children?" she asked.

"I'm not married."

"The two don't necessarily go hand in hand."

"No children."

"That you know of."

He exhaled. "Right."

The crowd started to head back into the building. "How freaky would it be to find out that you'd fathered a child say twenty years ago when you were cruising around in that gleaming new Beamer, acing your assignments, planning out your future with waves of twenty-four-carat-gold glitter."

"I might have a reputation, but I've always been responsible where sex is concerned."

"Right there we have a difference in understanding. How can a big-time player be responsible where sex in concerned?"

His smile was thin. "Takes practice."

"We're getting off topic. Point is that from day one you led a privileged life. Most kids aren't that lucky. Most children could use a hand on their way to reaching adulthood."

Inside the gymnasium, she and Jack sat to one side at the back in the bleachers while the leader of Ride for U.S. addressed the students. Tom Layton was a professional counselor Becca knew through various channels. He had incredible insight into the minds of young adults, a gift he used to full advantage. As he spoke to the audience,

Tom and Becca made eye contact. Tom winked to say hi but didn't miss a beat.

"Good, isn't he?" she whispered across to Jack. "Everything seems so *life or death* to teens. Tom gets that. A child needs all his strength going forward because the real test is later in life when he has to follow his own star, when he needs to develop a thick skin toward those who might want to trash his dream, for whatever reason."

Minus the sunglasses now, Jack trained his hooded gaze on her. "Would it surprise you to learn that you and I aren't so different, Becca?"

"It would surprise the living hell out of me."

His eyebrows drew together and damned if she didn't sense something real shift in Jack Reed. Not compassion or empathy exactly. That would have been too much to ask. It was more of a fleeting *connection* that fell through her fingertips, like loose grains of sand, before she could truly grasp it.

While Tom listed signs that everyone should watch for when identifying a peer who needed help, Becca scanned the audience. The geeks up front were all ears, some even taking notes. The lot in the middle alternated between sneaking looks at smartphones and zoning out, daydreaming about extracurricular activities. The mob in the back—the ones who really needed to listen—were restless. It was difficult to see a bright future when home life sucked everything into a vortex of gray. She and Tom wanted to help change that.

Thirty minutes later, as the principal thanked his guests and a round of applause went up, Jack immediately stood to stretch his spine. Becca looked up the entire length of him. God, he was tall.

"Still awake?" she asked, standing, too.

"Sure." He stretched again. "Coffee would be good though."

As they headed down the bleacher aisle, she helped bring the bigger picture into focus.

"The foundation works with school counselors across the country to get help to students who are under imminent threat. Who need our help now. This minute. We put on camps where they can talk about their problems in a safe and encouraging environment. Where they can share everything with others they identify with. It's important these kids know they're not alone."

At the bottom on the bleachers, Jack held up a hand. "Excuse me a moment? I need to make a call."

Okay. She'd drowned him with information, trying to make every second count. Now she needed to ease her foot off the pedal. Mix it up a bit.

"No problem," she said. "Go ahead. I'll wait here."

Jack drew out his cell and thumbed in a number as he strolled across the floor. By the time he'd disconnected, he'd wound back and was approaching a group who included Tom Layton. When the two men shook hands and spoke, Becca debated whether or not to join them. But they only talked for a moment before Tom sent a friendly wave her way and let Jack go. As Jack drew closer, she couldn't hide her smile.

"That was nice," she said.

"Sure. Nice guy." Jack rested his hand on her arm and eyed the exit. "Let's go."

Logic told Becca to remove herself from his touch. This wasn't a date.

Then again, giving her a guiding hand wasn't exactly an inappropriate gesture, either. If she wanted the chance to push her case going forward, she had to choose her battles. Jack had accepted her challenge, but he could walk away at any time.

And, secretly...

A part of her liked the contact. Crazy, dangerous, stupid. Still, there it was.

As he led her toward the gym doors, Becca made a suggestion.

"We could go back to the office for that coffee. My barista skills are renowned in that building."

"You're not afraid of being hit by a grenade," he said, "or ambushed by gunfire? That's why you waited outside this morning, isn't it? You wanted to keep this arrangement and the questions as quiet as possible."

Her step almost faltered. "I told you why I met you downstairs."

"You're not worried some people might think you're getting too friendly with the foe?"

"If I was worried about my reputation, I wouldn't invite you back, now, would I?" Sliding her arm away from his, she turned his assumption on its head. "Maybe it's you who's afraid to front up at Lassiter Media."

His slanted grin oozed sex appeal. "Yeah," he said. "That must be it."

As they entered the parking lot, Becca took stock. She'd decided to ease back on the info dump, and she'd got rattled at the idea of her loyalties ever being questioned, but she still needed to keep the dialogue open and evolving. She had to keep Jack close. *So, big breath and moving on.*

"Now that's settled," she said, walking alongside of him, "are we on for coffee?"

"If Danishes are involved."

"You're a fan?"

"Can you spell cheese, blueberry, apple toffee?"

Suddenly Becca could taste all her favorites. "How about cinnamon or custard?"

"Now you're talking."

"With my family owning a bakery, there was lots of cake growing up. *Too* much."

He gave her an odd look and then smiled. "You can never have too much cake."

Becca could have argued. She also wanted to know what that strange look was about. Instead she smiled as he opened the car door for her. If she let him in a little more, maybe he would open up to her, too. And then surely light and a sprinkling of goodness would fall among the shadows. Even where blackhearted Jack Reed was concerned.

Jack parked in a space outside of the Lassiter Media Building. After switching off the ignition, he lifted his chin to loosen his tie. He was serious about needing a coffee—extra strong. At each turn this morning, he'd been taken off guard.

Firstly, he was sure Sylvia had said that Becca had been a foster kid. Was she lying about the bakery? Something hinky was going on there.

Second, he, too, was a benefactor of Ride for U.S. When Tom Layton had spotted him and Becca in the bleachers together, Jack had seen speculation flare in the younger man's eyes. It wasn't a reach to think Tom had wondered whether he and Becca had partnered up in some charity-minded capacity. So, before Tom had the chance to wander over and all kinds of questions were asked, Jack had made an excuse and had "bumped" into him. Then, on the quiet, he'd let Tom know nothing had changed. *No one* needed to know who Reed Incorporated gave to, when, how or particularly why—unless it was the taxman.

If Becca wanted to stand behind general consensus and believe his character was a step away from sludge, Jack was used to being pegged as a villain. Hell, wearing that label where Becca was concerned was probably best. When the Lassiter deal went his way and the ax began to fall all around her, she might be hurt but at least she wouldn't be surprised.

On the upside, he had heard everything she'd said about problems facing young adults. Depression, self-harm, suicide…he wished he could wave a wand and all the damage—past, present and future—would be fixed.

Becca got out of the car before Jack had a chance to swing around and open her door.

"Will we personally choose our Danishes?" she asked over the roof of the car. "Or should we have them delivered?"

On the way back from the school, she'd mentioned a good bakery near the office.

"We'll go have a look," he said.

"Cheese, blueberry and apple toffee, right?"

Slipping on sunglasses, he met her at the trunk. "And cinnamon and custard."

She laughed, an effervescent, sexy sound that suited her far better than a scowl. "Just how much can you eat? Or am I buying for the whole office?"

"I'm buying," he said. "Might as well throw in a couple of chocolate chip muffins while we're at it."

"Now that's getting dangerous." They headed off toward the mall via the building's entrance. "And it's *my* treat. No argument. You're my guest." She playfully eyed him up and down. "A guest with a very big appetite."

"And growing by the minute."

Her smile changed in a knowing, measured way at the same time her gaze flicked to his mouth. Every one of Jack's extremities began to tingle.

Maybe she's the one doing the seducing.

Earlier, he had scoffed at Sylvia's suggestion, but the idea of Becca Stevens as calculating seductress out to save the world wasn't so far-fetched. Would she think that flirting, or even sleeping with him, might gain her information…curry favor…change his mind? After the kiss they had shared, he knew her hormones wouldn't object even if her conscience did.

Out of the corner of his eye, Jack saw a woman emerge from the building's main entrance. The slender build, dark brown hair and matching eyes were unmistakable. Angelica Lassiter was so absorbed in her thoughts, she almost ran into them without noticing. Recognizing Jack first, she sagged and let out a ragged sigh.

"Thank God. How did you know I'd be here?" she asked. Then she saw Becca.

Angelica was strong-willed, like her dad. But right now, with those dark-brown eyes wide and questioning, she looked as if she was teetering on an edge.

Jack spoke to Becca first. "Can we do this later?"

She said, "Of course," before offering Angelica an awkward goodbye. As Becca moved inside the building, Jack looped his arm through Angelica's.

"C'mon. Let's walk."

Four

"What are you doing with Becca Stevens?" Angelica asked as Jack ushered her away from the Lassiter Media Building and down the busy boulevard sidewalk.

"Becca's worried about the foundation's future," he said.

Angelica nodded deeply. "She does a brilliant job there. Her heart is totally in the right place. But, Jack, don't think for a minute she's on our side. She doesn't like you. Given our association, I'm sure she doesn't like me much at the moment, either."

Angelica could easily have grown up a spoiled pain. She'd come along later in Ellie Lassiter's life, after J.D. and his wife had been warned against ever trying to conceive. Ellie had died just days after giving birth to a healthy baby girl. Elevated blood pressure had brought on a stroke.

Years earlier, Ellie and J.D. had adopted her orphaned nephews, Sage and Dylan. After Ellie's death, J.D. and the boys had showered all their love and attention on Angelica, who had developed into a remarkably caring, career-minded woman.

It was no secret that J.D. had been grooming his daughter to take over Lassiter Media. When J.D. had died suddenly from a massive coronary, everyone was shocked to hear his final wishes at the will's reading. But, one by one, all had accepted the inexplicable terms. All except Angelica and, of course, Jack.

"Yep, Becca supports Evan."

"And if you want her to switch camps," Angelica went on, "you're wasting your time. When that woman makes up her mind about something, there's no changing it. And frankly, Jack, I don't see any point in trying."

"You've got it mixed up. Becca came to me. She wants me to see where the foundation's money goes. All the good it does."

He thought better of admitting he was hoping to pick up some Lassiter intel along the way. He wouldn't add to the tally of his baser tactics where Angelica's opinion of him was concerned.

She was mulling over his words. "Becca wants to inspire you enough that you'll back off from any takeover bid, and all the bad publicity and doubt plaguing the foundation will disappear along with you."

She stopped and sat heavily down on a vacant bench at a bus stop.

"I *hate* that the company is suffering," she said. "I hate that my family can barely look at me anymore." She exhaled a shaky breath as he sat alongside of her. "It's getting to me, Jack. Grinding me down until my head feels like it might explode."

"Trust me," he said. "We're in a good place with this."

"I rang Dylan this morning, a sisterly call to see how he and Jenna are doing."

Dylan had got involved with Jenna Montgomery, a florist in Cheyenne. Jack had heard that the couple had weathered some severe relationship storms before recently tying the knot.

"Of course, the conversation swung onto the will," Angelica went on. "I got so stirred up, I could have hit something. Out of everyone, I never thought Dylan would turn against me. We were so close when we were young. I thought we still were."

After high school, Dylan had set sail to see the world. Odd jobs in restaurants had grown into head chef opportunities in premiere establishments. Five years ago, J.D. asked him to head the Lassiter Grill Group with restaurants in L.A., Vegas, Chicago and now their hometown, Cheyenne. He'd inherited complete control of the restaurant business when J.D. died.

"Dylan told me again," Angelica said, "that I needed to accept Dad's wishes. That I should bury the hatchet and get on with my life." Staring into the noisy downtown traffic, she bit her lip and shook her head. "I needed to talk to Evan. Thrash it out. Know what he said? Evan said I should settle down. Sitting in *my* chair, in *my* office. Can you believe it?"

As a tear rolled down her cheek, Jack fished out a pressed handkerchief from his inside breast pocket.

Gritting her teeth, Angelica dabbed her face. "I can't get my mind around the fact that Evan somehow conspired with my father to do this. Or maybe Evan somehow conspired against us both."

Jack wanted to put his arm around her. Squeeze her hand. But Angelica didn't need sympathy. She needed firm direction. He sat forward, elbows on thighs, fingers thatched between knees.

"Evan's right," he said.

As the 302 bus growled by, she shot Jack a glance. "Excuse me?"

"You do need to settle down. Then you need to refocus and never let that target out of your sights. You can't afford to let emotion get in the way."

"Just sometimes, Jack…sometimes I wonder whether we're doing the right thing. Whether it's worth it."

"You wonder whether you ought to give up your inheritance because Sage and Dylan don't approve?" Pulling out all the stops, Jack turned toward her. "Sage was never close to J.D. He's a billionaire in his own right, for God's sakes, and yet he got twenty-five percent of Lassiter Media in the will. And Dylan? Why, he's happy as a pig in mud since he's snagged controlling interest of the Lassiter Grill Group. Then there's you. J.D.'s only child through blood. His little princess. Tell me how the hell it works when you get a lousy ten percent and the man you trusted enough to want to marry walks away with controlling voting interest of *your* father's company." Jack sneered. "I don't give a rat's furry behind whether or not Sage or Dylan or anyone else approves of your attempt to get what's rightfully yours."

Angelica's shoulders squared slightly and she blinked several times as if her eyes might be stinging.

"I miss Dad so much," she said. "I wish I could talk to him now. Let him make sense of it all. I'm torn between wanting to fold and being outraged that he could embarrass and hurt me like this. I worked my rear end off for that company. It was all I thought, ate. *Slept*." She swallowed back emotion and brushed away another tear. "I'm just so tired of it all."

Jack almost groaned aloud. He'd valued J.D.'s friendship, but if he'd been alive and standing in front of him now, Jack would have plowed him in the jaw, what Jack stood to make out of this deal be damned.

Angelica dabbed her cheek again. "I'm a wimp."

"Hey, would I team up with a wimp?"

When he bumped her shoulder, she almost grinned.

"Sylvia and I are working nonstop," he said, "finding ways to boost our position in the company's shares. It won't be long now. We're almost there. Okay?"

A genuine smile flickered at the corners of her mouth before her gaze narrowed, searching his.

"In the past, you've only ever wanted to tear down and sell off companies you'd acquired. Why is Lassiter Media any different?"

"You really need to ask?"

"Everyone's asking."

"J.D. was a close friend. I've known you since you were a skinny kid with braids. I'm doing precisely, to a *T*, what your father would want me to do."

"Except it goes against his final wishes."

"That can't have been his intent. Search your heart and tell me you don't agree."

Her gaze narrowed again.

"You would never betray me, would you, Jack?"

As a shiver ran up his spine, Jack looked her dead in the eye. "No, Angelica," he said. "I would never betray you."

Jack followed Angelica back to the Lassiter family mansion, which sat on two acres of Beverly Hills north of Sunset. J.D. had bought the Spanish Colonial revival twenty years ago when he'd created the L.A. office. Built in the 1930s, the mansion retained its original wrought-iron detail, leaded glass and homemade Spanish tiles. In recent years, however, Angelica had contributed much in the way of decorating its 11,000 feet of luxury living space. It had been more her home than J.D.'s.

When Jack and Angelica began to go over some figures and she asked him to stay for lunch, of course, he accepted. He even helped her prepare enough egg salad sandwiches to feed ten. Then they sat and ate in the lanai, taking in the sparkling pool and the flawless blue sky of late summer. By the time they had talked through everything and Angelica felt positive again about going forward, the sun was arcing toward the west.

As she accompanied Jack through the living room with its soaring ceiling to the front entrance, for the hundredth time he considered the part he was playing in this unfolding drama. Complex and uncomfortable, even for him. Still, as he had said to Angelica earlier, they need only keep their eyes on the target.

"I shouldn't have kept you this long." Angelica looked weary, resting her cheek against the opened door edge as Jack stepped onto the extravagant porch.

"I'm here anytime you need me."

"Becca Stevens must be wondering where you got to."

"She probably welcomed the break."

"I doubt that."

When Angelica sent him a fond smile, Jack held her shoulder. "You'll be okay."

"You were always a good friend to my father...to me. I don't know what I'd do without you."

"You'll never have to worry about that."

There was a spring in Jack's step as he crossed to his car. He had helped Angelica—or *not* helped, depending on which team a person rooted for. On top of that, even after having his fill of egg salad, Jack was still fanging for those Danishes.

Steering out onto the main road, he put through a call to the Lassiter Foundation and gave his name. He was transferred to Becca's assistant.

"Sorry, Mr. Reed. Ms. Stevens left for the day."

Jack checked the dash clock. A little after four. "She's gone home?" he asked.

"I couldn't say."

He reverse head-butted the seat. *Damn.*

"Do you have her private number?"

"Sorry, sir. I can't give that out."

Jack knew he could get it easily enough. Not the point. Nothing was more important to Becca than saving her foundation, which translated into putting all her efforts into trying to talk him around. Surely her nose wasn't put out because Angelica had needed him earlier.

So, what had come up that was so urgent? Was Becca playing hard to get? He wasn't that desperate for Danish.

When his cell rang a minute later, he connected without checking the ID.

It wasn't Becca.

"Hey, Jack. David Baldwin here."

Jack flinched but put a smile in his voice. "Hey. How's it going, David?"

"Call me Dave. Have you got a few minutes? I'd like to show you something."

"Sylvia already mentioned another factory tour."

"She let me know. You've seen enough there."

"And you'll have an offer by end of the month." Silence echoed down the line. "Dave, you there?"

"I wanted to speak with you about a personal matter."

Damn it. He should've checked that caller ID. "I'm not sure I can help with any personal issues."

"Actually it's about me helping you."

"I'm tied up at the moment, but sit tight and we'll get that offer—"

"This is about family, Jack. It's about…a journey."

Jack had heard it all before in a hundred different ways from just as many different people. The times they had spoken, David Baldwin had come across as a good guy who'd worked hard and considered his employees to be just that…family. Now, he wanted Jack to get involved, drag his financial butt out of the fire and save his business. Save the day.

And, hey, there was something about David Baldwin that gave Jack pause. Something in the deep brown of his eyes that made him care. But this association could end only one way and that was not with the two of them sharing Christmas dinners.

"I'll be in touch soon," Jack said. "Another call's coming through. Take care."

He disconnected. A single beat later, pain ripped through his chest—a stab followed by one almighty twist. Stopping at lights, he winced, massaging the spot.

Not heartburn or, God forbid, a heart attack. Just this Lassiter issue getting to him. The Baldwin business, too. If David wanted to save his family, best of luck. Jack couldn't help.

And, while she might never accept it—while she would want to see his head on a spike when this was done—Jack couldn't help Becca Stevens, either.

The next morning, Jack's cell phone woke him.

Rubbing his eyes, Jack grabbed it, checked the caller ID—lesson learned—and connected.

"Jack?" Becca sounded puzzled. "Did I wake you?"

He sat up, ran a hand through his hair. The bedside clock read eight-oh-five. *Holy crap.* He always had trouble getting to sleep, but what the hell time had he finally nodded off last night?

"I thought I'd call early," she went on. "I have a plan."

Jack smothered a yawn. "I like plans."

"Can I come over and tell you about it?"

"I thought you might have been, well…"

"Pissed at you after ditching me yesterday? I understand your situation with Angelica. She feels backed into a corner."

"The only way out is to fight."

"Or to accept. Even forgive."

He swung his feet over and onto the floor. "Ultimately, that's up to her."

"It'd help if you stopped pushing her."

Jack grinned. "I thought you said you understood."

He heard her sigh. At least she didn't argue.

"What time can I come over?" she asked.

She certainly was eager. "Why not the office?"

"It'd save time."

He couldn't argue with that. "I'll just jump in the shower."

It was on the tip of his tongue to suggest that he'd wait for her. *Bad Jack.*

"See you in thirty then," she said.

Naked, he crossed to the bathroom. "I'll be here." *With bells on.*

Jack answered his booming doorbell wearing tatty jeans that hung low on his hips. He hadn't bothered to put on a shirt. When he lifted an arm to lean against the jamb and his epic six-pack firmed up even more, Becca could have drooled.

Look into his eyes. Not the big, bronzed chest or that strip of skin south of his navel, damn it. Look at his eyes.

"Morning," he said. "You're late."

A lousy ten minutes. And she wouldn't give him the satisfaction of asking where the rest of his clothes were, either. Even his feet were bare; who knew toes could be sexy?

The other time she had visited, an older man with an impeccable air had seen her through to the back lawn. "I thought the butler would answer the door," she said.

"Merv's not a butler." His arm slid down as he stepped back to allow her inside. "He looks after things for me on the home front. It's his day off."

"Did you grow up having a person like Merv around

to mix your chocolate milk?" she asked, stepping into the double-story, marble-decked foyer that smelled of money.

"I did."

"Must be nice."

He laughed. "Still trying to guilt me out?"

"Just saying…"

"Merv does a great job. In return he is paid extremely well."

She pinned up a smile. "Then everyone's happy."

Jack must have been six-two or -three. In peep-toe flats that matched her simple white summer dress, Becca felt way less than her average height. When his scent filled her lungs, she fought the absurd urge to wither against him…even drag her lips all over those pecs. His chest was that good.

Before he shut the door, he did a double-take at her ride parked in the forecourt. "Tell me that's not a company car."

"My '63 Fiat Bambino is what's known as a true classic."

He squinted, looking harder—admiring the distinctive light mint-green shade, perhaps. "Are those dinky wheels even roadworthy?"

"I'm pretty sure it'll get us where we need to go."

He gave her a doubtful look. "*Pretty* sure."

"Are you ready?"

He shut the door and set his hands on the band of his jeans. She fought the urge to fan herself. She'd seen that body before, on a billboard advertising men's underwear.

"Ready to go where?" he asked.

"First of all," she pointed out, "you'll need clothes." *Or I'll go insane.* "Three to four changes."

"Sounds interesting."

"Oh, it will be."

With anticipation gleaming in his eyes, he nudged his

chin toward the stairs. "Come up while I pack. I might need further instruction."

As he headed off, Becca hesitated. But it wasn't as if he planned to throw her down on his bed and manacle her wrists to the posts. He wasn't that depraved. At least, she didn't think he was.

Steeling herself, she jogged up the stairs behind him.

"You didn't say where you're taking me," he said over one beautiful broad shoulder.

"On an adventure." *A journey.*

"Should I let anyone know?"

"Anyone, as in Angelica Lassiter?"

"She needs my support, now more than ever."

Becca's stomach pitched and she groaned. "God, I feel for her. I really do."

"But not enough to side with her."

"You know the answer to that."

At the top of the stairs, he turned left down a wide corridor. Examining the mouthwatering way his muscled back tapered to the incredible seat of those jeans, she kept close.

"Here's an idea," he said. "While you're trying to convince me to step back from a takeover, I could try to convince you to come join the dark side."

Join Jack Reed? *Ha!*

"I'm not the least drawn to the dark side."

He waited for her to catch up before continuing. "Not even a little bit?"

"Not even the teensiest baby thimbleful."

"Nothing in this world is simply black or white, you know."

She refrained from rolling her eyes. "Just pack, Jack."

They crossed a double threshold into a massive private suite. In this separate sitting room, blue brocade couches offered luxurious seating. Shelves filled with tomes lined an entire wall. An uneven pile of books lay stacked on an otherwise tidy desk. The room smelled of sandalwood. Masculine, soothing and unsurprisingly arousing.

Jack moved into an adjoining suite—the master bedroom. Becca took a calming breath and stayed precisely where she was.

"Will I need a dinner suit?" he called out while she ran a fingertip over book spines. Business, philosophy, a number of classics. One entitled *The Witchery of Archery*.

"No suit," she called back. "It'll be easy living all the way."

She moved to check out what was hung inside a large glass casing on a neighboring wall. "This bow looks like it belongs in a museum," she said loud enough for him to hear.

His deep disconnected voice filtered out from the bedroom. "It's thousands of years old, found preserved in ice in Norwegian mountains. The bow is made of elm. The arrow tip's slate. I won't say what I had to do to get hold of it."

She felt her eyes bulge. *Wow.* "This really does belong in a museum."

"I've had offers."

She took in the authentic Persian rug a few feet away. "Don't need the money, right?"

"It's not about money."

"It never is," she muttered, "when you eat caviar five days a week."

He went on, "It's about pride. It's about passion. A person should never give those away."

Passion… Becca peered out the window over his home archery field.

"So, have you ever split an arrow down the middle?" she asked, strolling over toward the view. "You know, like in the movies."

"That's a one-in-ten-thousand shot."

"So, that would be no?" she teased.

"I'm pretty good with apples though."

"On heads?"

"Just call me William Tell."

"I was thinking more Robin Hood, in reverse. Robbing from the poor to give to the rich."

"What about the theory that Robin Hood was nothing more than an outlaw?"

"In that case, I have the bases covered."

He emerged from the bedroom looking edible in a black polo shirt and tailored dark pants. Overnighter in hand, a wry smile on his face, he sauntered over.

"So now I'm a thief?"

"There is that theory," she said, "yeah."

As he lowered the case to the floor, his face came closer until the tip of his nose very nearly met hers. A tingling wave washed through her before settling in her chest.

"You're not worried that while we're away I might steal another kiss?" he asked close enough for his breath to brush her mouth.

Her suddenly sensitive nipples pushed against the lace cups of her bra. But now that she knew what to expect— knew just how to play this—it was within her power to resist.

She crossed her arms. "Like I said. Zip chance of defecting to the dark side."

While they were away, Becca planned to remind herself of that every minute of every day.

Five

Becca steered her Bambino north up Highway 1, tawny-colored hills on one side, awesome ocean bluffs and beaches on the other. With the windows rolled down, breathing in sweet oleander-scented air, she suggested that they play "Did you know?"

"Did you know," she began, "that there are no deaf birds or fish?"

Jack's dark hair ruffled around the sunglasses parked on his head. "I did *not* know that," he said, sounding suitably impressed.

"Did you know that one in every three hundred and fifty babies born have permanent hearing problems? Until twenty years ago, most children born with hearing problems weren't detected until they were two to three years of age. Now ninety-five percent of newborns are screened."

"That's good to hear." His grin was kick-ass sexy. "No pun intended."

After steering through a stomach-dropping curve, she

flicked over another look. Elbow hitched on the window ledge, foot tapping to 104 on the radio dial, Jack looked relaxed. Becca was stoked that he'd gone for this road trip idea even if it was simply because he needed the break from his desk. Of course, she knew Jack hadn't got to the top of his game by slacking off. No doubt he hoped this trip would be in some way beneficial, either by garnering information from her that might help advance his and Angelica's takeover plans, or by believing that he might actually pull off taking her to bed.

If she'd shared this smoldering chemistry with any other man, Becca might well have acquiesced. All kinds of sparks zapped around the room whenever she and Jack were together. But this week was not about romance. Definitely not about sex. It was about persuading a ruthless rich man not to add Lassiter Media to his wall of trophies. Becca wanted to reach Jack Reed's more human and merciful side. She wanted to help him accept that true pride came with peace of mind and compassion, not suffocating wealth and majority indifference.

Jack needed to find himself, and she was going to help shine the light. She'd started by planting him in the audience at a high school, making him a part of the swirl and the thrust. This morning she would introduce him to another foundation-funded scheme, as well as a person who had returned from the brink of despair to get her life back.

Later, Becca aimed to completely remove Jack from his cutthroat corporate element. She wanted to strip his defenses bare, make him forget who he was while nurturing his higher self. She had to believe there was some part of Jack Reed who would connect with the joys and importance of simple things, and also recognize that others less fortunate needed help to achieve even that connection.

She was excited about the little friend she had lined up for that part of their journey. Becca's friend, the owner of a gorgeous little dog, had come up with the idea. Chichi's antics could soften the hardest of hearts.

"Auditory areas of the brain," Becca went on now, "are most active not only when a child listens but also when he reads. Isn't that amazing?"

"How's your foundation involved?"

"It isn't *my* foundation. Not really."

"But the dream is to head your own charity someday?"

"If I did, it'd help all kinds of causes, like Lassiter's foundation does. I couldn't choose just one."

"If you had to?"

Concentrating on the snaking road, Becca ran through worthy causes in her mind.

"I'd want to give hope to homeless kids," she finally said. "I spent time in foster care." She pulled up in her seat and then took another sweeping turn. "I lucked out with my last family."

"The one with the bakery."

Ah... The smell of freshly baked bread and cinnamon-apple fritters in the morning. By then, she had felt transported to heaven.

"It was the first time and place I remember ever feeling truly safe. And loved." Such a beautiful, warm, *vital* feeling. "I was eleven, the age when a kid starts to mature, to change...when we question everything three times over and still have more to ask. But my parents seemed to have all the answers."

"How'd they manage that?"

"With patience and kindness. Plenty of communication. Talking. But mainly listening."

"Which brings us back to *did you know*."

She smiled. *Right*. "Did you know that the foundation is helping fund clinical trials of auditory brainstem implants in children?"

"You're really into kids."

"We all started out as one."

When he didn't reply, she glanced across again. He was studying the ocean. A pulse popped steadily above his jaw. Had she made him truly think or was she simply boring his pants off? Not that she needed that image in her head. It was tough enough battling the epic visual of his bare chest and arms when he'd opened his front door earlier that day. The memory alone made her breath come short.

"I got one for you," he said suddenly.

"One what?"

"A did you know."

Cool. "Shoot."

"Did you know, once a long time ago, I almost got married?"

Becca's grip on the wheel slipped and the Bambino swerved before she corrected and got back onto their side of the road. She pushed out a shaky breath.

"Jesus, Jack, don't throw those curveballs while I'm driving."

Jack Reed's reputation as a corporate raider was trumped only by his name as a player. He was always on the hunt for something or someone to jump into bed with, before moving on to some other project.

Seriously. *Marriage?*

"So…what happened?" She smirked. "Did she break your heart?"

"In a sense. She died."

Gravel sprayed as the car veered onto the shoulder. Was this a bad joke? Given the tight line of his mouth, she guessed not.

"Jack…" *God.* "I'm sorry."

"Like I said. It was a long time ago. A *lifetime* ago." His gaze sharpened on hers as his eyebrows knitted together. "You okay?"

"I just…wasn't expecting that."

Not for one minute.

He studied her white-knuckled grip on the steering wheel. "Want me to drive?"

"That could work." He might even enjoy it. "Except... this clutch slips a bit. The steering wheel wobbles a lot of the time. She's a temperamental beast."

"But full of heart."

Exactly. "I think she's worth the trouble."

When she looked across, Jack's thoughtful gaze probed hers. "I was thinking the same thing."

Becca parked the *antique-mobile* out front of a redbrick single-story building. With its barred, round-arch windows, it was a cross between last-century public housing and urban old-English church.

During the rest of the drive, they'd spoken more about charities, including the fact that J.D. had left a good deal of cash to the Lassiter Charity Foundation. That segued into a discussion that touched upon the recent grand opening of the Lassiter Grill in Cheyenne. Jack had attended the opening with Angelica, which hadn't gone down so well with the Lassiter "in" crowd. He mentioned that he hadn't been invited to Dylan's wedding to Jenna Montgomery; it had been very much a family-only affair.

Becca had then trilled about Felicity Sinclair's upcoming nuptials to Chance Lassiter. Jack couldn't see himself being invited to that shindig, either.

Now, as he and Becca walked up the rickety cement-block path, Jack pushed that other business aside to focus on a neat rainbow painted over the building's entrance.

He scratched his chin. "Are we here to listen to a sermon?"

Becca reached back to release her ponytail and shake it out. "We're here to test your powers of observation."

Like observing how her hair unraveled around her

shoulders like spools of gold silk? The way her every gesture and expression carried the conviction of what she believed in? Above all else, Becca believed in herself—what she was about and why.

She resembled Jack in that regard.

Not that he needed to explain himself to anyone—not for any reason. Although, when they'd played that game earlier in the car, he had given in to the impulse to throw a private snippet out there: if Krystal hadn't died, they would have been married. Things would have been different.

Jack rarely thought about that period of his life. It stirred up unpleasant feelings, doubts, memories—well, obviously.

"How would you rate yourself?" Becca asked. "On observation."

"I see what I need to see."

"What you *want* to see."

His gaze skimmed her lips. "That, too."

He swung open the front glass door and they crossed to a counter. A vase of marigolds sat at one end, a framed headshot announcing "Employee of the Month—Brightside House" on the other. Becca addressed the receptionist.

"Hi, Torielle. Mind if I take a guest through?"

The woman had a magic smile, the type that made a person want to beam back. "You know you're welcome here anytime, Becca. Anytime at all."

"Torielle Williams, this is Jack Reed."

Torielle's dark-chocolate gaze flickered—perhaps she recognized the name and its recent connection to the Lassiter scandal in the media. But her smile didn't waver.

"Pleased to meet you, Mr. Reed. Let me know if there's anything you need."

As they headed down a corridor, Jack felt Becca's energy swell and glow. She was a natural leader, a person who got the job done. Knowing she was out for his scalp would have upset a lesser opponent. Instead Jack found himself absorbing her spirit. What might they accomplish if Becca and he sat on the same team?

"This facility helps long-term unemployed women not only find work but also regain their self-esteem," she said. "No matter the color, creed, age or background, we do whatever needs to be done to get them back into contributing, earning and growing as individuals."

They stopped at a window that opened onto another room. Inside, a group was immersed in doing nails and makeup. Numerous rails of women's clothing were lined neatly off to one side.

"Every obstacle is tackled," Becca said, "from grooming and carriage to interview skills and continuing education."

Jack stole a look at Becca's hands resting on the window ledge. Her nails were cut short, no polish. Her makeup was minimal, too, if she wore any at all. Her kind of bone structure and flawless skin didn't need any help. Good diet, plenty of uninterrupted sleep. Jack imaged her opening her eyes each morning and bouncing out of bed. He usually hit the snooze button at least twice. Insomnia was a bitch.

Farther on, they stopped at another window and saw a well-dressed woman addressing a room full of women who were taking notes. Then the next room was a gym. Exercise classes were in full swing—spin bikes, Pilates, ball games.

"Everyone's enjoying themselves," he said.

"Exercise releases endorphins. Feeling good is addictive, Jack." Her shoulder nudged his arm. "You got to keep it pumping."

Jack grinned. "You like to push yourself."

"That's the way to success."

"As long as you don't burn out."

"No chance of that when you're doing what you love."

"And you love what you're doing."

"Every minute."

"Even troubleshooting problems like me?"

They faced each other and she tilted her head, as if she were trying to see him more clearly—see the good.

"You, Jack, are a challenge."

"But redeemable?"

"Everyone's redeemable." Her fingers tapped his shirt-front. "Even you."

Next was a stop at a newer facility separate from the main building. Groups of young children were painting, playing dress-up, making mud pies. Minders were engrossed in helping, sharing, laughing.

"A child-care facility?" he asked.

"And after-school facilities with a bus service to deliver and collect the kids. There's a nursery for the newborns, too."

As they walked along a fence lined with fragrant yellow flowers, Becca explained.

"In the States, more women than men are poor, and the poverty gap is wider here than anywhere in the Western world. When parents separate or divorce it's more likely that mothers will take on the financial responsibilities of raising the kids. Childcare costs can be crippling, never mind medical expenses. While we get a woman prepared to interview for jobs, we make certain any children are properly supervised and cared for."

A little girl with pink track shoes and big brown eyes saw Becca and waved her paintbrush hello over her head. Becca waved back and blew her a kiss before leading Jack back into the main building.

"Who was that?" he asked.

"Wait a minute and I'll let you guess."

They entered a room. Women sitting at half a dozen computer workstations glanced up and greeted them both.

Becca sat at a vacant desk and logged in while Jack stood behind her, attention on the computer screen. She opened up a file labeled "Before." There were countless entries, each catalogued by a headshot.

"These are just some of the women who the facility has helped," she said, enlarging a "Before" image. Not only did the woman look disheveled, her resigned expression said she'd accepted that disappointment was her lot in life.

"She never finished high school," Becca said, studying the screen. "For years she suffered in a domestic violence situation. Her husband put her in hospital more than once but she never pressed charges because she feared the next beating would be worse. Her teeth were broken. Can you imagine the agony of feeling discriminated against because of your smile? She was living in a shelter with her children when she came to us."

"Did she get a job?"

From her seat, Becca grinned up at him. "You don't recognize her?"

"No." Then he blinked, focused harder. "Wait…" Something in those eyes… "Torielle?"

"Just two years ago."

Of course. "The receptionist with the dynamite smile."

"We have several professionals, including dentists, who donate their time. Now Torielle helps out here part-time and is working toward completing a college degree."

"And the girl waving her paintbrush, saying hello…?"

"Chelsea, Torielle's four-year-old daughter. She has two older brothers in grade school, twins. The boys both want to become jet pilots. They're smart enough, too. Chelsea wants to be a ballerina—every little girl's dream, and why not?"

"A happy ending," Jack said as Becca clicked to Torielle's "After" picture. The difference, the pride—real pride—shone from the inside out.

"We want to set these facilities up all over the country," Becca said.

"But they need ongoing support."

"The way we see it, we give a little now and society gets a whole lot back later."

Becca pushed to her feet and smiled into his eyes, a beautiful smile Jack had seen before but not as clearly as he did this minute. Becca was one of those uniquely special individuals who bobbed up every now and then. Unselfish, exuberant. She was physically attractive but it was her attitude that made everything about her shine...even when she was chewing someone out.

"Are you ready for a change of pace?" she asked.

His gaze swept over her silken waves of hair. "What do you have in mind?"

"Something different." She winked. "Something fun."

Six

"My God. What the hell *is* that?"

Frowning at Jack's remark, Becca crossed over to the small, seemingly unsupervised dog. "You're lucky he's not sensitive," she said.

They had driven from Brightside House a short distance to a small, quiet parking lot located this side of a beach. When they'd gotten out of the car, this little guy had been waiting alone as planned. Chichi would play a role in Becca's weeklong challenge. Her overriding strategy was to reach Jack's more human, less sophisticated side. He couldn't help but lower his defenses with this cute dog around.

For the next two days of her remaining six, she would hide Jack away from all the temptations and reminders that drove his *conquer and take all* mentality. He needed to get back to basics, and appreciate that everyone deserved a chance to achieve at least that, too.

Now, studying the dog, Jack visibly shuddered. "Sorry, but that's got to be the ugliest mutt I've ever seen."

"Haven't you heard?" Crouching, Becca stroked the wispy tuft of hair on the dog's head. "Beauty is skin deep."

"Except when ninety-five percent of the skin is bald and dappled—" he shuddered again "—and please, not scaly, too."

"He's a Chinese-crested Chihuahua mix."

"If you say so." He flipped a finger at its head. "Do you think its tongue always lolls out the side of its mouth like that?"

She dropped a kiss between the puppy's ears. "Cute, huh?"

"God as my witness, I've never seen anything like it."

"Chichi will be joining us on our road trip."

Jack's head went back. "You know this dog?" As if to answer for her, Chichi sneezed and Jack shrank back. "Whatever it's got, let's hope it's not contagious. Does he smell?"

"Not as well as a bloodhound."

"That's not what I meant."

As she ran a palm down Chichi's hairless back, his pink tongue lolled out more. "Did you have a dog growing up?"

"Would it be too unkind to suggest those bobble eyes look possessed?"

"Jack?" *Focus.* "Growing up?"

"Yeah. We had a King Charles."

"To go with the thoroughbreds, right?"

Chichi's skinny tail with its pompom tip whipped the sandy ground; he got the joke.

Becca pushed to her feet. "He wants you to pick him up."

Jack crossed his arms and puffed out his chest. "You pick him up."

"That's pathetic."

Jack hashed it out some more and finally exhaled. He edged forward, gingerly hunkered down and scooped the dog up. Chichi's eyes grew heavy, contented, looking up into his. "Are you running some kind of weird dog make-over campaign?"

"We all need to be loved."

Jack shot her a look. "You're not trying to get me to adopt this thing, are you? Because my lifestyle isn't con-ducive, to say the least."

"He's on loan from a friend." The longtime owner of the café right next to this parking lot.

As Chichi's head and tongue craned up, Jack recoiled. "And the friend wants it back?"

"Oh, c'mon. You're not that harsh."

He arched a brow. "I have it on good authority that I am."

From many, including Becca. And yet Jack must have owned a soul at some point. He'd wanted to marry that woman, hadn't he? Ipso facto, he'd been in love, a self-sacrificing condition from all accounts. Of course, he could've simply been trying to screw with her brain. She wouldn't put it past him. And yet somehow, deep down, Becca knew he'd told the truth, at least about that.

Still gazing up at Jack, Chichi put his miniature paw on his chest. What a picture.

"He's really taken to you," she said.

The dog yipped and one side of Jack's mouth twitched—almost a grin. "He sounds like a mouse."

Moving closer, Becca ran a palm over Chichi's head. When the dog laid his ear against Jack's chest, her fingers skimmed that solid warmth, too, and for one drugging moment she imagined herself curled up in those capable arms, snuggling in against that sensational rock of a chest.

"He loves the sand and water," she said.

"That's my cue to take him for a walk while music plays over a slow-motion montage."

"I'm not aiming that high." Yet. She did, however, want to bring out Jack's softer, more compassionate side.

When Jack set him on the ground, Chichi trotted off down the wooden-slat path to the beach. Then he stopped and looked back, as if making sure he was being followed.

Shielding his gaze from the sun, Jack surveyed the quiet area. "We'll need a leash."

"It's a leash-free beach."

"So a bigger dog can just romp up and have him for lunch?"

"Hasn't happened yet."

"A hawk might swoop and carry him off. I'm *serious*."

Becca was laughing. Was Jack embarrassed or just being difficult? Either way, she was going to win. She skirted around the rear to give him a good push. But when she set her palms on his back, ready to shove, heat swirled up her arms, zapping her blood all the way to her core. At the same time, Jack spun around and, playing, caught her hands.

She should have stepped back then and put some physical distance between them. But his expression changed so quickly from games to that intense, dark gaze searching hers…when a thick vein in his throat began to throb, she couldn't help it. Becca felt mesmerized by the beat.

Chichi's yip broke the trance. The sound of waves washing onto shore faded back up. Again, she felt wind pulling through her hair. Light-headed, she edged back at the same time Jack reached to bring her closer. He missed catching her by a whisker.

Gathering herself, Becca nodded toward Chichi. "Go on," she said in an unintentionally husky voice. "He's waiting."

"What about you?"

"I have someone to see." Her friend, Chichi's owner.

He took two purposeful steps, closing the gap between them again. Had he suddenly grown six inches? Becca felt dwarfed…very nearly consumed.

"Becca, you said this was fun time."

Her heart was pounding so hard, she had to swallow against the knot lodged in her throat before tacking up a smile.

"So…" She shrugged. *"Have fun."*

But Jack didn't move. If he reached for her hand now, Becca wasn't sure which way it might go. How easy would it be to pretend they were a regular couple out for the day with their dog on the beach. But this wasn't about her. Definitely wasn't about them *as a couple.*

The intensity in Jack's expression finally eased. When he bent to slip off his shoes, Becca released that breath. As he trotted off down onto the beach, Chichi scampered back up, trying to scoot between his legs on each step. When Jack almost stumbled, Becca laughed. Glancing back, he laughed, too—a hearty, deeply stirring sound that in some ways touched Becca's heart.

She had to believe…

There must be hope for us all.

Amidst a clump of dried seaweed, Jack found a stick to toss while Becca disappeared in through the front door of a café located next to the parking lot. When what's-his-face let out a bark, Jack refocused and hurled the stick toward the water. He watched the dog scamper off, kicking up sand as he went. It was a perfect Californian day, Jack was a fan of the beach and, okay, this dog was half-cute in a sincerely *off* kind of way. But Jack's mind was stuck on Becca. First, he understood the visit to Brightside House. Becca had wanted to bring him up close and personal with the good work her foundation was doing, the real life peo-

ple the funds helped. The way she had highlighted Torielle's dramatic change in circumstances had been a nice
touch. It was obviously a worthwhile and solid program.

But what was she thinking lumping him with a dog?
Was this introduction somehow linked to opening his eyes
in connection to a pet adoption agency, perhaps? Whatever Becca was hatching here had to do with advancing
her cause of coaxing him away from a takeover bid.

She would be pleased to hear that this morning had
made him think.

More importantly, Becca made him *feel*. Whenever they
touched, even a brush, Jack felt it to the marrow of his
bones—they had sexual compatibility through the roof.
And a minute ago, he'd put a finger on at least one reason
for that. Becca wasn't *playing* hard to get. She *was* hard
to get. It wasn't happening, not in this lifetime, even while
they both felt temptation gnawing and growing between
them. With Becca, ethics came first, last and everywhere
in between.

If they should happen to come to some understanding
regarding the rescue of her beloved foundation, she would
worry that a rogue like him could always go back on his
word. She might suggest a contract with special clauses,
Jack supposed...in which case, perhaps he could slip in a
couple of special private conditions of his own.

Nah. That was low, even for him.

Jack was between throws and watching Becca from a
distance as she spoke with a woman on the veranda of the
café when his cell phone rang. After checking the caller
ID, he pressed the phone to his ear.

"Angelica just called," Logan said. "She wanted my
opinion again."

"And you said?"

Logan recited his standard response. "She needs to accept the terms of the will."

"But she resisted."

"She still can't believe J.D. would do this to her. She's convinced there's some kind of conspiracy going on."

Jack transferred the cell to his other hand and tossed the stick again. "Poor kid."

"Angelica's hardly a child."

"There's a part of me that still sees her that way."

Jack had felt for Angelica having grown up without her mother, although from all reports her aunt had done a great job as a substitute. J.D.'s longtime widowed sister-in-law, Marlene, still resided in a private wing of the homestead belonging to the Big Blue.

Of course, her son, Chance, had inherited a whopping sixty percent of the ranch. Real generous of J.D. It must have made Angelica wonder if what appeared to be favoritism was gender-related. It made Jack wonder, too. If J.D. had sired a son rather than a daughter, would he have structured his will differently, leaving out the complications that Angelica was experiencing now?

Jack hadn't thought about being a father himself, not since he'd been in love with Krystal back in college. He'd been a different person then. His own most recent will left everything to Sylvia and some friends as well as to charity.

Ha. Wouldn't that make Becca's day.

Chichi was dancing on his hind legs, tongue flapping, wanting to play *fetch* some more.

"I'm away from the office the rest of the week," Jack told Logan, throwing the slimy stick yet again. Logan didn't need to know why he was away. The attorney was tetchy enough about this final stretch as it was.

"But you'll keep your cell on," Logan said.

"Angelica knows I'm available to talk day or night."

"And if she wants to speak face-to-face?"

"I'm there. No question."

A pause. "Maybe it would be better if you *weren't* available for a while."

"Can't do that, Logan. We agreed to play by the rules."

"Yeah." He exhaled. "I know."

When Jack caught sight of Becca leaving the café and heading down toward the entrance to the beach, he signed off.

Becca joined him on the sand a couple of minutes later.

"You were on the phone," she said. "Business?"

"Always."

"Nothing too urgent?"

"It's in hand." He glanced at the café. "I was hoping you might bring back supplies."

"What about you, Chichi?" Becca asked, bending and patting her thighs. "Hungry, little fella?"

The dog sneezed and barked and then picked up the stick and dropped it at Jack's feet again.

"His batteries don't wind down," he told Becca. "I've tossed that stick a hundred times."

"A hundred?"

"Definitely fifty."

"So, you've got those endorphins pumping?"

As a sea breeze picked up, pulling her summer dress back against the curves and valleys of her body, Jack nodded. "You could say I'm pumped, yeah."

She waved for them both to follow. As Jack jogged after her, he glanced over a shoulder. Chichi was sitting, stuck beside that stupid stick. Jack whistled through his fingers.

"Yo. Get a move on, slowpoke."

Chichi scampered up and damned if he didn't leap into Jack's arms like a circus act. Jack pulled his head away from that feral tongue and then caught up with Becca.

"So, tell me about the foundation's link to animal shelters." If that's what this was about.

"No links to shelters. I simply thought that while we

were here you two could meet," she said innocently as she collected Jack's loafers because his hands were full. "Pets are good for humans."

"So are other humans."

"Yep. Having friends is important."

"What would you say to you and me becoming friends?"

She gave a small smile. "Oh, Jack, you know that's not possible."

"But it *would* be possible if I backed away from Lassiter Media?"

A glimmer of hope lit her eyes. "That sure would be a start."

As they walked up to the café, Jack ran over that last bit of conversation in his mind. If he were to spend time with Becca outside of this current context, he would have preferred to tick the "sex between consulting adults" box. And yet he had asked about them becoming *friends? And* he'd meant it. Clearly he had left off the "with benefits" part.

Jack was reading the name on the café's facade, *Hailey's Favorite Haunt,* when a van rolled up alongside the Bambino; the insignia of a top-rating tabloid entertainment news show was stenciled on the side. Jack's antennae twitched. Over the years, he'd tackled his fair share of reporters—truckloads since word of his possible takeover bid for Lassiter Media had leaked. But that crew wasn't here to hassle him. Normally he planned every minute of his day, from first call in the morning to final perusal of documents at night. However, Becca had drawn up this itinerary. No one knew he was here, not even Sylvia. The crew had probably pulled up to grab a coffee for the road.

Then a man jumped out the side door of the vehicle with a camera perched on his shoulder, and Jack paused. Next, a well-dressed woman with a mic climbed out the front passenger side, immediately focused on him and smiled like he was expecting her. Jack set his jaw.

Was this ambush somehow a part of Becca's weeklong deal? If so, he was not amused.

Seven

On their way up to the café, Becca heard someone call out Jack's name. She stopped to track down the source. A tall, slender woman in a bright tangerine skirt-suit and a man with a news camera balanced on one shoulder were ambling across the parking lot, headed their way.

An ice-cold feeling cut through her middle. No one other than her friend had known to expect her at this time. So what was a tabloid TV crew doing here? And what kind of spin would they put on her presence here with Jack?

Holding Chichi close, Jack asked, "Know anything about this?"

She shook her head.

"Lord knows how they'll twist this."

Jack growled. "God, I hate the media."

Becca's hackles went up. "You did happen to notice the name of the company you want to take over, didn't you? Lassiter *Media*. Not that you intend to keep it long." Keep it *whole*.

He repositioned Chichi against his chest. "We can be chewing each other out when that reporter reaches us or we can feed her crumbs and hopefully they'll slouch off."

The reporter and her cameraman were seconds away. Becca exhaled. "Any idea what crumbs?"

A wicked grin eased across his face. "I have a couple in mind."

"Mr. Reed, isn't it?" the reporter asked when she reached them. "Jack Reed. And you're Becca Stevens, head of the Lassiter Charity Foundation. Do you have a moment to answer a few questions?"

Jack replied for them both. "No trouble at all."

"Mr. Reed, you're aware of the publicity and unrest surrounding speculation that you and Angelica Lassiter may succeed in a takeover bid of Lassiter Media after she was shut out of running the company. Would you care to comment on this secluded get-together between yourself and a respected member of Evan McCain's umbrella management team?"

"Ms. Stevens and I have business to discuss regarding the foundation," Jack replied.

The reporter cocked her head and then made a point of eying Jack's loafers, which Becca still held.

"A leisurely day at the beach seems an odd way to discuss business," she said. "Could this be viewed more as a date? And if so, Ms. Stevens, how will you explain this kind of rendezvous to your Lassiter colleagues who are pretty down on Mr. Reed at the moment?"

Becca's blood pressure spiked. This might not look kosher at first glance, but her colleagues would never believe that she'd turned Benedict Arnold. They knew where her heart lay and it was not with Jack Reed.

"As Mr. Reed explained," she replied with barely a tremor in her voice, "today is strictly business."

The reporter's sky-blue eyes narrowed to slits. "So the

rumors regarding a romantic liaison between the two of you are unfounded?"

That hit her in the chest. *"What the—?"*

"My sole purpose today," Jack replied, "is to build on my already solid support of the Lassiter Charity Foundation. Now, we're late for an appointment. I'll thank you both to leave us to our privacy."

Becca rubbed a throbbing temple. She'd never suffered from migraines but she was sure she was getting one now.

How would Evan McCain react if or when this hit the airwaves? She had wanted to keep quiet about her long shot plan to crack Jack's enigmatic side and in some way at least sway his thinking. Now she would need to contact Sarah, her assistant, as well as Evan, to reassure them that she hadn't shifted camps, and never would.

Or maybe it would be wiser to simply call this all off now.

After Jack set Chichi down, Becca led him around the café's wide veranda to an ocean-facing table set with a reserved sign.

"You realize the dog has followed us," Jack said quietly, casting glances at the other guests sprinkled inside the café as well as out here in the fresh air.

"No problem," Becca said. "Trust me."

They were taking their seats when Becca's friend appeared in her trademark denim skirt and vest. They'd had a conversation earlier at this very table when she'd left Jack on the beach.

"Jack Reed," Becca said, "meet Hailey Lang."

"Pleased to meet you," Hailey said with the hint of a Texas twang. Her family had moved over from Houston twenty years ago when Hailey was eight. "I saw you tripped up by some pesky reporter."

"They appeared out of nowhere," Becca said, and then

noticed how Hailey averted her gaze before she spoke again, upbeat this time.

"How you doing there, Chichi?"

Now Jack looked between the dog and Hailey. "You know each other, too?"

"He's my baby," Hailey said while Chichi sat patiently by her feet, his tail fanning the wood planking. "He's a bit of a celeb around these parts."

Jack leaned back in his chair. "He does kind of grow on you."

"So, Chichi's going on a trip with you guys. One of his favorite things is riding shotgun."

"He's partial to sticks, too. Which reminds me..." Jack got to his feet. "If you'll excuse me, I need to wash up before lunch."

As Jack moved off, Hailey crouched down beside Becca's chair. "Becca, honey, I think I might need to apologize."

"For reserving us the best table in the house?"

"The reporter who gave you grief just now..." She leaned closer. "Thing is I have a regular who comes in most days around brunch time for our Delite Mushroom Omelet. Anita's daughter works for the same cable show. Anita talks about her all the time, how she's a hound, always after a big scoop. I think Anita overheard part of our conversation earlier about what you're doing here with Jack Reed. I think she tipped her daughter off."

Becca thought back. "You mean the redhead with a French twist, who was sitting a couple of tables over?" Becca had felt that woman's eyes on them a few times earlier.

"Anita McGraw has a keen ear for gossip. And if there's none around, she'll make dirt up." Hailey sighed. "Is it going to cause much trouble, hon?"

Nothing could be done about it now. And Becca didn't

want Hailey to feel responsible or to worry. "It'll be fine," she assured her friend as Jack returned to the table.

She would make those phone calls to Sarah and Evan's office. She'd decide then on whether or not to cancel this challenge.

Looking halfway relieved, Hailey pushed to her feet.

"Do I need a menu?" Jack asked, pulling his chair in. "I'm open to suggestions."

Hailey piped up. "Chef's salad and specialty pizza. That's with prosciutto, caramelized pear and goat cheese."

"I'm in," Becca said.

"Times two. So, how did you two become friends?" Jack asked, shaking out a napkin to place on his lap.

"Coming up two years ago, Becca broke down just over there, this side of the median strip." Hailey nodded toward a section of road. "Chichi let me know someone needed help. He zipped right up to me, turning circles like his tail was on fire."

"Water pump," Becca explained. "It'd been coughing all the way up the coast. The hood was spewing steam."

"I have a cousin just round the corner—the best mechanic in town," Hailey went on. "His specialty is old cars."

"*Classic* cars," Becca corrected. "He wanted to buy it, remember?"

"I sure do," Hailey said. "You wouldn't take the money even when he doubled the going rate. I don't *ever* see you giving up those wheels."

"There's no accounting for taste," Becca agreed. "Hailey ended up giving me a bed for the night while the repairs were done. Chichi slept at my feet."

Hailey sighed at Chichi, who was still gazing adoringly up at her. "That dog there is a fine judge of character."

Jack grinned. "And yet he likes me?"

"We were watching you two on the beach." Hailey winked at Jack. "He likes you a *whole* lot."

Becca had a moment of what psychologists term cognitive dissonance. She knew Chichi was a good gauge of character. She also knew he liked Jack. And yet Jack was not of good character. It made her brain hurt.

Hailey headed off. "I'll get this order under way and finish packing that ice chest for you all."

"Ice chest?" Jack asked, pouring water for them both from a carafe. "Are we going on a picnic?"

"Not a picnic, as such," Becca said and he grinned.

"Another one of your secret destinations?"

"With no chance of reporters this time." She lifted her glass. "One hundred percent guaranteed."

But first, she'd check with the boss.

Three hours later, watching out for media tails the whole way, Becca pulled the Bambino up in the middle of freaking nowhere—or, rather, somewhere east of Fresno.

Chichi was asleep on Jack's chest. The drool went from his neck to—he didn't want to think about it. With the dog's head and that tongue hanging out the window more than half the time, the car's side panel must be Slime City by now.

Jack surveyed the area. Dense woods. Lonely cabin. Cooler shadows creeping in.

"What is this?" he asked. "Boot camp?"

Becca jerked on the parking brake. "Actually...yeah."

While Becca got out of the car, Jack wondered how he could extricate himself without disturbing the dog. Which was crazy...except, with one leg kicking and eyelids twitching, the mutt looked like he was having a nice dream. When Becca opened the passenger side door, Chichi stirred, stretched and expelled a big smelly yawn. Then he jumped onto a carpet of pine needles and trotted off into the woods.

Becca was at the trunk. Jack eased out from the car and stretched out his own kinks, frowning as he watched the dog's cotton-top tail disappear among the trees.

"Aren't you worried about him?"

"Chichi's been here before," she said, handing over Jack's bag. "He knows his way around."

"Does he know his way around a mountain lion?"

"Don't forget the black bears and rattlesnakes."

She was screwing with him, but a chill rippled up Jack's spine just the same.

Heading for the door, she added, "He'll come the minute you call."

"If you're not worried, I'm not worried."

Jack grabbed the ice chest from the backseat and shut the door with a hip. "What did Hailey pack in here? Cement blocks?"

"Bread, fruit, cheese, refreshments—"

"Beer?"

"And wine."

They were most definitely set then. For what exactly, he had no idea.

"I got the high school visit and Brightside House. Forgive me if I sound slow, but what am I doing way the heck out here with a dog?"

"For two days and nights, I've kidnapped you," she said, heading for the front door. "Transported you away from your obsession with killer deals and accruing power so that you can get in touch with reality and learn some lessons on how to unleash your truer, less egocentric self."

"After which I will accept a higher calling and disavow my evil ways."

"*Ahh*...doesn't that sound heavenly?"

"It sounds like you're dreaming."

ROBYN GRADY   81

"Some of the world's biggest dreams have come true because someone believed and made others believe, too."

When a couple of huge examples came to mind, he couldn't argue the point. "And the mutt?"

"I knew he'd make you smile in a different way than you're used to."

"So, I'll change my mind about Lassiter Media because I played with a dog? Because I smiled differently?" *Come on*.

"Actions trigger emotions that link with the process of decision-making. I'm hoping that sometime this week, you'll not only smile differently, but start to *think* and choose differently, too."

Okay, fine. "Does Evan know about this cozy getaway?"

"He does now. I phoned him before we left the café. I didn't want him finding out from…other sources."

Like that tabloid show. "And he was okay with it?"

"He said he trusts my judgment and admires my determination."

"In that case, you get an A for creativity. Except you're forgetting one thing. Even when I want to, I never let emotions dictate my decisions."

Her expression didn't waver. "Then we'll simply call this a break from civilization."

Sure. Although he could do without the overgrown rat, he wouldn't object to hanging out here alone with this beautiful woman. Maybe he could put a spin on things and have *Becca* thinking differently by the time they left. And he wasn't talking business.

Inside, the place was quiet and dark enough at four in the afternoon to need to turn on the light. But Becca continued on from the front door without flicking a switch. Jack gave his eyes time to adjust. The room was sparsely furnished, no window dressings. Some walls were plastered. Others displayed exposed logs. It smelled like raccoons might have lodged in the cupboards over winter.

"Who owns this place? The foundation?"

He found Becca in a room that housed a double-bed covered with a patchwork quilt and matching pillows. A painting, featuring wilted poppies, hung above the headboard. Becca was setting her bag near a lopsided free-standing wardrobe.

"The cabin belongs to my parents," she said.

"When was it last used?" Jack sniffed the musty air. "1965?"

"Are you uncomfortable?" She faced him, hands on hips. "Out of your silver-spoon element?"

"Wasn't that the idea?"

With a wistful smile, she peered out the window at the trees. "We used to vacation here for a week every year. No television or hairdryers or—"

"Electricity?"

A camping lantern sat perched on top of a set of drawers. She flicked a switch and white light filled much of the space. "Ta-dah!"

Loving her bright smile, he moved closer. "Very rustic." He stopped before her, close enough to absorb the contentment and pride shining in her eyes. "Is there a second bedroom?"

"There is—complete with two sets of bunk beds, meant for kids, not a man of your sizable build."

His heart gave a running jump. "So, one bed?"

"And a cot." She nodded toward a corner. A saggy camper bed was tucked away among the shadows.

Oh. "Right." He scratched a temple. "That might work." *Not.*

"Guess we don't need to draw straws. I get the cot."

Jack growled as she moved across to inspect it. "Becca, I'm not letting you spend the night on that."

"Lots of people sleep on benches, in doorways, alleys, under bridges, in subways and behind Dumpsters—"

"Okay, okay." He'd heard enough. Guess her first point in bringing him here had been made. "I'll take the cot."

"You'll break it."

"If I do, I'll reimburse you." And see a chiropractor, end of discussion. "But it's a long way from lights-out. What do you have planned until then? Ghost stories around a campfire?"

Jack had a couple up his sleeve. She might even need two strong arms to help with the fright factor.

"A campfire?" she asked. "You mean outside with the bears and rattlesnakes?"

Jack paused. *Good point.*

"First we make the beds," she said. "Then a nice relaxing bath to wash off the travelers' dust."

An image of the two of them together caressing in a deep, sudsy hot tub faded up in his mind. Pure fantasy. Still, he didn't want to put a damper on her idea.

He rocked back on his heels. "Sounds good."

"Great. We'll need maybe ten buckets' full."

"Full of what?"

"Water. We don't exactly have a bath or a shower. We do, however, have a washtub."

Jack waited for the punch line.

His grin dropped.

She was serious.

"Aren't you going to let me know how many people go without adequate plumbing?"

"Don't need to. You worked it out yourself."

He grinned. *Lesson two: check.*

Becca moved to the drawers and found some sheets while he took his place on the other side of the bed. She fluffed out the lower sheet and proceeded to pull the elasticized end under the top corner of the mattress. He did the same on his side of the bed and then tackled the lower corner.

It was a cinch.

As she fluffed out the top sheet, she asked, "Ever made a bed before?"

He scoffed. "I'm sure I have."

"You'd have a housekeeper now, of course."

"Weekdays."

"How long has she worked for you? It's a woman, yes?"

"Mary's worked for me maybe four years."

"Long-time employee?"

"You could say that."

"So, Mary who?"

"Why do you want to know my housekeeper's last name?" What did that have to do with her plan to turn him around on the takeover question?

"I'm curious is all."

As they both stretched the sheet across the middle of the mattress, Jack searched his memory and came up a blank. "It'd be in my phone."

She moved to the end of the bed. "Uh-huh."

From across the mattress, Jack narrowed his eyes at her. "You know all your employees' names off the top of your head?"

"It's fine, Jack. Honest."

"Now you're patronizing me?"

"Is this you being defensive?"

"I'm more than happy with who I am."

She slipped her side of the sheet under the mattress. "Well, that's the main thing, isn't it."

"Why do I feel as if you just insulted me?" he asked, scooping under his end.

"You're smart enough to work it out."

"Just say I'm not."

She joined him on his side of the bed. "You live such a

privileged life, you take for granted clean sheets, and those who change them for you. Lots of children have to do their own laundry. Lots of people would do anything for any kind of bed to sleep on. Want to hear more."

He rubbed the back of his neck. "Not right now."

"Want to learn how to do a hospital corner then?"

Jack moved back to give her room. She bent to collect the dangling edge of the sheet and hold it out from the bed. Then she scooped the linen under the mattress and all the way up. At least he thought that's what she'd done. Call him a man, but even after the speech, Jack was more interested in the view of her legs and those buns.

Straightening, she turned to him. "Think you can do that?"

He feigned an uncertain look. "I might need help."

She moved back to her side, and nodded at the to-be-hospital-tucked bottom corner. "Go ahead. Have a go."

He crossed over and picked up the sheet at the wrong point.

"That's a little too far along," she said. "Let the sheet drop and naturally fold and try again."

He did as she instructed and then grabbed the sheet in a different spot.

"Here," she said patiently. "Like this."

She nudged in front of him and bent over again. Jack didn't see what happened next. He faintly heard some instructions. "...fold the lowest bit...smooth it under..." On autopilot, he moved in. His hand covered hers and they both tucked the sheet in.

"Like that?" he asked, close to her ear.

She didn't stiffen or jump away, so he closed his eyes and absorbed the moment. When she finally began to straighten, they disengaged and then simply stood there in the light and shadow, his hand holding hers as time ticked on and anticipation soared. When he coiled his arm around the front of her waist, he felt her intake of air. Pressing in behind her more, he imagined her biting her lip as she fought the urge to let nature take its course.

He brushed his lips over her temple, her cheek, all the while soaking up her scent. When he nuzzled her earlobe, he felt her quiver against him...heard her quiet, needful sigh. As he dragged his mouth down the side of her throat, bit by bit she tilted her head.

He nipped down the slope where neck met shoulder while his fingers left hers to skim the front of her dress. Through the cotton, he felt the start of her panties and, lower, the subtle rise of her mound. When she groaned—a low, wanting sound—half his blood supply rushed to a predetermined point.

"Jack...?" she murmured.

He hummed against her skin. *"Hmmm?"*

"The bed."

"What about the bed?"

"We were making it."

He dragged his grin back up to her ear. "I like making it with you."

When his fingers delved between her thighs, she made a husky noise in her throat that lit a fire in the pit of his belly. As his free hand slid up her side and under her breast, her head rocked back against his chest and her hand gripped his. Her voice was smoky now.

"This isn't what we're here for."

They were here to cut him off from reality and clobber him over the head with how little others had, how in need many of the less fortunate were.

"Okay." He nipped the side of her throat a little harder. "I'll stop."

When he didn't remove the hand between her legs, her grip over his tightened, not to drag him away but to hold his hand in place. His other palm dragged up over her breast and oh-so-lightly squeezed. She melted a moment before she pulled both his hands away and spun around. When she opened her mouth to speak, he got in first and lowered his head over hers.

Eight

When Jack pulled her close and his mouth captured hers, any objection Becca might have had dissolved like a teaspoon of sugar in hot water. As the kiss deepened, she reached to wind her arms around his neck. A moment more and she arched all the way in.

She would have denied it earlier, even to herself. The admission would have been incongruous, shameful. Inexcusable. She hadn't brought Jack here for this...and yet, secretly, Becca Stevens—the woman—had waited for this moment.

Now she couldn't think past the sensations sizzling through her system. Her breasts felt tender crushed against his chest. Suddenly her insides were filled with an emotion that felt like a swell of liquid fire.

Cupping her jaw, Jack held her mouth to his as he dropped back onto the bed, bringing Becca down along with him. Lips still locked, she tangled one leg around his and knotted her fingers in his clean dark hair while both his palms traced down her sides then slid over the rise of her behind.

Becca arched up and then ground down against him. Through their clothes she felt him already hard and ready. Reaching back, she clapped a hand over his where he was kneading the flesh above one thigh.

When he delved under her dress and down the back of her panties, a giant flash went off through her body. This all felt so new and necessary. So incredibly wrong and wonderfully right. She needed to get naked with Jack. She would *die* if she couldn't feel his hot skin on hers. She could barely breathe, the physical longing was so strong. So beautiful and bad and brilliantly intense.

As that first kiss broke down into hungry snatches, she wiggled to help him ditch her underwear. When he grabbed the hem of her dress and started to tug it over her head, she sat up and lifted her arms in the air. Straddled over his hips, her head back and eyes closed, she leaned in as he scooped her breasts out of their lace cups. His palms were big and hot and, dear heaven, just rough enough.

He was alternating between rolling and lightly plucking her nipples when she reached behind to unsnap her bra.

Her mistake was glancing down, seeing herself pretty much naked, thighs spread over a fully clothed man who, less than a week ago, she wouldn't have spat on let alone enjoyed mindless sex with.

Jack Reed. Number-one enemy…

What the hell am I thinking?

"I can't do this," Becca said, sweeping up the dress to cover what she could.

"Don't worry." He craned up to nuzzle her throat. "I'll guide you through."

"I mean this is a mistake."

His lips grazed her chin. "No mistake."

A hand curled around the side of her neck. Next she

knew, she was flipped onto her back and Jack was crouching, towering over her, unbuttoning his shirt, shrugging it off. His chest was so broad and bronzed, her fingertips tingled to sample every delicious mound and rung. When he maneuvered out of his pants and boxer shorts, she felt blood rush to her cheeks. This was moving much too fast.

He set a hand down next to her head. As one hot knee prized itself between hers, panic set in and both her hands shot out. She pushed against his pecs as he lowered himself onto her. A questioning look took hold in his eyes before he pulled slowly back and then frowned.

"You want to stop," he said—not a question, although the set of his mouth said it pained him to have to say it.

"One minute we were making the bed," she stammered. "The next…"

"You were kissing me."

"You kissed me!"

His grin flashed white. "You kissed me back."

She had. And, damn it, she wanted to kiss him again. Hard and deep and dirty. But this was wrong on so many levels, it made her head spin. And even if it were right…

Becca snatched a look down the length of his body and focused on that serious erection. As her heart pounded, she swallowed and then moistened her lips.

"Jack, we don't have protection."

"I have condoms."

"You do?" Wait. He *knew* this would happen?

"Better to be prepared than sorry," he pointed out.

Well, sure…except…it just reminded her how prepared Jack had been on so many other occasions. With so many other women.

She shook her head. *No.* "I can't do this."

"Do what?"

"This." She held her cheeks. "*Sex*. With you."

He hesitated and then, exhaling long and hard, he

brought her hand to his lips and tenderly kissed the palm. "I can't say I'm not bitterly disappointed," he murmured and then proceeded to kiss each fingertip.

Damn, he felt good, looked amazing, smelled divine. But even without the Lassiter complication, this was not a wise choice. Jack was a self-professed player. Sex was nothing more to him than sport. It meant as much as hitting a bull's-eye with an arrow.

While they'd been at the café, Becca had got away to make that phone call to Evan McCain. Then she'd explained the situation to her assistant. If the interview aired, she wanted everyone to know it was a beat up. But what would the world think if *this* ever got out?

She wiggled out from beneath him and set both feet on the floor. Avoiding his gaze, she put on her bra and shimmied back into her dress. It seemed that her panties, however, had disappeared. When she stood, she felt giddy... spacey...as if those last few moments had happened to somebody else on a distant planet.

Behind her, the bed squeaked; Jack had found his feet, too.

"I saw a lake when we drove in," he said as Becca listened to him shake out and then shrug back into his clothes. "I need to cool down and a washtub of water ain't gonna cut it."

He skirted around the bed, stood before her and then lifted her chin. His dark gaze was disappointed but also understanding.

"Why don't you come keep me company?"

Her stomach gave a kick and she found an excuse. "I should unpack...fix up this bed."

"Becca, I should warn you, if you say bed again in the next thirty seconds, I won't be held responsible for my actions."

Inside she shouted, *BED, BED, BED!*

Then she crossed her arms to stop herself from bringing him close.

"You go cool off," she said. "I'll be fine here."

He crossed to the bedroom door. "I'll find the mutt while I'm gone."

When she didn't reply, he kept going, through the main room and out the front door. Becca found her underwear, shoved her panties on and then sat on the side of the bed like a lump.

At the end of three solid minutes, her body was *still* vibrating—humming and smoldering with unruly heat. The unspent energy was driving her nuts! None of that was about to subside unless, or until, she did something about it.

She thought of the lake's cool mirrored surface, of swimming until she was too tired to move or so much as think about humping Jack Reed half the night. She made fists of her hands, tried to think rational thoughts. In the end, she grabbed two towels from the closet, her bikini from her bag and ran after Jack to catch up.

Becca got to the lake in time to see Jack cannonball off the pier and into the water. His clothes were hung on a branch near the bush she decided to hide behind. Waiting at the end of that pier, Chichi yipped, skidded forward and then jumped in, too.

That dog loved the water. Jack appeared to be a strong swimmer, too. He power-stroked a good length before flip-turning to head off in a different direction. He swam up to Chichi, who alternated between madly lapping at the water and barking excitedly. Treading water, Jack laughed, a sound that echoed across the lake, through the treetops and then down to wrap around Becca.

The water sure looked good. So did those dynamite arms and shoulders, that brilliant smile and slick dark brown hair. So good, in fact, Becca was forced to admit a truth.

Even if Jack Reed *was* a villain and these feelings were wrong and the world might shun her if anyone ever found out—there was no way around it. She liked Jack. She liked his smile and his wit. God help her, she liked his kiss.

Behind the bush, she changed into the bikini. When he started off again, swimming freestyle in the opposite direction, she darted down the pier, all the way to the end and, without stopping, dived into the deep.

Spearing through the cold water gave her a jolt, but, man, was it refreshing! Becca held her breath as long as she could. When she surfaced, Jack was right there, waiting not an arm's length away.

She yelped.

Chichi barked.

And Jack...well, he just grinned.

"How the hell did you do that?" she asked. He'd been at least ten yards away. Then it clicked. "You *knew* I followed you," she said, working hard to tread water.

"Bears make less noise."

"Why didn't you wait for me?"

"This was more fun."

Seriously? "Scaring me half out of my wits like that?"

"You weren't scared." As he waded closer, cool ripples lapped at her neck and chin. "You wanted to surprise me. I just turned it around."

He looked so relaxed and one step ahead of the game, she couldn't give it up that easily.

"I got to thinking that a swim would save filling up the washtub." When his smile spread, Becca tried to frown. "What's so funny?"

"You are." Although he'd be tall enough to stand at this depth, he began to paddle around her, his long, strong arms swerving inches beneath the surface. "Fess up. You wanted to come play."

He'd waded closer...near enough for Becca to reach out and touch.

"Maybe," she agreed. "This part of our week together is supposed to be about acknowledging your less complicated side. About seeing the bigger value in simple pleasures and understanding you can help bring them to others."

His smile changed again around the corners of his mouth. It was even sexier, more knowing. Mischievous and so hot.

But then he shook his head.

"What?" she asked, barely keeping her chin above the surface. Treading water, her limbs were feeling the burn now.

"I'm not doing it this time."

"Doing what?"

"You want me to sweep you over. You want me to kiss you. Only when we get started, you'll remember your higher purpose and make up some lame excuse why we ought to stop."

She objected to the one thing she could. "My excuses aren't lame."

He kept circling her, looking at her with that exasperating smile. He filled his mouth with water and squirted a fountain off to one side.

"Why don't you come over here?" he finally said.

Becca tried to stare him down but, in the end, she bit her lip and admitted, "This isn't very mature, is it?"

"Can we agree that we should be grown-up about the fact that we're attracted to each other?"

As he slid closer, she imagined his tongue rather than the water swirling over her belly, between her legs.

She nodded. *Damn it. Yes.*

"You know the consequences?" he asked.

She nodded again.

"And you still want this?"

Big breath. "Uh-huh."

Hot, strong fingers curled around her shoulders. Then their mouths joined and she was swept into the sublime haven of his arms.

He held her against his chest as their kiss played out— savoring, teasing, probing, until nothing else existed except the two of them and these sizzling, secret feelings.

When he broke the kiss, his lips stayed close. "Still okay?"

She rubbed her dreamy smile over his. "Okay isn't the word."

He tasted her lips again. "Wrap your legs around me."

She looped her arms around his neck and circled his hips with her legs, digging her heels in behind his thighs. He cupped her bottom and pulled her through the water, closer to him. As the length of his erection met the strip between her thighs, a jet of warm sparks flew through her veins. Her breath caught at the same time her head rocked back.

His hands slid under her behind. Then she felt his touch inside her bikini's crotch. His teeth dragged one half of her bikini top aside until the nipple was exposed and moist warmth covered that tip bobbing just above water level. While he drew that nipple back onto his tongue, his fingers slipped slowly up and down, over and between her folds. When his head pulled back a little and the edge of his teeth grazed her nipple, one finger slipped all the way inside of her.

She gasped, shuddered from top to toe, and then held his head in place against her breast.

The tip of his tongue rimmed the areola as he expertly massaged her down below. Every time his finger slid up, the tip grazed her G-spot, while one of his other fingers slipped up the outside, nudging the swollen bead hiding at the top of her folds. His pace was slow and steady, the perfect speed and pressure. Before long, she joined in with the rhythm, her hips rocking with his mesmerizing caress.

With each passing second, the sensations increased. As tingling heat ripped through her bloodstream, she needed to feel his mouth on hers again. She had to have him kissing her in a penetrating, all-or-nothing kind of way. Only the things his lips and teeth and tongue were doing added to the climb—a slope so steep, she had to gasp, the air was so thin.

When her orgasm broke, Becca curled into herself before she ground down against him and then released a cry that must have carried halfway to Montana. As she continued to shudder and groan, Jack watched a flow of raw emotions redefine her beautiful face. Holding her, loving her... This water might be chilly but he was rock-hard.

When he felt her floating down, he brought both his arms up around her waist to hold her against his chest. As her hot cheek nestled against the slope of his neck, he swirled her slowly through the water. Her ragged breathing gradually eased. Every now and then, her legs would twitch and then tighten around him again. He pressed a kiss to her crown, closed his eyes and wished every day could be as good as this.

After a few moments, she gave a big sigh, slid a palm over his shoulder and gradually lifted her face to his. Her smile was faraway. Satisfied. The loveliest smile he'd ever seen.

"You look like you could do with a nap," he joked.

"Are you kidding?" she asked groggily. "I may never let you sleep again."

Was she saying she wanted to do this every night? Jack could certainly arrange that. For a time, at least. Once they got back to the city, no doubt she would want to return to their former relationship…the one where she pretended to hate him.

She stretched her arms high over her head and then withered back against him, her lips landing on the pulse he felt beating at the side of his neck. The tip of her tongue tickled the spot.

"Hmm, you taste good," she murmured against his skin. "I want to taste every inch of you."

"Well, we're going to have to get out of the water for that."

She smiled up into his eyes. "Why?"

"A…we'll get all pruny. B…it's getting cold. C…something's nibbling at my toes and I don't need the distraction. D…"

"We don't have any protection," she finished.

Her dreamy gaze was growing clearer.

"We might have to shift camp, but look on the bright side," he said. "No one has to sleep on the cot."

Her legs tightened around him again. "I'll race you to shore."

"Okay, but I really don't think—"

Jack grunted as she used her feet against his abdomen to push off.

He let her have a head start and then sprang into action.

A moment later, when the water got too shallow for freestyle, he jumped up and stomped and splashed onto shore. Laughing and splashing too, she beat him by a nose. The prize was Jack crash-tackling her onto a patch of soft, long grass, working it so she landed on top of him, not vice versa. Then he rolled so she was pinned beneath him, his giggling prisoner.

In fact, Becca was laughing so much, she started to cough. He eased her up to a sitting position and patted her back. He didn't miss the fact that her body was even more sensational without all that water getting in the way. Personal preference, of course…and Becca Stevens was his.

"I brought towels," she said, spluttering again and then visibly shivering. Goosebumps erupted all down her arms.

Jack pushed to his feet and crossed over to sweep up the towels she'd left at the foot of the bush he had seen her hide behind earlier. When he turned to join her again, something struck him as strange. As…missing. Becca was sitting straighter, alert. With a curious gaze, she scanned the water.

Jack's throat thickened.

Where the hell was the dog?

Nine

"Can you see him anywhere?" Becca asked.

When Jack handed over a towel but didn't reply, she called Chichi's name nice and loud. Only eerie silence, sprinkled with cicada clicks, came back. She called again, and as the seconds ticked by, a feeling of dread filled her.

"He must be around somewhere," Jack said, lashing a towel around his hips before helping Becca to her feet as she wrapped her towel under her arms.

"I haven't seen him since I dived in," she said, scanning the woods for any sign.

Holding the towel around her chest, she crossed to the water's edge and called again. A sick feeling built high in her stomach and rose in her throat. When Jack, being supportive, gripped her shoulder, emotion prickled behind her nose.

Keep it together. Don't panic. Not yet.

Becca had lived alongside people, including babies and young children, who'd been forced to survive without adequate or clean water, with barely enough to eat, and little or no prospect of bettering their lives in a way most folks here took for granted. During her Peace Corps days, she'd kept strong, kept going. Rarely had she shed a tear, not because she hadn't felt anguish and despair, but because time spent crying was less time being productive. Being a positive role model.

And yet here she was, tears in her eyes, because she'd lost sight of a little dog.

But there was more to it than that. She'd been so self-absorbed in satisfying those urges, she hadn't given another thought to Hailey's dog. To her friend's four-legged baby. How would she explain that?

"Has he been here before?" Jack asked.

"Not to the lake, but he loves splashing around in the surf and diving into Hailey's pool at home. He likes the water."

"Yeah. I got that. He's probably dog-paddling up a storm right now, swimming across from the other side."

Becca crossed her arms, hugging herself, as she scanned the area again. Everything was so still. She called out his name, and then called it again, more loudly. As loudly as she could.

Jack gently turned her to face him. Holding her gaze with his, he gave a brave smile. "I'll find him, okay? You have my word."

His promise was supposed to make her feel better. But what was Jack's word really worth? He wasn't renowned for jumping on a steed and galloping to anyone's rescue. Angelica might disagree, but she was clinging to any port in the storm her father's death and will had brewed up.

"If we can't find him—" she said.

"We'll find him."

"But if we can't…how will I ever tell Hailey? She loves that dog like a child."

Jack skirted around in front of Becca and herded her back toward the trees, away from the lake. "You sit. I'll search. Deal?"

She didn't argue, but she had no intention of sitting back and doing nothing.

They quickly changed back into their clothes and Jack set off to circumnavigate the lake. Every now and then he brought cupped hands to his mouth and called out Chichi's name. As Becca headed off the other way, she sent up a prayer.

When she told Hailey this story, she needed it to have a happy ending.

It didn't look good.

Jack was halfway around the lake, calling out the pooch's name, searching the scrub nearest the water's edge. Not a peep. He'd assumed that Chichi had been paddling by himself in the lake before this.

Now he felt worse than any names reporters or broken businessmen had ever called him. Why hadn't he even given the little guy, who'd been paddling furiously, a second thought? Obviously because he had other things on his mind.

It was getting dark and he'd scoured most of the perimeter of the lake when he decided to head back. Becca had set off in the opposite direction. Looking back now and then, he'd seen her either wandering into or coming out of the woods, searching among the trees and shrubs. They'd both been calling for over an hour.

When they met back at the pier, Jack wrapped Becca in his arms. After a moment, she hugged him back. He grazed his lips through her hair. "We'd better go while there's still some light."

She nodded against his chest and then they walked hand in hand back down the trail. It might as well have been a funeral march. He couldn't help this situation, but he could at least try to keep Becca's mind on other things.

"We never had a cabin in the woods growing up," he said, giving her hand a squeeze.

"Don't suppose you need one when you own a five-star chalet in the snow."

She wasn't serious but there wasn't a hint of a tease in her voice, either. He tried again.

"What were the other kids in your family like?"

"I was the youngest, then Emily, Abigail and Faith."

"Still keep in touch?"

"Emily's in the U.K. now. She married a doctor."

"Good for her."

"Abigail is an elementary school teacher and Faith is travelling the world. She's in Burma at the moment, I think."

"Did you share any time with them here at the lake house?"

"Not recently. I've had Hailey up a couple of times."

She lowered her head and he tried to pick up their pace, to distract her from thinking about the dog and because night was falling fast. They needed to get back to the cabin.

"Anyone else?" he asked.

"A couple of friends from the office."

"Any male friends?"

She gave him a look. "You really want to know?"

He shrugged. *Your call.*

She didn't exactly grin. "Although it's rather personal... no. I've never brought any male friends to the cabin."

"You don't want to get personal?"

"I don't have anything to hide. What you see is what you get."

"What I see is a beautiful, feisty, determined woman who always puts others before herself."

Instead of a smile, the compliment brought on a frown. "Don't overdo it."

He blew out a breath. Guess it was going to be a long, cold night. So he might as well say what he felt.

"Has anyone ever told you that you have trouble accepting compliments?"

"I don't need compliments."

"Because you're tough."

"Because I already feel fine with who I am."

"Whereas I need lots of work."

She only looked the other way. Her hand felt limp in his. He had the sense she might be more comfortable severing the link. On one level, that annoyed him. Not an hour ago, she'd come apart in his arms as if it was her last feel-good moment before the world ended. He'd thought they'd been pretty tight then.

On the other hand, he understood...she felt gutted. He felt like crap, too.

By the time they made it back to the cabin, Becca wished she'd never heard the name Jack Reed. But not for the reasons he might have thought. She didn't blame Jack one bit for Chichi's disappearance. That dog had been her responsibility and she'd screwed up.

During the search, she'd not only thought ahead to Hailey's tears when she discovered the news, but also sifted through every grain of logic that said it was a good idea to kidnap Jack for a few days. She'd believed that coming here—experiencing this with her—would touch and bring out his more humble, benevolent side.

But Jack had been in the game a long time. Did she have any hope of swaying his plans to take over Lassiter Media and do what instinct told him to do: make a huge profit off selling the company piecemeal? No one could convince Angelica of Jack's deeper motives, just as no one could have told Becca she should have kept from sticking her nose in.

But not everything could be fixed, including, it would seem, her physical attraction toward Jack. Today she'd let her emotions rule her head in a spectacular way. On one level she didn't regret the time they'd spent in the lake together. She had never imagined that such intensity of sensation could truly exist. The height of her climax had turned her inside out.

On another far more practical level, while she had not set out to use the possibility of sex as a motivator, the fact remained that Jack had agreed to this challenge not because he thought for a moment she might be able to change his mind in a week about taking over Lassiter Media, but because a woman had confronted and intrigued him. Getting closer to her had been a challenge in itself. She'd pretty much handed herself to him on a platter. She was no different, in that regard, from any other woman he'd successfully seduced.

So why did she feel as if what had happened between them in the lake had been special? Why did she feel as if it truly mattered to him? Maybe because it had mattered to her. She felt a connection with Jack that made her want to leave their other, more complicated worlds behind.

When they got to the cabin, the door was ajar. In her stupid hurry to catch up with Jack, she'd bolted without shutting the damn thing. Now she walked in first.

"Want me to light a fire?" he asked, following her inside.

"It's not cold enough."

"Might get cold later."

He was trying to be supportive. He truly felt bad about how this afternoon had ended. He'd done his best to try to find poor Chichi.

Turning to him, she found a smile. "Thanks for trying to find him. I appreciate it."

In the shadows, she couldn't make out his face other than by the moonlight slanting in through the doorway.

"Becca...I'm sorry. I don't know what else to say."

"You don't need to say anything. Just sit with me awhile. Who knows? He might still come back." Chichi might not have drowned or been bitten by a snake or—

Becca caught a tear as it ran down her cheek. She apologized. "I'm not usually such a baby."

"You're not being a baby. You have feelings. Everyone has feelings."

"Even you."

"Yeah." She imagined she saw his smile. "Even me."

She reached up on tiptoe, rested a palm on his shirt and dotted a kiss on his cheek. "I'll get the lantern."

"You sit down," he said. "I don't need you tripping over something and breaking your leg."

"But I know this place—"

"And I'm telling you...*asking* you...please. Let me."

She surrendered and felt her way around to sit on the couch in front of the unlit fireplace. A moment later, a bright light from the main bedroom illuminated a wedge of the wooden floor in front of her. Telling herself that they would find Chichi tomorrow, and all would be well, she waited for Jack to return. Instead he called out.

"Becca, can you come here?"

She pushed to her feet and followed the light. Jack stood next to the set of drawers. He held the lantern high so most of the room was lit. Looking at the partly made bed, he grinned as he said, "Look who the cat dragged in."

Near the headboard, Becca saw two glowing eyes pop up. She blinked. And then she covered her mouth to smother the yelp—of delight, not fright.

Jack chuckled. "Seems Chichi decided to beat us home."

She rushed over, folded the cool little dog in her lap and smothered him in kisses. Wagging his tail, he lapped it all up.

"I know what this means," Jack said, moving closer.

Becca was still cuddling Chichi close. "What's that?"

"There won't be just the two of us sharing that bed tonight."

As low as she had felt a moment ago, now she felt as if she could fly. She didn't want to think about any regrets she might have in the morning. As Chichi jumped off the bed and leapt onto the camper cot, she only wanted to celebrate.

Ten

Becca reached up and pulled him down. As her mouth latched onto his, they fell back onto the bed.

Sometime later, when she let him come up for air, Jack arched a brow.

"Does this mean we have to get naked?"

They were lying facing each other. Now she sat up, grabbed the hem of his shirt and pulled it up. Then she dropped warm, hungry kisses all over his chest while her fingers kneaded his sides.

Her mouth slid lower and lower. The tip of her tongue was circling his navel when she unzipped his fly. Jack pushed up on his elbows. If she was about to do what he thought she would do, he was all for it. He helped her pull off his pants and boxer briefs. Then she snatched the dress off over her head. The bra landed on the coat stand in the corner. He wasn't sure where the panties went.

He was sitting at the foot of the bed while she stood before him. Ready to go, he fell back and then shot up again.

"Condoms," he said, ready to spring over to his bag for supplies.

But Becca was slotting herself between his parted thighs. Her breasts were at eye level. What was a man to do?

He dropped slow, moist kisses around one nipple while plucking and lightly pinching the other. Her fingers drove through his hair, over the back of his scalp then across to each shoulder as she arched into him and made noises in her throat that only excited him more.

His other hand fanned down the curve of her ribs, waist, hip. When his fingers slid between her legs and found her wet, he remembered why he'd sat up in the first place.

While he sucked and plucked and gently rubbed, he spoke around that nipple. "Rubbers…"

She pulled his head away, snatched a penetrating kiss that blew his mind and then lowered onto her knees on the floor. A second before her lips met the tip of his erection, he heard her murmur, "Not yet."

As her head lowered more, a series of bone-melting sensations rippled over his skin. At first she simply held him in her mouth. Then her tongue got into the act, swirling around the ridge, rolling one way then the other, tickling the tip. When she began to hum, the vibration at the base of her throat drifted along her tongue and teeth.

He clutched the sheet and clenched his jaw.

He wasn't normally this excited this soon. It had to be all the buildup—in the lake, coming home—and because she knew just what to do and how to do it, as if they had been together like this before. Of course, before this week, she would have jumped off a cliff rather than…well, do what she was doing now.

He shifted enough to scoop her around the waist and lift her up and onto the bed. As she lay there looking at him with hungry eyes, he cautioned her with a finger.

"Stay right there. Don't move."

With a cheeky grin, she crossed her heart.

He found his bag, ripped the condom box open and, crossing back, rolled the rubber on. Becca's arms were tucked under the pillow behind her head. Her hair had dried. In the lantern light, the mussed waves glistened around her face. Then she drew up one knee, angled her hips in a provocative pose, and he crawled up the mattress until he was kissing her again. He couldn't bring her close enough as they rolled together on the sheets.

His breathing was heavy by the time he urged her over onto her back and positioned himself between her thighs. As he entered her slowly, he watched her eyes widen, her back arch and lips part. Then she smiled. He wanted to say how beautiful she was, not just her face or her body, but the way she made him feel—truly alive for the first time in years.

When her legs wrapped around his thighs and her pelvis slanted up, he closed his eyes and gave himself over to sensation.

He'd wanted this, their first time together, to last all night. She fit him so well—everywhere. The physical friction building between them was the sweetest he'd ever known. And as heat began to blaze and then to rage, Jack found himself picturing them here together like this for more than two nights.

For longer than either one could ever allow.

Becca's entire body was left buzzing—floating. All the rumors were true. Jack Reed was not only smoking hot in bed, in her opinion, he was legendary.

They were lying on their backs side by side, both gazing blindly at the ceiling. Basking in the afterglow, they were still panting and smiling. Becca's skin was cooling. The payoff had been so unbelievably good, she only wanted to do it again.

"I wonder if that dog planned this," he said.

"What do you mean?"

"If Chichi hadn't wandered off," he explained, "we wouldn't be here doing this."

"If we hadn't lost him in the first place," she pointed out, "we would have done this beside the lake."

"And right now mosquitoes would be feasting on our backsides." He kissed her nose. "Our little friend did us a favor."

"After half scaring me death."

"He didn't know."

She laughed. "Jack Reed, crusader for misunderstood mutts."

"Make that misunderstood *ugly* mutts."

"Not kind, and yet I can see it on a T-shirt. On the letterhead of a charity. Maybe you should get one of your own."

"A dog?"

"And a charity."

He shifted up on an elbow and cupped his jaw in his palm. "Maybe I should."

His smile was so close, and with his heavy hand resting on the dip of her waist... Becca felt so lucky. And somehow also sad. If she didn't know Jack's background, if he wasn't so forthright in embracing his less-flattering side, she might be fooled into believing they were made for each other.

In reality, of course, two people couldn't be less suited to each other. This physical chemistry might be explosive, but what a person believed in was a thousand times more important than how skilled and connected they were in the bedroom. She stood for sacrifice and the betterment of society. Jack stood for self-gain, for power at the expense of anything and anyone who stood in his way.

"Does the lake have fish?" he asked, toying with a wave of her hair.

"My dad used to fish here all the time."

"Any poles around?"

"In the shed." She drew a wiggling line down the middle of his steamy chest. "You like fishing?"

"My father took me fly-fishing a couple of times."

"Fond memories?"

"Sure. We didn't get to spend that much time together."

"Why's that?"

"He ran his own company. That means putting in the extra hours when employees get to go home to their families."

"If it was his company, he could have made a choice to go home rather than stay."

"Not that simple. Before I came along, my father was bankrupt. They lost their house and more than a few fair-weather friends. At the same time my mother landed in the hospital with pneumonia. She almost died. On one of those fishing trips, Dad told me that when he thought she might not pull through, he'd made a vow. If only she lived, if they could spend a long and happy life together, he would take care of her the way she deserved."

"He blamed himself for her illness?"

"He felt responsible for his family. She recovered and their luck seemed to change. He started up another company, finance lending this time, and it took off. But he always had one eye on the past, the other on the future. He never allowed himself to drop the ball. His priority was making sure we were cared for."

"Even if he couldn't share what was most precious of all."

"His time? I knew he loved us both. But there were sacrifices. You can't have everything."

"Do you see much of them now?"

"They passed away ten years ago within months of each other."

"That must have been hard."

"We've all got to go sometime. Better to go in your seventies than…" His jaw tensed and he looked away.

Was he remembering the woman he had loved in college? Did he wonder what they might have shared and conquered together if she had lived? Becca wasn't sure he would have taken his father's route and dedicated his life to a company in order to ensure security for his family. She would rather believe that he'd have taken his own son fly-fishing often—spent quality time with those he loved.

Jack sat up. "Hey, you want a beer? A glass of wine?"

"Beer," she said, reaching over the side of the bed to find her dress.

"Stay put. I'll find the bathroom, clean up and bring back supplies. Can I take the light?"

"Be my guest."

While he was gone and she was left in the shadows, Becca shimmied under the top sheet and waited. She heard Chichi's collar rattle from the cot in the corner as he scratched himself. She'd had plans to set Jack to work while they were here. Chopping wood, fixing loose shingles, sanding back walls, cooking simple meals. Nothing so out of the ordinary for normal folk. Her goal had been to highlight the difference between the big-time "haves" and people who had to struggle. There were plenty of them out there.

There wasn't much work going on at the moment.

Soon, he was back carrying the ice chest in one hand, flashlight in the other. Becca took the light and he jumped in under the sheet and then set the chest down between them. As he cracked open one beer and handed it over, she picked up the thread of their conversation.

"Sounds as if you had good parents."

"I was lucky," he admitted, cracking open one for himself. They saluted each other and pulled down a mouthful. Becca didn't drink beer often, but in this setting, on this night, it felt right.

"I've never found out who my birth mother was," she said, resting the beer on her lap. "I didn't want to complicate anyone's life by dropping back in."

"Isn't it usually the other way around? A biological parent not wanting to make waves in the adult child's life?"

"I figure it might not be easy, but there are ways to track down a baby who's been gobbled up in the system. If she didn't want to know, it's better left alone."

"You never wanted to know the reasons?"

"Not anymore. Can't change yesterdays. And I didn't have such a hard time, even those first eleven years."

"Were you with lots of families?"

"Two others. I was provided for. Nobody abused me. But…" She brought the beer to her lips, swallowed another mouthful and confessed what she hadn't told anyone before. "I knew something was missing. Something key. Sometimes I felt…*invisible*." Sometimes she felt that way still. But not with Jack. Even right from the start. "It's hard to describe."

"Did you feel that way a lot?"

"Whenever I did, I read. Sometimes the same book over and over."

"What was your favorite?"

"When I was very young, *Cinderella*."

"A classic. Like the Bambino."

She smiled. "I fell in love with the idea of a fairy godmother. When all the lights went out at night, I'd sit up in bed and gaze out the window for what seemed like hours. I thought if only I wished hard enough, all my dreams would come true."

"What dreams?"

"I was an overweight, painfully shy girl. I wouldn't say boo to save myself. But in my dreams I was a princess, like Cinders. I simply needed my godmother to wave her wand and work her magic."

He was grinning. "Well, of course."

"If ever I saw a mouse," she went on, "I would close my eyes and wish for it to change into a beautiful white steed. I'd daydream that my dress was a gorgeous billowing gown made of white satin. Naturally a prince would happen along, fall on one knee and beg me to marry him."

Jack's eyes were smiling. "Naturally."

"The ring he'd ask me to wear was either a big diamond circled by priceless rubies, or a pearl surrounded by a sparkling sea of sapphires. Something right out of yesteryear."

"And then?"

Becca put her beer down. "Then I grew up, got a degree, joined the Peace Corps."

His expression changed. "Tell me about that."

"I served as a volunteer in the Dominican Republic for two years."

"That would be right after college?"

"Uh-huh. I helped to teach the youth how to make good choices. We talked to women about reproduction health and nutrition. There's so much poverty and unemployment. It's hard to imagine my life back there now. Those two years shaped me more than anything before or since. I know the true value of a safe, soft place to land."

"I had dreams of saving the world, too, once."

"*No*. Really?"

"I'd finished my engineering business degree. I was going to fly to Africa to help build housing."

Was he serious? "Jack, have you ever told anyone else that?"

"What? And destroy my image?"

She grinned. "So, you were going by yourself?"

"With my girlfriend. My fiancée. We were going to leave everything behind. Start fresh."

Lying on her side, Becca laid her cheek on her outstretched arm and searched his eyes.

"What was she like?"

He seemed to think back. "Krystal was soft. Delicate. She was studying criminal law. Her father was a defense attorney, and then became a judge later in his career. I never thought she was cut out for it. She didn't fit with the idea of courtroom drama and getting murderers off on a technicality. She was gentle. Easily hurt. Entirely giving."

Becca's heart was beating faster.

"You wanted to protect her."

Like Jack's father had wanted to protect his mom.

"I imagined us married with a couple of boys," he said. "I'd come home from work every day and she'd have a delicious dinner waiting. Later, while she took some downtime, I'd play with the kids."

Becca smiled softly. "I can imagine you doing that." She really could. "Can I ask...how did she die?"

His jaw tightened. "Her father was one mean son of a gun. Krystal was never good enough for the judge. She was an only child, so it was up to her to follow in her dad's giant footsteps. Carry on the legacy. She began to flunk classes. She wasn't looking after herself. When she came down with mono, it laid her up for weeks. Then we spent Thanksgiving at her parents'. Big mistake. Her father went from cool, to frosty, to flat-out belligerent. At the table, he started attacking her, telling her that she had to try harder. If that was her best, it wasn't near good enough."

Becca felt ill. "Poor girl."

"I gave him a piece of my mind. Then I was in *everyone's* bad books."

It was true. A person could say what they like about

their own family, but God help anyone else who tried to bring them down.

"Krystal was depressed for weeks after that. Then, a few days before Christmas, the dark cloud seemed to lift. She was smiling again. She said that she'd come to accept that she couldn't get away from disappointing her father, but that was okay."

Becca knew what was coming.

A muscle in his jaw flexed before Jack ended, "She didn't see that Christmas morning. I found her in the bathroom."

"Oh, Jack ..."

"Her father blamed me. Hell, *I* blamed me."

Was this the reason he'd looked so distant when they'd visited that school—the day she'd lectured him about vulnerable young adults? He had already learned that lesson on his own.

"You shouldn't blame yourself," she said, holding his hand. "She needed professional help."

"Instead her boyfriend added to the pressure." He exhaled. "So, you see, sometimes it's not so good to be handed your future, whether you think you want it or not. Big shoes are hard to fill."

Was that his way of justifying his position with Angelica? If they should succeed in overthrowing Evan McCain, was that perspective meant to stave off guilt over persuading Angelica to later sell off the pieces?

He studied her face for a long moment before casting a look at the ice chest. Shifting his hand from under hers, he flipped open the lid again and put a casual note in his voice.

"So, what else have we got? Eggs, bacon, tomatoes? You have gas in the kitchen?"

"Yeah. I do."

Becca was still processing everything he'd divulged.

How many more layers were there to this man? What other wounds was he covering up? Her first eleven years of her life hadn't been a picnic, but she hadn't had anyone close to her die. Jack had lost the woman he had loved as well as both his parents. Some people grieved by putting up a wall. Shutting off certain parts of themselves. Was that Jack?

"What say I whip you up an omelet?" he said.

She tried to be light. "You cook?"

"Not well."

"Can you chop wood?"

"If required."

It wasn't cool enough for a fire. Becca peered inside the ice chest. "There's crackers and strawberries and three kinds of cheese. And look at this…" She drew out a package. "Belgian chocolate."

"Even better than Danishes."

She broke off two pieces and slotted one bit in his mouth, the other in her own.

"I should mention that I have a chocolate addiction," she said around her mouthful.

"Chocolate's good for you."

He popped another square into her mouth and she smiled as she took in every line of his face.

"If you're a chocoholic," he said, "you need to try this."

He broke off another piece of chocolate and set a strawberry on top. "Open up," he said, and she did.

As she chewed and sighed, he made his own chocolate-strawberry stack.

"Oh, God." She sighed. "This is so good."

His lips came close to taste hers. "I totally agree."

Eleven

After their picnic and talk in bed, Becca fell asleep in Jack's arms.

He lay there for he didn't know how long, thinking back on how he'd opened up about that piece of his past. The words had come remarkably easy. The emotion hadn't been as painful as he'd remembered. Time healed all wounds? Maybe that was true. It was the scars he couldn't seem to kick.

Jack closed his eyes for a moment. When he opened them again, morning light was streaking in through the window, warming the room with a gauzy golden glow. Smiling, Jack stretched. *Man,* he felt good. And the reason was lying right here alongside of him.

He reached out to bring Becca close—and came up empty. The only sign of her was the impression left on the sheet.

Jack sat up.

The cot was empty, too. Other than birds chirping and

squawking outside, all was quiet. The screened window was open, letting in pine-scented fresh air. No smog. No traffic. No meetings.

No phone calls?

Was there even reception out here?

Jack swung out of bed, grabbed some jeans and pulled them on. Then he found his phone. Some texts and three voicemails. One from Logan, one from Angelica and one from David Baldwin.

Wearing cutoffs and a T-shirt that read "Choose Happiness," Becca entered the room. Her flawless face broke into a big smile. "You're up!"

Something pleasant tugged in Jack's gut. He crossed over, folded her up in his arms and nuzzled the top of her head. She felt soft and warm and smelled like sunshine. If Angelica was okay when he called back, maybe they could stay an additional couple of days. Or three, or four.

"I missed you," he murmured against her hair.

She laughed. "You've been awake two minutes."

"One minute."

Pulling away, she spotted the phone in his hand. When her smile cooled, he felt a spike of guilt—which he shouldn't.

"I wasn't sure if we got reception out this far," he said.

"It's patchy. Any messages?"

"A few."

While her eyes still shone, her mouth tightened. "Anything important?"

"You don't want to know."

"Angelica?" Jack nodded. "You going to call her back?" She held up her hands. "Sorry. Stupid question. She might be planning a coup for this afternoon. You wouldn't want to miss that."

Jack caught her as she turned to leave. "Becca, this was always a tricky situation."

She kept her gaze on the wooden floor. "I didn't think it'd get *this* tricky."

Ah, hell.

He brought her close again and, lifting her chin, searched those sparkling green eyes. "Are you sorry we came?"

"Up until a second ago, for so many reasons, I wasn't. I wanted to take you away from everything that drives your need to win. I wanted you to live a simple life and appreciate it, even for a couple of days. I thought you might see how little people need, and how easy it would be for everyone to have that if we all cared enough. But now..."

"What we shared last night was amazing. But I still have to help Angelica. I just *have* to."

"Because someone has a gun to your head?"

Jack struggled and then admitted, "I can't explain."

"No need. It's pretty obvious."

He studied her wounded, defiant look and then put the phone down on the side table.

Her gaze snapped from the phone back to him. "You're not going to call her?"

"Angelica can wait."

But then his phone rang. Becca swept it up and held it out for him, daring him to refuse, hoping that he would. He wanted to ignore the call, but now it had rung a bigger part wanted to reconnect and plug into what was going on beyond the walls of this cabin. He couldn't walk away from this deal, not even for Becca.

He took the phone, connected. It wasn't Angelica.

"Hope I didn't catch you too early," David Baldwin said. "I left a message—"

Annoyed, Jack cut in. "What can I do for you?"

"I'm having a get-together this afternoon. I know you're probably busy."

Chichi pranced in with a stick between his small, pointy teeth. Jack turned toward the window view. "A bit, yeah."

"But if you could make it over, just for a few moments… it's important."

"David, I really don't think—"

"Don't give me your answer now." He gave a time for the event. "At the shop. Hope to see you there."

David Baldwin could hope all he liked.

Chichi was going to town, chewing his stick on the cot. Becca, however, had disappeared.

As Jack headed for the doorway, she marched by, carrying the ice chest. He strode out and took it from her. *For Pete's sake.*

"What exactly is the rush?" he asked.

"It's time to go."

"You said two days and two nights."

"I've changed my mind. Things have gotten off track. This won't work."

Jack put down the chest and turned off his phone. "Weren't we fixing bacon and eggs?" Amid the giggling and kissing last night, there'd been some mention of cooking breakfast before she'd fallen asleep.

"I'd rather just get back on the road. You know…get back to reality."

"I didn't mean to upset you."

She knotted her arms over her chest. "I'm not upset with you. I'm upset with *me*. For a second there, I'd actually talked myself into believing that I might have reached your human side. A *caring* side that didn't have stealing and then raping Lassiter Media as next on his to-do list. But you can't wait to get back into it."

Jack flinched. Well, that stung.

"One day," he said, "I promise, we'll sit down and I'll give you the lowdown on this Lassiter business from my perspective. Just…not today. I can't today." He filed his fingers back through her silky hair and waited for her to meet his gaze. "Now, can I make us a coffee?"

"That won't fix anything."

"It sure won't hurt."

When he grinned, she bit her lip, exhaled and finally nodded. As they headed back to the kitchen, she said, "I guess there's still a part of me who believes in a fairy godmother. She was just here, expecting a miracle."

"Could be that's what I like most about you," he said. "Your faith." He stopped and turned her in the circle of one arm.

"You mean my temper," she said.

"Your tenacity."

"My stubborn streak."

"I like this about you, too."

His lips met hers and lingered there. Closing his eyes, he drank in all that sassy, strong-headed goodness. When he drew away, her eyes narrowed even as those succulent lips twitched.

"Next you'll be suggesting we take our coffee back to bed."

"Well, just remember." He lowered his head to kiss her properly. "It was your idea."

When she brought it up again, Jack didn't try to talk her out of leaving the cabin. She didn't need for matters between the two of them to get any more complicated than they already were, and he obviously needed to get back to see what Angelica was up to.

He'd tried to phone Angelica a number of times. When he'd failed to reach her, he'd grown more and more pre-occupied. He even admitted that he wondered if Angelica was purposely avoiding his calls now because she planned to do something he would stop if he could. When they finally got on the road after lunch, Becca couldn't shake the sense of guilt.

She had allowed her emotions to get the better of her where Jack was concerned. She'd taken him to the cabin not to give in to the attraction brewing between them, but to somehow help him gain perspective away from his cut-throat corporate world. She wanted to show him in a hands-on way he would remember that lots of people went without even the bare necessities. Had her scheme done any good at all, or had she only made matters worse?

Still, what Jack and she had shared at the cabin was more than physical. At least it had been for her. However much she abhorred Jack's business tactics and egocentric mind-set, whenever they had been together in an intimate sense, she hadn't been able to help falling just a little in love with him.

Chichi had sat on Becca's lap all the drive back to Santa Monica. When Jack pulled into the quiet beachside parking lot in a space right next to Hailey's café, the dog was quivering with excitement. Then Becca opened the car door; she couldn't stop Chichi from bolting up the ramp into the café's rear entrance.

Jack got out and hauled the ice chest off the backseat.

"Want to chow down while we're here?" Becca asked, joining him.

"Best to keep going."

He was eager to get back to L.A. He needed to call on Angelica, keep that Lassiter takeover ball rolling and on track. Becca had felt his preoccupation building for the whole drive back. Now, as they walked up the café's ramp together, he seemed disconnected.

As they made their way around the veranda, Hailey and Chichi appeared.

"How was the trip?" Hailey asked. "Hope Chichi behaved himself."

Jack set down the chest. As they took their usual seats and Hailey poured coffee, Becca let her friend know what had happened with Chichi the previous day at the lake... minus the bits about Jack and her being, well, otherwise occupied.

"I'm sorry," Becca said. "We should have kept a closer eye on him."

Hailey waved it off. "Way I see it, he probably just wanted to give you two some space."

When she flicked a knowing glance Jack's way, he held his expression, no hint of cheekiness or denial. But Becca's chest tightened. In his mind, he'd already moved on. What they had shared at the lake was in the past. He was back in corporate-raider mode and focused on bringing down his current target.

When neither Jack nor Becca commented, Hailey's expression grew concerned. "Oh, God," she murmured. "You don't know. There's no TV out at the cabin."

Jack's brow creased as he sat forward. "What happened?"

"It was on this morning," Hailey went on.

"You mean the interview from the reporter who ambushed us yesterday?" Becca asked.

"There were clips from that interview...." Hailey pressed her lips together. "It's the photos that got everyone talking."

Becca suddenly felt dizzy and she couldn't feel her face.

"What photos?" she groaned. She wasn't sure she wanted to know.

"You must have been followed," Hailey said. "They had shots of you both in that lake, taken with a telescopic lens, so they were kinda grainy. But it's pretty clear what you all were doing."

While Jack sat back like he'd been shot in the chest, the

knot of horror in Becca's stomach pulled apart and spread through every inch of her body. Everything around her, other than Jack's scowl, seemed to funnel back and fade to black.

Becca was always fighting the hard fight, standing up for morals and justice. Now she shut her eyes as that darkness enveloped her.

Despite keeping an eye out, Hailey said they must have been followed. Had they been followed back here, too?

She had to phone the office again and make certain Evans McCain understood. Things had gotten—confused, but she was still one hundred percent on his side.

"There's more," Hailey said, wincing.

Jack rubbed his brow. "Of course there is."

"Angelica Lassiter has called a press conference," Hailey went on, "scheduled for this afternoon."

Jack thumped the table and everyone, including Chichi, jumped. When he pushed to his feet, the action sent his chair skating and clattering into the one behind it.

Becca stood, too, hugged her friend and whispered in her ear, "I'll call you later."

Becca followed Jack around the veranda and down the ramp. Before he reached the driver's-side door of her Bambino, he stopped abruptly and spun around. She almost ran into him.

He held out his hand. "Keys."

Becca fumbled in her bag and slapped them in his palm. "You're going to see Angelica," she said.

"As soon as humanly possible."

Jack threw open the car door. As Becca skirted around and jumped in the passenger side, he turned the key in the ignition. The lights flashed up on the dash…but the engine didn't kick over. He growled and tried again.

Nothing.

He set his teeth, raised his fists, but held off somehow from smashing down on the wheel. If Becca was upset, Jack was livid. And then...

Things went from bad to a hundred times worse.

Twelve

"That's just great. That's *exactly* what I need."

Becca scowled across at him. "You're not the only one stuck in this car, you know."

"It's your car!"

As the tabloid show truck sailed into the parking lot and pulled behind them blocking their escape, Becca opened her mouth then simply sat back and crossed her arms tightly over her T-shirt while Jack brought up an app on his phone and sent a text for a cab.

He'd apologize for raising his voice later. Right now he needed to get them the hell out of this predicament. He didn't care who had tipped them off again or whether he and Becca had been followed the entire time. The director of the Lassiter Foundation had been seen repeatedly with the man who wanted to bring the whole lot down. He needed to get Becca out of this mess then he'd find Angelica before she purged in front of a microphone and said something they both might regret at that press conference.

When Angelica had wavered the other day, Jack thought he had been persuasive enough to get her back to where he needed her to be. Once again she had seemed set upon a path that would lead to a takeover of the company that was rightfully hers. But when she'd called this morning early and he hadn't been able to get in contact with her since, Jack had begun to worry. If Becca hadn't decided to call her cabin stay short, he'd have insisted.

As the camera crew and the reporter from the other day loped over, he threw open the door. "Get out of the car," he told Becca.

He met her around her side, grabbed her hand and headed for the road. She had to trot to keep up.

"Where are we going?"

"We're getting the hell out of Dodge."

As they reached the pavement, she yanked her hand from his. Her face was flushed but her bearing was almost regal.

"I'm not going," she said. "You've had Angelica dancing on your strings. Everyone knows she doesn't do anything without consulting you first. If Angelica's called a press conference without your permission or advice, it can only mean she's distancing herself from you. It might even mean that she's decided to step down from a takeover bid. I'm not going to tag along while you try to badger her into changing her mind."

The cab he'd ordered swerved into the gutter. Swinging open the door, he eyeballed Becca. "You coming?"

"I'll hold my head up and face the firing squad square on, thank you."

He had to admire her courage. "When you have a moment," he said, "I'll give you a lesson on how to avoid unnecessary trouble."

"You haven't done such a great job of it lately."

So it would seem. He should have flat-out refused

to give Becca an audience in the first place. Of course that would've meant missing out on getting to know her more—a once-in-a-lifetime experience. There'd never be another Becca.

"I'll call," he told her.

"Please don't."

"I can't change your mind?"

She only crossed her arms. Defiant to the end.

Jack hung his head, considered the repercussions and, leaving the cab door open, joined her again. "Then I'll stay, too."

Her eyes widened as her arms dropped to her sides. "I don't need you."

"Right now I think we need each other."

Stopping in position before them, the reporter shot out her first question.

"Mr. Reed," she began, "what do you have to say about the photos of yourself and Ms. Stevens circulating this morning?"

Jack surprised Becca. He didn't growl. Didn't try to divert the issue. He simply looped his arm around her waist, tugged her closer and announced, "Ms. Stevens and I are late for an engagement. So, if you'll excuse us…"

Then he crowded Becca toward the open cab door, leaving her no chance to argue. He scooted in the backseat after her. As he reached to close the door, the reporter persisted.

"Mr. Reed, wait…did you say engagement? You and Becca Stevens are engaged to be married? Does Angelica Lassiter know? Are you backing out of a takeover bid of Lassiter Media?"

The door slammed shut. The reporter's microphone hit the glass. Tires squealed as the cab pulled out.

"Where to?" the driver asked in an Eastern European accent.

"Beverly Hills."

Looking in the rearview mirror, the cabbie reached for a candy dispenser on the dash. He shook a mint into his mouth and sucked for a moment. "You are Jack Reed and the lady from the Lassiter charity, yes? I see pictures of you on TV."

Becca wanted to smack her forehead. Seemed everyone had seen those photos except them.

"No worries, Mr. Reed," the cabbie said with a lopsided grin. "I will lose those leeches. My mother-in-law, she worked for a big-time newspaper. She's still Mrs. Snoopidy Snoops." He sneered. "Always on my case, sticking in her nose where it might get cut off."

The cab swerved off the main drag down a side street.

"We get back on the highway a few miles down." The cabbie looked back at them over a shoulder. "Feel free to talk. What happens in cab, stays in cab."

After a few moments, Jack dared to look across at Becca. Her lips were tight, cheeks were pink. Her hands were balled up in fists at her sides.

"You tricked me," she growled.

"I did what I thought was right."

"You did what was right for *you*. I told you—" she pointed to Jack's brow "—you've got rocks in your head if you think I'm going with you to talk to Angelica. If you do, I'll tell her that she's being a fool. That she's destroying her family over the illusion of power. I'll ask her where the hell she put her priorities."

In this mood, Jack had no doubt that she would.

"I'll drop you off at your office," he said.

She slumped back and held her head. "They'll probably lynch me."

"Then I'll drop you home."

"That's not really addressing the problem, is it, Jack?"

He shut his eyes, his patience running thin now.

"I don't know what you expect me to do," he said. "If

you're waiting for a halo to magically appear above my head and a plea for forgiveness, don't hold your breath."

She stared at the ceiling, tears in her eyes. "I'm a fool. I was attracted to you and I let that ruin everything."

"Depends on how you look at it."

Her voice was thick, resigned. "There's only one way to look at it."

He didn't think so. "I want to see you again, Becca." And he didn't care who knew.

She froze, mouth half-open, eyes wide with shock. Then she shook herself and self-righteousness ruled again.

"You actually want to throw more fuel on this fire? Maybe you want to screw with my affections so much that I'll crumble and lead a munity of Lassiter management and employees against McCain?"

"That's crazy talk."

"Yeah, well, maybe I'm crazy."

"We're not going to get anywhere if—"

"That's it, Jack. We, you and I, are not going to get anywhere. Because this is over. O-V-E-R."

Angelica sent another text after Jack had dropped Becca home. She asked that he meet her at Lassiter Grill. He tried to ignore the ball of unease growing in the pit of his gut. The location was a sure sign. For her to suggest they meet there, she must have reconciled with her brother, Dylan, the one who'd been left controlling interest of the Lassiter Grill Group, including the restaurant here in L.A.

Jack would hear what she had to say. Then, if there was any doubt whatsoever about her caving in to the terms of J.D.'s will, he'd do his damnedest to talk her out of it.

When the cab dropped him off, Jack gave the driver a huge tip. As he walked into the restaurant, with its trademark rustic elegance, he spotted Angelica at a booth not far from the floor-to-ceiling stone fireplace. She sat staring into her coffee cup, looking like a jumper about to take that last step.

"Hello, Angelica," he said, sitting opposite her.

Angelica's head came up. Her expression was scathing. "What in the name of God were you thinking?"

Jack thatched his fingers on the table in front of him. "You're referring to Becca Stevens."

"The company, particularly the foundation, has been hit hard enough by this tug-of-war. Why in the name of everything sane would you go and sleep with that woman?"

"I didn't exactly plan it, Ange. Or not the way it turned out anyway."

She straightened in her seat. "I spoke with Logan. He was speechless."

And Jack was supposed to…what? Go to his room for time-out? "I am an adult. I don't need to ask permission."

"You sure as hell do when you're dragging my name down along with hers." She shook her head, incredulous. "I thought you said you weren't trying to get Becca on our side."

"I wasn't."

She blinked and frowned. "So, this was purely for sport?"

His teeth set so hard, his jaw ached. "I like Becca Stevens."

"Well, that's a shame because you just destroyed her."

It was bad, but not that bad. And Jack sure as hell didn't know why he was copping all the blame. "Becca's an adult, too. I didn't tie her down."

"She's no match for you." Angelica's anger turned into concern. "No one is."

Time to get back on topic. He took a breath and focused. "You wanted to see me."

"I want to… I mean, I'm pretty sure that I want to…"

"Walk away from your rightful inheritance?"

She raised her voice. "I want things back the way they were."

"We *can't* go back. We can only go forward. With commitment and justice on our side." He believed that to his bones.

Her head slowly tilted as she evaluated him through narrowed eyes. "You're saying the words, but somehow you don't sound as convinced."

That was news to him. But, granted… "It's been a long battle. When things are worth fighting for, it's never easy."

"Becca Stevens didn't get to you, did she? Here I am thinking you've used her, but I wonder—"

"If she had an effect on me?" Jack threw up his hands. "You know, in fact, *yes,* she did. She's a special lady with a big heart and too many other assets to count." He leaned forward. "But none of that changes what you and I are trying to achieve. *Will* achieve. Just think, Angelica. You won't have to live with the label of the snubbed daughter of J. D. Lassiter for much longer."

Her eyes glistened with moisture.

"You're not as strong as J.D.," Jack said. "You're stronger. And when you need a rest, like now, I'm here to stand guard on the battlements."

She blew out a shaky breath, then rested her elbow on the table and held her brow. "You don't know what it feels like to have to choose, Jack."

He might consider her fortunate. He was never given a choice.

When Logan had informed him of the part he was to play in this unfolding drama, Jack had wanted to refuse. But a friend was a friend; that didn't change once they died. And so he had agreed to comply with the special clause in J.D.'s will, which was meant solely for him and Angelica. Since that day he'd led her closer and closer toward a corporate showdown against Evan and anyone who stood behind him. The way Jack had looked at it, either outcome would be a victory.

Now…he only wished Becca Stevens didn't have to be part of the collateral damage.

Angelica called off the press conference, and Jack left her in a better state, although he didn't have a lot of faith in what the immediate future might bring. Angelica was an educated, capable woman. But he wondered how soon she would have crumpled and given in to the terms of the will if he hadn't been stirring her pot.

Jack ordered another cab, his intentions being to call in at the office—the first time ever wearing jeans, unlike Ms. Stevens. Not that he was in the mood to sit behind a desk. Truth be known, he felt like fishing…beside a quiet lake, simply to enjoy the atmosphere, the fresh air. The company.

As eventful as his time with Becca had been, he had an ice cube's chance in hell of rekindling those flames. Which got him thinking…just how long had it been since he'd been with a woman? The press played up his womanizing past. Jack's take? If a guy was single and able, damned if he'd want to sit at home singing to his cats. But he wasn't as ruthless in that department as the media made out. Of course it wasn't every day a man came across someone as intriguing as Becca.

She was in every way his match, including her annoying headstrong streak. And when they made love…she was wild and smart and incredibly generous. There were times when she exhausted him. She *always* inspired him.

And he sincerely doubted she'd ever want to see his hide again.

Jack was tossing around whether to tell the driver to ditch his earlier address and simply take him home when his cell phone beeped with a text. He prayed it wasn't

Angelica. Hoped against hope it might be Becca. It was neither.

David Baldwin. Again.

Still hope to see you this afternoon.
Best, Dave.

Jack felt bad for the man. He wished he could help the way David wanted him to. That was out of the question. But there was something more he could do. He had an afternoon to fill in anyway.

The cab dropped Jack off in front of the Baldwin Boats office and factory. The signage across the front of the main building was faded. The *o* in boats was gone completely. The yard was free of workers. He glanced at his watch. After quitting time for the factory.

As he neared the entrance, an odd, prickling feeling ran over his skin. He'd just take five minutes to tell Baldwin that not only was the deal still on the table, he would up the offer. Becca was right. How much money did one man need? And Dave had mentioned in one of the conversations that he had six kids. *Six*. What a scary thought. Four boys, two girls. What was it like growing up in a houseful of siblings? Noisy. Scary. Certainly never lonely.

When the receptionist spotted him strolling in through the automatic entry doors, she shot to her feet.

"Oh! Mr. Reed. Dave was expecting you. Well, he'd hoped..." She grinned like a kid who'd discovered every tree in the backyard had turned into a ball of cotton candy. "I'll go tell him you're here."

As she scurried off, Jack strolled around the reception area. Framed photographs hung on the walls, pictures of power catamarans, officials at boat launches. Quite a few of David, the earliest from perhaps twenty years ago. Before putting the contract together, he'd had a full background check compiled. David was only a little older than Jack, although he looked at least, ten years older. Stress could do that to a person. And while Jack lived with stress, it wasn't the kind where he had to scramble to find the next mortgage payment, or wonder when the utilities might be turned off. He didn't have to worry every week whether or not he could make the payroll. Jack knew that had been Dave's dilemma pretty much since the recession had hit and turned the economy on its head.

Dave ambled out from his office, a big smile plastered on his face. When he held out his hand, Jack took a hold and shook. There was a lot to be said about a man's handshake and Dave Baldwin's was firm without being cocky.

"Jack, glad you could make it," Dave said, ushering him down the corridor. He was a tall man. Almost as tall as Jack.

"Seems I'm too late for that get together," Jack said. Looked like everyone else had gone.

"Not too late at all."

They sat in tub chairs in Dave's office, a room that overlooked the factory yard. Outside Jack saw a couple of fixed cranes, several boat molds, numerous trailers, trolleys meant to shift upward of six tons. There was plenty of value in those assets. From previous conversations, Jack knew that Dave would never consider downsizing, which would mean putting people on unemployment. Men of Dave's ilk lived by two mottos: natural attrition only, and the captain must go down with the ship.

"Can I get you a coffee, Jack?"

"Got a beer?"

Dave brought two back from a bar fridge tucked under a counter covered with engineering plans. Jack cracked open the beer and downed a couple of much appreciated mouthfuls.

"Hmm. Cold," he said.

"I like it so cold that my lips turn numb."

Jack grinned. "Me, too."

"Cheryl and I have four boys, you know?"

"You mentioned."

"Oldest turning twenty-one next spring. Old enough to drink, to vote. It's scary how quickly time goes. I was twenty-one when I first got into this business. I worked my rear end off. When the owner decided to retire, he asked if I wanted to buy in. I learned everything from that man. He was like a father to me."

"That's a long time in one place. I understand why you think of your employees as family."

"Family..." Studying the floor near his feet, David nodded deeply. "It's the most powerful word in the dictionary, don't you think? Just the idea of family makes a person feel warm and included." He caught Jack's gaze. "And sometimes a little overwhelmed."

Dave was looking at him so curiously, as if his face was a mask he wanted peeled back to see what lay underneath. Jack, however, couldn't help thinking about the Lassiter family, how it had all come together only to be recently torn apart.

"You have two daughters, too," Jack said.

"They're the youngest. Twins. Only six. My wife worries that we're old parents. That we might not be around to see our youngest grandkids. I tell her that our memory and our love will live on. Those girls, the boys too, will always know where they came from and that they were loved."

Jack sipped his beer. Was that too much information? And yet after the week he'd had, sitting here, tipping back while Dave philosophized on the context of family seemed somehow acceptable. Even agreeable.

It was good to truly shirk off the Lassiter problem for a while. To forget how upset Becca had still been when he'd dropped her home. No matter how combustible the chemistry—no matter how much Becca had wanted what they'd shared—he couldn't believe she would ever want to lay eyes on him again. How could something so good end up so bad?

"You grew up an only child, right?" Dave was saying.

"My mother had health problems. My parents rated it a small miracle that I was conceived."

Jack always felt a kind of bond between Ellie Lassiter and his own mother because of that.

"Did you ever wonder what it would be like to have a sister or brother?"

Funny he should ask. "One of my first memories was asking my dad if he could stop on his way home from work and pick one up for me."

They both chuckled. Jack was enjoying the downtime, but he supposed it wouldn't do to get *too* friendly. He needed to wrap things up and get back on the road soon.

"Dave, I've been thinking about our deal. I'd like to throw a bit more into the hat."

Jack offered a figure—more than he'd even intended. When Dave simply sat there studying him with the hint of a smile on his lips, Jack shifted in his seat, cleared his throat. Perhaps he needed to clarify his position.

"I like you, Dave. You're a stand-up guy. But I'm not looking at this with the prospect of becoming business partners."

"You're not."

"No, I'm not."

"How about brothers?"

Jack's stomach knotted but he held his gaze. "I'm sorry. I can't become part of your family."

"You already are."

Jack breathed slowly out. Okay, this was getting awkward. He pushed to his feet. "I should head off."

Dave remained seated. "I'd rather you stay. We still have so much to talk about."

When Dave's oddly calm expression held, Jack confronted him. Something more than a business deal was going on here. "What's this all about?"

"I told you—"

"Family?"

"I only found out two months ago."

"Found out *what?*"

"Two months ago, my mother was in hospital. Complications with diabetes. She passed away."

Jack exhaled. What was he supposed to say to that? He lowered his voice. "I'm sorry. My own mother died ten years ago."

She'd been a loving, selfless person. Jack had shed tears at her funeral and wasn't ashamed to admit it. He was shell-shocked when his father had followed her only months later.

"Before she died," Dave went on, "she said she needed to pass something on. A story about me that also involves you, Jack."

"You're not making any sense."

"Your father never knew…"

For God's sake. "Spit it *out.*"

"Your father dated my mother when she originally lived in Cheyenne. They had a disagreement and broke up. It seemed his family didn't think she was good enough. Not long after that, he married your mother and my mom moved and married my dad." He sat back. "She didn't want her new husband to know that she was pregnant with John Reed's baby. That she was three months pregnant with me."

As Jack's ears began to ring, he simply stared and then coughed out a mirthless laugh. "You want me to believe…what? That I have a half brother…that you're my half brother and my father hid it from me my entire life?"

"He never knew."

Jack's ears and brow were burning. *What a crock.* There wasn't a single memory that so much as hinted that any of it was true. David Baldwin needed his head examined if he thought for one moment he would swallow this. Jack ought to walk away from the whole deal right now.

"For decades my mother followed your family's lives," Dave went on. "She particularly followed your accomplishments, Jack."

"Why are you doing this?"

"Because I want to make up for all those lost years. I thought you might want the same."

Jack wanted to tell him to get a grip on reality. But the emotion shining in Dave's eyes stopped him. It was affection. Compassion.

Brotherly love?

Jack collapsed back into the chair. After he drained that beer, he squeezed the empty in his hand and groaned out, "I'll need another drink."

Dave pushed to his feet, headed for the bar. "I'll make it Scotch."

Thirteen

Becca was gutted when Angelica Lassiter's press conference didn't take place. It didn't take her much to guess who had swooped in and got to J.D.'s haunted daughter before she could make any kind of announcement.

Catching up with a friend about the upcoming wedding, Felicity was in town again. When Fee arrived on her doorstep that evening, Becca was pretty much over the whole Lassiter mess. Over pretty much everything. For the first time in her life, she wanted to crawl in a hole and not bother coming back out.

As she opened the door, Fee simply stood there, looking disappointed and confused. Becca had kept her emotions under tight rein these past hours. Now despair rose in her throat, choking off air. Becca felt so miserable, she could only shrug and murmur, "Guess you heard."

The world must know by now…Jack Reed and Becca "Brainless" Stevens had blown off L.A. to get it on. And not in some motel room. Out in the great outdoors.

Shoot me now.

"I won't waste time asking if it's true," Fee said.

"I haven't seen the photos." Becca *never* wanted to see them. Never mind anyone else's opinions—what would her parents say?

In her favorite Raiders jersey and thick comfort socks, Becca led her friend through to the kitchen where Fee presented a bottle of red wine.

"Thought you might need a drink," she said. "I know I do."

"That'll go perfectly with the cheesecake."

Becca had already eaten half of it—the remaining half sat on the counter, next to a used plate.

Fee looked stupefied. "Tell me you didn't eat all that in one afternoon."

"It was a piece of cake." Becca gave her friend a withering grin. "That was a joke."

"Sorry," Fee said, "but you don't look like you've been yucking it up."

"Getting high on sugar is better than slitting my wrists."

"Don't talk like that. Nothing's ever that bad. Even this."

Becca thought of all the kids at risk of self-harm and suicide and flinched, ashamed. Of course, Fee was right. Nothing was worth taking your own life. That didn't mean that she didn't feel like hell.

Fee found two goblets while Becca cracked open the Merlot. She poured two generous servings and proposed a toast.

"To the world's weakest woman," Becca said and downed a mouthful.

Fee refrained. "Maybe alcohol isn't a good idea right now."

"Liquor has never been my problem." At the moment, nagging self-pity was.

"You are *anything* but weak."

"Except where Jack is concerned."

"Honey, forgive me for saying, but you're not alone there."

Good friends were always honest, and Fee was right on the money. She wasn't Jack's first conquest and she wouldn't be his last. One more notch on the bedpost.

"I knew Jack's reputation with women. He's a lady-killer. He wouldn't deny it. That's what my brain says. Then my heart got mixed up somewhere along the way and, suddenly, somehow, he looked like Prince Charming. It's crazy, but there's something about his voice—about his *everything*—that drags me in. I thought I could control it."

Fee narrowed her eyes. "You haven't fallen in love with him, have you?"

"Is falling in lust any better?" Becca set down her glass and covered her flushed face with her hands. "What am I going to do?"

Taking a hold of an arm, Fee hauled Becca over to the breakfast nook and sat her down.

"First you need to know that you have a lot of friends at Lassiter Media," she said, sitting down, too. "People who won't throw you under a bus, no matter what. But, yeah, this doesn't look good. I can't see Evan McCain being so understanding."

"Evan and I spoke. He wasn't pleased, to say the least. He knows I had all the right intentions. It was my execution that was off."

Whenever Becca thought about facing her coworkers' disappointed faces—their curious glances—she shuddered.

"I'd already arranged to have the rest of the week off." And she hadn't had a vacation break since starting at the foundation, so there were days up her sleeve. "Evan suggested I go back into the office Monday. I guess he'll have figured out what to do with me by then."

"And Jack Reed?" Fee asked.

Just the sound of his name sent her blood pounding. "I would be happy if I never had to see that sexy, bloodsucking smile ever again."

Fee arched a brow. "So, you're not in love with the man? You kind of skated around that question earlier."

Becca crossed to the counter and forked cheesecake into her mouth. It didn't hit the spot. Didn't ease the pain.

"I wish I'd never laid eyes on him," she said, avoiding the question again. "I wish I could go back and erase everything that's happened this past week."

"So, when he calls—and he *will* call—you're unavailable? It's just I know what you're going through. Being a slave to your own emotions, wishing you could feel differently but not being able to get past the longing. It's all consuming. An irritating, breathtaking reality that just won't go away."

Understanding, Becca smiled softly. "You went through that with Chance."

"Oh, yeah. In the end, my surrender set me free."

"You're saying that I should, what? Follow my heart where Jack is concerned?" Becca shivered even as added warmth swirled through her veins at the thought of being with him again. "He's nothing like Chance Lassiter."

"But you're not attracted to Chance. For all his apparent faults, you're attracted to Jack." Fee joined her friend by the counter. "Have you asked yourself why you're so angry right now?"

"I know why. I allowed this to happen."

"You mean you couldn't *stop* it from happening."

Fee didn't get it. There was such a thing as responsibility. "I know you must be feeling like all the world is filled with roses and love songs right now. I am so, so happy for you and Chance. But there is no way this side of forever that Jack and I will ever end up a happy couple. We have less than nothing in common. I despise what he stands for. His antics with Angelica have done so much damage to the foundation, and he couldn't care less."

Fee took a few seconds and then cocked her head. "As hard as it is, I think you ought to force yourself to look at those pictures of you and Jack in that lake."

The thought of thousands ogling those ultraprivate moments made Becca want to puke. Or was that the cheesecake?

"They must be plastered all over the internet by now."

"To my mind," Fee went on, "they show two people who look as if they belong with one another. Call me Cupid, but I don't think you and Jack are done just yet."

There were two reasons Jack tucked in his tail and went home to Cheyenne.

First, he needed time and space to absorb what he'd learned from David Baldwin. Dave believed that he and Jack were half brothers...that they shared a biological father. Dave had finished by saying that, if Jack agreed, he wanted to provide DNA material for testing.

Jack's first thought had been that it was some kind of scam meant to glean or extort money. His second thought was to wonder how his life might change if Dave's theory were true. He had no aunts or uncles. Since his parents had passed away, no extended family at all.

Although he'd never dwelled on it, Jack had always felt a sense of aloneness most during holidays. Everyone had somewhere to go Christmas day. He worked his private life so that he wasn't short on invitations. But even at his age, Christmas without family felt kind of hollow. A nonevent.

Waiting for the DNA results was harder than Jack had imagined. Anticipation was made worse by the second reason he'd left L.A. Jack hated how he and Becca had parted company. He had hurt her, embarrassed her, and he cared too damn much to ever want to risk doing that again. That meant staying the hell away.

And so he'd gone to bunk down in the place he'd once called home.

The single-story ranch-style house was modest compared to some of the neighboring places. Certainly a far cry from the luxury of either of his L.A. abodes. But when he set his bags down inside his childhood bedroom and looked around at the high school pennants on the wall and his first CD player, Jack felt a sense of peace…grounded in a way he could never be in California.

He simply chilled for the first couple of days. The freezer was stocked and the fridge had enough beer to last. By the third day, he got itchy feet. He revved up the ten-year-old pickup his dad had left in the garage. Slapping a Stetson atop his head, Jack drove north, headed for the Big Blue.

Thirty miles on, the famous ranch came into view. Originally two hundred acres, the Big Blue now encompassed 30,000 acres, breeding Wyoming's most sought after Hereford cattle. J.D.'s nephew Chance resided in the original ranch house. The main house where Chance's mother lived was an 11,000-square-foot two-story structure made of hand-cut logs and wood shingles, built when Ellie and J.D. had adopted the boys. Many times Jack and J.D. had taken brandy out on the flagstone deck, off from the great room, to discuss sport and finance. That seemed so long ago now.

Jack sat outside the gates with the truck idling for a full five minutes. He'd come to fill a curiosity and see the Big Blue again, but he had no intention of paying a call. He wouldn't be welcome, not like in the old days when he had been viewed a friend of the family rather than foe— Angelica being the current exception, of course.

Maybe he'd go visit Logan downtown. The ambitious attorney and he might not be buddies, as such, but at least

Logan understood Jack's current situation with regard to Lassiter Media like no one else could.

Jack was ready to perform a U-turn when another, newer truck pulled into the wide driveway. When Jack recognized the driver, he wound down his window, as did she.

"How you doing, Marlene?"

"I'm real good, Jack. You coming inside?"

Marlene had turned sixty this year. She wore her brown hair in a short, no-nonsense style. Her hazel eyes were round and kind. After her husband had died twenty-four years ago, she'd moved in here from the original house to take care of J.D.'s children. Rumor said that she also cared for J.D. in a wifely fashion. More power to 'em.

"I was on my way into town," he let her know.

"Gonna grab a steak from the Grill?"

And risk seeing Dylan if he was in town? Not likely.

"I was going to stop by Logan Whittaker's office."

"Give him my regards." Marlene propped an elbow on the window ledge. "I sure don't like the position J.D.'s will has put you boys in."

Jack appreciated her concern but this was neither the time nor place to get into it. "It'll all work out," he assured her.

She leaned in closer and lowered her voice as if someone might overhear. "I know what this is about. At least, living with J.D. and his concerns, I'm pretty sure I know."

Jack took a moment and then smiled. He wondered if Marlene had worked it out, or whether J.D. had mentioned something before that final fatal night when he collapsed at Angelica and Evan's wedding rehearsal dinner. Either way, at this point in time, Jack was under obligation to keep quiet. If things unraveled the way he believed they would, the true nature of the part he had played in this tug-of-war would be revealed soon enough.

What would Becca say?

"J.D. was a good daddy," Marlene said. "He loved his princess more than anyone. More than anything. I'm glad she has a good friend to look after her now that he's gone."

That touched Jack in a way he hadn't anticipated. He was used to being viewed in a far less positive light. His mother had always said a kind word went a long way.

Sitting back, Marlene put her truck into gear. "Take care, Jack. Be sure and come back when this is all over."

For Jack, that couldn't be soon enough.

David Baldwin contacted Jack at the end of that week. The results were in and they confirmed his suspicion. When Jack heard, he flew back to L.A. and went directly to his brother's house.

He met the kids—Jack's very own nieces and nephews— and then enjoyed a big family meal of mashed potatoes and meat loaf in a room full of conversation and laughter and so much...well, *love*. By the end of the evening, he'd accepted that these people were indeed family. He planned to get to know them all a whole lot better.

Saying good-night on the front porch, Jack wanted his brother to know one important thing.

"I'm not upset with your mother for keeping her secret all those years. I get she was only trying to protect the people she cared about most."

"I'm sorry I never met your father." Dave eased into that familiar lopsided smile. "*Our* father. I wish we'd had the chance to know one another."

Those thoughtful eyes, his warm laugh... "Dad was a lot like you, you know."

Dave's eyebrow's lifted. "Really?"

Jack brought his brother close for a man hug. In some ways, this news was like receiving a gift from beyond the grave. The opposite of Angelica's situation.

When her father had died, she'd received what might equate to a kick in the pants. But the show wasn't over yet. Jack still hoped it would all work out for her, even if that meant it wouldn't work out for him. He'd like to believe that discovering that he had a brother—family—had changed his view on how he conducted business. In one important way, it had: he wouldn't be taking over and ransacking Dave's company. Other plans were in store there. Family was family.

He would not, however, reconsider his move on Lassiter Media. Evan McCain had cemented his stand and Jack Reed was standing by his. He had no choice.

Jumping in his car, Jack switched on his phone. Angelica had left a message asking him to call her as soon as possible. She answered on the first ring.

"How was Cheyenne?" she asked.

"Quiet."

He had let her know before leaving where he'd be. He could have been back in L.A. if she'd needed him here within a couple of hours.

"How's things with you?"

He heard her draw down a breath. "I had planned to speak to you in person about this…you've done so much to try to help. But there's really no need for you to waste time coming over."

He braced himself. "I'm listening."

"I've decided I'm going to step back."

Jack's chin went up. "Go on."

"I can't do it. I *won't* do it. My family means more to me than raging or crying over something I thought should be mine."

"Angelica—"

"No, Jack. Not this time. Let me finish. Dad was the smartest man I've ever known. I loved him. I respected him. It's time for me to make peace with his final wishes, with my family but, most of all, with myself. It's over. I'm backing away from the fight."

He waited before replying, "In the end, that's your decision."

"I'm glad you understand. And there's one more thing."

"Anything I can do to help."

"I want you to know that if you ever try to take over Lassiter Media anytime in the future, I'll do everything in my power to make certain that you fail. So will my brothers."

Jack rapped his fingertips on the steering wheel. "And Evan?"

"As long as Evan is the CEO of Lassiter Media, I will support him in that capacity."

A smile eased across Jack's face even as he kept his tone solemn. "Is there any way I can convince you to reconsider?"

"Nothing in this world you or anyone else can say will change my mind."

As soon as she disconnected, he put through a call to Logan. The attorney sounded apprehensive.

"I'm hoping this is good news," Logan said.

"The *best*."

Logan's voice dropped. "Are you saying what I think you're saying?"

"I just got off the phone from Angelica. She's made up her mind. She's throwing in the towel. Tossing it away for good."

"There's no way to talk her around?"

"None."

"You're certain?"

"To quote Angelica, it's over." Smiling, Jack shut his eyes and dropped his head back on the rest. *And thank God for that.*

* * *

As soon as Jack Reed appeared, his impressive physique filling the doorway of her office, Becca shot to her feet.

Today she had returned to work. It had been difficult facing her co-workers. Even harder would be her scheduled appointment to meet with Evan later in the day. She was prepared for the worst. If she were in his position, regardless of any good intentions, she would throw herself out the door.

Now that time had passed since that last incident outside of Hailey's café, she'd assumed that Jack had swept her from his mind. Trust him to show up here, at the Lassiter Media Building, and make a big performance. Did the man have no shame? Did he not care at all about her future? Her feelings?

As he shut her office door, Becca backed up a step. "How did you get in here?"

"Security downstairs was either asleep or didn't recognize my mug shot. I made my own way from this floor's reception area. I think your cohorts were all too stunned to stop or question me. Not that it would have done any good if they'd tried."

She snatched up her phone extension at the same time she told him in a firm clear voice, "Kindly leave."

If he wouldn't go, she would call security. The police. Hell, she'd bring in the National Guard if she had to. Word would have reached Evan. If her goose hadn't been cooked here before now...

"You need to hear what I have to say," Jack said, striding over to join her behind her desk. "You'll want to crack open a bottle of champagne when I'm through."

She was shaking inside and out. "I'll say it one more time. Leave, Jack. Leave now before this turns ugly."

Like the last time they'd seen each other. She loathed recalling how the reporter had smirked at their predicament that afternoon. Only now, with Jack standing so close, more pleasant memories began to rise to the surface, like how incredible and secure those strong arms had felt whenever he'd held her. Without meaning to, she breathed in his scent and suddenly she was reliving the heat she'd enjoyed whenever his mouth had claimed hers.

But all that was past. She had washed her hands of him. Nothing could make her want to go through that torment again. Not even that heart-thumping, devilish grin.

"I do wish you wouldn't smile at me like that," she said, turning away and punching that call through to security.

Reaching over, he took the receiver and dropped it back in its cradle.

She blinked at him. "Excuse me? You can't just waltz in here and tell people they need to listen to you. You don't own the place yet."

"Looks like I won't own it anytime in the future, either." His eyes shone down into hers as he edged nearer still. "Will I order up the ice bucket now?"

The floor tilted beneath Becca's feet. She had to unravel her arms and lean against the desk before her knees gave way. Was she reading this right?

"You mean...there's not going to be a takeover?" He'd stepped back from helping Angelica in her fight to take over Lassiter Media? No. Surely that was too easy. Too good to be true. Becca looked at him through narrowed eyes and took two full steps back.

"I don't believe you."

"You don't have to. I have no doubt it'll make this evening's news."

She waited, listening to her pulse beat in her ears. He wasn't laughing. Wasn't lying?

"You mean it?"

"Every word."

As reality sank in, happy tears welled in her eyes. Unimaginable pressure lifted off her shoulders. "When...?"

"Angelica and I spoke last night."

A laugh escaped from Becca's lips. She wrapped her arms around his neck and laughed some more. He felt so solid. So reliable and, at the end of it all, understanding. She wanted to kiss him until their lips were bruised.

Then she remembered Angelica. As much as Becca wanted this outcome for so many reasons, poor Angelica must be feeling gutted. Jack was her last hope of regaining control of this company.

She stepped back but held his right hand in both of hers. "How did Angelica take it? She must be upset."

"It was Angelica's call. Not mine."

"Oh?" Okay. That made a difference. "Did you try to talk her out of it?"

"Of course I tried. But this time there was no turning back. She'd made up her mind to put family first, corporate aspirations second."

Becca dropped his hand.

"You mean she's just giving up...walking away from the fight?" *And no thanks to you?*

When he nodded, Becca gathered herself. Those warm fuzzy feelings cooled. Other less favorable feelings were taking their place. Suddenly Jack didn't look so reliable.

"Well, I know why I'd want champagne, but you tried to talk her out of it." *And not for the first time.* "Why are you so happy?"

"It's really quite simple." Jack leaned back against the desk, crossed his ankles then his arms. "J.D. always meant for Angelica to run Lassiter Media, but he didn't want her to make the same mistakes he'd made."

"What are you talking about?"

"J.D. devoted all his time and energy to business, right?"

"Right."

"Corporate matters overshadowed every facet of his life. After the first heart attack, when Angelica stepped up to the plate, she became so engrossed in work, J.D. became worried that, when he went, his daughter would leave behind everything, including family, in the pursuit of corporate power."

Jack caught Becca's hand and drew her over to the couch.

"She did seem totally committed," Becca said, sitting down beside him.

"When J.D. made changes to his will in those final months, he also had a secret codicil drawn up. Logan Whittaker and I were the only ones who knew it existed. If and when Angelica accepted the will's terms and supported the family and Evan going forward, it would trigger the codicil. She would then be awarded controlling voting interest in Lassiter Media, which had been J.D.'s wish all along."

Had he said this was simple? "Only when she accepted the terms of the will...?"

"The way J.D. saw it, Angelica needed to understand and appreciate the importance of family first and foremost. He wanted her to run the company but, above all else, he wanted her to enjoy the rewards of a balanced life."

Becca slumped back. Poor Angelica. She thought she understood now what J.D. had been trying to accomplish, but what a test! Not only had it driven a wedge between Angelica and her brothers, she had gone to war with a man she wanted to marry. If J.D. had wanted his daughter to embrace the benefits of family, to Becca's mind, he'd gone about it in a weird way.

"You were part of this scheme?" she asked.

"It was my job to push her as hard as I could in the other direction."

"Toward a hostile-takeover bid? That's...*twisted*."

"J.D.'s plan, not mine. He wanted her to struggle with it, if necessary. He wanted her to be sure."

"J.D. probably expected Angelica to be married before he died and the will went into effect. Did he consider the stress it would bring to Angelica's marriage to Evan?" She thought for a moment. "Or did he want to test the honesty of Evan's intentions somehow, too?"

"I only know he chose me to push the barrel."

"He obviously thought you were the man for the job." As unbelievable as it seemed, the plans and its resolution were sinking in. Jack hadn't been the bad guy in all this drama. He'd been a *good* guy willing to *look* like the bad guy. Which made him *extra* good.

He hadn't planned to steal from the rich to give to the poor exactly, but neither had he plotted to trick Angelica into a takeover and then sell off the pieces under her feet. For Jack, that was big. Heck, it was huge!

Becca's smile stretched from ear to ear. If Jack felt relieved, she felt euphoric!

Falling forward, she planted a closed-mouth kiss on his lips. "Sorry. I'm just so happy this nightmare has turned out so well. Angelica gets control of her company."

"Don't apologize." Tipping close, he brushed his lips over hers. "Best part is, when word gets out, any negative publicity the foundation has weathered will be reversed."

"But Evan…"

"He gets a big payout."

"I don't know how much compensation would be enough for losing this company *and* the woman he loved. Maybe still loves."

Jack tried to sound convincing. "Evan will bounce back."

"And you…do you know what you are?" She cupped his jaw and then grazed her thumb over the stubble of his chin. "You're a hero."

He drew back a little. "I was only following instructions."

"I wish I'd known."

"I wish I could have told you."

Her heart was throbbing, aching in her throat. God, his lips looked good. And now it didn't matter who took their picture. The truth was out and her Jack was back.

As her palm trailed down his shirt, she shifted closer still. His body heat steamed through his shirt, warming her all over, making her sigh.

"So, what are you doing now?"

His lips brushed hers as he answered, "I'm kidnapping you."

"A copycat strategy. I like it." She squeezed his thigh and thought to add, "Not that I'm in favor of the general nature of your business."

"The corporate-raiding stuff. Then you might like my other news. But I'm afraid it'll take most of the day to relay every detail, so you might want to inform your assistant that you'll be unavailable."

When he kissed her again, deeply this time, the fireflies humming around in her stomach began to burst into flame.

Coming up for air, she murmured, "Should we leave a ransom note?"

"Let's say, *gone fishing.*"

Thirty minutes later, they were naked in his bed.

Fourteen

He and Becca walked out of that office and away from the Lassiter Media Building without a care in the world.

Or it sure had seemed that way at first.

Jack had hoped that Becca would take his news concerning Angelica well. He had wondered whether she might have struggled with believing him. He'd imagined her telling him to leave and not come back even after the facts had been verified. He'd been pleasantly surprised, to say the least, when she'd accepted the truth so readily. He had read her eyes, her body language, in those first moments when she'd been trying so hard to hate him.

In reality, she missed him, like an addict missed her drug. He knew because he felt the same way. All the pieces had fallen into place. This morning, he'd arranged for his bank to wire a sizable sum to the Lassiter Charity Foundation—specifically to help Brightside House and its endeavors. It was a good cause. And there was the added benefit of making Becca happy, because when she was happy, he was happy. Happier than he'd ever been.

He took her to his penthouse and let a valet park his car while he grabbed Becca's hand and rushed her to his private elevator. As soon as the metallic door whirred open and he had her inside, alone, he gathered her close, grazed his palms up and down the back of her red designer dress and forced himself to wait a moment more.

"You're more beautiful than I remembered."

She fanned her fingers over his chest, watching the action before looking up at him from beneath her lashes. "Aren't you going to kiss me?"

He gripped her tush and drove her hips against him. She laughed and then coiled her arms around his neck. With those killer heels, she was the right height to feel *just* how much he wanted to kiss her.

"If I start here and now," he growled against her lips, "we might be riding this elevator all day."

"So?" She tilted her head. "You own the building, don't you?"

Good point.

His mouth was one thumping heartbeat away from taking hers when the doors whirred open. He swept her up into his arms and strode to the center of the living room.

"Do you have a Merv here?" she asked.

"There's just the two of us."

The morning light flooding in through the wall-to-wall windows caught a flicker of unease in her eyes. "No cameras?"

He lifted her until the tips of their noses touched. "We have nothing to be ashamed of. Do you hear me?"

"I hear you. That's all behind us now."

So true. He did have some additional news to share, but it could wait.

He kissed her, lightly at first, a feathery brush of lips.

The contact sent rounds of pleasure ricocheting throughout his veins. Then he covered her mouth with his completely and leaned in as those sensations fired harder, longer. A thousand times deeper.

They had until morning. By then everyone would know that Evan was out, Angelica was in and Becca would need to attend to issues stemming from the switch. But what he would give to convince her to take a week or two leave. So they could spend every moment in bed.

With his mouth working over hers—while she was still in his arms—he crossed to the corridor that led to the master suite. He set her down at the foot of the bed and ran his hands up her back. With his brow resting on hers, he drew the zipper of her dress all the way down and then slipped it off her arms. Red linen rustled and fell around her feet.

He hadn't meant to get hung up at this point, but that lingerie was ten miles past sexy. He took a step back to get a better look. With a sultry grin, she cocked one hip and set her hands on her hips.

"You like?"

"You love to mix it up as far as office attire is concerned, don't you?" he asked, taking in the provocative picture from top to toe. "One day jeans, the next..." He wagged a finger. "What exactly do you call those things?"

"A garter slip. Satin and mesh." She performed a slow turn. "The color is raspberry."

He moved close again, letting his palms drift over the curvy satin all the way down to the strip of firm flesh left bare at the top of each thigh. A hand-span below that, the bands of her silk stockings began. He grazed his jaw lightly up one side of her cheek and then scooped her hair aside. Sliding the strap of her garter slip off a shoulder, he lowered his mouth to that smooth sweep of skin. She smelled fresh and...the only word that fit was *classy*. He ran the tip of his tongue along the ledge joining shoulder

to neck then all the way up the side of her throat. He felt
her shiver, a delicious, delicate quiver that only cranked
the heat up all the more.

"Take off your shirt," she murmured. "Sit on the edge
of the bed."

He nipped her earlobe. "You like to be the boss?"

"I'd like to take turns."

Jack had no objection to letting her go first.

He backed up toward the bed, at the same time releasing the buttons on his cuffs and shirt front. He took a seat
while Becca made a tantalizing show of slipping down
the second shoulder strap. After slipping off her shoes,
she strolled forward and lifted her leg, setting her foot on
the quilt next to his thigh. She flicked the stocking snap
and leaned forward. Using her palms, she rolled the silk
all the way down.

Jack was torn—should he look at that scrumptious toned
leg or the closer, perhaps even more tempting view of her
breasts wanting to spill out of their low-cut bra cups? Then
there was the glimpse he'd caught of her panties when she'd
switched legs to lower her other stocking.

He wound out of his shirt and tossed it on the floor.
Then he reached for her hands but her fingers slipped
through his as she moved back, a grin on her face.

Happy to play, he leaned back on his hands while she
caught the hem of her slip and eased the satin up over her
belly, ribs, breasts, until she stood holding the slip in one
hand, wearing only panties.

The room's shutters were slanted, letting in strips of
light that highlighted parts of her beautiful body. She
moved forward with so much poise and confidence, Jack's
anticipation turned a cartwheel and ramped up again. It
had near killed him to keep away these past days. But the
wait had been worth every minute.

He heeled off his shoes and got rid of his pants, briefs

and socks before she'd closed the distance and crawled up onto his lap. As she tasted his lips, she used her weight to ease him down onto his back. Straddling him, she kissed him deeply. Her arms curled around his head while her breasts brushed over his chest. When she tried to draw away, he gripped the top of her arms to bring her back. She only laughed and slid down the length of his body. Her lips trailed his throat, the center of his chest, over the ruts of his abs....

Then her tongue was looping a slow, purposeful circle around his navel, setting off a series of fireworks. His fingers filed through her hair as his hips rocked up.

She slid down more until the seam of her lips skimmed the tip of his erection. He felt her fingers wrap around the base of his shaft, squeeze and then drag up at the same time her amazing mouth went down.

He gripped the quilt and grit his teeth. This was scorching, intense. He could feel the beginnings of a climax burning, begging for release. He focused on the sublime rhythm she'd created, the tow of her hand working in perfect sync with the pump and pull of her mouth. Her other hand was spread over his chest, rhythmically kneading one side like a kitten preparing its bed.

As her mouth drew away, cooler air met warm wet flesh. It was a good thing she stopped when she did. He'd almost forgotten how much he wanted to satisfy her rather than the other way around. He caught her around the waist as she straightened. Then he cupped her breasts, grazing palms over distended nipples. He slid a hand down the front of her panties. She was swollen, wet. As ready as he was.

He urged her over onto her back and dropped a line of slow, moist kisses around each breast before angling lower. He hooked a finger into the side of her panties' crotch, pulled aside the satin and tenderly kissed her there. He heard her sigh before she arched into his caress. He tasted her again, relishing the scent and feel of her beneath his lips before he whipped off her last scrap of clothing and found a condom in a drawer.

When he was sheathed, he joined her again. She felt warm and soft and her eyes held nothing but trust. He positioned himself between her thighs while she ran her fingers through his hair.

He felt as if a furnace were burning inside of him. Her brow and the valley between her breasts were damp, too. He pushed inside of her, closing his eyes and tilting his face toward the ceiling as he buried himself to the hilt.

Her legs coiled around the back of his and she whispered to him how wonderful he felt, how she never wanted this to end. He built the friction as they moved together until he felt as if he was a part of her and she a part of him.

He was aware of her inner walls squeezing, of her fingers digging into his shoulders and her head rocking back. He watched the line crease between her brows, studied the smile lifting the corners of her parted lips. As he upped the tempo and force of each thrust, he felt her panting breath warm on his face. He lowered his mouth close to hers at the same time her legs clamped down hard.

Then he closed his eyes and held her tight as they both let go at once.

Fifteen

"You're not going to believe this," Becca said, gaping at a message on her smartphone.

Jack rolled over and stole another glorious morning kiss and then murmured against her lips, "You've decided you want to order in Danishes?"

"All my cravings have been well and truly satisfied." She tasted his lips again then amended, "For now."

They had stayed in Jack's penthouse the entire day *and* night. They'd ordered in dinner and had devoured barbecue ribs and butter pecan ice cream sitting out on the balcony, their feet propped up on the railing. Around ten, they'd fallen asleep on a soft-as-clouds leather lounge while they watched *Forrest Gump*. An hour ago they'd taken a long, sudsy shower together before Jack had dialed up the AC and pulled her under his duck-down duvet.

Becca hadn't checked back in with Sarah. Worse, she'd turned off her phone until now. She'd had an amazing time playing hooky with her bad boy, but it seemed lots had happened while she'd been away.

"Sarah says word is out about Angelica being reinstated as CEO. With you out of the picture, donations are already pouring back in." She sent Jack a sympathetic look. "No disrespect intended."

"None taken." He snuggled into her neck, tickling and arousing her as he nuzzled. "And so, all is right with the world."

Sighing, she beamed up at the ceiling while he nibbled her shoulder. "This has all turned out so well. I'm waiting for the bubble to burst."

He looked into her eyes. A soft, sexy smile tugged one corner of his mouth. "I guess sometimes there are happy endings."

"I guess there really are."

He kissed her again, long and slow and deep, before sitting up against the headboard alongside of her. "What are you doing Thanksgiving?"

"Are you asking me on a date?" she teased.

"I'm not sure. Is a family occasion classified as a date?"

"You don't have any family."

"As of yesterday, I officially do."

He passed on everything that had happened between himself and David Baldwin this past week. Jack Reed had a brother? Nieces and nephews?

"My God, Jack. That's *fantastic*. Why didn't you tell me sooner?"

"I wanted this other Lassiter stuff to be settled first." He lifted her hand and dropped a kiss on the underside of her wrist. "One victory at a time."

"You're not an only child anymore. How does it feel? Amazing, right?"

"The truth?"

"Of course."

"It feels almost too good." He leaned in to kiss her shoulder. "Like it feels almost too good to be holding you again."

She moved to run her fingers through his hair. "We should accept good things when they come our way."

"I'm beginning to understand that."

Their next kiss felt like the first of all their tomorrows. Which was thinking too fast, too soon. But she couldn't help wanting to take a hold of this fantasy and actually believe they could live it.

As the kiss broke, she curled into his arm and leaned her cheek against his chest.

"So, what's happening with your brother's business?" she asked.

"Take a guess."

"You're going to become partners."

"Uh-huh."

Her jaw dropped. "You're kidding."

"I offered to gift him the funds. He refused. Then he put it in a way I couldn't turn my back on. He said that through no fault of our own we were separated. Now it was within our power to be close, and stay close. Working together, becoming partners, would mean we'd be in touch most days, not just holidays. He doesn't want to simply maintain the connection. He wants to build on it. So do I."

"You're really going to be building a company up?" She laughed. "Call a medic!"

He tickled her until she begged him to stop.

"It's time we got something clear," he said, bundling her up in those big beautiful arms again. "I may make money out of applying a keen business eye to enterprises that can provide a larger profit operating as smaller entities."

"Say that again slowly."

"That does not, however, make me Scrooge."

"I know, I know. You give to charity. In fact, Sarah

mentioned in her text that Reed Incorporated had made the biggest of the foundation's recent donations so far." She dropped a kiss on his scratchy chin. "Thank you."

"You're very welcome. And I want you to know that this latest, shall we call it *coming together of minds,* had no influence on the size of that donation. Although, it would be remiss of me not to mention that I am open to bribes."

"Like this?"

She shifted to straddle his lap all the while kissing her way slowly and thoroughly around his neck and chest. He groaned.

"*Exactly* like that. Keep it coming."

As his fingers trailed up and down her back, a thought popped into Becca's head. She'd wondered about it last night halfway through the movie, but it had drifted off again until now. When she felt him growing harder against her belly, she straightened. If she didn't ask this minute, she might never get around to it.

"I'm not sure on one thing," she said, as his palms trailed down her sides.

"What's that?"

"Your job was to keep pushing Angelica toward a take-over bid, right?"

"Right."

He leaned in to draw a nipple into his mouth. She quivered and closed her eyes. It was hard to think straight when he did that.

"You've been actively acquiring shares and positioned your company so it would be ready to move," she said. "I would have thought very soon."

He was running his tongue around her other nipple now. "These things take time."

"It's just…Jack, what would have happened if Angelica hadn't backed down? What if she'd gone ahead with the takeover and you both won?"

"Then she and I would have become partners."

"And you'd have managed all the Lassiter interests to-gether." When he didn't answer, she looked down.

"Jack?"

"We would have worked together, yes."

She waited for him to add something more. Like, *But I would never turn around and do what I've done with every other company I've obtained through fair means or foul.* When nothing came, every hair on her head stood on end. Damn it! She *knew* this was too good to be true.

She shifted off of him and scrunched the duvet up under her arms.

"You were planning to sell off parts of Lassiter Media, weren't you?"

He scratched his head. "I can't say it didn't cross my mind that we could make a huge fortune without a whole lot of work."

"You mean by ripping apart someone else's work of a lifetime."

"There would have been discussions."

Oh, come on. "Angelica is no match for you."

"You've said that before but what about the way she stood up to me yesterday? Her father would have been proud."

Becca's throat was aching now. Suddenly she felt empty. Betrayed. Or was that merely foolish?

"You would have made it difficult, made it ugly, then you would have talked her into folding before the selling price was affected."

"You give me too much credit and Angelica not enough." He sat up straighter.

"What would have happened to the foundation?"

"We would have worked something out there."

"An offer I couldn't refuse?"

"I'm not a criminal, Becca. I'm only being honest with

you. It doesn't matter now because the game is played out and Angelica is where she was always meant to be."

"She'll never know how close she came to bringing it all down on her head."

"And that's the end of it." He reached for her. But his smile didn't look sexy now; she imagined it looked patronizing. Predatory.

She edged away and got to her feet, dragging the duvet along to cover herself. "There is no moving along until we get past this."

"Why worry about something that cannot, will not, happen? This, you and me, we're not about business."

"I know what I'm about. Ethics. Principles. Making the tough decisions so I can wake up in the morning and look at myself in the mirror. Guess what? That's gotten harder since I hooked up with you."

He opened his mouth, shut it again and then stood, too. "Shine a little light on something for me here. You never liked me, and you don't like me now because I'm a selfish, money-hungry, insensitive moron."

"You're not a moron."

"Thanks for clarifying that." He skirted the end of the bed until he stood an arm's length away. "Tell me, how could you lower yourself to sleep with me? And not just once. I must be losing my mind because I thought it was good. *No.* I thought it was *great*. The best."

That took her aback. She struggled for a response.

He moved closer, looming. "You know more about me than anyone. You might not trust me but, damn it, Becca, I trusted you. And for my trouble, you want to rake me over the coals."

She huffed. He would see it that way. "This isn't about you. Not anymore. It's about my feelings, my future, my decisions."

"Right, because my feelings don't count."

"You don't have feelings." She winced. That was going too far. "Or not like you should. If you did, you wouldn't be arguing with me now."

"You think J.D. was an angel?" he drawled. "Do you want to hear about the low deals he cut so that you could crow about all the great works your charity does? There has to be a *take* in order to have a *give*. Someone has to make the money to give it away, and no one makes money, real money, by sitting on a delicate behind letting other people make the choices that need to be made."

She spoke through her teeth, which had to be a damn sight better than speaking through tears. "Don't try to justify your behavior."

"I'm not. I won't. Not to anyone."

She marched toward the bathroom.

He called after her. "Where are you going?"

"Back to reality. *My* reality. Where people own up to their flaws and maybe try to do something about them."

He slapped his thighs. "Right. *Good.* I'm evil because I had good parents, was born with a brain and a drive to succeed."

"You were born with a will to *dominate*."

He shook his head as if he couldn't believe it. "I'm not wrong about most things," he said quietly. "But I was wrong about you."

"You thought you could convert me."

"I thought you could *care* about me." He stabbed a thumb at his chest. "*Me*. Not the money or connections or the name, Jack Reed."

Tears were so close, she could taste them. "Well, whaddya know?" The door swung shut as she finished. "You were wrong!"

Sixteen

"If I'm your sidekick, I hope this doesn't make me Friar Tuck."

Standing at the shooting line on the back lawn of his Beverly Hills house, Jack spun around and frowned. What was Sylvia doing here?

He lowered his bow as she crossed over to join him. She was right to carry her shoes. Those high-priced heels would ruin his lawn—not that he imagined for a minute that had been her motive for taking them off.

"Merv the Man let me through," Sylvia let him know.

"What's up?"

She eyed the distant target. Arrows were scattered all over the place. The bull's-eye, however, remained untouched.

"I was wondering when the boss might be coming back in," she said.

"You don't need help running the office. You have one of the most efficient business minds I know."

"Flattery doesn't work with me, Jackie boy."

"I'm doing other things."

"Like building boats with David Baldwin?"

Sylvia knew that story.

"That's the one good thing to come out of this month's firestorm."

Sylvia offered him a genuine smile. "No one's happier for you than I am."

He redirected his attention to the target. He and Sylvia did bottom-line analysis, not deep and meaningful conversation.

He sucked air in between his teeth. "I have other projects I'm working on."

"Any involve Becca Stevens?"

Eye still on the target, he growled. "No."

"You've been in contact with her, though."

"After I made myself clear, she made herself crystal clear."

In the briefest of summaries, he had also let Sylvia know that, due to the fallout surrounding the twist in J.D.'s will, his and Becca's "challenge" had come to an acrimonious end. He hadn't given up the finer details.

"I admitted to her that I would have followed through with the Lassiter Media takeover if Angelica hadn't changed her mind."

Of course, Sylvia didn't look the least bit surprised. "And since she ditched you, you haven't been able to think straight, right?"

"It's a matter of willpower."

He strode back to the line and fired a shot—which sailed over the top.

Damn!

Sylvia crossed over to join him. She took a long moment to study the target.

"Silly idea," she said, "but why don't you call her?"

Don't you know I want to?

"Sometimes in a relationship," he explained, "we say things we don't mean. Words can hurt. They can cut to the bone. But people can apologize, deeply, sincerely, and then get back to the good stuff. Becca and me...we went way beyond that."

Sylvia examined his face, particularly his mouth.

"Wait a minute," she said, and wriggled a finger. "Your bottom lip. Is that a pout? Are you *pouting,* Jack?"

Sylvia was like that. She never let herself, or anyone else on her radar, feel sorry for themselves. She could give a friend money, advice, she would work through the night if a job needed to be done. But no one could ask her for pity.

Jack crossed to the bench and sat down heavily. He swallowed against the lump lodged in his throat and then dealt out the bottom line.

"Becca told me exactly what she thinks of me. I could get over the argument, but she never will. She could never reconcile who she is, what she stands for, with being with a wrecking ball like me."

Sylvia sat down beside him.

"I could chase her," Jack said. "We'd fall into bed again. It'd be good for a while. Then she'd remember who I am, what I've done and the shame would creep back in. The guilt. She'd resent our being together. She'd resent me." He let his bow drop to the ground. "Not a recipe for happiness."

"Sorry," Sylvia said. "I was wrong. I thought you must really care for that woman. I thought she was the reason your schedule has been up the creek and we haven't seen your designer pants in the office for weeks."

"I'm the same Jack Reed," he said. But that was a lie.

"You're hiding."

"I am not *hiding.*"

"What are you so afraid of?"

"I'm *not* afraid."

"C'mon. Spit it out."

"No."

"Do it."

Fine! "I'm afraid I'll destroy her. That I'll let her down. I'll let her down and then…" He sighed. "Then I'll have made things even worse. I'm not good at long-term, Sylvia. I'm controlling. I have a controlling personality."

"I bet she'd like the chance to work things out."

His grin was entirely humorless. "I humbly disagree."

"She's taking a sabbatical from the foundation. Rumor is she's going to work in a mission overseas."

"What's the plan, Sylvia? I pack a bag, follow her and we save the world together?"

"I thought you might like to say goodbye at least."

"Why the hell would I want to do that?"

She gave a wry grin. "I've known you to be flippant, ruthless, but never cruel. Never stupid."

"I so don't need this." He pushed to his feet.

She got to hers. "I'm trying to help you."

"I don't need help."

"Everyone needs help sometime, for some reason. Some of us are even big enough to accept it. Don't be a dope. Go to Becca before she leaves, even if she slams the door in your face." She touched his arm, lightly at first and then more firmly. "Take the word of a lonely woman who always needs to be right. Talk to her. You'll regret it if you don't."

Standing on the beach, Becca watched Jack pull up, get out of his car and study Hailey's café before wandering down over the sand to join her.

When she'd answered his call earlier, her hand had shaken, she'd wanted to hang up so bad. But there'd been something different in his voice. Something...real. Had she imagined the self-effacing tone?

It didn't matter now. She'd agreed to meet him. But she had wanted to choose the place. To finish here in Santa Monica on a more adult, less hostile note would bring this episode full circle. And then hopefully she would be able to put aside this constant ache in her chest...in her heart.

She held her breath as he stopped in front of her. In that moment, she saw only his eyes, heard only the waves.

"Where's the Bambino?" he asked.

"I sold it."

"Get outta here. Really?"

"To Hailey's brother."

"Wow. Big step."

"Yeah." She slotted her hands in the front pockets of her denim pedal pushers and dragged a bare foot through the sand. "Moving on."

His smile faded and that different tone she'd heard on the phone was there again.

"Thanks for seeing me," he said.

"Guess you heard about the sabbatical."

He nodded as the wind combed his hair. "Where are you off to?"

"Haven't decided yet."

"The foundation will sure miss you."

Will you miss me, Jack?

She cut off that thought and focused on the ocean until she'd gathered herself again.

"I'm hosting a final auction night next week," she said, speaking to the waves. It hurt too much to look at him here like this. "Then I need time away."

She heard distant barking and turned toward the café. Chichi was scampering down the ramp and onto the sand. He sped right up to Jack, who dropped onto his haunches to play wrestle with him. Becca figured that Chichi would find a stick and the rest of this short time she and Jack had here together would be mediated by this brash third party. Not a bad thing.

But suddenly Chichi turned a tight circle and shot off again. Becca hadn't heard anything, but dogs had good ears; Hailey must have called him back.

"I want you to know," she said, "I'm not angry with you." Not anymore. "In fact, I want to apologize. Being so self-righteous isn't very pretty. I have no right to judge others when my behavior has been less than glowing. I was frustrated." And hurt mostly.

Looking up at her, his dark gaze turned stormy. "Then why are you leaving?"

"I need to work on myself. The best way to do that is to help others. Sort out what's important and what's not." He sat all the way down on the sand, facing the waves with his legs bent, forearms resting on his knees.

"I had a long conversation with a friend," he said. "She thinks we ought to give it a go."

Becca's legs went weak. She'd expected something but nothing as direct as this. After all those nasty things they'd said to each other?

"You and me?" she asked. "Like a *couple?*"

He reached out his hand. She took a hold and knelt beside him, still processing what he'd just said.

"I want us to be together," he went on. "I want to make it work."

She let that sink in. Obviously he didn't know what he was saying.

"What do you mean 'make it work'?"

"I mean negotiate. Compromise. Maybe move in together."

Whoa.

If he wasn't beating around the bush, neither would she.

"Do you want forever?"

A line formed between his brows but he didn't look away.

"That girl I told you about," he said. "I told you I'd proposed. In fact, we were going to be married the next day."

His eyes were reflective now, glassy, like he was living in the past and wasn't in a hurry to come back. Becca felt sick to her stomach. It was bad enough to have a loved one take her own life, but to be faced with that tragedy a day before they were supposed to begin life's most wonderful journey together... *Unimaginable.*

"You still love her," Becca said, wanting to cry for him all these years later.

"She was my best friend." He blinked slowly. "I wonder sometimes if she hadn't met me whether she'd still, you know...be around. The truth is I pushed her too hard. I thought I was helping. So, this is a tough one for me." He blinked a few times as a pulse beat in his jaw. "I want to push you to stay, but there's also that part of me that says— that *always* says—don't try to hold on. It's best to let go."

Becca held her stomach. She didn't think she'd felt so sorry for anyone in her life.

She got to her feet and forced out the words before they got stuck in her throat. "I honestly wish you nothing but happiness."

He looked more resigned than disappointed. "What's happiness? That's the sixty-four-thousand-dollar question."

"It's being at peace with yourself."

Before she walked away, she squeezed his shoulder and prayed that Jack found his.

Seventeen

One week later, Becca was ready to make an announcement.

This Lassiter Charity Foundation Auction Night had been wildly successful, with exceptional items up for grabs and an astounding amount of money having been raised. The high-neck black sheath she wore somehow suited her bittersweet mood. The foundation would not only survive, it would flourish under Angelica's reinstated reign at Lassiter Media. But this was also Becca's last public appearance as director of the Los Angeles-based charity she believed in so much.

A moment ago, Sarah had suggested it was time to offer the guests a final thank-you. Becca had been on her way to the lectern when she'd glimpsed someone standing alone in the back of the ballroom.

He was exceptionally tall with dark hair. His masculine physique was made all the more eye-catching by the tuxedo he wore. As he headed for an exit, she actually considered for a third of one second to simply let him go. However, in her professional capacity here this evening, that wouldn't be right.

Becca wove through the crowd. In her hurry, she bumped into one gentleman's paunch and then immediately knocked darling Mrs. Abernathy and her glass of punch. She apologized profusely to both and kept rushing toward the exit. She caught up the moment the man pushed open the door.

"Jack. *Jack!*"

He turned around. He was so handsome...when he smiled, the entire room seemed to light up.

"I've tried to contact you today," she said. "I spoke to your PA. Jack, I can't thank you enough for your generosity."

"She passed on your invitation. I'm glad the bow and arrowheads brought in a good price."

Good price? More like incredible. "I've never seen such a bidding war. I'm so glad they went to a museum, even if it's overseas."

"I'm glad, too."

They held each other's gazes while music wove through the room and crystal flutes tinkled.

"I'd better let you get back to your guests," he said at last, and turned toward the exit again.

"Wait." She had something she wanted to ask. "Have you heard from Angelica?"

"We spoke today. She's feeling right at home in the CEO's chair. Sage and Dylan are happy for her, too. I'm not sure what's happening with Evan McCain, other than there are rumors he's going to start up his own company with the money J.D. left him via that codicil. Guess he was very generously compensated but he still feels burned by the whole thing."

"It'd be nice if those two got back together. But I understand why she might think Evan somehow conspired with her dad to get controlling interest of the company. That's a lot of hurt to get over on both sides."

"Miracles happen."

When his broad shoulders rolled back and he glanced at the door, she threw in another question.

"How's your brother?"

"We touch base every other day. And I'll see the whole crowd on Turkey Day. And Christmas will be here before you know it. I'll have to do some research on buying gifts for people under sixteen."

"You'll have fun with it."

Sarah appeared at Becca's side.

"Sorry to interrupt. Becca, we need you to announce the total amount that was raised tonight. The mayor's about to leave."

Becca nodded. "I'll be right there."

"Duty calls," Jack said. "Good luck, Becca."

She took a deep breath and let it out on a wistful smile. "Same to you."

When the last of the guests left the ballroom, Sarah gave Becca a congratulatory hug.

"This has to be the most successful fund-raising night in history."

Becca laughed. "I wouldn't go that far."

"I just hate that you're leaving the charity. It's been such a buzz working with you. I've learned so much. But I understand. You have things you need to do. It must be hard leaving, though. Letting go."

"I'll find another job in charity when I get back."

"I mean leaving Jack Reed. You two have some amazing chemistry going on."

Becca hadn't spoken much to Sarah about her dealings with Jack. Of course her assistant had seen those shots taken at the lake...who hadn't? But the look on Sarah's face now—it was as if she believed in fairy dust or something. Real life wasn't like that.

The women said good-night. Sarah had shared a ride with a couple of the other girls from the office. Becca said she'd get a cab home.

Alone in the elevator, Becca hit the button for the ground floor. A moment later, she was crossing the quiet hotel foyer. The click of her heels on the marble tiles echoed through the large glitzy space.

But she didn't want to go home just yet. She wanted to do what she'd never given herself permission to do before: be idle and simply waste time window-shopping on one of the world's most famous streets, Rodeo Drive. It was strange to think that next week it would be a hard task to buy necessities that most people who lived in the States took for granted.

This street was lined with fairy-lit trees and filled with the boutiques of some of the most revered names in the fashion world. She studied the displays, clothes, jewelry, ridiculously priced handbags. And then she came across a window filled with exquisite gowns...beautifully crafted. Most of them were white.

One in particular caught her eye.

The gown was antique-white with a fitting, puff-sleeved satin bodice adorned with a sparkling sea of crystals. The skirt was extra full, flaring from low on the waist. The outer layer was gauzy with a satin band three-quarters down and a floral wreath in the same satin embroidered on the lower front half. It was a reflection of a bygone era when a member of the fairer sex had been encouraged to be fragile and endlessly romantic in the hope of finding her prince.

A dress like that, a dream like that, would need nothing more than the perfect ring. And, needless to say, the perfect groom.

Becca let the illusion wash over her a little more. She saw herself in that gown, her face beaming and eyes filled with love. Beside her stood a man, exceptionally tall, with dark hair, his masculine physique made all the more eye-catching by the tuxedo he wore. And then, the reflection spoke her name. As in...

It *actually* spoke.

Becca spun around. Embarrassment and panic set in so fast, her cheeks caught light. "I thought you'd gone."

Jack only smiled and commented on the window display. "That's some dress."

How must it have looked, her fawning over a whimsical wedding gown alone late at night?

"It's a good street to window-shop," she mumbled.

Jack followed when she set off at a brisk pace, putting the dress behind her.

"I thought it might be something you were thinking of for Felicity's wedding," he said, easily keeping up.

"Oh, she wouldn't have anything so...big."

"Would you?"

She kept her gaze dead ahead. "I might."

"It was very, well, sparkly. I don't think I've seen you wear a piece of jewelry other than a watch."

Slowing her pace, she slid over a defiant look. "I might be saving it all up for one revoltingly gaudy occasion."

"A dress like that would need a pretty impressive ring." He stopped and pulled a small box out of his pocket. "Maybe like this."

As he opened the clasped lid, Becca's jaw dropped. The most amazing piece of jewelry sat glittering up at her from its white satin bed.

"It's sapphires and a pearl." His finger circled the setting. "But you also like diamond and rubies, right?" He pulled out another box. When she stood rigid, overcome with shock, he prodded her. "Go on. Open it."

This couldn't be happening. It felt like everything was moving in a weird kind of slow motion. Someone reached to open the lid. Becca realized it was her. A beautiful white diamond shone up at her. It was mounted in a pool of blood red rubies. Both rings were just as she had imagined they would be way back when she was a girl.

Becca finally formed some words. "Jack…what is this?"

"I want to marry you."

She swallowed against the ache of so many emotions clogging her throat. "We said goodbye…God, I've lost count how many times."

"I worked it out. It's really quite simple. The fact is I love you. And if you love me, why wouldn't we try to work through this…through anything to stay together?" One dark eyebrow lifted as he leaned closer. "You do love me, don't you, Becca?"

Tears stung behind her eyes. No matter how much she tried to hide the truth, everyone else seemed to see it. What was the point in denying it now?

"Of course I love you," she told him. "So much it hurts."

His dark eyes glistened as he gave her a grateful smile. "Let's fix that."

His mouth took hers and, in that instant, sparks tingled and fell through her body. Nothing seemed impossible. She could surmount any problem. Achieve any dream.

When he broke the kiss, Becca felt light-headed, floating, as if her feet no longer touched the ground.

"Are you going to choose?" he asked with his lips still close to hers.

She couldn't argue with him. Not this time. She wanted to say, *I choose you. I choose love.* But he meant the rings. As she looked down to study them again, her vision grew misty with tears. They were both so beautiful. So…*her.*

"I don't think I *can* choose."

"Then you'll have both. As soon as you say yes." He put the boxes in his pocket and drew her close. "I love you, Becca. I want you to be my wife. I don't want to lose you. We *can't* lose each other."

"You really want to do this?" she asked.

"Yeah." He dropped a kiss on her brow and murmured, "I really, really do."

"I have a condition."

He grinned. "Sure."

"That we respect and honor each other for the rest of our lives."

"Just give me the chance."

"We'll both make the rules."

"I only have one."

"Tell me."

After he whispered in her ear, she laughed and wound her fingers into his jacket's lapels. "I think I can handle that." Then she cupped his jaw and fell into a tender gaze that held nothing but adoration for her. "I guess sometimes there really are happy endings."

"Oh, baby." Jack got ready to kiss her again. "Now I know there are."

* * * * *

FROM SINGLE MUM
TO SECRET HEIRESS

KRISTI GOLD

To my fellow Lassiter authors, particularly Kathie DeNosky, my good friend and brainstorming buddy. I can always count on you to have my back, as long as you've had your coffee. Couldn't have done this one without you.

One

What a way to begin the end of April—with limited funds and leaky plumbing.

Yet Hannah Armstrong couldn't quite believe her sudden change in fortune. Twenty minutes after placing the 5:00 p.m. service call, and hearing the dispatcher's declaration that they would *try* to send someone out today, her doorbell sounded.

She left the flooded galley kitchen and carefully crossed the damp dining-room floor that was littered with towels. After entering the living room, she navigated another obstacle course comprised of a toy plastic convertible painted shocking pink, as well as a string of miniature outfits that would be the envy of the fashion-doll world. "Cassie, sweetie, you have to pick up your toys before you can spend the night with Michaela," she called on her way to answer the summons.

She immediately received the usual "In a minute, Mama," which came from the hallway to her right.

Hannah started to scold her daughter for procrastinating, but she was too anxious to greet her knight in shining tool belt. Yet when she yanked the front door open, she was completely taken aback by the man standing on her porch. The guy had to be the prettiest plumber in Boulder. Correction. All of Colorado.

She quickly catalogued the details—a six-foot-plus prime specimen of a man with neatly trimmed, near-black hair that gleamed in the sun and eyes that reminded her of a mocha cappuccino. He wore a navy sports coat that covered an open-collared white shirt, dark-wash jeans and a pair of tan polished cowboy boots, indicating she'd probably pulled him away from a family function. Or quite possibly a date since he didn't appear to be wearing a wedding band.

"Ms. Armstrong?" he asked as soon as she stepped onto the porch, his voice hinting at a slight drawl.

Considering her ragtag appearance—damp holey jeans, no shoes, hair piled into a disheveled ponytail and a faded blue T-shirt imprinted with Bring it On!—Hannah considered denying her identity. But leaky pipes took precedence over pride. "That's me, and I'm so glad to see you."

"You were expecting me?" Both his tone and expression conveyed his confusion.

Surely he was kidding. "Of course, although I am really surprised you got here so quickly. And since I've obviously interrupted your Friday-night plans, please know I truly appreciate your expediency. Just one question before you get started. What exactly do you charge after normal business hours?"

He looked decidedly uncomfortable, either from the question or her incessant rambling. "Anywhere from two-fifty to four hundred regardless of the hour."

"Dollars?"

"Yes."

Ridiculous. "Isn't that a bit exorbitant for a plumber?"

His initial surprise melted into a smile, revealing dimples that would make the most cynical single gal swoon. "Probably so, but I'm not a plumber."

Hannah's face heated over her utterly stupid assumption. Had she been thinking straight, she would have realized he wasn't a working-class kind of guy. "Then what are you? *Who* are you?"

He pulled a business card from his jacket pocket and offered it to her. "Logan Whittaker, attorney at law."

A slight sense of dread momentarily robbed Hannah of a response, until she realized she had no reason to be afraid of a lawyer. She gained enough presence of mind to take the card and study the text. Unfortunately, her questions as to why he was there remained unanswered. She'd never heard of the Drake, Alcott and Whittaker law firm, and she didn't know anyone in Cheyenne, Wyoming.

She looked up to find him studying her as intently as she had his card. "What's this about?"

"I'm helping settle the late J. D. Lassiter's estate," he said, then paused as if that should mean something to her.

"I'm sorry, but I don't know anyone named Lassiter, so there must be some mistake."

He frowned. "You are Hannah Lovell Armstrong, right?"

"Yes."

"And your mother's name is Ruth Lovell?"

The conversation was growing stranger by the minute. "Was. She passed away two years ago. Why?"

"Because she was named as secondary beneficiary should anything happen to you before you claimed your inheritance."

Inheritance. Surely it couldn't be true. Not after all the years of wondering and hoping that someday…

Then reality began to sink in, as well as the memory of her mother's warning.

You don't need to know anything about your worthless daddy or his cutthroat family. He never cared about you one whit from the moment you were born. You're better off not knowing….

So shell-shocked by the possibility that this had something to do with the man who'd given her life, Hannah simply couldn't speak. She could only stare at the card still clutched in her hand.

"Are you okay, Ms. Armstrong?"

The attorney's question finally snapped her out of the stupor. "I'm a little bit confused at the moment." To say the least.

"I understand," he said. "First of all, it's not my place to question you about your relationship with J. D. Lassiter, but I am charged with explaining the terms of your inheritance and the process for claiming it. Anything you reveal to me will be kept completely confidential."

When she realized what he might be implying, Hannah decided to immediately set him straight. "Mr. Whittaker, I don't have, nor have I ever had, a relationship with anyone named Lassiter. And if you're insinuating I might be some mistress he kept hidden away, you couldn't be more wrong."

"Again, I'm not assuming anything, Ms. Armstrong. I'm only here to honor Mr. Lassiter's last wishes." He glanced over his shoulder at Nancy, the eyes and ears of the neighborhood, who'd stopped watering her hedgerow to gawk, before turning his attention back to Hannah. "Due to confidentiality issues, I would prefer to lay out the terms of the inheritance somewhere aside from your front porch."

Although he seemed legitimate, Hannah wasn't comfortable with inviting a stranger into her home, not only for her sake, but also for her daughter's. "Look, I need some time to digest this information." As well as the opportunity to investigate Logan Whittaker and determine whether he might be some slick con artist. "Could we possibly meet this evening to discuss this?" Provided she didn't discover anything suspicious about him.

"I can be back here around seven-thirty."

"I'd prefer to meet in a public venue. I have a daughter and I wouldn't want her to overhear our conversation."

"No problem," he said. "And in the meantime, feel free to do an internet search or call my office and ask for Becky. You'll have all my pertinent information and proof that I am who I say I am."

The man must be a mind reader. "Thank you for recognizing my concerns."

"It's reasonable that you'd want to protect not only yourself, but your child." He sounded as if he truly understood, especially the part about protecting Cassie.

She leaned a shoulder against the support column.

"I suppose you've probably seen a lot of unimaginable things involving children during your career."

He shifted his weight slightly. "Fortunately I'm in corporate law, so I only have to deal with business transactions, estates and people with too much money to burn."

"My favorite kind of people." The sarcasm in her tone was unmistakable.

"Not too fond of the rich and infamous?" he asked, sounding somewhat amused.

"You could say that. It's a long story." One that wouldn't interest him in the least.

"I'm staying at Crest Lodge, not far from here," he said. "They have a decent restaurant where we can have a private conversation. Do you know the place?"

"I've been there once." Six years ago with her husband on their anniversary, not long before he was torn from her life due to a freak industrial accident. "It's fairly expensive."

He grinned. "That's why they invented expense accounts."

"Unfortunately I don't have one."

"But I do and it's my treat."

And what a treat it would be, sitting across from a man who was extremely easy on the eyes. A man she knew nothing about. Of course, this venue would be strictly business. "All right, if you're sure."

"Positive," he said. "My cell number's listed on the card. If your plans change, let me know. Otherwise I'll meet you there at seven-thirty."

That gave Hannah a little over two hours to get showered and dressed, provided the real plumber didn't show up, which seemed highly unlikely. "Speaking of calls, why didn't you handle this by phone?"

His expression turned solemn once more. "First of all, I had some business to attend to in Denver, so I decided to stop here on the way back to Cheyenne. Secondly, as soon as you hear the details, you'll know why I thought it was better to lay out the terms in person. I'll see you this evening."

With that, he strode down the walkway, climbed into a sleek black Mercedes and drove away, leaving Hannah suspended in a state of uncertainty.

After taking a few more moments to ponder the situation, she tore back into the house and immediately retreated to the computer in her bedroom. She began her search of Logan Whittaker and came upon a wealth of information, including several photos and numerous accolades. He graduated from the University of Texas law school, set up practice twelve years ago in Dallas, then moved to Cheyenne six years ago. He was also listed as single, not that it mattered to Hannah. Much.

Then it suddenly dawned on her to check out J. D. Lassiter, which she did. She came upon an article heralding his business acumen and his immeasurable wealth. The mogul was worth billions. And once again, she was subjected to shock when she recognized the face in the picture accompanying his story—the face that belonged to the same man who had been to her house over twenty years ago.

That particular day, she'd returned home from school and come upon him and her mother standing on the porch, engaged in a heated argument. She'd been too young to understand the content of the volatile conversation, and when she'd asked her mom about him,

Ruth had only said he wasn't anyone she should worry about. But she had worried…and now she wondered….

Hannah experienced a surprising bout of excitement mixed with regret. Even if she had solid proof J. D. Lassiter was in fact her father, she would never have the opportunity to meet him. It was as if someone had given her a special gift, then immediately yanked it away from her. It didn't matter. The man had clearly possessed more money than most, and he hadn't spent a dime to support her. That begged the question—why would he leave her a portion of his estate now? Perhaps a guilty conscience. An attempt at atonement. But it was much too late for that.

She would meet Logan Whittaker for dinner, hear him out and then promptly tell him that she wouldn't take one penny of the Lassiter fortune.

At fifteen minutes until eight, Logan began to believe Hannah Armstrong's plans had changed. But from his position at the corner table, he glanced up from checking his watch to see her standing in the restaurant's doorway.

He had to admit, he'd found her pretty damned attractive when he'd met her, from the top of her auburn ponytail to the bottom of her bare feet. She'd possessed a fresh-faced beauty that she hadn't concealed with a mask of makeup, and she had the greenest eyes he'd ever seen in his thirty-eight years.

But now…

She did have on a little makeup, yet it only enhanced her features. Her hair hung straight to her shoulders and she wore a sleeveless, above-the-knee black dress that molded to her curves. Man-slaying curves that reminded Logan of a modern version of those starlets from days gone by, before too-thin became all the rage.

When they made eye contact, Hannah started forward, giving Logan a good glimpse of her long legs. He considered her to be above average in height for a woman, but right then she seemed pretty damn tall. Maybe it was just the high heels, although they couldn't be more than two inches. Maybe it was the air of confidence she gave off as she crossed the room. Or maybe he should keep his eyes off her finer attributes; otherwise he could land himself in big trouble if he ignored the boundary between business and pleasure. Not that he had any reason to believe she'd be willing to take that step.

Logan came to his feet and rounded the table to pull out the chair across from his as soon as Hannah arrived. "Thanks," she said after she claimed her seat.

Once he settled in, Logan handed her a menu. "I thought for a minute there you were going to stand me up."

"My apologies for my tardiness," she said. "My daughter, Cassie, had to change clothes three times before I took her to my friend's house for a sleepover."

He smiled over the sudden bittersweet memories. "How old is she?"

"Gina is thirty. Same as me."

Logan bit back a laugh. "I meant your daughter."

A slight blush spread across Hannah's cheeks, making her look even prettier. "Of course you did. I admit I'm a little nervous about this whole inheritance thing."

So was Logan, for entirely different reasons. Every time she flashed those green eyes at him, he felt his pulse accelerate. "No need to be nervous. But I wouldn't blame you if you're curious."

"Not so curious that I can't wait for the details until after dinner, since I'm starving." She opened the menu and began scanning it while Logan did the same. "I'd forgotten how many choices they offer."

He'd almost forgotten how it felt to be seated at a dinner table across from a gorgeous woman. The past few years had included a few casual flings for the sake of convenience with a couple of women who didn't care to be wined and dined. Sex for the sake of sex. And that had suited him fine. "Yeah. It's hard to make a decision. By the way, did you get your plumbing fixed?"

She continued to scan the menu. "Unfortunately, no. They called and said it would be tomorrow afternoon. Apparently pipes are breaking all over Boulder."

With the way she looked tonight, she could break hearts all over Boulder. "Do you have any recommendations on the menu?"

"Have you had bison?" she asked as she looked up from the menu.

"No. I'm more of a beef-and-potatoes kind of guy."

"Your Texas roots are showing."

She'd apparently taken his advice. "Did you check me out on the internet?"

"I did. Does that bother you?"

Only if she'd discovered the part of his past he'd concealed from everyone in Wyoming. *Almost everyone.* "Hey, I don't blame you. In this day and time, it's advisable to determine if someone is legitimate before you agree to meet with them."

"I'm glad you understand, and you have quite the résumé."

He shrugged. "Just the usual credentials."

"They certainly impressed me."

She undeniably impressed him. "Have you eaten bison before?"

"Yes, I have, and I highly recommend it. Much leaner and healthier than beef."

"I think I'll just stick with what I know."

Her smile almost knocked his boots off. "Perhaps you should expand your horizons."

Perhaps he should quit sending covert looks at her cleavage. "Maybe I will at some point in time." Just not tonight.

A lanky college-aged waiter sauntered over to the table and aimed his smile on Hannah. "Hi. My name's Chuck. Can I get you folks something to drink? Maybe a cocktail before dinner?"

Bourbon, straight up, immediately came to Logan's mind before he realized booze and a beautiful woman wouldn't be a good mix in this case. "I'll have coffee. Black."

Hannah leveled her pretty smile on Chuck. "I'd like a glass of water."

The waiter responded with an adolescent grin. "Have you folks decided on your meal?"

She took another glance at the menu before closing it. "I'll take the petite bison filet, medium, with a side of sautéed mushrooms and the asparagus."

Logan cleared his throat to gain the jerk's attention. "Give me the New York strip, medium rare with a baked potato, everything on it."

Chuckie Boy jotted down the order but couldn't seem to stop staring at Hannah as he gathered the menus. "How about an appetizer? I highly recommend the Rocky Mountain oysters."

That nearly made Logan wince. "I believe I'll pass on that one, Chuck."

"I second that," Hannah said. "A salad with vinaigrette would be good."

Chuck finally tore his gaze away from Hannah and centered it on Logan. "Can I bring you a salad, too, sir?"

No, but you can get the hell out of Dodge. "Just the coffee and a glass of water."

The waiter backed away from the table, then said, "I'll have that right out."

"What an idiot," Logan muttered after the guy disappeared into the kitchen.

Hannah frowned. "I thought he was very accommodating."

"He definitely wanted to accommodate you and it didn't have a damn thing to do with dinner." Hell, he sounded like a jealous lover.

Hannah looked understandably confused. "Excuse me?"

"You didn't notice the way he was looking at you?"

"He was just being friendly."

She apparently didn't realize her appeal when it came to the opposite sex, and he personally found that intriguing. "Look, I don't blame the guy. You're an extremely attractive woman, but for all he knows, we're a couple. The fact that he kept eyeing you wasn't appropriate in my book."

Her gaze momentarily wandered away and the color returned to her cheeks. "But we're not a couple, and he wasn't *eyeing* me."

"Believe me, he was." And he sure couldn't blame the guy when it came right down to it.

She picked up the cloth napkin near her right hand, unfolded it and laid it in her lap. "If he was, I didn't notice. Then again, I haven't been out much in the past few years."

"Since your…" If he kept going, he'd be treading on shaky ground. The kind that covered a major loss from the past. He knew that concept all too well.

She raised a brow. "Since my husband's death? It's okay. I've been able to talk about it without falling apart for the past four years."

He definitely admired her for that. Even after nine years, he hadn't been able to discuss his loss without flying into a rage. "I admire your resiliency," he said, all the while thinking he wished he had half of her tenacity.

Chuck picked that moment to bring the drinks and Hannah's salad. "Here you go, folks. Dinner will be right out."

As bad as Logan hated to admit it, he was actually glad to see the jerk, if only to grab the opportunity to turn to a lighter topic. "Thank you kindly, Chuck."

"You're welcome, sir."

After the waiter left the area, Logan returned his attention to Hannah. "So it's my understanding you recently obtained your degree."

She took a quick sip of water and sent him a proud smile. "Yes, I did, and apparently you've done your homework on me, too."

"I had to in order to locate you." Thanks to J. D. Lassiter not providing much information when they discovered the annuity's existence.

She picked up a fork and began moving lettuce around on the plate. "That old internet is a great resource for checking people out."

He only wished she would thoroughly check him out, and not on the computer. And where in the hell had *that* come from?

He cleared his throat and shifted slightly in his seat. "I take it you're satisfied I'm not some reprobate posing as an attorney."

"Yes, but frankly, I'm curious as to why you relocated from Dallas to Cheyenne, Wyoming. That must have been quite a culture shock."

He didn't want to delve into his reasons for leaving his former life behind. "Not that much of a shock. You find cowboys in both places."

"Were you a cowboy in another life, or just trying to blend in now?"

"I've ridden my share of horses, if that's what you mean."

She smiled again. "Let me guess. You were born into an affluent ranching family."

"Nope. A not-quite-poor farming family. Three generations, as a matter of fact. My parents ran a peach orchard in East Texas and raised a few cattle. They're semiretired now and disappointed I didn't stick around to take over the business."

"What made you decide to be a lawyer?"

He grinned. "When I wore overalls, people kept mistaking me for a plumber, and since clogged drains aren't my thing, studying the law made sense."

Her soft laughter traveled all the way to her striking green eyes. "Something tells me you're not going to let me live that one down."

Something told him he could wind up in hot water if he didn't stop viewing her as a desirable woman. "I'll let you off the hook, seeing as how we just met."

"And I will let you off the hook for not giving me fair warning before you showed up on my doorstep."

He still had those great images of her branded in his brain. "You know, I'm really glad I didn't decide to handle this over the phone. Otherwise, I wouldn't have met you, and something tells me I would have regretted that."

Hannah set down the fork, braced her elbow on the edge of the table and rested her cheek in her palm. "And I would have missed the opportunity to get all dressed up for a change and have a free meal."

She looked prettier than a painted picture come to life. Yep. Trouble with a capital *T* if he didn't get his mind back on business. "After you learn the details of your share of the Lassiter fortune, you'll be able to buy me dinner next time." Next time? Man, he was getting way ahead of himself, and that was totally out of character for his normally cautious self.

Hannah looked about as surprised as he felt over the comment. "That all depends on if I actually agree to accept my share, and that's doubtful."

He couldn't fathom anyone in their right mind turning down that much money. But before he had a chance to toss out an opinion, or the amount of the annuity held in her name, Chuck showed up with their entrées.

Logan ate his food with the gusto of a field hand, while Hannah basically picked at hers, the same way she had with the salad. By the time they were finished, and the plates were cleared, he had half a mind to invite her into the nearby bar to discuss business. But dark and cozy wouldn't help rein in his libido.

Hannah tossed her napkin aside and folded her hands before her. "Okay, we've put this off long enough. Tell me the details."

Logan took a drink of water in an attempt to rid the dryness in his throat. "The funds are currently in an annuity. You have the option to leave it as is and take payments. Or you can claim the lump sum. Your choice."

"How much?" she said after a few moments.

He noticed she looked a little flushed and decided retiring to the bar might not be a bad idea after all. "Maybe we should go into the lounge so you can have a drink before I continue."

Frustration showed in her expression. "I don't need a drink."

He'd begun to think he might. "Just a glass of wine to take the edge off."

She leaned forward and nailed him with a glare. "How *much?*"

"Five million dollars."

"I believe I will have that drink now."

Two

She'd never been much of a drinker, but at the moment Hannah sat on a sofa in the corner of a dimly lit bar, a vodka and tonic tightly gripped in her hand. "Five million dollars? Are you insane?"

Logan leaned back in the club chair and leveled his dark gaze on hers. "Hey, it's not my money. I'm only the messenger."

She set the glass down on the small table separating them, slid her fingers through the sides of her hair and resisted pulling it out by the roots. "You're saying that I can just sign some papers and you're going to hand me a fortune."

"It's a little more complicated than that."

After having the five-million-dollar bombshell dropped on her head, nothing seemed easy, including deciding to refuse it. "Would I have to go before some probate court?"

"No, but there are some stipulations."

She dropped her hands into her lap and sat back on the cushions. "Such as?"

"You have to sign a nondisclosure waiver in order to claim the inheritance."

"Nondisclosure?"

"That means if you take the money, by law you can't disclose your connection to the Lassiters to anyone."

She barked out a cynical laugh. "I refuse to do that. Not after living my entire life in the shadow of shame, thanks to my biological father's refusal to acknowledge me."

"Then you have reason to believe J. D. Lassiter is your father?"

Good reason. "Yes, there is a chance, but I don't know for certain because I have no real proof. Regardless, I do know I won't take a penny of his hush money."

Logan downed the last of his coffee, sat back on the opposing sofa and remained quiet a few moments. "What does your future hold in terms of your career?"

A little hardship, but nothing she couldn't handle. "I'm going to teach high-school human physiology and probably health classes as well."

He released a rough sigh. "It takes a lot of guts to stand in front of a room full of teenage boys and talk about the facts of life, especially looking the way you do."

Hannah appreciated his skill at doling out the compliments, even if she didn't understand it or quite believe it. "I assure you I can handle whatever teenage boys want to throw at me."

"I don't doubt that," he said. "But it's not going to be easy. I know because I was one once."

She imagined a very cute one at that. "Most men still retain some of those prepubescent qualities, don't you agree?"

He grinned, giving her another premiere dimple show. "Probably so. Do you have a job lined up?"

That caused her to glance away. "Not yet, but I've had my degree for less than two weeks, and that's when I immediately started the search. I expect to find something any day now."

"And if you don't?"

She'd harbored those same concerns due to the lack of prospects. "I'll manage fine, just as I've been managing since my husband died."

He sent her a sympathetic look. "That must have been a struggle, raising a child and going to school."

She'd been lucky enough to have help. Begrudging help. "My mother looked after my daughter when necessary until Cassie turned two. I lived off the settlement from my husband's work accident and that, coupled with Social Security benefits, allowed me to pay for day care and the bills while studying full-time. I obtained grants and student loans to finance my tuition."

"If you don't mind me asking, do you have any of the settlement left?"

She didn't exactly mind, but she felt certain she knew where he was heading—back into inheritance land. "Actually, the payments will end in October, so I still have six months."

He streaked a hand over the back of his neck. "You

do realize that if you accept this money, you'll be set for life. No worries financially for you or your daughter."

If Cassie's future played a role, she might reconsider taking the inheritance. "My daughter will be well provided for when she turns eighteen, thanks to my in-laws, who've established a million-dollar-plus trust fund in her name. Of course, I'm sure that will come with conditions, as those with fortunes exceeding the national debt are prone to do."

"Guess that explains your aversion to wealthy people."

Her aversion was limited to only the entitled wealthy, including Theresa and Marvin Armstrong. "Daniel's parents didn't exactly approve of my marriage to their son. Actually, they didn't approve of me. It was that whole illegitimate thing. They had no way of knowing if I had the appropriate breeding to contribute to the stellar Armstrong gene pool. Of course, when I became pregnant with Cassie, they had no say in the matter."

He seemed unaffected by her cynicism. "Are they involved in your daughter's life at all?"

"Theresa sends Cassie money on her birthday and collector dolls at Christmas that carry instructions not to remove them from the box so they'll retain their value. What good is a doll you can't play with?"

"Have they ever seen her?"

"Only once." And once had been quite enough. "When Cassie was two, they flew us out to North Carolina for a visit. It didn't take long to realize that my mother-in-law and active toddlers don't mix. After Theresa accused me of raising a wild animal, I told her

I'd find a good kennel where I could board Cassie next time. Fortunately, there wasn't a next time."

Logan released a deep, sexy laugh. "You're hell on wheels, aren't you?"

She took another sip of the cocktail to clear the bitter taste in her mouth. "After growing up a poor fatherless child, I learned to be. Also, my mother was extremely unsocial and rather unhappy over raising a daughter alone, to say the least. I took an opposite path and made it my goal to be upbeat and sociable."

He grinned. "I bet you were a cheerleader."

She returned his smile. "Yes, I was, and I could do a mean backflip."

"Think you could still do it?"

"I don't know. It's been a while, but I suppose I could don my cheerleading skirt, though it's probably a little tight, and give it the old college try."

He winked, sending a succession of pleasant chills down Hannah's body. "I'd like to see that."

"If you're like most men, you just want to see up my skirt." Had she really said that?

He sent her a sly grin. "I do admire limber women."

A brief span of silence passed, a few indefinable moments following unmistakable innuendo. Hannah couldn't recall the last time she'd actually flirted with someone aside from her husband. And she'd been flirting with a virtual stranger. An extremely handsome, successful stranger.

A very young, very peppy blonde waitress sauntered over and flashed a grin. "Can I get you anything, sir?"

"Bring me a cola," Logan said without cracking a smile.

She glanced at Hannah. "What about you, ma'am?"

"No, thank you."

"Are you sure?" Logan asked. "You wouldn't like one more round?"

She was sorely tempted, but too sensible to give in. "I'm driving, remember?"

"I could drive you home if you change your mind."

"That would be too much trouble," she said, knowing that if he came anywhere near her empty house, she might make a colossal mistake.

"It's not a problem."

It could be if she didn't proceed with caution. "I'm fine for now. But thanks."

Once the waitress left, Hannah opted for a subject change. "Now that you know quite a bit about me, what about you?"

He pushed his empty coffee cup aside. "What do you want to know?"

Plenty. "I saw on your profile you're single. Have you ever been married?"

His expression went suddenly somber. "Once. I've been divorced for eight years."

She couldn't imagine a man of his caliber remaining unattached all that time. "Any relationships since?"

"Nothing serious."

She tapped her chin and pretended to think. "Let me guess. You have a woman in every court."

His smile returned, but only halfway. "Not even close. I work a lot of hours so I don't have much time for a social life."

"Did you take a vow of celibacy?" Heaven help her, the vodka had completely destroyed her verbal filter.

When the waitress returned with the cola, Logan pulled out his wallet and handed her a platinum card to close out the tab, or so Hannah assumed. "Keep it open for the time being," he said, shattering her assumptions.

Once the waitress retreated, Hannah attempted to backtrack. "Forget I asked that last question. It's really none of my business."

"It's okay," he said. "I've had a few relationships based solely on convenience. What about you?"

He'd presented a good case of turnabout being fair play, but she simply had little to tell when it came to the dating game. "Like you, I haven't had time to seriously consider the social scene. I have had a couple of coffee dates in the past year, but they were disastrous. One guy still lived at his mother's house in the basement, and the other's only goal was to stay in school as long as possible. He already had three graduate degrees."

"Apparently the last guy was fairly smart," he said.

"True, but both made it quite clear they weren't particularly fond of children, and that's a deal breaker. Not to mention I'm not going to subject my child to a man unless he's earned my trust."

He traced the rim of the glass with his thumb. "It's logical that you would have major concerns in that department."

"Very true. And I have to admit I'm fairly protective of her. Some might even say overprotective." Including her best friend, Gina.

Logan downed the last of his drink and set it aside. "I'm not sure there is such a thing in this day and time."

"But I've been known to take it to extremes. I've even considered encasing her in bubble wrap every day before I send her off to school."

Her attempt at humor seemed to fall flat for Logan.

"You really can't protect them from everything, and that's a damn shame."

His solemn tone spurred Hannah's curiosity. "Do you have children from your previous marriage?"

He momentarily looked away. "No."

Definitely a story there. "Was that a mutual decision between you and your wife?" Realizing she'd become the ultimate Nosy Nellie, she raised her hands, palms forward. "I'm so sorry. I'm not normally this intrusive."

"My wife was an attorney, too," he continued, as if her prying didn't bother him. "Having kids wasn't in the cards for us, and that was probably just as well."

"How long were you married?"

"A little over seven years."

She started to ask if he'd been plagued with the legendary itch but didn't want to destroy her honorable-man image. "I'm sorry to hear that. I'm sure the divorce process can be tough."

"Ours was pretty contentious. But it wasn't anything compared to losing someone to death."

He almost sounded as if he'd had experience with that as well. "They're both losses, and they both require navigating the grief process. I was somewhat lucky in that respect. I had Cassie to see me through the rough times."

"How old was she when your husband died?" he asked.

"I was five months pregnant, so he never saw her." She was somewhat amazed she'd gotten through that revelation without falling apart. Maybe her grief cycle was finally nearing completion.

"At least you were left with a part of him," Logan

said gruffly. "I assume that did provide some consolation."

A good-looking and intuitive man, a rare combination in Hannah's limited experience. "I'm very surprised by your accurate perception, Mr. Whittaker. Most of the time people look at me with pity when they learn the details. I appreciate their sympathy, but I'm not a lost cause."

"It's Logan," he told her. "And you're not remotely a lost cause or someone who deserves pity. You deserve respect and congratulations for moving on with your life, Hannah."

Somewhat self-conscious over the compliment, and oddly excited over hearing her name on his lips, she began to fold the corner of the cocktail napkin back and forth. "Believe me, the first two years weren't pretty. I cried a lot and I had a few serious bouts of self-pity. But then Cassie would reach a milestone, like her first steps and the first time she said 'Mama,' and I realized I had to be strong for her. I began to look at every day as a chance for new opportunities. A new beginning, so to speak."

The waitress came back to the table and eyed Hannah's empty glass. "Sure I can't get you another?"

She glanced at the clock hanging over the bar and after noticing it was nearly 10:00 p.m., she couldn't believe how quickly the time had flown by. "Actually, it's getting late. I should probably be going."

"It's not that late," Logan said. "Like I told you before, I'll make sure you get home safely if you want to live a little and have another vodka and tonic."

Hannah mulled over the offer for a few moments. Her daughter was at a sleepover, she had no desire to watch TV, and she was in the company of a very attractive and attentive man who promised to keep her safe. What would be the harm in having one more drink?

"I should never have ordered that second drink."

Logan regarded Hannah across the truck's cab as he pulled to a stop at the curb near her driveway. "It's my fault for encouraging you."

She lifted her face from her hands and attempted a smile. "You didn't force me at gunpoint. And you had no idea I'm such a lightweight when it comes to alcohol."

Funny, she seemed perfectly coherent to him, both back in the bar and now. "Are you feeling okay?"

"Just a little fuzzy and worried about my car. It's not much, but it's all that I have."

He'd noticed the sedan had seen better days. "It's been secured in the valet garage, and I'll make certain it's delivered to you first thing in the morning."

"You've done too much already," she said. "I really could have called a cab."

In reality, he hadn't been ready to say good-night, although he couldn't quite understand why. Or maybe he understood it and didn't want to admit it. "Like I told you, it's not a problem. You don't know who you can trust these days, especially when you're an attractive woman."

She gave him a winning grin. "I bet you say that to all the women who refuse a five-million-dollar inheritance."

"You happen to be the first in that regard." Absolutely the first woman in a long, long time to completely capture his interest on a first meeting. A business meeting to boot. "I'm hoping you haven't totally ruled out taking the money."

"Yes, I have. I know you probably think I've lost my mind, but I do have my reasons."

Yeah, and he'd figured them out—she was refusing on the basis of principle. He sure as hell didn't see that often in his line of work. "Well, I'm not going to pressure you, but I will check back with you tomorrow after you've slept on it."

She blinked and hid a yawn behind her hand. "Speaking of sleeping, I'm suddenly very tired. I guess it's time to bid you adieu."

When Hannah reached for the door handle, Logan touched her arm to gain her attention. "I'll get that for you."

"Whaddya know," she said. "Looks like chivalry is still alive and well after all." She followed the comment with a soft, breathless laugh that sent his imagination into overdrive.

Before he acted on impulse, Logan quickly slid out of the driver's seat, rounded the hood and opened the door for Hannah. She had a little trouble climbing out, which led him to take her hand to assist her. Weird thing was, he didn't exactly want to let go of her hand, but he did, with effort.

He followed behind her as they traveled the path to the entry, trying hard to keep his gaze focused on that silky auburn hair that swayed slightly with each step she took, not her butt that did a little swaying, too.

Right before they reached the front porch, Hannah glanced back and smiled. "At least I'm not falling-down drunk." Then she immediately tripped on the first step.

Logan caught her elbow before she landed on that butt he'd been trying to ignore. "Careful."

"I'm just clumsy," she said as he guided her up the remaining steps.

Once they reached the door, he released her arm and she sent him another sleepy smile. "I really enjoyed the evening, Logan. And if you'll just send me what I need to sign to relinquish the money, I'll mail it back to you immediately."

He still wasn't convinced she was doing the right thing in that regard. "We'll talk about that later. Right now getting you to bed is more important." Dammit, that sounded like a freaking proposition.

"Do you want to come in?" she asked, taking him totally by surprise.

"I don't think that's a good idea." Actually, it sounded like a great idea, but he was too keyed up to honestly believe he could control his libido.

She clutched her bag to her chest. "Oh, I get it. You're afraid you're going to be accosted by the poor, single mom who hasn't had sex in almost seven years."

Oh, hell. "That's not it at all. I just respect you enough not to put us in the position where we might do something we regret, because, lady, being alone with you could lead to all sorts of things."

She leaned a shoulder against the support column and inclined her head. "Really?"

"Really. In case you haven't noticed, I've had a hard time keeping my eyes off you tonight." He was having a real *hard* time right now.

She barked out a laugh. "I'm sorry, but I'm having a difficult time believing you would be interested in me."

She couldn't be more wrong. "Why wouldn't I be?

You're smart and savvy and pretty damn brave to raise a child on your own and finish college at the same time."

"Keep going."

He could...all night. "You're a survivor and very beautiful, although you don't seem to know that. And that's not only hard to find in a beautiful woman, it's appealing."

"And?"

"Right now I'd like to kiss you," he blurted out before his brain caught up with his mouth. "But I'm not going to."

"Why not?" she asked, looking thoroughly disappointed.

"Because if I kissed you, I might not want to stop there. And as I've said, I respect you too much to—"

Hannah cut off his words by circling one hand around his neck and landing her lips on his, giving him the kiss he'd been halfheartedly trying to avoid.

Logan was mildly aware she'd dropped her purse, and very aware she kissed him like she hadn't been kissed in a long, long time—with the soft glide of her tongue against his, bringing on a strong stirring south of his belt buckle. He grazed his hand up her side until his palm rested close to her breast, and he heard her breath catch as she moved flush against him. He considered telling her they should take it inside the house before someone called the cops, but then she pulled abruptly away from him and took a step back.

Hannah touched her fingertips to her lips, her face flushed, her emerald eyes wide with shock. "I cannot believe I just did that. And I can't imagine what you must be thinking about me right now."

He was thinking he wanted her. Badly. "Hey, it's chemistry. It happens. Couple that with a few cocktails—"

"And you get some thirty-year-old woman acting totally foolish."

He tucked a strand of hair behind her ear. "You don't have to feel foolish or ashamed, Hannah. I'm personally flattered that you kissed me."

She snatched her bag from the cement floor and hugged it tightly again. "I didn't give you a whole lot of choice."

"You only did what I wanted to do." Trouble was, he wanted to do it again, and more. "For the record, I think you're one helluva sexy woman and I'd really like to get to know you better."

"But we've just met," she said. "We don't really know anything about each other."

He knew enough to want to move forward and see where it might lead. "That's the get-to-know-each-other-better part."

"We don't live in the same town."

"True, but it's only a ninety-mile drive."

"You're busy and I have a five-year-old child who is currently in school, plus I'm looking for a job."

He remembered another search she should be conducting, and this could be the key to spending more time with her. "There's something I've been meaning to ask you all night."

"Have I taken total leave of my senses?"

He appreciated her wit, too. "This is about your biological father."

That seemed to sober her up. "What about him?"

"Just wondering if you have any details about his life."

She sighed. "I only know that my mother hooked up with some guy who left her high and dry when she became pregnant with me. According to her, he was both ruthless and worthless."

Some people might describe J. D. Lassiter that way. "Did she ever offer to give you a name?"

"No, and I didn't ask. I figured that if he wanted nothing to do with me, then I wanted nothing to do with him." Her tone was laced with false bravado.

He did have a hard time believing J.D. would be so cold and uncaring that he would ignore his own flesh and blood no matter what the circumstances. "Maybe there were underlying issues that prevented him from being involved in your life."

"Do you mean the part about him being an absolute bastard, or that he was married?"

Finally, a little more to go on. "Do you know that to be a fact? The married part."

"My mother hinted at that, but again, I can't be certain."

"Then maybe it's time you try to find out the truth. You owe it to yourself and to your daughter. Because if J.D. is actually your father, you have siblings."

Hannah seemed to mull that over for a time before she spoke again. "How do you propose I do that?"

"With my help."

She frowned. "Why would you even want to help me?"

"Because I can't imagine what it would be like to have more questions than answers." In some ways he did know that. Intimately. "And since I'm an attorney, and I know the Lassiters personally, I could do some subtle investigating without looking suspicious."

"It seems to me you would be too busy to take this on."

"Actually, I have a light caseload this week." Or he would as soon as he asked his assistant to postpone a few follow-up appointments. "But I would definitely want you to be actively involved in the search."

"How do you suggest I do that from here?"

Here came the part that would probably have her questioning his motives. "Not here. In Cheyenne. You could stay with me for a few days and I'll show you the sights and introduce you to a few people. You could so some research during the day while I'm at work."

Hannah's mouth opened slightly before she snapped it shut. "Stay with you?"

He definitely understood why that part of the plan might get her hackles up. "Look, I have a forty-five-hundred-square-foot house with five bedrooms and seven baths. You'd have your own space. In fact, the master bedroom is downstairs and the guest rooms are all upstairs. We could go for days and not even see each other." Like he intended for that to happen.

"Good heavens, why would a confirmed bachelor need a house that size?"

"I got a good deal on the place when the couple had to transfer out of state. And I like to entertain."

"Do you have a harem?"

He couldn't help but laugh for the second time tonight, something he'd rarely done over the past few years. "No harem. But I have five acres and a couple of horses, as well as a gourmet kitchen. My housekeeper comes by twice a week and makes meals in advance if I don't want to cook."

"You know how to cook?" she asked, sounding doubtful.

"Yeah. I know my way around the stove."

She smiled. "Mac and cheese? BLT sandwiches? Or maybe when you're feeling adventurous, you actually tackle scrambled eggs?"

"My favorite adventurous meal will always be Italian. You'd like my mostaccioli."

She loosened her grip on her bag and slipped the strap on her shoulder. "As tempting as that sounds, I can't just take off for Cheyenne without my daughter. She won't be out of school for five weeks."

"Is there someone who could watch her for a few days?" Damn, he almost sounded desperate.

"Possibly, but I've never left Cassie alone for more than a night," she said. "I don't know how she would handle it. I don't know how *I* would handle it. Besides, I'm not sure I could accomplish that much in a few days even if I did decide to go."

He might be losing the battle, but he intended to win the war. "You could drive up for day trips, but that would require a lot of driving. If you stayed with me a couple of days, that would give us time to get to know each other better."

"Residing in a stranger's house would require a huge leap of faith."

He closed the space between them and cupped her face in his palm. "We're not strangers anymore. Not after you did this."

He kissed her softly, thoroughly, with just enough exploration to tempt her to take him up on his offer.

And once he was done, he moved away but kept his gaze locked on hers. "There could be more of that if you decide you want it. Again, no pressure. I'm just asking you to think about it. You might have the answers you need about your heritage, and we might find out we enjoy each other's company. Unless you're afraid to explore the possibilities…"

Logan realized he'd hit a home run when he saw a hint of defiance in Hannah's eyes. "I'm not the cowardly type, but I am cautious because I have to be. However, I will consider your suggestion and give you my answer tomorrow."

"Do you mind giving me your number? So I can call and let you know when your car's on its way." And in case he needed to further plead his case.

She dug through her purse for a pen and paper and scribbled down the information on the back of a receipt. "That's my home and cell number," she said as she handed it over. "Feel free to send me a text."

As Logan pocketed the paper, Hannah withdrew her keys, turned around and unlocked the door with a little effort, then walked inside without another word.

Logan was left alone on the porch to ponder why being with her again seemed so damn important. He had his choice of beautiful women back in Cheyenne, although most hadn't come close to capturing his interest like Hannah Armstrong.

He could chalk it up to chemistry, but he inherently knew that was only part of it. He did appreciate her keen sense of humor, knock-'em-dead body and those expressive green eyes that could drop a man in his tracks. He appreciated her all-fire independence and that she had the temperament of a mother bear when it came to her kid. In some ways, that attracted him more than anything else. But above all, she'd experienced the loss of a loved one. Their true common ground.

Hannah might understand his grief because she'd lived it, but if he told her his story, would she see him in the same light? Or would she turn away when she learned the truth?

Only time would tell if he'd find the courage to confess his greatest sin—he'd been partially to blame for the death of his only child.

Three

Her car was back, and so was the man who'd been foremost on her mind all morning long. All night, too.

Hannah peered out the window and watched Logan emerge from her aged blue sedan dressed in a long-sleeved black shirt, faded jeans secured by a belt with a shiny buckle and dark boots. Her heart immediately went on a marathon, the direct effect of an undeniable attraction she'd experienced all too well last night. That attraction had given her the courage to kiss him, something she normally wouldn't have the audacity to do. But by golly she had, and she'd liked it. A lot.

Hormones. That had to be it. Those pesky freaks of nature that made people act on impulse. She made a point to banish them as soon as she climbed out of bed. Granted, when he'd called to say he was bringing the car back, she'd made certain she looked more presentable than she had during their first meeting. She'd dressed in simple, understated clothing—white capri pants, light green, short-sleeved shirt and rhinestone-embellished flip-flops. Of course, she had put on a little makeup and pulled her hair back in a sleek, low ponytail. The silver hoop earrings might be a little much, but it was too late to take them off unless she ripped them out of her earlobes.

When the bell rang, Hannah automatically smoothed her palms over the sides of her hair and the front of the blouse. She measured her steps to avoid looking too eager, even though she wanted to hurl herself onto the porch and launch into his arms. Instead, she gave herself a mental pep talk on the virtues of subtlety before she slowly opened the door.

He greeted her with a dimpled grin and surprisingly stuck out his hand. "Mornin'. I'm Logan Whittaker, in case you've forgotten."

Hannah didn't know whether to kick him in the shin or kiss that sexy look off his face. She chose option three—play along for now—and accepted his offered handshake. She noticed the calluses and the width of his palm as he gave her hand a slight squeeze before he released her. "Good morning, Mr. Whittaker, and thank you for returning my car."

"You're welcome, but after last night, you should call me Logan."

Cue the blush. "I'm trying to forget about last night."

"Good luck with that because I sure can't forget it. In fact, it kept me tossing and turning most of the night."

She'd experienced the same restlessness, not that she'd admit it to him. "Do I need to drive you back to the lodge?"

"Nope," he said. "One of the valet guys will be here in about ten minutes."

Must be nice to have people at your beck and call, but she supposed that perk came with money. "Are you sure I can't drop you off? It's the least I can do."

"I'm sure, but I'm not leaving until we discuss your inheritance and my proposal."

No amount of money would ever convince her to agree to sign a nondisclosure form, even if she had no intention of aligning herself with the Lassiters. And that's the way it would stay. "I haven't changed my mind about the money, and the jury's still out on the other, to coin a legal phrase."

"Well, since you haven't ruled it out, I think you should let me in to argue my case. I'm housebroken and I won't destroy the furniture."

The sexy dog. "I suppose that's okay, but I have to warn you, the place is a mess, thanks to my child and the plumbing problems."

He had the gall to grin again, revealing those damnable dimples and perfectly straight, white teeth. "I promise you won't regret hearing me out."

She already did when he brushed past her and she caught the subtle scent of his cologne. Even more when once they moved inside, he turned and asked, "Where do you want me?"

An unexpected barrage of questionable images assaulted Hannah, sending her mind in the direction of unadvisable possibilities. Clearly those inherent female desires she'd tried to bury in everyday life weren't completely dead. That was okay, as long as she didn't act on them. Again.

She swallowed hard and bumped the door closed

with her bottom. "Let's go in the dining room." A safe place to interact with Mr. Charisma. "Actually, the floor's wet in there, so we can stay in here." First, she had to clear the worn floral couch of kid debris.

Before she could do that, Logan presented a frown that didn't detract from his good looks one iota. "Leaky pipe?"

"You could definitely say that. I managed to cut off the water under the sink, but this morning I got up only to discover the valve is leaking, too. Now the flood waters are trying to take over my kitchen."

"Tough break."

When Logan began rolling up his sleeves, Hannah's mouth dropped open. "What are you doing?"

"I'm pretty handy when it comes to pipe problems."

"That's not what you said yesterday."

"I've learned not to reveal my skills. Otherwise I'll be hounded every time someone has a plumbing issue. But for you, I'm willing to take a look."

She'd already taken a look. A covert look at his toned forearms threaded with veins, and the opening in his collar that revealed tanned skin and a slight shading of hair she'd tried not to notice last night. "Now I get it. You're really a repressed plumber masquerading as a lawyer."

His reappearing smile had the impact of a jackhammer. "No, but I am good with my hands."

She'd bet her last buck on that. "Thanks for offering to help, but it's not necessary. A real plumber should be here today."

Now he looked plain cynical. "Good luck with that, too. They don't get in a big hurry on a Saturday." He winked. "Besides, I'll save you that weekend rate and check it out for free."

He did have a valid argument, and she really liked the free part. What would be the harm in letting him peruse her pipes, or anything else of hers he'd like to peruse? She seriously needed to get a hold on her self-control. "Fine, but you're going to get wet. I did."

"Not a problem. Getting wet isn't always a bad thing."

Logan's suggestive tone wasn't lost on her. "Since you insist, be my guest." She pointed toward the opening to the dining room. "Just swim through there and keep going. You can't miss the kitchen sink."

Hannah followed behind Logan, covertly sizing up his butt on the way. A really nice butt, not that she was surprised. He happened to be one major male specimen, and she'd have to be in a coma not to notice. Still, she refused to let a sexy, dark-eyed, dimpled cowboy attorney muddle her mind. She'd let him fix her sink and say his piece before sending him packing back to Cheyenne without her.

Logan grabbed a wrench from the counter, lowered to his knees and stuck his head into the cabinet beneath the sink. Hannah leaned back against the counter to watch, unable to suppress a laugh over the string of oaths coming out of the lawyer's mouth.

"Sorry," he muttered without looking back. "I need to tighten a fitting and it's not cooperating."

"Is that the reason for the leak?"

"Yeah. It's a little corroded and probably should be replaced eventually. But I think I can get it to hold."

At least that would save her an after-business-hours service call. "That's a relief."

"Don't be relieved until I say it's repaired."

A few minutes passed, filled with a little more cursing and the occasional groan, until Logan finally emerged from beneath the cabinet and turned on the sink. Seemingly satisfied, he set the wrench aside and sent Hannah another devastating smile. "All done for the time being. Again, it needs to be replaced. Actually, all the pipes should be replaced."

Hannah sighed. "So I've been told. The house was built over forty years ago and it's systematically falling apart. I just paid for a new furnace. That pretty much ate up my reserves and blew my budget."

He wiped his hands on the towel beside the sink. "If you claim the inheritance, you'd never have to worry about a tight budget."

She couldn't deny the concept appealed to her greatly, but the cost to her principles was simply too high. "As I've said, I have no intention of taking my share." Even if J. D. Lassiter did owe her that much. But money could never make up for the years she'd spent in a constant state of wondering where she had come from.

Logan leaned back against the counter opposite Hannah. "And what *are* your intentions when it comes to my invitation?"

"I just don't see the wisdom in running off to Cheyenne on what will probably be a wild-goose chase."

"But it might not be at all. And you would also have the opportunity to meet some of the Lassiters, in case you decide you'd like to connect with your relatives since you wouldn't be bound by the nondisclosure."

"I'm not interested in connecting with the Lassiters."

He studied her for a few moments, questions in his eyes. "Aside from your in-laws, do you have any family?"

Hannah shook her head. "No. I'm an only child and so was my mother. My grandparents have been gone for many years."

"Then wouldn't it be good to get to know the family you never knew existed?" he asked.

She shrugged. "I've gone all these years without knowing, so I'm sure I'll survive if I never meet them."

"What about your daughter? Don't you think she deserves to know she has another family?"

The sound of rapid footsteps signaled the arrival of said daughter. Hannah's attention turned to her right to see the feisty five-year-old twirling through the dining area wearing a pink boa and matching tutu that covered her aqua shirt and shorts, with a fake diamond tiara planted atop her head. She waved around the star wand that she gripped in her fist and shouted, "I'm queen of the frog fairies!"

Cassie stopped turning circles when she spotted the strange man in the kitchen, yet she didn't stop her forward progress. Instead, she charged up to Logan, where she paused to give him a partially toothless grin. "Are you a frog or a prince?"

Possibly a toad in prince clothing, Hannah decided, but that remained to be seen. "This is Mr. Whittaker, Cassie, and he's a lawyer. Do you know what that is, sweetie?"

Her daughter glanced back and rolled her eyes. "I'm not a baby, Mama. I'm almost six and I watch the law shows on TV with Shelly. That's how I learned about lawyers. They look mad all the time and yell 'I object.'"

Hannah made a mental note to have a long talk with the sitter about appropriate television programs for a kindergartner. When Cassie began twirling again, she caught her daughter by the shoulders and turned her to face Logan. "What do you say to Mr. Whittaker?"

Cassie curtsied and grinned. "It's nice to meet you, Mr. Whittaker."

Logan attempted a smile but it didn't make its way to his eyes. In fact, he almost looked sad. "It's nice to meet you, too, Your Highness."

Being addressed as royalty seemed to please Cassie greatly. "Do you have a little girl?"

His gaze wandered away for a moment before he returned it to Cassie. "No, I don't."

"A little boy?" Cassie topped off the comment with a sour look.

"Nope. No kids."

Hannah sensed Logan's discomfort and chalked it up to someone who hadn't been around children, and maybe didn't care to be around them. "Now that the introductions are over, go pick up your toys, Cassandra Jane, and start deciding what you'll be wearing to school on Monday since that takes you at least two days."

That statement earned a frown from her daughter. "Can I just wear this?"

"I think you should save that outfit for playtime. Now scoot."

Cassie backed toward the dining room, keeping her smile trained on Logan. "I think you're a prince," she said, then turned and sprinted away.

Once her daughter had vacated the premises, Hannah returned her attention to Logan. "I'm sorry. She's really into fairy tales these days, and she doesn't seem to know a stranger. Frankly, that worries me sometimes. I'm afraid someday she'll encounter someone with questionable intentions. I've cautioned her time and again, but I'm not sure she understands the risk in that behavior."

"I understand why that would worry you," he said. "But I guess you have to trust that she'll remember your warnings if the situation presents itself."

Hannah sighed. "I hope so. She's everything to me and sometimes I'd like to keep her locked in her room until she's eighteen."

He grinned. "Encased in bubble wrap, right?"

She was pleasantly surprised he remembered that from the night before. "Bubble wrap with rhinestones. Now what were you saying before we were interrupted by the queen?"

"Mama! Where's my purple shorts?"

Hannah gritted her teeth and spoke through them. "Just a minute, Cassie."

"Look, maybe this isn't a good time to discuss this…." Logan said.

She was beginning to wonder that same thing. "You're probably right. And it's probably best if I say thanks, but no thanks, to your proposal, although I sincerely appreciate your offer."

When Logan's phone beeped, he took the cell out of his back pocket and swiped the screen. "The driver's here."

"Then I guess you better go." She sounded disappointed, even to her own ears.

He pocketed his wallet then unrolled his sleeves. "Do you have a pen and paper handy so I can give you my info?"

Hannah withdrew a pencil from the tin container on the counter and tore a piece of paper from the nearby notepad. "Here you go, but don't forget, I already have your card."

He turned his back and began jotting something down. "Yeah, but you don't have my home address."

She swallowed hard. "Why would I need that?"

He faced her again, caught her hand and placed the card in her palm. "In case you change your mind and decide to spend a few days as my guest in Cheyenne."

Oh, how tempting that would be. But... "I would have to ask my friend Gina if Cassie could stay with her. And I'd have to suspend my job search, even though that's not going anywhere right now." Funny, she sounded as if she was actually considering it.

He took a brief look around before he leaned over and brushed a kiss across her lips. "If you do decide to come, don't worry about calling. Just surprise me and show up."

With that, he strode through the living room and out the door, leaving Hannah standing in the kitchen in a semi-stupor until reality finally set in. Then she snatched up the cordless phone and pounded out a number on her way to the bedroom, where she closed the door. As soon as she heard the familiar hello, she said the only thing she could think to say.

"Help!"

"He wants you to do *what?*"

Sitting in a high-back stool at the granite island in her best friend's kitchen, Hannah was taken aback by Gina Romero's strong reaction to her declaration. Normally the woman rode her mercilessly about finding a man. "I'll speak more slowly this time. He wants me to go to Cheyenne for a few days and investigate the possibility that the man I'm inheriting from might be my biological father." She sure as heck wasn't going to reveal that inheritance was basically a fortune.

Gina swept one hand through her bobbed blond hair and narrowed her blue eyes. "Is that all he wants to investigate?"

Hannah would swear her face had morphed into a furnace. "Don't be ridiculous, Gina."

"Don't be naive, Hannah."

"I'm not being naive." Even if she wasn't being completely truthful. "He really is trying to help me."

Gina handed her eight-month-old son, Trey, another cracker when he began to squirm in the nearby high chair. "So tell me what's so special about this mystery attorney who wants to *help* you."

That could take hours. "Well, he's fairly tall, has dark hair and light brown eyes. Oh, and he has incredible dimples."

Gina gave her a good eye-rolling, the second Hannah had received today. "Okay. So he's a hunk, but does he have anything else to back that up?"

"As a matter of fact, he does. He's a full partner in a very prestigious law firm in Cheyenne."

"How's his butt?" she asked in a conspiratorial whisper.

The memory brought about Hannah's smile. "Stellar."

"Well, then, why aren't you home packing?"

"You'd think that would be enough, but I still have quite a few reservations."

"Unless you're lying and he's really in his eighties and drives a Studebaker, you should go for it."

"He's thirty-eight and drives a Mercedes. But he's also childless and divorced."

"Not everyone who's divorced is an ogre, Hannah," Gina said. "You can't judge him by your experience with that Henry what's-his-name you went out with for a while."

Gina could have gone all year without mentioning that jerk. "I only went out with him twice. But you know I worry when I meet a man who couldn't make his marriage work."

Gina frowned. "There are all sorts of reasons why marriages don't work, and it might not have even been his fault."

She couldn't argue that point since she had no details about Logan's divorce. "But what if it was his fault? What if he has some horrible habits that can't be overlooked?" Or worse, what if he cheated on his wife?

When the baby began to fuss, Gina rifled through the box of crackers and handed another one to her son. "Tell me, did this attorney do anything weird at dinner like that Henry guy you dated? Did he pick his teeth and belch? Or did he try to unsnap your bra when you hugged him good-night?"

"I didn't hug him good-night."

"Too bad."

"But I did kiss him."

Gina slapped her palm on the table, sending the baby into a fit of giggles. "You've been sitting here for ten minutes and you're just now telling me this?"

"It was a mistake." A huge one. "I had a couple of drinks and I guess it stripped me of all my inhibitions."

Gina sent her a sly look. "Question is, did you strip following the kiss?"

Heaven forbid. "Of course not. I just met the guy and I'm not that stupid."

"Yet you're considering going away with him," Gina said, adding a suspicious stare.

"I wouldn't be going away with him. I'd be staying at his house, which is very big, according to Logan."

"Wonder if his house is the only thing that's big."

Hannah playfully slapped at Gina's arm. "Stop it. This has to do with filling in the missing pieces of my family history, not getting friendly with Logan."

"Sure it does, Hannah. Just keep telling yourself that and you might start to believe it."

Leave it to Gina to see right through her ruse. "So what if I am attracted to him? Is there anything wrong with that?"

Gina made a one-handed catch of Trey's cracker when he tossed it at her. "There's absolutely nothing wrong with that. In fact, it's about time you start living again, girlfriend."

Same song, fiftieth verse. "I have been living, *girl-friend*. I've finished school and raised my daughter and I'm about to start a new career."

"Don't forget you cared for your ungrateful mother during the final months of her illness." Gina reached across the island and laid a palm on Hannah's forearm. "What you've done for your family since Danny's death is admirable. Heck, I'm not sure I could do the same thing if something happened to Frank. But now you need to do something for yourself."

Hannah still harbored several concerns. "What if I make this trip, decide that he's someone I want to spend a lot more time with and end up getting hurt?"

"That will happen only if you let him hurt you."

"True, but you have no idea how I felt being around him last night. I could barely think."

"Chemistry will cloud your mind every time."

Chemistry she could handle. "I'm worried it's more than that, Gina. I wish I could explain it." How could she when she couldn't explain it to herself? "I sense he really is a compassionate person, and maybe he's had some hard times during his life, too."

Gina took Trey from the high chair, placed him in the playpen and then signaled Hannah to join her in the adjacent den. She sat on the sofa and patted the space beside her. "Come here and let's have a heart-to-heart."

Hannah claimed her spot on the couch and prepared for a friendly lecture. "Bestow me with your sage advice, oh, wise one."

Gina sent her a smile. "Look, while we were growing up, you always walked the straight and narrow, always striving to be the best cheerleader, best student and an all-around good girl."

She bristled over her friend's words. "And what was wrong with that?"

"Because you did all those things to please your mother, and it never seemed to matter. Then you married Danny at the ripe old age of twenty. You worked hard to please him by quitting college so he could go to trade school when his parents cut him off because he married you."

She could feel her blood pressure begin to rise. "I loved Danny with all my heart and he loved me."

"Yes, he did, and he appreciated your efforts, unlike Ruth. But don't you think it's time you have a little adventure?"

Adventure had been a word sorely missing from

her vocabulary. "Maybe you're right, but what do I do about Cassie?"

Gina looked at her as if she'd lost her mind. "I can't count the times you've kept Michaela when Frank and I went out of town for a long weekend, including the one when I got pregnant with Trey. It's way past time for me to return the favor and watch Cassie for however long it takes for you to thoroughly investigate the attorney."

Hannah couldn't stop the flow of sexy, forbidden thoughts streaming through her imagination, until reality came calling once more. "But you're going to be saddled with two giggling girls and a baby. That doesn't seem fair."

Gina stood and began picking up the toys bouncing across the hardwood floors while Trey kept hurling more over the side of the playpen. "I'm used to this little guy's antics, and the girls will be in school during the day. Unless you plan to be gone until they reach puberty, it shouldn't be a problem."

"If I do go—" and that was a major *if* "—I only plan to stay a couple of days. A week, tops. But you're still going to have to deal with them at night, not to mention you have a husband to care for and—"

Gina held up a finger to silence her. "Frank has been trained well. And besides, he's been talking about trying for another kid next year. I might as well get in some practice before he knocks me up a third time."

The sound of those giggling girls grew closer and reached a crescendo as one red-headed ball of fire and one petite, brown-haired follower rushed into the room dressed in too-big formal attire, their faces showing the signs of a makeup attack.

"Aren't we pretty, Mama?" Cassie asked as she spun around in the red sequined strapless grown.

"Very," Hannah lied when she caught sight of the charcoal smudges outlining her daughter's eyes. "But did you have permission to raid Gina's closet?"

"Those came out of my cedar chest, Hannah," Gina said. "Cassie's wearing my prom dress and Michaela's wearing yours, in case you didn't recognize it."

Hannah did recognize the black silk gown all right, but she didn't remember giving it to her friend. "What are you doing with it?"

Gina looked somewhat chagrined. "I borrowed it and forgot to give it back."

Michaela's grin looked as lopsided as her high ponytail, thanks to the scarlet lipstick running askew from her mouth. "Can I keep it, Hannah?"

"Yes, honey, you most certainly can." The terrible memories of her part-octopus prom date, Ryan, were still attached to the gown, so no great loss.

"Do you have something you'd like to ask your daughter, Hannah?" Gina inquired.

Hannah supposed it wouldn't hurt to get Cassie's reaction to the possibility of her traveling to Cheyenne. "Sweetie, if I decided to take a trip out of town for a few days, would you mind staying here with Michaela and Gina?"

Cassie ran right out of her oversized high heels and practically tackled Hannah with a voracious hug. "I want to stay, Mama! When are you going?"

Good question. She pulled Cassie into her lap and planted a kiss on her makeup-caked cheek. "I'm not sure yet. Maybe tonight, but probably tomorrow."

Cassie looked crestfallen. "Go tonight, please. Me

and Mickey want to have a wedding. Gina said we could use her dress."

Hannah glanced at Gina. "You said that?"

"Yes, I did. But they've been forewarned that the groom will either be a stuffed animal or the baby brother, no boys from the neighborhood."

Cassie came to her feet and gave Hannah a hopeful look. "So can I stay, Mama? I'll be good and I'll help Mickey clean her room and I'll go to bed when I'm told."

Hannah couldn't in good conscience make a promise she might not keep. "We'll see. Right now you need to wash that purple eye shadow off your lids and go for something a little more subtle, like a nice beige. But before you do that, I want to take a picture."

While she fished her cell phone from her pocket, the girls struck a pose and put on their best grins. And as soon as she snapped the photo, the pair took off down the hall, sounds of sheer excitement echoing throughout the house.

She then noticed the blinking blue light indicating she'd received a text. And she couldn't be more surprised when she noted the message's sender. "Speak of the sexy devil."

Gina moved close to her side. "Devil as in the attorney?"

"Yes."

"What does it say?"

"'Dinner should be ready around seven. Italian. I also have a good bottle of wine. The only thing missing is you.'"

"Now I'm worried," Gina said.

Hannah pocketed the phone and stared at her friend. "You have something against Italian food?"

"I'm part Italian, silly. No, I'm worried because the devil didn't mention good sex."

She elbowed Gina in the side. "Would you please get off the sex thing? We have two impressionable, minor children in the house and they hear everything within a fifty-mile radius."

Gina pushed off the sofa and picked up the whimpering baby. "Come on, Hannah. Put on your big-girl panties and get with the program."

Something suddenly dawned on her. "Oh, my gosh, all I have are big-girl panties. Not a sexy pair in the drawer."

Her friend claimed the rocker across from the sofa and positioned the baby on her shoulder. "It's not even close to noon yet, so you have a few hours left to remedy that. Have you used the department-store gift card I gave you on your birthday?"

She was somewhat ashamed she'd held on to it for three months. "No, but before you get *your* big-girl panties in a wad, I've been too busy to shop."

"You better get busy if you want to be in Cheyenne by sundown," Gina said as she set the rocker in motion and rubbed her sleepy son's back.

A barrage of memories assaulted Hannah, recollections of a time when she'd rocked her baby girl, plagued with emotions that ran the gamut from bliss to utter sadness that her daughter's father would never know those precious moments. She secretly longed to have another child someday, and to be able to share that with a special someone. She suspected Logan Whittaker might not be the one to fulfill that dream.

"What's wrong now, Hannah?"

She looked at Gina through misty eyes. "Nothing really. Just remembering when Cassie was a baby, I guess. Time has a way of zipping by before you even realize it's gone."

"True, and time's a wastin' for you," Gina said. "Go shopping and buy those sexy panties along with a few nice outfits. Then go home and pack and get thee to Cheyenne."

If only it were that easy. "Do you really think this is the right thing to do?"

Gina sighed. "I think you'll never know unless you try, so just stop thinking and do it."

Her best friend was right. Nothing ventured, nothing gained, and all that jazz.

She might live to regret the decision, but darned if she wasn't actually going to do it.

Four

Never in a million years had Logan believed she'd actually do it. But there Hannah stood on his threshold, wearing a fitted, long-sleeved blue silk blouse covering tapered jeans, a small silver purse clutched in her hands. Talk about feeling underdressed in his faded navy T-shirt, tattered jeans and rough-out work boots. She'd parked her car beneath the portico and set two bags at her feet, which sported some deadly black heels, causing Logan to think questionable thoughts he shouldn't be thinking before she even made it into the house.

"You're here," he said, slight shock in his tone.

"I guess I should have called," she replied, clear concern in her voice.

"I told you to surprise me."

"Yes, but you looked absolutely stunned when you opened the door."

He grinned. "I thought you were the maid."

Fortunately she returned his smile. "I suppose we're going to have to work on that mistaken identity thing."

He personally would have to work on resisting the urge to kiss her at every turn. "We can do that after dinner."

"As long as I don't have to cook, it's a deal."

After grabbing Hannah's bags, Logan stepped aside and nodded toward the open door. "Come inside and make yourself at home."

The minute she entered the house, Hannah's gaze traveled upward toward the two-story foyer flanked by twin staircases with modern black banisters. "Wow. This is amazing."

He'd pretty much taken the view for granted and enjoyed seeing it through her eyes. "Yeah, it's impressive. But overall the place is more comfortable than elaborate."

She shot him a cynical look. "It's practically a mansion."

He started up the wood-covered stairs to the right. "I'll show you to your room before I give you the grand tour."

Hannah followed behind him to the second floor, where Logan stopped at the landing, allowing her to move in front of him for a purely selfish, and very male reason—to check out her butt. "Just go right and keeping walking until you reach the end of the hall."

She paused to peer inside the first of the three spare bedrooms. "Very nicely appointed. I really like the navy stripes mixed with yellows."

A color pallet he wouldn't have personally chosen, but if it worked for her, it worked for him. "The house was basically move-in ready. You can thank my decorator for the finishing touches. That's definitely not my thing."

"She's very good at what she does. I'm sure she has clients lined up for her services."

"Actually, she doesn't decorate for a living. She's a good friend of mine."

"A really good friend?"

When he heard the mild suspicion in Hannah's tone, he knew exactly what she was thinking. "Her name is Marlene and she's sixty years old. I'll introduce you in the near future." He decided to withhold the fact the woman was the late J. D. Lassiter's sister-in-law.

She passed the bathroom and peeked inside, then did the same with the next guest room, and pulled up short when she came to the closed door. "What's in here?"

A room he hadn't had the heart to touch, even if it did unearth bittersweet memories he'd just as soon forget. "It's a kid's bedroom that I haven't redone yet. I figured since I have three more guest rooms, I'm not in any hurry."

When she glanced back at him, Logan could tell she wasn't buying it. "Are you sure it's not your secret man-cave?"

"That's downstairs," he said, relieved she wasn't as suspicious as he'd assumed.

"Mind if I take a look?" she asked.

"Knock yourself out."

When Hannah opened the door and stepped inside, her expression said it all. The place was a little girl's fairy tale come to life, from the four princesses painted on the walls, to the pink cushioned seat built in beneath a ceiling-high window overlooking the courtyard at the front of the house.

"Cassie would absolutely love this," Hannah said as she looked around in awe. "That was one lucky little girl."

At least someone's little girl had been that lucky. "It's not exactly my taste, but then as a kid I preferred all things rodeo and baseball."

She turned and smiled. "Is that the décor you chose for your man-cave?"

His presumed "man-cave" would suit both genders. "You can see for yourself after we get you settled in, so keep going because we're almost there."

She turned and bowed. "My wish is your command, captain."

Grinning, he headed back into the hall and strode to the door he'd intentionally kept closed just so he could enjoy her reaction when he opened it. As expected, Hannah looked completely awed when he revealed the orange-tinted skies and the Rocky Mountain backdrop in clear view through the floor-to-ceiling windows.

"That is unbelievable," she said.

So was Logan's immediate physical reaction to the breathless quality of her voice. Keeping a firm grip on his control, he set her bags on the bench at the end of the king-size bed. "I have to agree with you there. It's better than the view from my bedroom, but you'll see that for yourself." When he noticed the trepidation in Hannah's eyes, he decided to backtrack for the second time in the past five minutes. "It's included on the tour, unless you want me to leave it off."

She shook her head. "No. Since we're both grown-ups, I can go into your bedroom without the fear of being grounded."

He wouldn't mind keeping her there for an indeterminate amount of time, a fact he'd keep to himself for now. "The bathroom's to your left."

She breezed through the bedroom, opened the double doors and then looked back with a smile. "Is this where you hold all your parties?"

He wouldn't mind holding a party there for the two of them. "Nope, but I probably could fit six people in the steam shower, and at least four in the jetted bathtub."

Hannah moved inside and ran her hand over one of the two granite-topped vanities. "I feel like I've died and gone to five-star-hotel heaven."

He thought he might die if he didn't get a little lip action real soon. "It's yours to enjoy for the duration."

She turned and leaned back against the vanity. "I could use a good soak in the tub."

And he'd gladly soak with her. "If you can wait until after dinner, that would be preferable. And speaking of that, it won't be too long before it's ready."

Hannah straightened and smiled. "Great, because I'm starving."

Man, so was he—for her undivided attention. "Then let's get going with the tour." Before he suggested they say to hell with dinner and take advantage of that tub. He definitely didn't want her to believe he intended to take advantage of her.

Logan showed Hannah to the upstairs den and then escorted her downstairs. He did a quick pass through the great room, pointed out his office and the game room, pausing as he arrived at the last stop before he led her to kitchen. "And this is my favorite place, the media room," he said as he opened the heavy double doors.

Her gaze traveled over the dark gray soundproof walls as she strolled down the black-carpeted, declining aisle. She paused to run her hand along the arm of one beige leather chair before facing him again. "Media room? This is more like an honest-to-goodness movie theater. All that's missing is a popcorn machine."

He nodded to his left. "In the corner behind that curtain, next to the soda fountain."

"Of course."

Hannah sounded almost disapproving, which sent Logan into defense mode. "Hey, the whole setup was here when I bought the house, including a huge collection of movies." Most of which he'd never watched because he didn't like watching alone. He planned to remedy that…and soon.

After folding her arms beneath her breasts, she slowly approached him. "I'd love to check out your collection."

"Not a problem, but right now I better check on dinner before I burn everything to a crisp and we have to call out for pizza."

She made a sweeping gesture toward the exit. "After you."

She followed quietly behind him as he led the way back through the great room and into the kitchen. As she'd done in the media room, Hannah took a visual trek through the area, her eyes wide with wonder. "State-of-the-art appliances, enough cabinets to store supplies for an army and a stainless island that I would sell my soul to have. Are you sure you don't have a robot hidden away somewhere to prepare your food?"

At least she'd said it with a smile, and that relieved him. He'd never been one to seek approval, but for some reason her opinion mattered. "No robot. Just me and sometimes the maid. I learned to cook after the divorce. It was either that or starve."

Hannah claimed the chrome-and-black bar stool across from the oven and folded her hands before her. "I hope it tastes as good as it smells."

He rounded the island, rested his elbows on the silver counter and angled his lower body away. "The recipe's never failed me before." He couldn't say the same for his self-control because he was having one hell of a fantasy involving her and that bar stool.

"What are we having?" she asked.

He personally was having a major desire to kiss her. "The mostaccioli I told you about."

"Fantastic. I've never had it before, but it's always good to try something new."

"And it's great to share something new with someone who's never experienced it before."

"I'm looking forward to a lot of new experiences while I'm here."

As their gazes remained connected, tension as apparent as the smell of the pasta hung in the air, until Hannah broke their visual contact by leaning around him. "According to your timer, we still have five minutes."

He straightened and glanced behind him before regarding her again. "True, and it needs to rest for another ten." Now what to talk about during those few minutes that would keep him from taking an inadvisable risk. "How did your daughter feel about you coming here?"

Hannah frowned. "She couldn't get me out of town fast enough. I can't compete with best friends and their baby brothers."

"I guess sometimes kids need a break from their parents."

She sighed softly. "I agree, but this is the longest break from each other we've ever had. I am glad to know she's in good hands, and that she's going to have a great time in my absence dressing up like a teenage harlot."

"Oh, yeah?"

Hannah pulled her cell phone from her pocket, hit an app and turned it around. "I took this photo this morning of my kiddo and her best friend, Michaela."

Logan started to laugh but the urge died when he homed in on the little girl standing next to Hannah's daughter. The resemblance might be slight, but the memories overwhelmed him. Recollections of his black-haired baby girl they'd appropriately named Grace.

He swallowed hard before handing Hannah the phone. "Gotta love their imaginations."

"Yes, but I don't like the fact she's trying to grow up too fast."

He'd give up everything he owned for the opportunity to watch his daughter grow up, but she'd been torn from his life after only four brief years. Now might be a good time to tell Hannah about her, but he wasn't ready yet. He wasn't sure he would ever be ready to make that revelation. "While we're waiting on dinner, do you want a glass of wine?"

"Sure," she said with a soft smile. "As long as you're also partaking tonight. I've decided it's best I not drink alone."

He'd learned that lesson all too well. "I'm not much of a wine drinker, but I do like a beer now and then."

"Whatever works for you."

Everything about Hannah Armstrong worked for him, and he'd just have to take out that thought and analyze it later. At the moment he needed to play the good host.

Logan crossed the room to a small bar where he'd set out an expensive bottle of red and poured a glass. Then he bent down and pulled out his favorite lager from the beverage refrigerator.

He returned to his place across from Hannah and slid the wine toward her. "Let me know if this meets your standards."

"I'm sure it will since I can only afford the cheap stuff," she said. "And before you mention that I can afford the best if I take the millions, don't waste your breath. I still haven't changed my mind."

"That's fine by me." And it was, to a point. "If you do refuse the inheritance, the funds will be merged into the Lassiter Foundation and given to charity."

She looked slightly amazed. "I didn't think J.D. would have a charitable bone in his body after the way he apparently treated my mother."

"And you," Logan said. "But he always has been somewhat of a philanthropist, and a good parent, which is why I'm surprised he would ignore his child."

"Perhaps he did have his reasons, and chances are I won't know. Maybe I don't want to know."

He didn't want to spoil the evening by being bogged

down by emotional chains from the past. "Let's concentrate on the present and worry about the rest later."

Hannah grinned and lifted her glass. "Here's to procrastination."

This time Logan did laugh as he touched his beer to her wine. "And to good food, new friends and more good food."

She took a sip of her wine and set the glass down. "Just don't feed me too well. If I put on an extra five pounds that means I'll have to lose fifteen instead of ten."

"You don't need to lose weight," he said, and he meant it. "You look great."

She lowered her gaze for a moment. "Thank you, but I really need to get back in shape so I can comfortably do those backflips."

That made him grin again. "I've got quite a few acres if you want to practice after dinner."

"Do you really think that's a good idea in the dark?"

No, but he could think of several things he'd like to do with her in the dark. Or the daylight. "You're right. I have another place to show you anyway."

She bent her elbow and supported her jaw with her palm. "Where do you plan to take me?"

Places she hadn't been before, but he didn't want to jump the gun, or get his hopes up…yet. "It's my second favorite place."

She narrowed her eyes. "You aren't referring to your bedroom since you left it off the tour, are you?"

He'd done that intentionally in an effort not to move too fast. "Not even close."

"Can you give me a hint?"

Without regard to the taking-it-slowly plan, he

reached over and brushed a strand of silky auburn hair from her cheek. "You surprised me tonight. Now it's time for me to surprise you."

Hannah had to admit she was a bit surprised when Logan suggested an after-dinner walk. She was even more shocked by his skill as a chef. Never before had she sampled such great food at the hands of a culinary hobbyist, who also happened to be a man.

She imagined his skills went far beyond the kitchen, particularly when it came to the bedroom. And although she'd been curious to see his sleeping quarters, she appreciated that he hadn't presented her with that possible temptation. Of course, she had no reason to believe he actually wanted to get her in his bed. She could hear Gina laughing at her naiveté the minute that thought vaulted into her brain.

According to Logan, the temperature had dropped quite a bit and now hovered around forty-five degrees, sending Hannah upstairs to change right after they cleaned the kitchen together. Hopefully the weather would begin to warm up in the next few days with the arrival of May. She rifled through her unpacked bag and withdrew a sweatshirt. After putting that on, she exchanged her heels for a pair of sneakers, did a quick makeup check, brushed her hair and then sprinted back down the stairs.

She found Logan waiting for her at the back door right off the mudroom adjacent to the kitchen, exactly where he'd told her to be. "I'm ready to walk off all that delicious food."

He inclined his head and studied her. "You really thought it was that good?"

Men. Always looking to have their egos stroked, among other things. She would actually be game for both…and obviously she was turning into a bad, bad girl. "I believe I said that at least five times during dinner, when I wasn't making the yummy noises."

His beautiful smile lit up his intriguing brown eyes. "Just making sure."

After Logan opened the door, Hannah stepped in front of him and exited the house. She was totally stunned, and extremely thrilled, when he rested his palm on the small of her back as he guided her toward a somewhat visible rock path illuminated by a three-quarter moon.

Unfortunately he dropped his hand as they began their walk toward a large expanse of land, but the Rocky Mountains silhouetted against the star-laden sky proved to be a great distraction. "It's really nice outside, even if it's a little cold."

"Feels good to me," he said.

She glanced at him briefly before turning her focus straight ahead to prevent tripping. "I can't believe you're not freezing since you're only wearing a light-weight jacket."

"The wind's not nearly as bad as it usually is around here. And I'm also pretty hot-blooded."

She had no doubt about that. He was hot, period. "What's that building in the distance?"

"A barn."

"Is that where you're taking me?"

"Nope."

She didn't quite understand why he seemed bent on being evasive. "Are you purposefully trying to keep me in suspense?"

"Yeah, but it'll be worth it."

A roll in the hay in the barn would be well worth it to her, and she'd best keep her questionable opinions to herself.

They continued to walk in silence until a smooth-wire fence stopped their forward progress. "This is my second favorite place," Logan said as he propped one boot on the bottom rail and rested his elbow on the top.

Hannah moved beside him and waited for her vision to adjust to the dark before taking in the panorama. The lush pasture traveled at an incline to what appeared to be a stream lined by a few trees. Not far away, she noticed two shadowy animals with their heads bent to graze on the grass. "Are those your horses?"

"Yeah. Harry and Lucy."

"Didn't they star in a fifties sitcom?"

Logan's laughter cut through the quiet. "I'm not sure about that, but they both came to me already named."

After she turned toward him and leaned against a post, his profile drew her attention. It was utterly perfect, from forehead to chin. "How long have you had them?"

"I bought Harry when I turned eighteen. He was a year-old gelding. I broke him and trained him to be a pretty good cutting horse. He's twenty now."

She had no idea what a cutting horse was, but she didn't want to show her ignorance. "What about Lucy?"

He went suddenly silent for a few seconds before speaking again. "I've had her about ten years, I guess. She's a retired pleasure horse and pretty kid-proof."

"That sounds about my speed."

He lowered his foot and faced her. "You've never ridden a horse?"

She internally cringed at the thought. "Twice. The first time I was sixteen and I went on a trail ride with friends. A controlled environment is a good place to start, or so they told me. They didn't, however, tell Flint, my ride. He decided to take off ahead of the pack and it took every ounce of my strength to get him to stop. After that, the trail master tied him to his horse to make sure he behaved."

"But you still got on a horse again?"

"On a beach in Mexico. I rode a really sweet mare and by the end of the ride, I'd trusted her enough to actually gallop." She closed her eyes and immersed herself in the memories. "The wind was blowing through my hair and the sun was on my face and I remember feeling the ocean spray on my feet. It was incredible."

"You're incredible."

She opened her eyes to find him staring at her. "Why?"

"Most people aren't brave enough to get back on a horse after a bad experience. I'm starting to wonder if anything scares you."

She was scared by the way she felt around him—ready to jump headfirst into possible heartache. "Believe me, I have fears like everyone else. I've just tried not to let them paralyze me."

Logan inched closer and streamed a fingertip along her jaw. "Would you be afraid if I kissed you again?"

She might die if he didn't. "Not really."

He bent and brushed a soft kiss across her cheek. "Would it scare you if I told you that you're all I've thought about for the past two days?"

"Would it scare you if I said I've been thinking about you, too?"

"I'm glad, because I can't get thoughts of us, being really close, off my mind." When he laced their fingers together, the implications weren't lost on Hannah.

"It's been a long time, Logan. I don't take intimacy lightly."

"I respect that," he said, not sounding the least bit disappointed. "That's why I only want to kiss you. Tonight."

After he said it, he did it, and he did it very well. The first time she'd kissed him, she'd fumbled through the motions. The first time he'd kissed her, he'd been quick about it. But not now.

He explored her mouth with care, with the gentle stroke of his tongue, allowing her to capture all the sensations. She responded with a soft moan and a certain need to be closer to him. On that thought, she wrapped her hands around his waist while he wound one hand through her hair and planted the other on her back.

When Logan tugged her flush against him, the cold all but disappeared, replaced by a searing heat that shot the length of Hannah's body and came to rest in unseen places, leaving dampness in its wake.

Too long since she'd been kissed this way, felt this way. Too long since she'd experienced a desire so strong that if Logan laid her down on the hard ground beneath their feet and offered to remove her clothes, she'd let him.

Clearly Logan had other ideas, she realized, when he broke the kiss and tipped his forehead against hers. "I need you so damn bad I hurt."

She'd noticed that need when she'd been pelvis-to-pelvis with him. "Chemistry definitely can commandeer your body."

He pulled back and studied her eyes. "But I don't want to screw this up, Hannah, so we're going to take this slowly. Get to know each other better. But sweetheart, before you leave, I plan to make love to you in ways you won't forget."

Hannah trembled at the thought. "You're mighty confident, Mr. Whittaker."

"I just know what I want when I want it, and I want you." He ran the tip of his tongue over the shell of her ear and whispered, "I think you want me just as badly. So let's go before I change my mind and take you down on the ground and get you naked."

Her body reacted with another surge of heat and dampness over Logan's declaration. Yet they walked back to the house, hand in hand, like innocent young lovers who'd just discovered each other, not mature adults who were approaching the point of no return.

Hannah knew better than to cross that line too soon. She knew better than to lead with her heart and not her head. Yet when Logan said goodbye to her at the bedroom door, she almost tossed wisdom out the window for a night of wild abandon. Instead, she let him go and sought out the place where she would spend the night alone longing for things she shouldn't. Wanting, needing, Logan's words echoing through her cluttered mind...

But sweetheart, before you leave, I plan to make love to you in ways you won't forget...

Deep down she had no doubt he was a man of his word. But if she took that leap into lovemaking, would her heart suffer another devastating blow?

Five

"What do you mean you didn't do it?"

That was the last thing Hannah wanted to hear first thing in the morning, especially from her best friend.

After turning the cell on speaker and setting it on the bed beside her, she slid a sneaker onto her foot and began lacing it. "He happens to be a gentleman, Gina. And I didn't call to talk about my sex life. I called to talk to my daughter."

"You don't have a sex life, and you can't talk to Cassie because she's not here right now."

She tightened the shoestrings just a little too tight. "Where is she?"

"Out with bikers she met bar-hopping last night."

Infuriating woman. "I'm serious, Regina Gertrude Romero."

"You know how I hate it when you use my middle name."

"Yes, I do," she said as she pulled on the remaining shoe. "Now tell me my daughter's actual whereabouts before I tell everyone in your book club that you want to be a pole dancer when you finally grow up."

Gina let out an exaggerated sigh. "She's with Frank at his sister's house. Since it's going to be close to eighty degrees today, and we don't know how long this heat wave is going to last, the kids are going to swim."

Hannah was poised to hit the panic button. "Are you sure it's warm enough there because it's not nearly that warm here."

"I checked the weather, Hannah. And don't forget, you're almost a hundred miles away."

She hadn't forgotten that at all, and now the distance between her and her child really worried her. "I hope the adults pay close attention because Cassie—"

"Can swim better than you and me," Gina said. "Stop being such a worrywart."

Her patience was starting to unravel. "Did you pack sunscreen? You know how easily she burns."

"Yes, I did, and I put the fire department on alert, just in case."

One more acerbic comment and she might very well come completely unglued. "Real funny, Regina. And why are you home?"

"Trey kept me up a good part of the night, so Frank let me sleep in while the baby is sleeping. I'll be heading out in an hour or so. By the way, where is your attorney now?"

He wasn't *her* attorney, but Hannah saw no reason to debate that point. "I'm not sure. I just got out of the shower and I haven't left the bedroom yet."

"I could see where you'd still be in the bedroom if

he was in there with you, but it's almost ten o'clock. Don't you think he might be wondering if you've flown the coop, leaving the rooster all alone?"

Hannah had thought about that, but so far she hadn't heard a thing coming from downstairs. "Maybe he's sleeping in, too. But I won't know until I get off the phone."

"Hint taken. Call me this evening and I'll put your daughter on the phone, unless, of course, you're engaged in some serious cross-examination."

"I'm hanging up now, Gina." As soon as she ended the call, Hannah hopped to her feet, ready to face the day—and Logan.

After a quick makeup application and hair brushing, she sprinted down the stairs, tugging at her plain light blue T-shirt and wishing she'd worn a better pair of jeans. But casual seemed to suit Logan. Very well.

She wound her way through the cowboy palace, following the scent of coffee in hopes of locating the master of the manor. When she arrived in the kitchen, there he was in all his glory, sitting with his back to her at the island. He wore a navy plaid flannel shirt and a cowboy hat, which almost sent Hannah completely into a female frenzy over her Wild West fantasy coming to life.

She stood in the kitchen opening just long enough to take a good look at his broad back before she slid onto the stool across from him. "Good morning."

He lifted his gaze from his coffee cup and smiled, but only halfway. "Mornin', ma'am. How did you sleep?"

Like a woman who couldn't get his kisses off her

blasted mind. "Pretty darn well, thank you. That mattress is as soft as a cloud."

"I'm glad you found the accommodations satisfactory." He nodded at the counter behind her. "There's some coffee left if you want me to get you a cup."

"I'll get some in a minute," she said when she noticed the keys resting near his right hand. "Have you been out already this morning?"

"Not yet, but unfortunately I'm going to have to get a move on. I got a call from Chance Lassiter. He's Marlene's son and the ranch manager at the Big Blue. He needs some extra help herding a few calves that got out of a break in the fence last night."

It figured her plans would be foiled by a Lassiter. So much for spending a relaxing Sunday getting to know him better. "How long will that take?"

"Hard to say, but it could be quite a while since we'll need to cover a lot of land. And the ranch is about thirty minutes north of here. Feel free to turn on the TV while I'm gone, or use the computer if you want to do some research on the Lassiters. If you need supplies, they're in the desk drawer."

She wondered why he would invite her—a virtual stranger—into his private domain. "You're absolutely sure you don't mind me hanging out in your office?"

He sent her a sexy-as-sin grin. "I don't have anything to hide. All my professional files are password protected, but if you have a hankerin' to hack into those, knock yourself out. The legal jargon on mergers and acquisitions is pretty damn riveting. Just be forewarned you're going to need a nap afterward."

She wouldn't mind taking a nap with him. "Do you want me to whip something up for dinner?"

"Don't worry about me. As far as you're concerned, there's quite a bit of food in the refrigerator, so help yourself."

Hannah admittedly was a bit disappointed he hadn't asked her to join him on the day trip. "Thanks."

"I really hate having to leave you, but—"

"I'm a big girl, Logan. I can entertain myself until you return."

He reached over the counter and ran a fingertip along her jaw. "When I get back, I have some entertainment in mind for you."

She shivered like a schoolgirl at the thought. "And what will that entail?"

After he stood, Logan rounded the island, came up behind her and brought his mouth to her ear. "You'll just have to wait and see, but it will be worth the wait."

After Hannah shifted toward him, Logan gave her a steamy kiss that made her want to initiate his kitchen counter. Or the floor. But he pulled away before she could act on impulse.

He snatched up his keys and winked. "I'll let you know when I'm heading home."

"I'll be here." And she couldn't think of any place she would rather be at the moment, aside from home with her daughter. Or in bed with him.

Naughty, naughty, Hannah.

After Logan left out the back door, she hurried to the great room to peer out the picture window facing the front drive. She waited until he guided the massive black dual-wheel truck and silver horse trailer onto the main road before she returned to the kitchen for coffee. She poured a cup and doctored it with lots of sugar and cream, then ate the apple set out in a fruit bowl.

Now what? TV watching seemed about as appealing as contemplating the cosmos. She did bring a book, but she wasn't in the mood to read. Doing a little research on Logan's computer called to her curiosity. After finishing off the coffee, she went in search of his office and retraced her steps from when Logan showed her around. Following a few wrong turns, she finally located the room beyond the formal dining room.

The French doors were closed, but not locked, allowing Hannah easy entry into the attorney's inner sanctum. A state-of-the-art PC sat in the center of a modern black desk that looked remarkably neat. Two walls of matching bookshelves housed several law manuals, as well as quite a few true-crime novels.

She dropped into the rolling black leather chair and scooted close to the computer, ready to start looking for more info on the Lassiters. Yet something else immediately drew her attention.

In Hannah's opinion, a man's desk drawer was equivalent to a medicine cabinet—worthy of investigation. But did she dare poke around? That would undeniably be considered an invasion of privacy. Sort of. Hadn't he said to help herself to any supplies? Of course, she didn't need any paper or pens yet, but she did have a strong need to satisfy her nosiness.

With that in mind, Hannah slid the drawer open slowly, and like the desk, the thing was immaculate. She took a quick inventory after she didn't notice anything out of the ordinary on first glance. A few pens in a plastic divider, along with some binder clips. A box of staples. A stack of stationery stamped with his name, along with coordinating envelopes.

Not quite satisfied, Hannah pulled the drawer open

as far as she could, and glimpsed the corner of something shiny. She lifted the brown address book to find a small silver frame etched with teddy bears and balloons, the bottom stamped with a date—February 15, twelve years ago. She withdrew the photo of a pretty newborn with a dark cap of hair, a round face, precious puckered lips and what looked to be a tiny dimple imprinted on its right cheek. Unfortunately, she couldn't quite determine the gender due to the neutral yellow gown, but she would guess this baby happened to be a little girl. The question was, *whose* little girl?

Logan had been adamant he had no children, leaving Hannah to assume the infant could be a sibling's child, if he had any siblings. She could clear up the mystery when he came home, but since the frame had been tucked away out of sight, she would have to admit she'd been snooping.

Right now she had another mystery that needed her focus, namely trying to find any clues indicating John Douglas Lassiter was her mother's sperm donor.

With that in mind, Hannah booted the computer and brought up her favorite search engine. She decided to dig a little deeper this time, expand her inquiries, and learn as much about the Lassiter family as possible, beginning with where it had all begun. She read articles about the self-made billionaire and his various ventures, from newspapers to cattle to his media corporation in California. He'd married a woman named Ellie, adopted her two nephews and lived through the loss of his wife, who sadly died at forty-two just days after giving birth to a daughter.

She took a few moments to study a recent publicity photo of that daughter, Angelica Lassiter, who could possibly be her sister. The sophisticated-looking woman was tall and slimly built, with dark hair and eyes—nothing that physically indicated Hannah might be kin to the reported "brains" behind Lassiter Media. Apparently Angelica had broken off her engagement to Evan McCain, interim chairman and CEO of the company, after a reported dispute over the terms in her father's will. High drama indeed.

Hannah surfed a little longer, trying to establish some connection between J.D. and her mother, yet she found nothing whatsoever to prove that theory.

Stiff-necked and bleary-eyed, Hannah noticed the time and realized a good part of the day had already passed her by. And as far as she knew, Logan hadn't returned home yet. She sat back in the chair and closed her eyes, remembering his lips fused with hers, his body pressed flush against her body, how badly she had wanted him last night. How badly she wanted him still, though she shouldn't...

The phone shrilled, startling Hannah so badly, she nearly vaulted from the rolling chair as she fumbled the cell from her pocket. Disappointment washed over her when Gina's name—not Logan's—displayed on the screen. "No, we haven't done it yet."

"Done what, Mama?"

Great. This was not the way she wanted to introduce her child to human sexuality. "Hi, sweetie. I miss you. Do you miss me?"

"Uh-huh, a little."

That stung Hannah like a hornet. "Are you back at Gina's?"

"Nope. We're still at Aunt Linda's house and we're swimming a lot."

Funny how Cassie had adopted the Romero family's relatives. But then she had very few relatives aside from Danny's parents. For the most part, they didn't count. "Are you sunburned?"

"A little on my nose. I'm gonna get more freckles, right?"

She was somewhat surprised that her daughter sounded almost happy about it. "If you continue to stay in the sun, yes, you probably will."

"Or if I swallow a nickel and break out in pennies."

"Where did you hear that, Cassie?"

"Frank told me. I like Frank. I wish he was my daddy. I mean, I love my daddy in heaven, but I want a real one. Mickey said she'd share him."

Hannah's heart took a little dip in her chest when she recalled how difficult it had been to grow up without a father. At least Cassie knew who her dad was, even if she'd never known him. She also had many pictures of Danny available to look at any time she desired. "Well, honey, maybe someday that might happen."

"Are you gonna marry your prince?"

Cassie sounded so hopeful Hannah hated to burst her fairy-tale bubble. "If you mean Mr. Whittaker, he's a lawyer, not a prince, and he's only my friend."

"But he's really cute and he doesn't have a kid. Everyone should have a kid."

From the mouth of her matchmaking babe.

Hannah heard a background voice calling for Cassie to come on, followed by her daughter saying, "Gotta go, Mama. We're eating pizza!"

"Okay, sweetie, tell Gina that—"

When she heard a click, Hannah checked to see if the call had ended, which it had. The conversation had been too brief for her liking, and too telling, yet she understood Cassie's excitement over being a part of a complete family.

At some point in time, perhaps she could provide that family for her daughter, but she didn't believe it would happen in the foreseeable future. And definitely not with Prince Logan. Though she didn't know the details of his divorce, she sensed he wasn't willing to travel that road again. Regardless, she would enjoy their time together and let whatever happened, happen. Now that she knew Cassie was faring well without her, she wasn't in a rush to head home.

"What is the rush to leave, Logan Whittaker?"

If he answered the question, it would require explaining his houseguest to Marlene Lassiter. And although she was as good as gold, she had a penchant for trying to direct his private life. "I'm just ready to take a shower and prepare for work tomorrow." And get home to a woman who'd weighed on his mind all day long.

She patted her short brown hair before pulling out a chair for him at the dining table in the corner of the kitchen area. "You've got time to eat. I made my famous meat loaf and cornbread."

Logan hadn't realized he was hungry until she'd said the magic words. Nothing like good old country cooking. He hadn't checked in with Hannah yet, so she wasn't expecting him. That didn't discount the fact he was still in a hurry to get home to her. "Do you mind fixing me a plate to go?"

That earned him Marlene's frown as she hovered above him. "Do you have a meeting of some sort?"

"Not exactly."

"Could—wonder of wonders—you have a date?"

If he didn't throw her a bone, she'd keep hounding him. "I have a friend staying with me and I'd like to get in a visit before I go to bed." Among other things.

Marlene smoothed a hand down her full-length apron. "Well then, I'll just make up two plates since I wouldn't want *him* to go hungry."

Damn. He might as well correct the gender issue. "I'm sure *she'll* appreciate it."

Marlene pointed a finger at him. "Aha! I suspected you're harboring a woman."

That sounded like he was holding Hannah against her will. He turned the chair around backward and straddled it. "Before you start getting any wrong notions, she's just a friend."

Marlene walked into the nearby pantry, returned with two paper plates and began dishing out food from the stove. "Are you sure about that friend designation? One of the hands said you seemed distracted, and nothing distracts a man more than a woman."

Double damn. "Just because I temporarily lost one of the heifers that left the herd doesn't mean I was distracted. It happens."

She shot him a backward glance. "It doesn't happen to you. But I'm glad you're finally getting back into the dating scene."

He could set her straight, or let her think what she would. He chose the first option. "Look, I'm handling a legal matter for her. That's why she's here."

After covering the plates with foil, Marlene turned and leaned back against the counter. "Is there potential for it being more than a client-attorney relationship?"

"It might, but I'm not in the market for anything permanent at this point in time." If ever.

"Does she know this, or are you leading her on?"

She had an uncanny knack for seeing right through him. "I'm not going to do anything to hurt her, if that's what's worrying you. Besides, she doesn't strike me as the kind of woman who's looking to nab a husband. Not only is she widowed, she also has a five-year-old daughter to consider."

Marlene frowned. "Have you told her about Grace?"

He should've seen that coming. "You know I don't talk about that with anyone but you, and that's only because you prodded me about my past." After he'd had a few too many during a party she'd hosted that happened to have fallen on Grace's birthday. He'd spent the night on her couch and woken the next morning with a hangover and more than a handful of regrets over baring his soul.

"Maybe you should talk to someone else about her, Logan," she said. "Keeping all that guilt and grief bottled up isn't doing you any good. You can't move forward if you stay stuck in the past."

"I'm not stuck." He tempered his tone, which sounded way too defensive. "I like to keep my private life completely private."

"And if you keep that attitude, you're never going to be happy." She took the chair next to his. "Honey, you're a good man. You have a whole lot to offer the right woman. You can't let yourself get bogged down in mistakes you think you might have made. One day you're going to have to forgive yourself, go on with your life and take a chance on love again."

He *had* made mistakes. Unforgivable mistakes.

"Isn't that the pot-and-kettle thing, Marlene? You never remarried after Charles died."

Marlene turned her wedding band round and round her finger. "No, I didn't. But that doesn't mean I cut myself off from love."

Exactly what he'd assumed, along with everyone else in town. "You mean you and J.D."

"I didn't say that."

She didn't have to. Logan saw the truth in her hazel eyes. He'd also seen something else in her at J.D.'s funeral, that soul-binding sorrow that he'd known all too well. "Come on, Marlene. You lived here with J.D. all those years after you both lost your spouses. No one would fault the two of you for being close."

"He was totally devoted to the kids and Ellie's memory." She sighed. "His wife meant everything to him and he never really got over her."

Which meant Marlene's love could have been one-sided. "Are you going to deny he cared for you, too?"

She shook her head. "No, I'm not, because he did care. But I couldn't compete with his cherished ghost. Regardless, we had some very good times."

That led Logan to believe the pair had been lovers, not that he'd ever request verification. "I tell you what, when you decide to have a serious relationship again, then I'll consider it, too." He figured he was pretty safe with that pact.

Marlene smiled sagely. "You never know what the future holds."

After checking the clock on the wall, Logan came to his feet. "I better get back to the house, otherwise Hannah might not speak to me again."

"Hannah?" she asked, more concern than curiosity in her voice.

"Yeah. Hannah Armstrong. Why?"

She attempted another smile but it fell flat. "Nothing. I've always thought it's a lovely name for a girl."

Logan wasn't buying that explanation, but he didn't have the energy to question her further tonight. He'd set aside some time later and have a long talk with her. Marlene Lassiter's relationship with her brother-in-law could be the key to solving the mystery of Hannah's past.

Yeah, he'd wait a little while before he sought more information from Marlene. If she did hold the answers, then Hannah would no longer have any reason to stay. And he damn sure wasn't ready for her to leave.

She wasn't quite ready to leave the heavenly bath, but when Hannah heard sounds coming from downstairs, she realized the dashing attorney was finally home.

After extracting herself from the jetted tub, she hurriedly dried off and prepared to get ready to greet him. And since she'd had headphones stuck on her ears until a few minutes before, and she hadn't checked her cell for messages in the past hour, she had no idea when Logan had returned.

She quickly dressed in a white tank with built-in bra and black jeans, then had a crisis of confidence and covered the top with a coral-colored, button-down blouse. She brushed her teeth, applied subtle makeup and opted to leave her hair in the loose twist atop her head. Danny had often told her she looked sexy with her hair up…and she really shouldn't be thinking about him while in the home of another man. An undeniably sexy man who'd commandeered her common sense from the moment she'd met him. And that lack of common sense had her slipping the first three buttons on the blouse to reveal the lace-edged tank beneath. An obvious indication of a woman bent on seduction.

Bracing her palms on the vanity, Hannah leaned forward and studied the face in the mirror. The same face that looked back at her every morning. Yep, she looked the same, but she felt very different. Her nerves sang like a canary and she felt as if her skin might take a vacation without her.

What was she thinking? It took a good three months for her and Danny to consummate their relationship. She'd only known Logan for three days. Yet she was older, and wiser, and lonely. She wanted to be in the arms of a man she was beginning to trust. Why she trusted him, she couldn't say. Intuition? Or maybe she was simply so foggy from lust that she wasn't thinking straight at all. That didn't keep her from sliding her feet into a pair of silver sandals and dabbing on perfume when she thought she heard him calling her name.

After rushing out of the bathroom and jogging through the bedroom, Hannah stopped in the hall to catch her breath. Seeming too enthusiastic might lead to misunderstanding. She might be happy to see him. She might be game for a little more serious necking. But she didn't know if she had the courage to go any farther than that.

She took her sweet time walking down the stairs and basically strolled to the great room. When she didn't find Logan there, she entered the kitchen to find it deserted as well. She did discover a pair of boots in the mudroom and his keys hanging on the peg, and detected the sound of the dryer in the adjacent utility room that was about as large as her den back in Boulder. At least she hadn't imagined he'd returned, but maybe she *had* imagined he'd called her.

Determined to locate the missing lawyer, she explored all the rooms he'd shown her, to no avail. That left her with only one uncharted location—his bedroom. She didn't dare go there. If he needed to speak with her, he could come and get her.

Two hours had passed since she'd eaten the ham sandwich, so she retrieved a bottle of water from the fridge and then perused the pantry for some sort of snack. She targeted the bananas hanging on the bronze holder and snapped off the best of the bunch.

Hannah had barely made herself at home on the bar stool when she heard heavy footfalls heading in her direction. The thought of seeing Logan gave her a serious case of goose bumps. When he walked into the kitchen, dressed in only a low-slung navy towel, she thought she'd been thrust into some nighttime soap opera starring a half-naked Hollywood hunk. He had a twelve-pack's worth of ridges defining his torso, a slight shading of hair between his pecs and another thin strip pointing downward to ground zero. Broad shoulders, toned biceps. Oh, boy. Oh, man.

While she sat there like a mime, appropriately clutching a phallic piece of fruit, Logan flashed her his dimpled grin. "You're here."

"You're wearing a towel." Brilliant, Hannah.

He pointed behind her. "I've got clothes in the dryer. I thought maybe you'd gone to bed already."

She noticed what looked to be a red tattoo on his upper right arm, but she couldn't see the details unless she asked him to turn toward her. Right now speaking at all was an effort, and the frontal view couldn't be beat. "It's not even six o'clock. I never go to bed that early."

"Maybe that theory was a stretch, but you didn't answer when I called you. And you didn't respond to my text."

She was surely responding to him now. All over. "I was taking a bath. The jets in the tub were going and I was listening to my MP3 player."

He cocked a hip against a cabinet and crossed his arms over his extremely manly chest. "Did you enjoy the bath?"

Not as much as she was enjoying the view right now. "Yes. Very relaxing. You should try it."

"I've got a big tub in my bathroom, but I'm not a bath kind of guy."

Maybe not, but he was one gorgeous guy. "Most men aren't into taking baths."

"True," he said. "Showers have always suited me better. A lot less effort. Easy in, easy out."

That conjured up images Hannah shouldn't be having. "I prefer showers, too, but I like a good bath now and then."

When he pushed away from the counter, she held her breath. She released it when he started toward the laundry room. "My clothes are probably dry now, so I better get dressed."

Please don't, she wanted to say, but stopped the comment threatening to burst out of her mouth. "Good idea."

The dryer door opened, followed by Logan calling, "If you're hungry, there's a plate of food in the refrigerator Marlene sent with me."

Hannah unpeeled the banana she still had in a death grip. "Thanks, but I've already eaten." She took a large bite of the fruit. Probably too large.

"Did you do any online research today?" he said over the sound of shuffling clothes.

"Yes, I did," she replied, her words muffled due to banana mouth.

"Find anything interesting?"

She swallowed this time before speaking. "Not much other than business articles." And a photo in his drawer that had piqued her interest.

While Hannah finished the fruit fest, Logan returned a few minutes later, fully dressed in beige T-shirt and old jeans. "I have an idea on how we might get some information on J.D.," he said.

She slid off the stool, opened the walk-in pantry and tossed the peel into the trash before facing him again. "What would that be?"

He leaned over the island using his elbows for support. "I'll let you know after I investigate further. It could end up being a dead end."

The man was nothing if not covert in his dealings. Must be the attorney thing—confidentiality at all costs. "Fine. Just let me know if you turn something up."

"I will." He straightened and smiled. "Are you in the mood for a little entertainment?"

She'd already been quite entertained by his recent show of bare flesh. "Sure. What do you suggest we do?"

"Watch a movie in the media room."

Not exactly what she had in mind, but what she'd been envisioning wouldn't be wise. "I'm all for a movie. Lead the way."

Six

Logan had chosen the lone theater chair built for two, along with a shoot-'em-up suspense film. But he hadn't bargained for the racy sex scene that came during the movie's first fifteen minutes.

He glanced to his right at Hannah, who had a piece of popcorn poised halfway to her mouth, her eyes wide as wagon wheels. "Wow. What is this rated?"

"R, but I thought that was due to the violence factor."

She popped a kernel into her mouth and swallowed. "I can't believe he didn't take off the shoulder holster when he dropped his pants. What if the gun goes off?"

"It does give a whole new meaning to 'cocked and ready.'" And he might have gone a bit too far with the crudeness.

Surprisingly, she released a soft, sultry laugh. "Ha, ha. It's hard for me to imagine a man taking a woman in an alley in broad daylight, gun or no gun."

That didn't exactly surprise him. "Anything's possible when you want someone bad enough." Exactly how he felt at the moment.

She tipped the red-striped box toward him. "Want some of this?"

His current appetite didn't include popcorn. "No thanks."

As the on-screen bumping and grinding continued, Logan draped his arm over the back of the seat, his hand resting on Hannah's shoulder. When he rubbed slow circles on her upper arm, she shifted closer to his side and laid her palm on his thigh. If she knew what was happening a little north of her hand, she might think twice about leaving it there. And if the damn movie didn't return to the run-and-gun scenes real soon, no telling what he might do.

No telling what *Hannah* might do was his immediate thought when she briefly nuzzled his neck, then brushed a kiss across his cheek. His second thought... the cheek kiss wasn't enough.

Logan tipped Hannah's face toward him and brought her mouth to his, intending only to kiss her once before going back to the film that fortunately now focused on the suspense plot. But the lengthy sex scene had obviously ignited the sparks between them, and from that point forward, everything began to move at an accelerated pace.

They made out like two teenagers on a curfew to the sounds of gunfire and cursing. He couldn't seem to get close enough to Hannah and that prompted him to pull her up onto his lap. He wound his hands through her hair and continued to kiss her like there was no tomorrow.

With Hannah's legs straddling his thighs, the contact was way too intimate for Logan to ignore. Every time she moved, he grew as hard as a hammer. To make matters worse, she broke the kiss, rose up and pulled away the band securing her lopsided ponytail. Obviously she was testing his sanity when she unbuttoned her blouse, slipped it off and tossed it aside, leaving her dressed in a thin tank top that left little to the imagination.

Seeing her sitting there with her tousled auburn hair falling to her shoulders, her lips slightly swollen and her green eyes centered on his, Logan's strength went the way of the popcorn that had somehow ended up on the floor. And just when he'd thought she was done with the surprises, she slid the straps off her shoulders and lowered the top.

He'd dimmed the lights before he'd cued the movie, but he could still make out the details. Incredible details. Unbelievable, in fact. Too tempting to not touch. That's exactly what he did—touched both her breasts lightly while watching her reaction. When Hannah tipped her head back and exhaled a shaky breath, Logan personally found it hard to breathe at all, and even harder not to take it further.

Pressing his left palm against her back, he nudged her forward and replaced his right hand with his mouth. Logan circled his tongue around one pale pink nipple, drawing out Hannah's soft groan. When he paid equal attention to her other breast, she shifted restlessly against his fly. If she didn't stop soon, it would be all over but the moaning. He damn sure didn't want to stop completely. He had a perfectly good bed at their disposal...and a perfectly good reason to halt the insanity before he couldn't. She deserved better than a quick roll in a chair, and he had no condoms available.

On that thought, he returned Hannah to the seat beside him and leaned back to stare at the soundproof ceiling while his respiration returned to normal.

"What was that?" Hannah asked, her voice somewhat hoarse.

Logan straightened to find her perched on the edge of the seat. Fortunately she'd pulled her top back into place, otherwise he wouldn't be able to concentrate. "That was uncontrollable lust."

"And, might I add, two adults acting like oversexed sixteen-year-olds," she said. "All we need now is to climb into the backseat of your car and have at it."

He didn't need to entertain that notion, but damned if he wasn't. "Hey, it happens."

"Not to me," she said. "I have never, ever been that bold."

He liked her boldness. A lot. "Not even with your husband?"

"Not really. We were both young when we met, and not very adventurous."

Interesting. "What about the men before him?"

Her gazed faltered for a moment. "Danny was my first. There wasn't anyone before him and there hasn't been anyone since."

Man, he hadn't predicted that. She kissed like someone who'd been around the block. Apparently she was a natural, even if she was somewhat of a novice. "Had I known that, I would've stopped sooner."

She frowned. "Why?"

"Because I don't want to do anything you don't want to do."

This time she released a cynical laugh. "I would think it's fairly obvious I wanted to do what I did, or I wouldn't have done it."

"Neither of us was thinking clearly." But he sure was now.

"Probably not, but since we're both consenting adults, I certainly don't consider our behavior shameful by any stretch of the imagination."

"I'm not sure I'm ready for this." He'd heard those words before, but never coming out of his own mouth.

Hannah looked perplexed. "Excuse me?"

He leaned forward, draped his elbows on his parted knees and focused on the popcorn-riddled carpet. "I'm not sure this is the right thing for either of us. More important, I don't want to hurt you, Hannah."

She touched his shoulder, garnering his attention. "I'm a big girl, Logan. I don't have any wild expectations of happily-ever-after. I want to feel desired by a man I can trust to treat me well. I know that man is you."

Yet she didn't know what he'd been concealing from her. She didn't know the demons still chasing after him. And she had no idea that his feelings for her were going beyond animal attraction.

He needed time to think. He needed to get away from her in order to keep his libido from prevailing over logic. Being the second man in her life would be a big burden to bear. He'd gained skill as a lover through experience, but he sucked when it came to the possible emotional fallout. If they continued on this course, they would only grow closer, and she might begin to have expectations he couldn't meet, regardless of what she'd said about not having any.

For that reason, he grabbed the remote from the adjacent chair, turned off the movie and stood. "I have an early day tomorrow and I'm pretty tired. We'll continue this discussion later."

Hannah stood and propped both hands on her hip. "That's it? You're going to run out on me without explaining why you've suddenly gone from hot to cold?"

He couldn't explain unless he made a few revelations that he wasn't prepared to make at this point. "I have some thinking to do, Hannah, and I can't do it with you in the same room."

"Suit yourself," she said as she moved past him and headed toward the exit.

He couldn't let her leave without telling her one important fact. "Hannah."

She turned at the door, anger glimmering in her eyes. "What?"

"I just don't want you to have any regrets."

"I don't," she said. "But I'm beginning to think you do."

Logan only regretted he might not be the man she needed. The man she deserved. And he had to take that out and examine it later before he made one huge error in judgment.

For the past two days, Hannah had barely seen Logan. He'd left for work before she'd awakened, and returned well after she'd retired to her room. She'd whiled away the lonely hours researching her possible family until she was certain her eyes might be permanently crossed. Her only human contact had come in the form of Logan's fiftysomething housekeeper,

Molly, who'd been extremely accommodating, right down to preparing meals in advance.

Of course, on several occasions she had spoken to Cassie, who had reinforced that she was having the time of her life with her best friend. Out of sight, out of mind, Hannah realized, at least when it came to her daughter and the attorney. And that hurt.

But after spending the morning in the public library perusing archived newspapers, Hannah had the perfect excuse to seek out Logan. She'd intentionally dressed in her professional best—a white sleeveless silk blouse, charcoal-colored skirt and black three-inch heeled sandals that Gina had fondly termed "do-me shoes." Hopefully she wasn't wasting those on a possible lost cause named Logan.

She didn't bother to call ahead before she arrived at the Drake, Alcott and Whittaker law firm located not far from the library. After playing tug-of-war with the strong Wyoming wind for control of the heavy wood door, she simply marched up to the very young, very pretty brunette receptionist and presented her best smile. "I need to see Mr. Whittaker please."

The young woman eyed Hannah suspiciously. "Do you have an appointment?"

She finger-combed her gale-blown hair back into place as best she could without a brush. "No, I don't. But I'm sure if you'll give him my name, he'll see me." If luck prevailed.

"What *is* your name?" the receptionist asked, sounding as if she believed Hannah might be some crazed stalker.

"It's Ms. Armstrong. Hannah Armstrong."

"Just a moment please." She picked up the phone and

pressed a button. "Mr. Whittaker, there's a Ms. Armstrong here and she... Of course. I'll send her right in." She replaced the phone and finally put on a pleasant demeanor. "His office is down the hall to your right, the second door on the left."

"Thank you."

Hannah traveled down the corridor with a spring in her step, feeling somewhat vindicated, until she realized she probably looked a whole lot disheveled. She paused long enough to open her bag for the appropriate tools, then brushed her hair and applied some lip gloss before continuing on to Logan's office. A brass plate etched with his name hung on the closed door, but the raised blinds covering the glass windows lining the hallway gave her a prime view of Logan, who happened to be on the phone.

She wasn't sure whether to wait until he hung up, or barge in. She opted to wait, until Logan caught her glance and gestured at her to come in.

Hannah stepped into the office, closed the door behind her and chose the chair across from the large mahogany desk. In an attempt not to appear to be eavesdropping, she surveyed the office while Logan continued his conversation. She had three immediate impressions—massive, masculine and minimalist. Neutral colors with dark blue accents, including the sofa and matching visitors' chairs. Blue-and-white-tiled fireplace with a barren mantel. A few modern Western paintings. Overall, a nice place to visit, but she wouldn't care to work there. The whole area could use some warming up.

Hannah couldn't say the same for herself. Seeing the sexy attorney dressed in coat and tie, his dark hair combed to perfection, his large hand gripping the phone, she had grown quite warm.

He seemed to be listening more than speaking until he finally said, "I understand, Mom, and I promise to do better with the calls. Tell Dad to stop giving you grief, and I'll talk to you next week. I love you, too." He then hung up and sent her a somewhat sheepish grin. "Sorry about that."

"I think it's nice you're close to your mother." The kind of relationship she'd wanted with hers, but never really had. "Are you an only child?"

"Actually, no," he said. "I have an older sister. She and her husband are both geologists living in Alaska with their five kids."

That could explain the picture in his desk drawer. "Wow. Five kids, huh?"

He grabbed a pen and began to turn it over and over. "Yeah. All boys."

She could have sworn that the baby in the photo she'd found in the desk had been a girl. "I suppose when you live somewhere as cold as Alaska, you have to find creative ways to keep warm."

"True, but constant procreating seems pretty extreme to me."

Hannah let out a laugh, but it died on her lips when she noticed his obvious uneasiness. "I was hoping you might introduce me to some more Lassiters."

He loosened his tie, a sure sign of discomfort. "It's been crazy busy around here."

Like she really believed that after he'd told her his schedule happened to be light this week. "Are you sure you haven't been avoiding me?"

He turned his attention back to the pen. "Not intentionally. I'm sorry that I haven't spent much time with you."

So was she. "Anyway, that's not exactly why I'm here. I came upon something at the library this morning that I found interesting." She dug through her bag and withdrew the copy of the archived article, then slid it across the desk. "This is a picture of J.D. and his brother, Charles, at a rodeo here in Cheyenne over thirty years ago. Charles won the roping competition."

Logan studied it a few moments before regarding Hannah again. "And?"

She reached across the desk and pointed at the text below the photo. "Look at the list of winners."

Logan scanned the text before looking up, sheer surprise in his expression. "Your mother was a barrel racer?"

"Yes, she was, but she gave it up after I was born." Only one more thing Ruth had blamed on her daughter. "Now I'm wondering if she met J.D. through his brother during one of these competitions."

Logan seemed to mull that over for a moment. "I planned to question Marlene Lassiter about J.D.'s past. They were very close, so she might know something about an affair."

"I'd appreciate that, Logan." She would also appreciate a better explanation for his behavior the other night in the media room. "Now that we've settled this matter, we do need to move on to our other issue."

"What issue would that be?"

She refused to let him play dumb. "The one involving our attraction to each other, and your concerns that I don't know my own mind."

"Hannah, I'm worried that—"

"I'll have regrets...I know. You're worried I'm going to get hurt. But as I told you during our last conversation, I don't have any expectations. I don't need poetry or candy or any promises. I only want to enjoy your company while I'm here, whatever that might involve."

"I don't want to do anything to hurt you."

Time to set him straight. "I'm not some fragile little flower who needs to be sheltered from life, both the good and the bad."

"I never thought of you as fragile, Hannah. But you have to know that I'm not in the market to settle down and have a family."

How well she understood that. "Fine. I get that. I'll hold off on picking out the engagement ring. Now I have a question for you."

"Shoot."

She scooted to the edge of her chair and stared at him straight on. "Do you still want me?"

He tossed the pen aside. "You really have to ask that?"

"Yes, and I want an answer."

When he rolled the chair back and stood, Hannah expected one of two things—Logan was going to kiss her, or show her to the door. Instead, he walked to a control panel mounted on the wall, pushed a button and lowered the electronic blinds, securing their complete privacy. Then he moved in front of her chair, clasped her wrists to pull her into his arms and delivered a kiss so soft and sensual, she thought her knees might not hold her. As if he sensed her dilemma, he turned her around and lifted her onto the desk.

Her skirt rode up too high to be considered ladylike, but frankly she didn't care. She was too focused on the feel of Logan's palms on her thighs, the strokes of his thumbs on the inside of her legs that seemed timed with the silken glide of his tongue against hers. *Higher,* she wanted to tell him. *Please,* she almost pleaded. But before she could voice her requests, he broke the kiss.

"Are you convinced I still want you, Hannah?"

This time she decided to play dumb in hopes he'd make more attempts at persuading her. "Almost."

"Maybe this will help." He took her palm and pressed it against his erection, showing her clear evidence of his need.

"I'm convinced." And veritably panting.

He placed her hand back into her lap. "Do you know what I really want right now?"

Hopefully the same thing she wanted—for him to have his very wicked way with her on top of his desk. "Do tell."

"Lunch."

Clearly the man was bent on driving her straight into oblivion. "Are you serious?"

Logan lifted her off the desk and set her on her feet. "Dead serious. There's a café right down the street that serves great burgers where we can eat and talk. I've been meaning to take you there."

Hannah wanted him to just take her. Now. But a talk was definitely warranted. She sent a pointed look in the direction of his fly. "Are you sure you're up to it? Oh, wait. Obviously you are."

He let go a boisterous laugh. "You'll need to walk in front of me for a few minutes. Just don't shake your butt."

Oh, how tempting to do that very thing. Instead, she picked up her purse and took her time applying more lip gloss. After she popped the cap back on and dropped the tube into her bag, she smiled. "Are you recovered now?"

"Enough to retain my dignity, so let's get out of here before I change my mind, lock the door and tell Priscilla to hold all calls while I hold you captive for a few more hours."

"Promises, promises," Hannah teased as they walked into the hall and started toward the lobby.

When they rounded the corner, an attractive sixty-something, brown-haired woman wearing a tasteful red tailored coat dress, nearly ran head-on into Hannah. "I'm so sorry, honey," she said. "I shouldn't be in such a hurry."

"You're always in a hurry, Marlene."

She patted Logan's cheek and smiled. "Not any more than you are, young man. Particularly the other evening when you rushed out of my house like your hair was on fire."

Hannah sent a quick glance at Logan, then returned her attention to the first Lassiter she'd encountered thus far.

Logan moved behind Hannah and braced his palms on her shoulders. "Hannah, this is Marlene Lassiter. Marlene, Hannah Armstrong."

The woman gave her an odd look before she formed a tentative smile and offered her hand. "It's nice to finally meet you."

Hannah accepted the brief shake, but she couldn't quite accept that the woman found the situation nice at all. "And it's a pleasure to finally meet you, too. Logan has told me a lot of good things about you."

"Well, you can't believe everything he says," Marlene added with a sincere smile directed at Logan.

"Were you here to see me, Marlene?" Logan asked.

"No," she said. "I'm having lunch with Walter, provided he's ready to go. The man still works like a field hand when he should be considering retirement."

The sparkle in Marlene's eyes, and the telling comment, led Hannah to believe the couple must know each other beyond any business arrangements. "I suppose that comes with the territory."

Marlene fiddled with the diamond necklace at her throat. "Yes, I suppose it does. And I better see if I can hurry him along."

"Again, it's nice to meet you," Hannah said as Marlene hurried past them.

"You, too, Hannah," she said over one shoulder before disappearing into the office at the end of the hall.

Hannah and Logan remained silent until they exited and stepped foot onto the sidewalk, where Logan turned to Hannah. "I suspect there's a story there with Walter and Marlene."

Considering Marlene's uneasy expression when they met, Hannah wondered if the woman might actually know the story of her life.

Before Logan could open the glass door to the Wild Grouse Café, a brown-haired man walked out, blocking the path. At first he didn't recognize him, until he realized the guy happened to be a client, a premiere chef, and the second Lassiter he'd encountered that day. "Are you checking out the competition, Dylan?"

"Hey, Logan," he said with a smile as he shook Logan's offered hand. "Actually, I grabbed a bite here because it's still one of the best eateries in town, at least until the grand opening of our newest restaurant. I've

barely had time to eat since I've been working on grabbing some good press for this venture to circumvent
the bad press over the will dispute."

Bad press compliments of Dylan's sister, Angelica.
"I hear you on the bad press, and finding time to eat.
I'm actually going to have lunch for a change."

"So they do let you out of the law cage?"

"It happens now and then." When he remembered
Hannah was behind him, he caught her arm and drew
her forward. "Dylan, this is Hannah Armstrong. Hannah, this is Dylan Lassiter, CEO of the Lassiter Grill
Corporation, a veritable restaurant empire."

Dylan grinned. "Pleased to meet you. And where
have you been hiding her out, Whittaker?"

"I'm his maid," Hannah said as she returned his
smile.

Dylan frowned. "Seriously?"

Leave it to Hannah to throw out a comeback, but
then he'd really begun to appreciate her easy wit. "She's
a teacher during the day."

"And Logan actually moonlights as a plumber," she
said.

They exchanged a smile and a look over their inside
joke, interrupted by Dylan clearing his throat. "Logan,
as a word of warning, I just had lunch with my sister.
She's still loaded for bear over the will, in case you
want to reconsider and find somewhere else to dine."

Great. Another Lassiter, and this one wasn't going
to be pleasant. "I can handle Angelica." As long as
he used kid gloves. He just hoped she wasn't wearing
boxing gloves.

Dylan slapped him on the back. "Good luck, Whittaker. And it was damn good to see you again. Nice to
meet you, too, Hannah."

After Dylan rushed away, Logan escorted Hannah into the restaurant and walked up to the hostess stand to request a table. He glanced across the crowded dining room and immediately spotted Angelica Lassiter sitting alone, wearing a white tailored business suit and a major scowl. Unfortunately, she spotted him as well. Too late to turn tail and run, he realized, when she slid out of the booth and approached him at a fast clip.

She bore down on him like a Texas tornado, her dark hair swaying and brown eyes flashing. "Logan Whittaker, you didn't return my last call."

An intentional oversight, not that he'd tell her. "I've been busy, Angelica, and you should address all questions regarding the will to Walter."

"Walter won't listen to me," she said. "He keeps saying there's nothing I can do to change the paltry percentage of Lassiter Media I inherited and I should learn to live with the fact Evan controls the majority of the shares, and the voting power that affords him. I still can't believe Daddy did this to me."

Frankly, neither could Logan. Nor could he believe how Angelica, a strong, independent businesswoman, reportedly the spitting image of her mother, could sound so much like a lost little girl. "I'm sure he had his reasons, and I know they don't seem logical or fair. All I can say is hang in there."

This time Hannah stepped forward on her own volition. "Hi, I'm Hannah Armstrong, a friend of Logan's."

Angelica gave Hannah's offered hand a gentle shake and presented a pleasant smile. "It's truly a pleasure to meet one of Logan's friends. Perhaps we can have dinner at some point in time."

"I'd like that." And she would, for reasons she

couldn't even reveal—namely this woman could actually be her sister.

Angelica turned back to Logan. "I'm asking you as a friend to talk to Walter and see if I can somehow contest the will. That company should be mine, not Evan's." And with that she was gone as quickly as she'd come, fortunately for Logan and for Hannah.

Once they were seated across from each other in the booth Angelica had just vacated, Hannah folded her hands on the table before her. "What were the odds I'd meet two of J.D.'s offspring in one day?"

Slim to none. "Now that you have met them, what do you think?"

She seemed to mull over that query for a minute. "Well, Dylan seemed nice enough, and so did Angelica, although she did seem pretty angry. I assume it had something to do with the breakup and that will dispute that I came across in a newspaper article. Am I right?"

He wasn't at liberty to hand her all the dirty details. "That's part of it. But just so you know, she's actually a very nice woman. Smart and savvy and she spends a lot of time involved in charity work."

"Don't forget she's very pretty," Hannah added.

"Yeah, you could say that." And he'd probably said too much.

"Have you dated her?" Hannah asked, confirming his conjecture.

"No. She's ten years younger and not my type."

She braced her bent elbow on the table and propped her cheek on her palm, reminding him of that first night they'd had dinner together. "Exactly what is your type?"

Hard to say, other than she seemed to be fitting the

bill just fine. "Keen intelligence, a nice smile. Green eyes. And most important, a smart-ass sense of humor."

Hannah leaned back and laid a dramatic hand above her heart. "I do declare, Mr. Whittaker. You sure have high standards."

He narrowed his eyes. "And you're getting a Texas accent."

"I wonder why." She went from smiling to serious in less than a heartbeat. "It's really hard for me to believe the people I met today could be my half siblings. And it makes me angry that my mother withheld vital information years ago, preventing me from making my own decision whether or not to connect with them."

If she only knew the vital information he'd been withholding from her, she wouldn't be too thrilled with him, either. But little by little, he'd begun to think he could trust her enough to tell her about his own sorry past. Eventually. "If you did decide to sign the nondisclosure, you'd never have a chance to get to know them. And since you're determined not to sign it, you really should give getting to know them a shot."

Hannah pondered that statement for a few moments before speaking again. "That's an option I'm not ready to explore. And signing the nondisclosure waiver would be the price I'd pay if I claimed my inheritance."

He wondered if she'd come to her senses and changed her mind. "Are you reconsidering taking the money?"

She shook her head. "No. Although it's tempting, I still don't feel I can claim it in good conscience, or sign the nondisclosure. Knowing the annuity will be turned over to charity does make my decision much easier."

She didn't sound all that convincing to Logan. "You

still have some time to think it through before you have to leave." And he wasn't looking forward to her leaving, though he had no right whatsoever to ask her to stay.

After finishing their food, they engaged in casual conversation, covering movies and music they liked, before their discussion turned to Hannah's child. Logan listened intently while Hannah verbally demonstrated her devotion to her daughter. Not a day had gone by when he hadn't thought about his own daughter, Gracie, and what she would look like now at age twelve. If she'd be chasing boys, or chasing cows with her grandpa. If she'd be smart as a whip like her mom, and love all things horses like him. The signs had pointed to that equine love, but he'd never known for sure, and never would. Gracie had only ridden Lucy one time, and that was a shame on many counts. A mare that willing and able and gentle should be ridden more often....

"Did I lose you somewhere, Logan?"

His thoughts scattered and disappeared after Hannah made the inquiry. "Sorry. I just came up with a really good idea." And he had. A banner idea.

"What would that be?" she asked.

He stood, held out his hand and helped her out of the booth. "I'm going to take the rest of the day off and we're going to have some fun."

"What, pray tell, do you have in mind, Mr. Whittaker?"

"Sweetheart, we're going to take a long, long ride."

Seven

This wasn't at all what Hannah expected when Logan mentioned going for a ride. She'd envisioned satin sheets and afternoon delight in his bedroom that she had yet to see. She *hadn't* expected to be sitting atop a plodding mare that kept stopping to graze as they headed toward the creek.

"You're doing fairly well for someone who hasn't been on a horse for a while."

She shot him a withering look. "Remind me of that when I have a sore butt for the next few days."

Logan's rich, deep laugh echoed across the pastureland. "Nothing a good soak in the tub won't cure. Or a massage."

"Know a good massage therapist?"

That question brought a frown to Logan's face. "Why would you need one when you have me?"

Her day suddenly brightened significantly, along with the sun. "Are you good at giving massages?"

"So I've been told."

She didn't care to ask who had told him. "That's nice to know in case I do need your services."

He winked. "Oh, you're going to need them all right. And I promise you're going to enjoy them."

"I'm counting on you to make good on that promise." And counting on herself not to let her heart get tangled up in him. Of course, that would be easier said than done.

They continued to ride in companionable silence, and after traveling over most the surrounding land, Logan finally dismounted in one smooth move a little farther away from where they'd stood the other night. Hannah did the same with much less poise, grabbed the reins and tugged a single-minded Lucy in Logan's direction before the mare launched into another grass attack. "Why did we stop?"

Logan guided the gelding to the gate opening up to the pasture that led to the creek. "I want to show you another special place."

"Good," Hannah replied. "My bottom was just about to give out."

After leading the horses through the gate, Logan turned and closed it, then said, "Let Lucy go for now."

As predicted, the mare went to the nearest clump of grass. "She's a regular chow hound."

"She needs to be ridden more often," Logan said as he detached a rolled blanket from the back of his saddle and tucked it beneath his left arm. "We can take another ride this weekend on my nearest neighbor's property. He has a larger spread and he told me to feel free to use it anytime."

Hannah's spirits plummeted when she realized she was set to leave in three days. "I plan to go home on Saturday."

He clasped her hand in his and gave it a gentle squeeze. "You can stay until Sunday."

She just might at that. One more day wouldn't matter to Cassie. If anything, her daughter might be disappointed to see her if it meant going back to her normal routine. "We'll see."

Logan guided her down the incline a hundred yards or so from the fence and stopped beneath a cottonwood tree not far from the narrow creek. He released her hand to spread the blanket over the ground. "I've been known to come here to think."

Hannah looked around the area, amazed at the absolute quiet. "It does seem to be a good place to clear your head."

"Among other things."

She turned to see Logan had already planted himself on the blanket, removed his boots and reserved a space beside him. "Take off your shoes and take a load off," he said.

She really wanted to remove more than her shoes. More like her clothes. And his. It had now been confirmed—she could star in her own made-for-TV movie about a very bad girl titled *Hannah and Her Outrageous Hormones*.

After she toed out of her sneakers, she dropped down next to Logan as a little flurry of butterfly nerves flitted around in her belly. "So are we going to meditate now?"

Logan's eyes appeared to grow darker in the shade, and undeniably more intense. "That's up to you."

With that, he brought her down onto the blanket in his arms, where she rested her head on his chest. They stayed that way for a time, the sound of his heart beating softly in Hannah's ear, his arm stroking her shoulder back and forth in a soothing rhythm.

She lifted her head to find him staring at the overhead branches. "Dollar for your thoughts. To account for inflation."

His smile made a short-lived appearance before he turned sullen again. "I was thinking how quickly life can change in one moment."

Hannah returned her head to his chest. "I know that all too well. One day you're sending the man you married off to work, the next you learn you'll never see him again."

"What exactly happened to him?" he asked. "If you don't mind talking about it."

She didn't mind, at least not now. "He was rewiring a commercial building that was under renovation and something went wrong. After the electrocution, they rushed him to the hospital and tried everything they could to save him, but it was too late."

"Does anyone know what went wrong now?"

"At first the insurance company claimed Danny was at fault, but his coworkers said he did everything he should have been doing in accordance with the wiring diagram. So they offered me a two-hundred-thousand-dollar settlement and I took it."

"You should have sued them."

Spoken like an attorney. "With a baby on the way and a new mortgage, I couldn't afford to ride it out, possibly for years, or risk losing the suit and ending up with nothing. Danny had a small insurance policy, but it barely covered funeral expenses, let alone any hospital bills I incurred after having Cassie."

"And your mother couldn't help out financially?"

A cynical laugh slipped out before she could stop it. "She always acted as if she didn't have a dime. However, she gifted us the down payment on our house out of the blue. I was able to repay her in a manner of speaking when I took care of her after her cancer diagnosis."

"You did that and attended school?" he asked, his voice somewhat incredulous.

"She only lasted two more months during the summer, so I wasn't in school." Hannah thought back to that time and the bittersweet memories. "Funny, I always felt as if I'd been a burden to her because she was so unhappy and bitter. Yet the day before she died, she told me thank you, and said she loved me. I don't recall her telling me that the entire time I was growing up. She was never the demonstrative type."

He released a rough sigh. "I can't imagine a parent not telling a child they loved them. But maybe she was so consumed by anger over being jilted by your father, she couldn't see what a gift she had in you."

Hannah's heart panged in her chest. "I don't know about being a gift, but I tried my best to be a good girl so I could win her approval. Unfortunately it never seemed to be enough."

He gave her a gentle squeeze. "As hard as it was, her attitude probably made you a stronger person. Definitely a good person. One of the best I've met in a long time."

He was saying all the right things, and he'd said

them with sincerity. "You're kind of remarkable yourself."

"Don't kid yourself, Hannah. I'm just an average guy who's made more than my share of mistakes."

Those mystery mistakes he had yet to reveal, leaving Hannah's imagination wide open. "Haven't we all screwed up a time or two, Logan? You just have to learn from those mistakes and move on. And eventually you have to stop blaming yourself for your shortcomings. That was fairly hard for me."

"Why were you blaming yourself?"

She truly hated to drudge that up, but soul-cleansing seemed to be the order of the day. "The morning Danny died, I got on him about leaving his shoes on the living room floor and missing the clothes hamper. I should have said I loved him, but the last words he heard from me had to do with cleanliness. I can count on one hand the times I didn't say I loved him before he left for work."

He brushed a kiss over her forehead. "You had no way of knowing he wouldn't be coming home."

If only she had known. "I finally acknowledged that, but it didn't lessen the guilt for a long time. If it hadn't been for Gina verbally kicking my butt, I might still not be over it."

"She's a good friend, huh?"

The very best and one of the few people she'd trust with her child. "Yes, she is. Granted, she does like to throw out advice whether I ask or not."

"How does she feel about you being here with me?"

She thought it best to hand him the abridged version. "Oh, she's all for it. In fact, if she'd had her way, we would've been having wild monkey sex from the minute I walked through your door."

"That would've worked for me."

She looked up to see his grin and poked him in the side. "That's rich coming from the guy who left me high and dry in his home theater."

"Believe me, that wasn't an easy decision."

Revelation time. "Just so you know, the way you make me feel…well…I thought I might never feel that way again."

He tipped her chin up and said, "That's my goal right now, to make you—" he kissed her forehead "—feel—" he kissed her cheek "—real good."

When Logan finally moved to her mouth, all Hannah's pent-up desire seemed to come out in that kiss, a hot meeting of tastes and tongues and mingled breath. Soon they were not only lip-to-lip, but also facing each other body-to-body until Logan nudged Hannah onto her back. He kissed the side of her neck as he slid his calloused hand beneath her T-shirt, at first breezing up her rib cage until he found her breasts. When he kissed her thoroughly again, he also circled her nipple with his fingertip through the lacy bra, and she reacted with an involuntary movement of her hips. Dampness began to gather in a place too long neglected, and she felt as if she might spontaneously combust due to the heat his touch was generating.

Her breathing, as well as her pulse, sped up as he skimmed his palm down her belly. She would swear her respiration stopped when he slipped the button on her jeans and then slid the zipper down.

Logan left her lips and softly said, "Lift up," and when Hannah answered his command, he pushed her pants down to her thighs, leaving her brand-new, leopard-skin panties intact.

For a few minutes, he seemed determined to keep her in suspended animation, toying with the lace band below her navel without sliding his hand inside the silk, no matter how badly Hannah wanted it. He finally streamed a fingertip between her thighs and sent it in a back-and-forth motion. He knew exactly how and where to touch her, but he only continued a brief time before he took his hand away. She responded with a somewhat embarrassing groan of protest, yet she soon discovered she had nothing to complain about when Logan worked her panties down to join her jeans.

From that moment forward, every bit of her surroundings seemed to disappear. The only sound she heard happened to be Logan whispering sensual words in her ear about what he wanted to do to her, what she was doing to him right then. Some of the comments could be considered crude, but she regarded them as the sexiest phrases she'd ever heard. He knew all the right buttons to push and, boy, did he push them well. The pressure began to mount, bringing with it pure pleasure on the heels of an impending climax, compliments of Logan's gentle, right-on-target strokes. And when the orgasm hit all too soon, Hannah inadvertently dug her nails into his upper arm and battled a scream bubbling up from her throat.

She'd never been a screamer. She'd never been in a pasture with her pants down around her knees either, being tended to by one outrageously gorgeous, sexy guy who knew exactly how to treat a woman.

Hannah was suddenly consumed by the overwhelming need to have him inside her. Yet when she reached for his fly, he clasped her wrist to stop her. "Not here," he said. "Not now. This was all for you."

She focused on his beautiful face, the deep indentations framing his mouth. "But—"

"It's okay, sweetheart. I'm going to be fine until we get back to the house."

She lifted her head slightly, with effort, to look at him. "What are we going to do when we get there?"

"I'm going to show you my bed." He favored her with a grin. "That is, if you want to see it."

Who was he kidding? "I seriously thought you would never ask."

Logan could have gone with spontaneity, but he wanted this first time between them to be special. More importantly, he needed Hannah to know she meant more to him than a quick roll on the ground, instant gratification, then over and out. She'd begun to mean more to him than she probably should.

Taking her by the hand, he led her into the master bedroom and closed the door behind them, determined to shut out the world and any lingering reservations.

Hannah remained silent when he tossed back the covers then guided her to the side of the bed. "Take off your shoes." And that would be the last thing she'd remove by herself if he had any say in the matter, which he did.

While she sat on the edge of the bed and took off her sneakers, he sat in the adjacent chair to pull off his boots. Once that was done, he lifted her from the bed and back onto her bare feet. He saw absolute trust in her eyes after he pulled the T-shirt over her head and tossed it aside. He noticed some self-consciousness in her expression as he removed her bra, and unmistakable heat when he slid her jeans and panties to the floor. She braced one hand on his shoulder for balance as she stepped out of the remaining clothes, a slight blush on her cheeks when he swept her up and laid her on the bed.

The sun streamed in from the open curtains covering the windows facing the pasture, casting Hannah's beautiful body in a golden glow. He needed to touch her. Had to touch her. But first things first.

Her gaze didn't waver as Logan stripped off his shirt, but she did home in on the ink etched in his upper arm. He'd have to explain that later. Right then he had more pressing issues. After shoving down his jeans and boxer-briefs, he opened the nightstand drawer, withdrew a packet and tossed it onto his side of the bed. He returned his attention to Hannah, who looked more than a little interested in his erection, her eyes wide with wonder.

She caught his glance and smiled. "I didn't realize you were that happy to see me."

Happier than he'd been in a long, long time. "I'm ecstatic to be here."

"So am I."

Relieved to hear that confirmation, Logan claimed the empty space beside Hannah and remained on his knees to allow better access. As he slid his fingertip between her breasts, pausing to circle each nipple, then moved down her torso, Hannah's breath caught. And when he replaced his hand with his mouth to retrace his path, he would swear she stopped breathing altogether.

When it came to sex, the advantage always went to women—they required little to no recovery time. And although his own body screamed for release, he was bent on proving that fact.

Logan nudged her legs apart to make a place for himself, then planted a kiss right below her navel. He didn't linger there long because he had somewhere more interesting to go. An intimate place that needed tending. When his mouth hit home, Hannah jerked from the impact. But he didn't let up, using his tongue to tease her into another climax. And as far as he could tell, this one was stronger than the last, apparent when she dug her nails even deeper into his shoulder.

He'd waited as long as physically possible to make love to her completely, and that sent him onto his back to reach for the condom. In a real big hurry, he tore the packet open with his teeth and had it in place in record time. He moved over her, eased inside her and called up every ounce of control to savor the feel of her surrounding him.

He'd learned long ago how to take a woman to the limits, but he also learned how to shelter his emotions in recent years. His sexual partners—and they'd been very few and far between—had been a means to an end. No commitments. No promises. Only mutual physical satisfaction. Up to that moment, he hadn't realized how empty his life had become. Until Hannah

He minimized his movements as he held her closely. He wanted it to last, if not forever, at least a little while longer. But nature had other ideas, and the orgasm crashed down on him with the force of a hurricane.

Logan couldn't remember the last time he'd shaken so hard, or the last time his heart had beaten so fast. He sure as hell couldn't recall wanting to remain that way for the rest of the day, in the arms of someone he'd known for such a short while. But at times, he'd felt as if he'd known Hannah for years.

When she moved slightly beneath him and sighed, he took that as a cue his weight might be getting to her. But after he shifted over onto his back, she asked, "Where are you going?"

He slid his arm beneath her and brought her against his side. "I'm still here, Hannah."

She rose up and traced one half of the broken-heart tattoo on his upper arm, etched with an *A* on one side, and a *G* on the other. "Are these your ex-wife's initials?"

He'd expected that question, and he decided on a half-truth. "No. They belong to a girl I used to know." His baby girl.

She rested her cheek on his chest, right above his heart, which was pounding for a different reason now. "She must have been very special, and I'm sorry she broke your heart."

After another span of silence passed, Logan thought she'd fallen asleep. She proved him wrong when she asked, "You've never really considered having children of your own?"

Alarm bells rang in his head. "I'm not cut out for fatherhood."

She raised her head again and stared at him. "How could you possibly know that if you haven't even tried it? Or do you just not like kids?"

"I like kids a lot. They're way the hell more honest than adults. But it takes more than liking a child to raise them right."

She settled back on the pillow. "I personally think you'd be good at it, for what it's worth."

In a moment of clarity, Logan realized Hannah deserved the truth. She had to know the real man behind the facade. It pained him to think about reliving those details. He'd be tearing open an old wound that still refused to heal. He also could be inviting her scorn, and that would be even worse. Still, he felt he had no choice but to be open and honest.

"Hannah?"

"Hmmm…" she murmured as she softly stroked his belly.

"There's something I need to tell you, and it's not going to be pretty."

Hannah sensed he'd been concealing a secret all along, but was she prepared to hear it? She certainly better be, she realized, when Logan handed her the T-shirt and panties, then told her to put them on with a strange detachment that belied the sadness in his brown eyes.

While she dressed, Logan pulled on his jeans before sitting on the bed's edge and turning his back to her. A long period of silence passed and for a minute she wondered if he'd reconsidered confessing whatever it was he felt the need to confess.

"I had a daughter at one time."

Hannah bit back an audible gasp. She'd expected an affair, a business deal gone bad. Maybe even bankruptcy, although that didn't make much sense considering he'd purchased a million-dollar home. But she could not have predicated he'd lied about being a father. Then again, that could explain the framed photo she'd found in his desk drawer. "Did you lose custody?"

"I lost her because she died."

And Hannah only thought she couldn't be more stunned. "When did this happen, Logan?"

"Almost eight years ago," he said in a weary tone. "She was only four years old."

She swallowed around her shock right before her

ability to relate to his loss drew her to his side. She laid a hand on his shoulder. "I'm so sorry, Logan." It was all she could think to say at a moment like this. Now she understood why so many people had been at a loss for words following Danny's death.

He leaned forward, hands clasped over his parted knees as he kept his eyes trained on the dark hardwood floor beneath his feet. "Her name was Grace Ann. I called her Gracie."

The truth behind the tattoo. Devastating loss had broken his heart. Not a woman, but a precious child. "I know how badly it hurts to lose a husband, but I can't even begin to imagine how difficult it would be to lose a child."

"That's because it's unimaginable until it happens to you." His rough sigh echoed in the deathly quiet room. "When Jana got pregnant, we'd barely been out of law school. We were both ambitious and career-minded. A kid hadn't been a part of the plan. But when Gracie was born, and they put that tiny baby girl in my arms, I thought I'd be terrified. Instead, I was totally blown away by how much I loved her at that moment. How I would've moved mountains to keep her safe. And I failed to do that."

Hannah desperately wanted to ask for details, but she didn't want to push him. "Things happen, Logan. Horrible things that we can't predict or prevent."

"I could have prevented it."

Once more Hannah didn't know how to respond, so she waited until he spoke again. *If* he spoke again.

A few more seconds passed before he broke the pain-filled silence. "I bought her one of those little bikes for her fourth birthday. The kind that still had training wheels. She loved that bike." He paused as if lost in the memories before he continued. "A couple of days later, I was supposed to be home early to help her learn to ride it. I'd just made junior partner, and I was assigned the case of a lifetime that would've netted the firm a windfall. The pretrial hearing went on longer than expected that afternoon, so I wasn't going to make it home before dark. My job took precedence over my daughter."

The guilt in his tone was instantly recognizable to Hannah. "You're not the first man to put work over family when the situation calls for it. Danny missed dinner many times because he had to put in overtime to secure our future."

"But I had earned plenty of money by then, and so had my wife. I could have turned the hearing over to the associate working the case with me, but I was so damn driven to prove the senior partners had been justified in choosing me over two other candidates. And that drive cost my child her life."

She truly needed to know what had happened, but did she dare ask? "Logan, I'm really trying to understand why you feel you're to blame, but I'm having some problems with that with so little information to go on."

Logan glanced at her again before returning his focus to the floor. "When I drove up that night, I saw the ambulance and police cruiser parked in front of the house. I tried to tell myself one of the neighborhood teens had been driving too fast and had had an accident. But my gut told me something inconceivable had happened, and it turned out I was right." He drew in a ragged breath and exhaled slowly. "I pulled up to the curb, got out of the car and started toward the ambulance, only to be met by an officer who told me not to go any farther. He said Grace had ridden the bike into the street and a woman driving by didn't see her, and she didn't even have time to put on her brakes."

Hannah felt his anguish as keenly as if it were her own. "Oh, Logan, I don't know what to say." And she honestly didn't. Again.

"Her death was instant, they told me," he said, as if he couldn't stop the flow of words. "She didn't suffer. But we all suffered. My marriage definitely suffered. Jana screamed at me that night and told me she'd never forgive me."

That threw Hannah for a mental loop. "She blamed you?"

He forked both hands through his hair. "We blamed each other. She blamed me for the bike and not being at a home on time. I blamed her for not watching Gracie closely enough. We both blamed the nanny for leaving early."

While Hannah pondered all she had learned, Logan went silent for a few more seconds before he released a ragged breath. "We had an alarm on the pool," he said. "We bought a top-rate security system and had every inch of the house child-proofed. But it wasn't enough. It came down to one unlocked door to the garage and Gracie climbing on a step stool to open the garage door, and she'd never been a climber."

Hannah had one burning question she had to ask. "Where was your wife at the time Gracie left the house?"

"Checking her email. She said Gracie was watching a DVD in the den only minutes before she went into the home office, and I had no reason not to believe her. Jana had always been a good mother, even if she had the same drive to succeed as I did. Basically, a few minutes of inattentiveness on Jana's part, and blind ambition on my part, irreparably changed our lives forever."

To Hannah, Logan's wife seemed more at fault than he did. But then she really couldn't completely blame her when she had been guilty of the same inattentiveness. "Children can be natural-born escape artists, no matter how vigilant the parent. Cassie got away from me in the grocery store once when I wasn't paying attention to her. It took a half hour and a security guard to find her. I was lucky someone didn't kidnap her when it would have been so easy."

"Gracie knew better than to leave the house without an adult," he said. "Until that night, she never had. I should have suspected she might pull something with the bike when I talked to her that afternoon."

"You spoke to Gracie?"

He smiled a sad smile that shot straight to Hannah's heart. "Yeah. I called Jana to say I was going to be late and she put Gracie on the phone so I could explain. When I told her I couldn't help her ride the bike that night, she was mad as a wet hen and told me she'd do it herself. I said that wasn't allowed and if she tried it, I'd take the bike away. She pouted for a few minutes but when I promised to help her the next day, and take her to the zoo that weekend, she seemed happy enough. Her last words to me were 'I love you, Daddy Bear.' She had a thing for Goldilocks."

Hannah's eyes began to mist like morning fog. "I know it's not the same thing as having her in your life, but at least you'll always have Gracie's wonderful last words to keep in your memory bank."

"But it's never been enough," he said, his voice

hoarse with emotion. "I finally did forgive Jana, but it was too little, too late. And when it came right down to it, she'd been right. I never should have bought Gracie the damn bike."

A solid stretch of logic, but logic didn't count for much when it came to guilt and grief. "When are you going to forgive yourself, Logan?"

He looked at her as if she'd presented a totally foreign concept. "Forgiveness is earned, Hannah. I'm not there yet."

She wanted to inquire as to how long it might take before he reached that point, but he looked completely drained. "I can tell you're tired." Of the conversation and the pain.

He swept both hands over his face. "I'm exhausted."

Hannah stretched out on her back on the bed and opened her arms to him. "Come lie down with me for a little while."

For a split second she thought he might ignore her request, but instead he shrugged out of his jeans and surprisingly accepted the solace she offered.

Curled up together, they slept for a while, until the sun had been replaced by darkness. Logan made love to her again, at first slowly, gently, completely, before a certain desperation seemed to take over. "I can't get close enough," he said, even though they were as close as two people could be.

"It's okay," she kept telling him, until his body went rigid and he released a low moan.

In the aftermath, he brought his lips to her ear and whispered, "Stay with me, sweetheart."

She caressed his shadowed jaw and almost started to cry over the tenderness in his request. "I'm not going anywhere, Logan."

"I meant don't leave on Saturday. Stay another week."

Temptation came calling, but wisdom won out. "I need to get home to Cassie."

"I know I don't have any right to ask, but I need you to be here for a little longer."

I need you....

Those three powerful words shattered Hannah's resolve. Cassie would be fine without her for another week, perhaps even happy to have the extra time with her best friend, that much she knew. Gina would be okay with her extended stay as well.

Logan needed her, and it felt so good to be needed. She instinctively knew she couldn't save him, but maybe if she loved him enough...

Loved him? If she wasn't completely there, she was well on her way, perhaps to her own detriment. She might regret giving in to that emotion, but she would never regret knowing him or what they had shared. What they would share.

"All right, Logan. I'll stay."

Eight

"Logan Whittaker, what brings you all the way out here in the middle of the week and the middle of the day?"

A quest for information he sensed Marlene held. He'd revealed his sorry secrets to Hannah several days ago, and now he wanted Marlene to do the same. "I'm taking a late lunch. Guess I should have called first."

"Don't be silly," she said as she held open the door. "You're practically family."

After he stepped through the door, Marlene pointed to the doors leading to the outdoor entertainment area. "Since it's such a lovely day, let's talk outside," she said as she showed Logan onto the flagstone deck adjacent to the massive great room. He settled on a rattan chair while she took the one to his left.

The 30,000 acres comprising the Big Blue ranch

spread out before them as far as the eye could see. The original homestead where J.D. and Ellie Lassiter had raised their family, now occupied by Marlene's son, Chance, sat in the distance beneath the blue sky that inspired the ranch's name. He'd learned the history early on, but it had never impacted him like it did today. "I'd like to build a house on a place like this in the future. Far away from everything with no signs whatsoever of the city." No suburban streets where playing kids could get hurt, or worse, and that unexpected thought gave him pause. He didn't intend to have any more kids. Not now. Not ever.

"It is peaceful," Marlene said. "All the Lassiter children enjoyed living here."

Speaking of Lassiter children...

Logan glanced back and peered inside through the uncovered floor-to-ceiling windows, looking for signs of other life—namely J.D.'s only daughter. "Is Angelica staying here right now?" Not only did he not want a repeat of their last conversation, but he also didn't want to risk her accidentally overhearing that her own father had taken a mistress, and produced a child. That would categorically send her over the edge. Of course, that would only happen if Marlene came clean.

"Angelica is back in L.A. for a couple of days," she said. "And quite honestly, that's a good thing. That girl has been in a constant tizzy lately. She needs a break. *I* need a break."

"I totally understand. J.D.'s decisions on who inherits his millions have created a lot of questions." Especially for Hannah.

Marlene reached over and patted his arm. "Now why are you here, honey?"

A perfect lead-in to the reason for his impromptu visit. "It's actually about those aforementioned questions. I'm pretty sure you have information about Hannah Armstrong's parentage, namely her connection to J.D. And if you do know anything about that, tell me now because she has a right to know."

She began to wring her hands like an old-time washer. "It's probably past time Hannah learns the truth, and I do know the details. But I wouldn't feel right discussing those particulars with you before I speak with her."

His suspicions had been upheld, and the answers were within Hannah's grasp. A good thing for Hannah because she would know the truth. A bad thing for him because she'd have no reason not to return to Boulder immediately. But delaying the revelation would be selfish on his part. "If I bring her by, will you tell her the whole truth?"

Marlene raised a brow. "She's still here?"

"Yeah. I asked her to stay another week." An unforgettable week of lovemaking and conversation and making a connection with a woman who'd become very special to him. A week that had passed way too fast. But since he had so little to offer her, he would be forced to let her go eventually.

"What makes this one so different from the rest, Logan?" Marlene asked, cutting into his thoughts.

He could recite every one of Hannah's attributes, but that would take hours, so he chose to list only a few. "She's funny and kind but also damn tough. Not many people could handle losing a husband, raising a child on their own, caring for an ill parent and finishing college in the process. Without even trying, she also has the means to make a person want to tell their life story." Much like the woman sitting next to him.

She raised a brow. "Did you tell her yours?"

He streaked a palm over his neck. "Yeah. She knows about Grace." And it had almost killed him to tell her.

Marlene smiled a mother's smile. "I am so glad, Logan. And since she's still sticking around, I assume that she holds the opinion you're not to blame, like I do. Am I right?"

"Yeah, you are." Even if he still didn't agree with that lack of blame assumption. "But she's also compassionate."

"She's a woman who understands loss," Marlene said. "I do as well. We're all unwitting members of a club drawn together by that loss, and sadly that also includes you, too. Hannah intimately understands your pain, and you're very lucky to have found her."

"Don't read too much into this relationship. On Saturday, she's going back to her life and I'll go back to mine."

"Your currently lonely life?" She topped off the question with a frown. "You'd be a fool to let her go, Logan, when she could be a part of your future."

Here we go again. "We had this conversation last week."

"And we'll continue to have it until you listen to reason."

If that's the way she wanted to play it, he'd reiterate all the reasons why a permanent relationship wouldn't work with anyone, especially Hannah. "Marlene, my job doesn't allow for a personal life, and I don't intend to quit for another twenty years, if then."

"Work isn't everything," she said. "Family is."

His profession had indirectly destroyed one family. He wasn't going to risk that possibility again. "Look, I enjoy being with Hannah, but I'm not sure I'll ever be able to make a serious commitment again. I've already been through one divorce and I don't want a repeat. And most important, Hannah's a single mom. She's going to have expectations I might not be able to meet."

Marlene narrowed her eyes and studied him for a few moments. "Part of your reluctance has to do with her daughter, doesn't it?"

Only someone as astute as Marlene would figure that out. "Could you blame me for being concerned? What if I became close with Cassie and my relationship with Hannah doesn't work out? That would be like—"

"Losing Grace all over again?"

She'd hit that nail on the head. "It wouldn't be fair to either one of them."

Marlene leaned forward, keeping her gaze on his. "Honey, life is about balance and a certain amount of chance-taking when it comes to matters of the heart. But life without the possibility of love isn't really living at all. We aren't meant to be alone. Just keep that in mind before you dismiss Hannah due to your fears."

"I'm only afraid of hurting her, Marlene." Afraid he might fail Hannah the way he'd failed his former wife and daughter.

"Maybe you should let her decide if she wants to take a chance on you."

Needing a quick escape, Logan checked his watch and stood. "I have an appointment in less than an hour, so I better get back to the office. When do you want to have that talk with Hannah?"

Marlene came to her feet. "Bring her over for lunch

on Saturday. I'll take her aside after that and speak with her privately. Better still, why don't you bring her daughter, Cassie, too? You could surprise her as a Mother's Day gesture, and give yourself some extra time with her as well."

He'd totally forgotten about the holiday. Marlene's suggestion would buy him more time with Hannah, and he knew she would appreciate the gesture. "I'd have to figure out how I could manage that without her knowing."

Marlene patted his cheek. "You're a smart man, Logan. You'll come up with a plan."

And that plan suddenly began to formulate in his mind. Marlene's suggestion just might work after all. But could he deal with being around a little girl so close in age to Grace when he'd lost her? He wouldn't know unless he tried, and this time he needed to consider Hannah, not himself.

Logan gave Marlene a quick hug. "Thanks for doing this for Hannah. She really needs to know how she came to be."

"You're welcome, honey. And once she learns the whole truth, she's going to need you to lean on."

Being there for her, like she had been there for him, was pretty much a no-brainer. "She's already figured out J.D. was her father. You'll only ease her mind if you confirm it."

Marlene sighed. "On second thought, maybe it's better I provide you with some information first so you'll be prepared. As long as you promise not to say anything to her before I do."

He just wished she would make up her mind. "Fine,

as long as you tell me everything, down to the last detail."

"J.D. didn't father Hannah."

Apparently they'd been traveling straight down the wrong-information path. "Then who was it?"

"My husband, Charles."

She'd spent the day doing laundry and packing her clothes—her final day in Cheyenne.

When Logan sent her a text saying he'd be home by 3:00 p.m., Hannah waited for him on the great-room sofa, wearing only his white tailored button-down shirt. She felt somewhat foolish, but what better way to greet him on their last night together? Even after days of nonstop searching, tomorrow she would return home with no answers about her father and no idea if she would ever see Logan again.

He'd seemed somewhat distant the past two days, or at the very least distracted. She couldn't help but believe he'd been planning his goodbye, and she should be preparing for it now. As soon as she implemented her current and somewhat questionable plan, she would. In the meantime, she refused to think about the impending heartache brought on because she'd been naive enough to fall in love with a man who might never love her back.

Ten minutes later, when she heard the front door open, Hannah stretched out on the cushions on her side and struck what she hoped would be deemed a sexy pose. Logan strode into the room, tossed his briefcase aside and stopped dead in his tracks when he caught sight of her. "Howdy, ma'am."

She brushed her hair back with one hand and smiled. "Howdy yourself."

He walked up to the couch and hovered above her. "I have never said this to a woman before, but you're going to have to get dressed."

She pretended to pout. "You don't like what I'm wearing?"

"Oh, yeah," he said. "But I have a surprise for you and it requires that you put on some clothes."

She straightened and lowered her feet to the floor. "I have a surprise for you, too. I'm not wearing any panties."

He hesitated a moment, his eyes growing dark with that familiar desire. "We don't have a whole lot of time, and I need to take a shower."

Hannah slipped two buttons on the shirt, giving him a bird's-eye view of her breasts. "Imagine that. So do I. We could go green and do it together."

His resistance dissolved right before her eyes, and he proved he was no match for their chemistry when he clasped her hands and tugged her off the sofa. "Then let's go conserve some water."

They rushed through the house, pausing to kiss on the way to Logan's bedroom. Once there, they began to shed their clothes article by article, until they reached the bathroom, completely naked and needy.

He pressed a series of buttons on the nearby chrome panel, sending several showerheads set into the stone walls into watery motion.

While the digital thermostat adjusted the temperature, Hannah stood behind Logan, her arms wrapped around his bare waist. "If I use your soap and shampoo, I'm going to smell like a guy."

He turned her into his arms and grinned. "Better than me smelling like a girl. Of course, you could go get your stuff, but that would take time we don't have." He punctuated the comment by placing a palm on her bottom and nudging her against his erection.

What a man. A sexy, incredible man. "I get the point. Now don't just stand there, take me in the shower."

"That's precisely what I plan to do."

All talk ceased as they took turns washing each other with soap and shampoo that smelled like Logan— clean, not cologne-like. For all intents and purposes, Hannah didn't care if she carried the trace scent of him on her flesh all night, or back home with her tomorrow for that matter. She rejected all thoughts of leaving, and fortunately for her, Logan aided in that cause with his gentle caresses and persuasive kisses that he feathered down her body. He kneeled before her and brought her to the brink of climax with his mouth, then suddenly straightened and pressed the control that cut off the sprays.

His rapid breathing echoed in the large stone shower before he groaned the single word, "Condom."

Hannah did a mental calculation and realized it would be the worst time to take a chance. "We absolutely have to have one before we go any further."

"I know. Getting you pregnant is the last thing I need."

She couldn't deny that his firm tone stung a little, but she also acknowledged he had his reasons for being so resolute—he wanted no more children, period. "Should we take this to the bedroom?"

"Good idea."

They had barely dried off before Logan gathered her

up in his arms, carried her to the bedroom and didn't even bother to turn down the covers. He simply deposited her on the navy comforter and put the condom in place in record time, then faced her on the mattress, one arm draped over her hip.

"I want to really see you when we make love," he said, followed by a brief yet stimulating kiss.

With the room bathed in sunlight, Hannah didn't view that as an issue. "It's still daytime."

"I want you to be in charge."

She gave him an intentionally furtive grin. "You want me on top."

"You got it."

Not a problem, she thought, as she rose up and straddled his thighs. Quite an extraordinary fit, she realized after he lifted her up and guided himself inside her. From that moment on, instinct took over as Hannah took the lead. She suddenly felt as if she'd become someone else—a truly sensual being with the capacity to be completely in control. Yet that control began to wane as Logan touched her again and again, and didn't let up until the last pulse of her orgasm subsided. Only then did she realize he was fairly close to losing it, and she took supreme advantage, using the movement of her hips to send him over the edge. She watched in wonder as the climax began to take hold. His respiration increased, his jaw locked tight and he hissed out a long breath as his body tensed beneath her, yet he never took his gaze from hers.

Feeling physically drained, Hannah collapsed against Logan's chest and rested her head against his pounding heart. He gently rubbed her back with one hand and stroked her hair with the other, lulling her into a total sense of peace.

After a time, he rolled her over onto her back, remained above her and touched her face with a reverence that almost brought tears to her eyes. "You're phenomenal, sweetheart."

But not phenomenal enough to figure into his future. "You're not so bad yourself, sexy guy."

She took his ensuing smile to memory to bring back out on a rainy day. "I wish..." His words trailed off, along with his gaze.

"You wish what?"

"I wish I'd met you years ago, back when we were both young and unattached."

Before his life had taken a terrible turn, she assumed. "Well, since you're eight years older, and I married at the ripe old age of twenty, that would have made me jailbait if you'd dated me before I met Danny."

"I guess you're right about that, and from what I gather, you loved your husband very much."

"I did," she said without hesitation. "But I also know he'd want me to be happy and go on with my life."

He turned onto his back and draped an arm over his forehead. "You deserve to be happy, Hannah. And someday you're going to find someone who will do that for you."

Clearly he believed he didn't qualify, when in truth he did. Not exactly goodbye, but pretty darn close.

She sat up and scooted to the edge of the bed so he wouldn't see the tears starting to form in her eyes.

"Hannah, are you okay?"

No, she wasn't. Not in the least. But she would be because she was a survivor. "I'm fine. I just thought

I'd get dressed since I do believe you mentioned we have some place to be."

When she started to stand, Logan caught her wrist before she could come to her feet. "Believe me, if things were different, if I were the right man for you—"

She pivoted around to face him and faked a smile. "It's all right, Logan. I told you before this thing started between us I had no expectations where we're concerned." And, boy, had she lied without even realizing it.

"You're one in a million, Hannah, and never forget that."

One thing she knew to be true, she would never forget him.

An hour later, Hannah climbed into Logan's Mercedes and they set out for who knew where. She dozed off for a bit and awoke to find they were close to Fort Collins in Colorado, heading in the direction of Boulder.

She hid a yawn behind her hand before shooting a glance at Logan. "If you wanted me to go home, all you had to do was ask."

He gave her a quick grin before concentrating on the road. "That's not where we're going."

"Do you mind telling me were we *are* we going?"

"You'll see real soon."

Five minutes later, he exited the interstate and pulled into a rest stop, leading Hannah to believe Logan needed a break. He shut off the ignition, slid out of the sedan without saying a word, rounded the hood and then opened her door. "Time to get out and take a walk."

"I don't need a walk."

"You'll want to take this one whether you need it or not."

She tapped her chin and pretended to think. "Let me guess. You've arranged for an intimate dinner to be catered at a roadside park."

"Not hardly."

"A picnic beneath the halogen light set to the sights and sounds of eighteen-wheelers, complete with the smell of diesel fuel?"

He braced a hand on the top of the door. "You can sit there and crack jokes, or you can come and see your surprise."

She saluted like a practiced soldier. "Whatever you say, Your Excellency."

Hannah exited the car with Logan's assistance and followed behind him, completely confused over where he could be taking her. Then she saw the familiar silver SUV, the sweet, recognizable face pressed against the back window, and it all began to make sense.

Gina came around from the driver's side, opened the door and released a squealing redhead dressed in white sneakers, floral blue shorts and matching shirt, and of course the tiara planted on her head. "Mama!"

Hannah kneeled down and nearly fell over backward due to her daughter's voracious hug. "I missed you so much, sweetie!" she said as she showered Cassie's cheeks with kisses. "But what are you doing here?"

The little girl reared back, wiped her wet face and displayed her snaggletoothed grin. "It's an early Mother's Day gift. Gina told me I'm gonna spend the weekend with you and the prince!"

"And it was all His Royal Hotness's idea," her best

friend said as she approached carrying Cassie's suitcase and booster seat.

Hannah straightened and turned to Logan. "How did you manage to make this happen without my knowledge?"

He streaked a hand over his nape. "It took some work and some sneaking around. I had to steal your phone when you weren't looking so I could get Gina's number."

"Then he called and asked me to bring Cassie halfway," she added. "Now here we are and Frank's at home with a crying son and a pouting daughter who's mourning the temporary loss of her best gal pal."

Only a short while ago, Logan had claimed he couldn't be the kind of man she needed, and then he did something so wonderfully considerate and totally unselfish to prove himself wrong, wrong, wrong. "This is a very welcome surprise, Mr. Whittaker. Thank you very much."

He took the bag and seat from Gina. "You're very welcome."

Cassie tugged on Logan's shirt sleeve to garner his attention. "I'm hungry, Prince Logan."

"Then we should probably get on the road so we can get the queen something to eat." His follow-up bow brought back Cassie's vibrant grin.

Hannah took the suitcase from Logan's grasp. "If you don't mind getting her settled into the car, I'll be along in a minute right after I receive a full report from Gina." She then set her attention on her daughter. "And Cassie, stay close to Logan when you're crossing the parking lot."

"You can count on that," he said with all the determination of a man who believed he'd failed to protect his own little girl.

When Cassie slid her hand into Logan's hand, Hannah saw the flash of emotion in his eyes and she could picture how many memories had assaulted him in that moment. After they walked away—the cowboy attorney with the slow, easy gait, and the bouncing queen wannabe—she turned back to her friend. "*Your Hotness?* Really?"

Gina shrugged. "Seemed pretty appropriate to me."

"You know, I'd be mad at you over that comment if I didn't so appreciate everything you've done. Not only this evening, but over the past two weeks."

"The question is, Hannah, was it worth it? Did you finally find what you were looking for?"

She shook her head. "I still don't know who my father might be, and I've accepted the fact I might never know."

Gina rolled her eyes. "I don't mean only the thing with your long-lost dad. I'm referring to you and the lawyer. Do you see a future with him in it?"

Sadly, she didn't. "He's not the kind to settle down, Gina. He's a remarkable man who's been through a lot, but he's closed himself off emotionally. And that's okay. I didn't expect anything to come of it anyway."

Her friend nailed her with a glare. "You did it, didn't you?"

This time Hannah rolled her eyes. "We had this discussion at least three times last week and once this week. Yes, we did it. Often."

"I'm not talking about the sex," Gina said. "You've gone and fallen in love with him, haven't you? And don't hand me any bull because I can read it all over your face, you ninny."

Hannah's hackles came to attention. "I am not a ninny, and I didn't fall in love with him." Much.

"You lie like a cheap rug."

"You're too meddlesome for my own good." Hannah hooked a thumb over her shoulder. "My daughter is waiting for me."

Gina held up both hands, palms forward, as if in surrender. "Fine. Go with your daughter and the hunk. But when you get home tomorrow, we're going to have a long talk about the virtues of emotionally safe sex."

That worked for Hannah, and after that talk, she could very well need to have a long, long cry.

By the time they arrived home, Logan had been steeped in so many recollections, he'd begun to feel the burn of regret. Watching Cassie at the café ordering a kid's meal and coloring on the menu, he remembered Gracie at every turn. And he missed her. God, did he miss her.

The ache grew worse when he carried a sleeping Cassie up the stairs and to the second surprise of the evening.

"You can put her in my bed," Hannah said from behind him.

That wasn't a part of the plan. "She'll sleep better in here." He opened the door to the room he'd kept as a tribute to his own daughter.

Hannah gaped when she saw the double bed covered by a white comforter imprinted with pink slippers to match the décor. "When did you do this?" she whispered as she turned down the covers.

He laid Cassie carefully on the sheets, her thumb planted firmly in her mouth, her eyes still closed against the light coming from the lamp on the nightstand. "I'll tell you in a minute."

After Hannah pulled off her daughter's shoes, then gave her a kiss on the cheek, they walked back into the hall.

Logan closed the door and turned to her. "The owner of a furniture store in town happens to be a client. I arranged to have the bed delivered right after we got on the road tonight."

"And the bedspread?"

"I bought it yesterday during lunch." Another gesture that had rocked him to the core.

Hannah folded her arms beneath her breasts. "I don't mean to seem ungrateful, because I do appreciate your consideration. But my question is, why would you buy a bed when we're only going to be here one night?"

"I thought maybe you'd agree to stay another night."

She sighed. "I need to get home and resume my job search."

He started to grasp at hopeless straws. "Maybe you and Cassie could visit now and then when you have the chance. I could teach her to ride Lucy."

"What would be the point in that, Logan? You've already established this relationship isn't going to go anywhere. So why would I get my daughter's hopes up and lead her to believe there could be more between us?"

She evidently wanted him to say there could be more, and he couldn't in good conscience promise her that. "I guess you're right."

"Yes, I am right. Now that we've cleared that up,

I'm going to get ready for bed and I'll see you in the morning."

He shouldn't be surprised by her curt dismissal, since he'd made it perfectly clear earlier that he couldn't be the man in her life, but he hadn't expected this rejection to twist his gut in knots. However, despite his wounded male pride, he still could provide the information she'd sought from the beginning. "Marlene Lassiter wants us to have lunch at the Big Blue ranch tomorrow."

She frowned. "I really planned to get on the road early."

"Can you wait to leave until later?" he asked, trying hard not to sound like a desperate idiot. "The ranch is a great place for a kid to play. Cassie would enjoy it." He'd learned long ago if you wanted to melt a good mom's heart, you only had to mention her kids.

He realized the ploy had worked when she said, "I guess a few extra hours won't matter. Besides, I might grab the opportunity to ask Marlene a few questions about J.D., if you don't think I'd be overstepping my bounds."

She had no idea that's exactly what Marlene intended to do—answer all her questions—and he couldn't help but feel guilty over not being forthcoming with what he knew. "Actually, it's a real good idea. Since you haven't signed the nondisclosure, I'm sure she'd be willing to tell you what she knows."

"Provided she actually knows something."

Little did she know, tomorrow she would not only learn about her real father, she would also discover she had a brother. "You might be surprised."

"Probably not," she said. "But I guess I'll find out."

When she started away, he caught her hand and pulled her into his arms. She allowed it for only a moment before she tugged out of his hold and said, "Sleep well, Logan."

For the first time in several days, Hannah retired to her own bedroom, and Logan left for his, without even a kiss good-night.

Sleep well? No way. Not with the prospect of letting her go hanging over his head. But he still had another day in her presence. He would make it his goal to show her and her daughter a good time, and try one more time to convince himself why he didn't deserve her.

Nine

When Marlene Lassiter showed her into a private study at the main house for an after-lunch chat, Hannah could barely contain her curiosity. She wondered if perhaps the woman might hand her the third degree about her relationship with Logan. If so, Marlene would be encountering a major dead end with that one. Truth was, after today, the relationship would be null and void.

"Have a seat, dear," Marlene said as she gestured to one of two brown leather chairs before she crossed the room, nervously tugging at the back hem of her white cotton blouse that covered her black slacks.

After Marlene paused at what appeared to be a bar, Hannah took a seat and conducted a quick visual search of the room. The office was rustic and large, like the rest of the Lassiter family homestead, with bookcases flanking another stone fireplace. That fireplace was much smaller in scale than the one in the great room, where they'd left Logan watching some animated film with Cassie, who'd adhered herself to his side like kid glue. He'd spent most of the morning keeping her entertained by letting her climb up to her castle—in this case, huge round bales of hay—under his watchful eye. If he'd minded the make-believe, or the recollections the interaction had most surely produced, he hadn't let on. He'd just patiently played the knight to the imaginary queen, wielding an invisible sword while sporting a sadness in his eyes that couldn't be concealed, at least not from Hannah.

"How big is this place?" she asked when Marlene bent down and opened the door to the built-in beverage refrigerator.

"Eight bedrooms, at least ten baths, I think because I always lose count, and around 11,000 square feet."

She'd known the glorified log cabin was huge when they'd driven through the gates of the Big Blue, but not that huge. "You have enough room to establish your own commune."

Marlene smiled over one shoulder. "Would you like a glass of wine, dear?"

Hannah normally didn't drink in the middle of the day, but it was well after noon, so what the heck? "Sure, but just a little. I have to head home this evening."

"I'll pour just enough to take the edge off."

Hannah wanted to ask why on earth she should be edgy, yet when Marlene returned with the drinks, looking as solemn as a preacher, she assumed she would soon find out.

She accepted the wine and said, "Thanks," then took

a quick sip. The stuff was so dry it did little to wet her parched throat.

Marlene took a larger drink then held the glass's stem in a tight-fisted grasp, looking as if she could snap it in two. "You might be wondering why I asked you in here, Hannah."

That was a colossal understatement. "I assume it has something to do with Logan."

"Actually, no, it doesn't. It has to do with—"

"Mom, are you in there?"

Marlene sent her an apologetic look before responding to the summons. "Yes, Chance, I'm here."

The door opened wide to a six-foot-plus, brown-haired, athletically built man wearing a chambray shirt with the sleeves rolled up to his elbows, worn leather boots and faded jeans. "Just wondering if the coals are still hot on the grill."

"Yes, they are," Marlene said. "And Chance, this is Logan's new girl, Hannah. Hannah, this is my son, Chance, and if he doesn't learn to wipe his boots better at the back door, I'm going to ban him from the house."

Hannah wanted to correct her on the "Logan's girl" thing, but when Chance Lassiter turned his gaze on her, she was practically struck mute. She met eyes the exact same color of green as hers, and although his hair was a light shade of brown, the resemblance was uncanny. Not proof positive she could be a Lassiter, but pretty darn close.

She had enough wherewithal to set the glass down on the coffee table and offer her hand. "It's nice to meet you, Chance."

He leaned over and gave her hand a hearty shake.

"Pleasure's all mine," he said before regarding his mother again. "Did you have burgers or steak?"

Marlene shrugged. "Steaks, of course. What I always have when we have guests. I saved you one in the fridge to cook to your liking. Two flips on the grill and it's done." She turned her attention back to Hannah. "Chance owns and runs the whole ranching operation, including developing the cattle breeding program. He raises the best Black Angus in the country, but I hope you know that after sampling our steaks."

Fortunately she hadn't been formally introduced to the cows before she'd literally had them for lunch. "Unequivocally the best."

Chance grinned with pride. "We aim to please. So now I'm going to leave you ladies to your girl talk while I go grab a bite. I take it that little redheaded girl napping on the sofa beside Logan belongs to you, Hannah."

Clearly Cassie had finally wound down, a very good thing for the poor lawyer. "Yes, she's all mine, and she's quite a live wire."

"She's as pretty as her mama," he said. "Logan is one lucky guy. Think I'll go tell him that before I grab a bite and get back to riding the range."

Chance Lassiter could talk until he was blue in the face, but luck had nothing to do with their inevitable parting a few hours from now.

After Chance closed the door behind him, Hannah smiled at Marlene. "He seems to be a great guy. Is he your only child?"

"Yes, he is. And he's done very well considering he lost his father when he was only eight. I believe you were around six years old at the time."

How would she possibly know that? Unless... "Marlene, has Logan mentioned anything to you about why I'm here in Cheyenne?"

She momentarily looked away. "Yes, he has, but don't hold that against him because he was only trying to help."

Logan's determination to come to her aid only impressed Hannah more. "Then you know about the annuity J.D. bequeathed to me?"

"I do, although no one else in the family knows about it."

"And the nondisclosure I have to sign to accept it?"

"J.D. added that clause to protect me."

And that made no sense to Hannah. "Why would he feel the need to protect you?"

Marlene downed the rest of her wine and set the glass aside on the end table positioned between the chairs. "Because my husband, Charles, was your father."

Hannah's mind reeled from the shocking revelation, jarring loose a host of unanswered questions. "And you knew about this for how long?"

"Charles came to me and told me about his brief affair with Ruth a few days after he ended it," she said. "Both of us learned about the pregnancy two weeks after you were born."

She didn't know whether to apologize to Marlene for her mother's transgressions, or scold her for not saying something sooner. "And you're absolutely sure Charles was my father?"

"I demanded a paternity test, and when it confirmed he was without a doubt your dad, Charles insisted on being a part of your life."

Hannah took a moment to let that sink in. "Apparently that never happened since I don't remember any man claiming to be my father spending time with me."

Marlene fished a photo from the pocket of her slacks and handed it to her. "You were two years old when this was taken."

She could only stare at the lanky yet handsome cowboy seated on a park bench, a smiling little girl on his lap. She didn't recognize him, but she positively recognized herself. "I have no memories of this or him." And she hated that fact with a passion.

"That's because your mother quit allowing visits when Charles refused to leave me for her."

Her fury returned with the force of an exploding grenade. "She used me as a pawn?"

"Unfortunately, yes," Marlene said. "If Charles wouldn't give in to her demands, then she wouldn't let him see his daughter."

Hannah wasn't sure she could emotionally handle much more, but she had to ask. "And he didn't think to fight for me?"

"No, dear, that's not the case at all. Charles consulted several lawyers on several occasions through the years. Ironically, he even spoke with one family law attorney who used to work at Logan's firm. They all basically told him the same thing. A mother's rights, especially a mother who'd conceived a child and was essentially *dumped* by a married man, would trump the biological father's rights."

She couldn't fathom the time she'd lost getting to know her father, all because of the law. "That's archaic."

"That's the way it was in that day and time." Marlene laid a hand on Hannah's arm. "But Charles never stopped hoping that might change, and he never stopped sending you money up until his death. I took over the payments after that."

Hannah was rapidly approaching information overload. "My mother claimed my father never gave her a penny of support."

Marlene sent her a sympathetic look. "I am so sorry you're learning this now, but Ruth received a monthly check every month from the day you were born, until J.D. learned you'd left college and married, which she failed to tell him."

Obviously all-consuming bitterness had turned her mother into the consummate liar. "She failed to tell me any of this." And now for another pertinent question. "Do you happen to know why J.D. came to our house when I was in the first grade? I remembered him when Logan first approached me about the annuity and I did an internet search."

"He went to tell her about Charles's death in my stead," she said. "Ruth only wanted to know who was going to sign the check. J.D. insisted on contributing the full amount and then some, but I refused to let him. That's when he established the annuity in your name."

"But why on earth would he list my mother as the secondary beneficiary?"

"I assume he believed it would allow him control over the situation. I honestly believe he didn't want to create a scandal for me, since he didn't know Charles had confessed to me about the affair and you. Regardless of what my husband had done, Charles and J.D. were always thick as thieves."

And that left one very important consideration—

the wronged wife. "Marlene, I can't imagine what you went through all those years, knowing your husband created a baby with another woman. And then you were charitable enough to see to that child's welfare." Even if the child had never known. And how horrible to learn her own mother had betrayed her. At least now she knew how Ruth had come by the down payment for the house. A weak gesture in light of the lies.

"Believe me, Hannah," Marlene continued, "I'm no saint. It took me years to forgive Charles, and I resented the hell out of your mother. I also resented you in many ways, and for that I am greatly ashamed."

Hannah set the photo next to her wineglass and clasped Marlene's hand. "I don't blame you at all. I *do* blame my mother for the deceit. Although it does explain why she never seemed happy, especially not with me. No matter what I did, I never felt it was good enough."

"Yet somehow you turned out so well, dear," she said. "I can tell you're a wonderful mother and a genuinely good person. Believe me, Logan knows that, too."

Regardless, that wasn't going to be enough to keep him in her life. "Logan is a very good man with a wounded soul. I hope someday he realizes he deserves to be happy again."

"With your help, I'm sure he will."

If only that were true. "I hate to burst your bubble, Marlene, but when I leave here, I doubt I'll be coming back anytime soon."

Marlene frowned. "I was hoping you'd return now and then to get to know your brother."

Her brother. She'd been so embroiled in the details she hadn't given Chance a second thought. "Does he know about me?"

"No, but I plan to tell him in the very near future. And I hope you'll tell Logan how you really feel about him before you go."

Time to admit the agonizing truth. "He's only going to be a special man I had the pleasure of meeting, and that's all he'll ever be."

Marlene had the skeptical look down to a science. "Don't try to fool an old fool, Hannah. I can spot a woman in love at fifty paces."

Hannah fixed her gaze on the almost-full glass next to the photo, but she had no desire to drink, only sob. "It doesn't matter how I feel about him. Logan has all but given up on love. And that's sad when he needs it so very much."

"I'm asking you not to give up on him," Marlene said. "Men have been known to come around, once the woman of their dreams has flown the love nest. But before you do that, you need to tell him how the cow ate the cabbage and convince him that you're worth fighting for. Then make sure you turn around and leave so he'll have time to chew on it awhile."

"I suppose I could give that a shot."

"You'd be surprised how effective it can be."

Hannah could only hope. That's about all she had left to hold on to. Actually, that wasn't exactly the case. She picked up the photo and studied it again. "Do you mind if I keep this?"

"Not at all, dear." Marlene stood and smiled. "Now let's go find that hardheaded attorney so you can have the last word."

Hannah had the strongest feeling it could very well be her last stand.

* * *

"Looks like it's going to rain."

In response to Logan's observation, Hannah looked up. The overcast skies reflected her gloomy mood, but she needed to snap out of the funk in order to tell Logan exactly what had been brewing in her mind, with a little help from Marlene.

She kicked at a random stone as the two of them walked a path leading away from the house. "Hopefully it won't be more than a spring shower. Just enough rain that lasts long enough for Cassie to get in a good nap."

"Chance is hoping for a deluge."

"You mean my *half brother,* Chance?" she asked, as she took a glimpse to her right to gauge Logan's reaction.

"I figured Marlene told you everything."

His poker face and even tone told Hannah he'd been privy to that knowledge. "How long have you known Charles Lassiter was my father?"

"Since Wednesday."

"And you went three days without telling me?" She'd thought she'd meant more to him than that. Obviously she'd been wrong.

"Now before you get all worked up," he said, "Marlene made me promise I wouldn't say anything to you before she could explain. It was damn hard keeping you in the dark, but I had to respect her wishes."

She shrugged. "What's three days when compared to thirty years? I still cannot believe my own mother never told me about him, or the fact that she received checks from Charles and then Marlene during my formative years and beyond."

Finally, Logan showed something more than detachment to her disclosures. "That part I didn't know, Hannah. I'm sorry you had to find out after the fact."

She was sorry she couldn't change his mind about settling down. Or having children. Yet expecting someone to alter their ideals made little sense. "It's done, and I'm over it. I have a great daughter, own my home and a degree. Now I just need to find a job and my life will be complete." That rang false, even to Hannah's ears.

"You know, you could look for a job here," Logan said.

The suggestion took her aback, and gave her hope. "Why would I do that when my life is in Boulder?"

"So you can get to know your new family since you're not going to take the inheritance."

So much for hoping he might actually see a future with her. "That really only includes Chance, since I have no idea how my cousins will take the news." And who was to say her brother would even want to have a relationship with her?

"I still think that if you moved closer, we could get together every now and then."

Not at all what she wanted to hear. "For the occasional booty call?"

He scowled. "You know me well enough to know I respect you more than that. I just thought we could see where it goes."

She knew exactly where it would go. Nowhere. "Let's review, shall we? I eventually want to marry again and have at least one more child. You, on the other hand, would prefer to live your life alone, moving from one casual conquest to another with no commitment, in typical confirmed-bachelor fashion. And since I don't intend to follow in my mother's footsteps and wind up as someone's mistress, that puts us directly at odds. Do you not agree?"

He stopped in his tracks to stare at her, anger glinting in his dark eyes. "I've never seen you as some kind of conquest and definitely not as a potential mistress. I only thought that if we spent more time together—"

"You'd suddenly decide by some miracle to become a family man again?"

"I told you why—"

"You don't want to settle down. I know. You're too wrapped in guilt and grief to give me what I need. But what about *your* needs?"

He shifted his weight from one leg to the other. "What do you think I need?"

He'd asked for it, and she was glad to give it to him. "You need to get over yourself. You're not the only one who's lost someone they loved more than life itself. But life does go on unless you say it doesn't. And that's what you've been saying for the past eight years. Do you think keeping yourself closed off to all possibilities is honoring your daughter's memory? Believe me, it's doing just the opposite."

His eyes now reflected pent-up fury. "Leave Grace out of this."

"I can't, Logan, because deep down you know I'm right. And if I never see you again, it's going to be tough, and it's going to break my heart just like that memorial tattoo on your arm. But I'm not a quitter, and I didn't peg you as one, either, when I stupidly fell in love with you."

He looked astonished over her spontaneous admission. "You what?"

No need to stop when she was on a roll. "I love you.

Oh, I fought it with everything in me. I chalked it up to lust and liking your home theater. And of course my appreciation of your plumbing skills. What woman wouldn't want a man who could fix her leaky pipes? And I really valued your determination to make sure I found out the truth about my heritage." She hitched in a breath. "But do you know when I quit questioning my feelings?"

"No."

"Today, when I watched you playing with my daughter, and I saw this longing in your eyes that took my breath away. Whether you believe it or not, you're meant to be a father, and somewhere beneath that damned armor you've build around your heart, you want to be one again. But that will never happen unless you stop beating yourself up and being afraid of making a mistake."

Tension and silence hung between them despite the whistling wind. Hannah allowed the quiet for a few moments before she finished her diatribe. "Logan, I only want what's best for you, believe it or not. And I hate it that I hurt you by laying out the truth. I also pray you find the strength to love again. Maybe I'm not the woman you need, but you do need someone."

For the first time ever, he appeared to be rendered speechless. Either that, or he was simply too irate to speak.

When he failed to respond, Hannah decided to give up, though that went against her nature. But she wasn't too stubborn to recognize when it was time to throw in that towel. "If it's not too much of a bother, I'd like to go back to your place, collect my things and my car, and get back to Boulder before dark."

This time she didn't bother to wait for his answer. She simply spun around and headed back to the house to gather her child in order to go home and lick her wounds.

Yet as she afforded a glance over her shoulder, and she saw him standing there in the rain, looking forlorn instead of furious, she wondered if maybe she'd expected too much from Logan too soon. Given up on him too quickly. She wanted desperately to believe he might eventually come around to her side.

And that possibly could be too much to ask.

Yesterday afternoon, Logan had told Hannah goodbye after giving her and Cassie a brief hug, not once giving away the sorry state of his heart. Since then, he'd been carrying around a brand-new bushel full of regrets that kept running over and over in his head. He wound up spending the night seated on the floor in the now-vacant child's room, alone and lonely. He dozed off now and then, always awakening with a strong sense that he'd made the biggest mistake of his life when he let Hannah go without putting up a fight.

He'd blamed her for treading on his pride, when all she'd done was shine a light on the hard truth. In many ways, he had stopped living. But he hadn't stopped loving, because he was—without a doubt—in love with her. He loved her wit and her gentle ways. He loved the way she made love to him. He loved the fact she could melt his heart with only a smile. He hated that he hadn't uttered one word of that to her before she'd driven away, and now it might be too late.

Although he was dog-tired, that didn't keep him from sprinting down the stairs when he heard the doorbell chime. He hoped to see Hannah on his doorstep, but instead he peered through the peephole and found Chance Lassiter. As much as he liked and respected the guy, he wasn't in the mood for company. But when he noticed the wind had begun to push the rain beneath the portico, he decided he should probably let him in.

Logan opened the door and before he could mutter a greeting, Chance said, "You look like hell, Whittaker."

He ran a hand over his unshaven jaw and figured he looked like he'd wrestled a bear and lost. "Good to see you, too, Lassiter."

Chance stepped inside without an invite, shrugged off the heavy weatherproof jacket and shook it out, sprinkling drops of water all over the travertine tile. He then dug a pair of tiny blue socks from his jeans pocket and offered them to Logan. "Mom told me Cassie left these at the house. Is Hannah still here?"

He wished that were the case. "She went home yesterday afternoon."

"Damn. I really wanted to talk to her. When's she going to be back?"

"I don't think she'll be coming back anytime soon." Voicing it made the concept all too real. "At least not to see me."

"Trouble in paradise?"

Paradise had disappeared the minute she'd walked out his door. "Guess some things aren't meant to be."

"That's really too bad," Chance said. "I was hoping maybe you'd be my brother-in-law in the near future, that way I wouldn't hesitate to call you when I need help with the cows."

Chance's attempt at humor sounded forced to Logan, and with good reason. Suddenly learning you have a sister because your late father was a philanderer would be a damn bitter pill to swallow. "You don't hesitate to call me for help now, and I take it Marlene told you the whole story about your father and Hannah's mother."

"Yeah, the whole sorry story." Chance let go a caustic laugh. "You spend your life idolizing your dad, only to learn the guy was a good-for-nothing cheater. But at least I got a sibling out of the deal. That's if she wants to acknowledge me as her brother. Had I known the facts before she took off, I would've spoken with her yesterday while she was still at the ranch."

Had Logan known how bad he would hurt, he might not have let her take off. "I've got her phone number and address if you want to get in touch with her."

"I'll do that," he said. "Question is, what are you going to do about her?"

"I'm not sure what you mean."

Chance shook his head. "For a man with a whole lot of smarts, you're not real good at pretending to be stupid."

He didn't much care for the stupid designation, even if it might ring true in this instance. "Didn't know you planned to deliver insults along with the socks."

"Well, if the shoe fits, as Mom would say."

Logan also didn't appreciate the pun. "Look, Hannah and I had a good thing going, but now it's over."

Chance narrowed his eyes, looking like he was prepared to take his best shot, or throw a punch. "You do realize you're talking about my sister. If you used her and then threw her away like garbage, that's grounds to kick your ass."

"I don't use women and I sure as hell didn't use

Hannah, so simmer down. In fact, I stayed awake all night thinking about her."

Chance seemed satisfied by that response, at least satisfied enough to unclench his fists. He also looked a little too smug. "Man, do you have it bad for her."

Dammit, he'd walked right into that trap. "That's one hell of a major assumption, Lassiter."

"Are you going to tell me I'm wrong?"

Not unless he wanted to hand Chance one super-sized lie. "No, you're not wrong."

"Well, hell, that sure explains why you look like something the mountain lion dragged in that the bloodhound couldn't stomach."

He really should have checked a mirror on his way downstairs. "Are you done deriding me now?"

"Nope. Not until you admit how you really feel about Hannah."

"I love her, dammit." There, he'd said it, and a hole in the tiled entry hadn't opened up and swallowed him. "Are you happy now?"

"As happy as a squirrel in the summer with a surplus of nuts. Do you still want to be with her?"

More than he could express. "Yeah, I do."

"Now what are you going to do about it?"

Logan didn't have a clue. "I'm sure you're itching to tell me."

"I don't even begin to understand what makes a woman tick," Chance began, "but I do know if you want her back, you've got to do it soon, before she has time to think about how you've wronged her."

"I'll call her as soon as I call my mom." Talk about serious avoidance.

Chance glared at him like he'd just proposed a plot

to commit murder. "Man, you can't do this over the phone. You have to go see her. Today."

"But—"

He pointed a finger in Logan's face. "You're going to show up at her house with something that will force her to forgive you."

"Flowers?"

"Yeah. Flowers are good, especially since it's Mother's Day. Do you have any planted in some garden?"

"Hell no. I'll have to buy them somewhere." Fortunately he had a connection who could accommodate him.

"What about one of those fancy silk suits?"

Logan's patience was wearing thin. "I'm an attorney, Chance. I have a damn suit."

"Sorry, but I had to ask because I've never seen you wear an entire suit, bud. Anyway, you'll show up in your suit with flowers—"

"For a die-hard bachelor, you're sure quick to dole out the advice."

"I just want my sister to be happy," Chance said in a surprisingly serious tone.

So did Logan. But would all the frills be enough to persuade Hannah to give them another chance? "What if she throws me out before I have my say?"

Chance slapped his back with the force of a steamroller. "Whittaker, according to Mom, Hannah loves you something awful, too. If you play your cards right, she'll let you come crawling back to her. Now I'm not saying you need to propose marriage because you've known each other a short time. My mom and dad only knew each other a month before they tied the knot and we now know how that one worked out."

Funny, Marlene hadn't mentioned that to Logan during their many conversations. "No kidding? Only a month?"

"No kidding," he said. "And then he cheated on his wife, not that I think you'd do that to Hannah."

"Not on your life." She was all he needed. All he would ever need.

"And to top it off," Chance continued, "Mom told me yesterday that in spite of my father's faults and weakness, she never doubted his love for her. It's just hard for me to believe love that strong exists."

Logan was beginning to believe it existed between him and Hannah, provided she hadn't fallen out of love with him overnight. "I hope you eventually forgive Marlene. She was just trying to protect you from the ugly truth."

"I'll forgive her eventually," Chance said. "As far as my dad's concerned, I'm not sure that will ever happen."

Logan knew all about that inability to forgive, and he could only hope Chance eventually came around like he had. But Hannah... "I hope like hell Hannah forgives me for taking so long to realize we need to be together."

"She'll forgive you the minute you show up at her door wearing your heart on your sleeve."

"Guess that's better than eating crow."

"You'll be doing that, too, Whittaker, so pack some salt. And groveling couldn't hurt. Hope that suit isn't too expensive in case you have to get down on your knees when you beg."

The suit didn't mean as much to him as Hannah. His pride no longer mattered much where she was concerned, either. "Are you sure you don't want to go with me, Lassiter? In case you want to talk with her after I do."

Chance grinned, grabbed his coat and backed toward the door. "You're on your own with this one, bud. Now go get a shower and shave, then go get your girl. Who knows? She might even be waiting for you."

Ten

Hannah walked out the door to meet Gina for their traditional Mother's Day brunch, only to stop short of the sidewalk when she caught sight of the black Mercedes parked at the curb. And leaning against that sedan's driver's door was the beautiful, wounded, brown-eyed man who'd invaded her thoughts the majority of the night. He wore a beige silk suit with matching tie and a white tailored shirt, a bouquet of roses in one hand, a piece of white paper in the other. If not for the dress cowboy boots, she might believe this was Logan Whittaker's clone. Yet when he grinned, showing those dimples to supreme advantage, that was all the confirmation she needed. But why was he here? She aimed to find out.

Hannah stepped across the yard, her three-inch heels digging into the grass made moist by the deluge that had arrived during the night. Fortunately the clouds had begun to break up, allowing the sun to peek through.

When she reached Logan, she shored up her courage and attempted a smile. "What are you doing here, Mr. Whittaker?"

"Thought you might need a plumber."

"My pipes appear to be holding, so no more water in the floor." On the other hand, her heart was flooded with a love for him that just wouldn't leave her be. "Since you're wearing a suit, I thought maybe you got lost on your way to some wedding."

"Nope, but I was pretty lost until I found you."

Her flooded heart did a little flip-flop in her chest. But she wasn't ready to give in to his pretty words and patent charms. Yet. "Who are the flowers for?"

"You," he said as he handed them off to her. "Happy Mother's Day."

She brought the roses to her nose and drew in the scent. "Thank you."

He leaned around her. "Where's Cassie?"

"Two houses down at the Romeros'. She's going to spend a few hours there while Gina and I have lunch together."

"Who's going to be watching her?"

His protective tone both surprised and pleased Hannah. "Gina's husband, Frank. He's used to watching their baby and the girls when Gina and I have plans."

"That sounds like a damn daunting job."

"He's a great dad, but he's had lots of practice." *And you would be a great dad, too,* she wanted to say.

Amazingly the familiar sadness didn't show in his eyes. "I guess practice makes perfect."

He still had a lot to learn. "Not perfect, Logan. No parent is ever perfect."

"I'm starting to realize that."

Oh, how she wanted to believe him. Yet she continued to resist the notion he had finally seen the light.

Hannah pointed at the document now clenched in his fist. "What's that?"

"The annuity terms that include the nondisclosure clause." He unfolded the paper, tore it in half and then tossed the remains into the open back window. "And according to your wishes, it's no longer valid."

Hannah couldn't resist teasing him a little. "Darn. I decided last night to sign it and take the money."

"Are you serious?"

She stifled a laugh. "No, I'm not serious. I could always use that kind of money, but I have everything I need without it, especially since Cassie's future is secure, thanks to my in-laws."

He inclined his head and looked at her as if he could see right through her phony assertion. "Everything?"

Except for those things money couldn't buy—like his love. "Enough to get by until I find a job. And mark my words, I will find a job even if I have to flip burgers."

"Marlene told me there's an opening at one of the rural high schools between my place and the Big Blue. They need a biology teacher. You should go for it."

"You're saying I should just uproot my child, sell my house and move to the middle of nowhere?"

"As I mentioned earlier, you'd have the opportunity to get to know your brother. We can continue to get to know each other better, too."

And he would have to do better than that. "We've already had this discussion, Logan. I want—"

"A man who can promise you a solid future and more kids."

"Exactly."

Some unnamed emotion reflected in his eyes. "I can be that man, Hannah. God knows I want to be."

The declaration tossed her into an emotional tailspin. "If that's true, then what made you suddenly change your mind?"

"What you told me about not honoring Grace's memory. I sat up all night in that room with the princesses on the wall and had a long talk with my daughter, as crazy as it seems."

How many times had she had those conversations with Danny in the distant past? "It's not crazy at all. It's long overdue."

"Anyway, for the first time since the funeral, I cried like a baby. But that meltdown didn't occur last night only because of Gracie. It had a lot to do with losing you."

Hannah could tell the admission was costing him as much as it was costing her. She wanted to throw her arms around him, tell him it would be okay, but she wasn't quite ready to do that yet. "Are you sure you're prepared to make a commitment to me and Cassie if and when the time comes?"

"I'm all in, Hannah," he said adamantly. "I also know I can be a good dad to Cassie. And do you want to know how I figured that one out?"

"Yes, I would."

He looked down and toed a random clump of grass before bringing his gaze back to hers. "When I was playing with Cassie yesterday on the hay bales, she slipped a few times and I caught her. Once I couldn't reach her, but she managed to pick herself back up after she tumbled to the bottom. Granted, it scared the hell out of me for a few minutes, but it also made me acknowledge that kids are actually pretty resilient, and the truth is, you can't logically be there for your children all the time." He exhaled roughly. "You can only do the best you can to protect them, and sadly sometimes that isn't enough, but you can't spend your life being paralyzed by a fear of failure."

A lesson everyone should learn. Unfortunately, he'd learned it the hard way. "Cassie's completely enamored of you, Logan. She told me on the drive home that you would make a good daddy, and she's right. But I've known that all along. I'm just glad you finally realized it."

His smile was soft and sincere. "She still thinks I'm some kind of prince."

"So do I. Or maybe I should say a prince in progress. You still need some work, but the flowers helped your cause."

He reached over and clasped her hand. "If I tell you I can't imagine my life without you, would that help, too?"

Hannah held back the tears, with great effort. "Immensely."

He brought her closer. "How about if I tell you I love you?"

So much for keeping those tears at bay. "Really?"

He gently kissed her cheek. "Really. I didn't expect to fall so hard and so fast for someone, because I never have. Hell, I didn't expect you at all. And although neither of us knows what the future will bring, I do know what I want."

Hannah sniffed and hoped she didn't look like a raccoon. "For me to buy waterproof mascara from now on?"

He responded with that smile she had so grown to

adore. "No. I want to give us a fighting chance. I promise to do everything in my power to make it work."

"I promise that, too." And she did, with all her heart and soul. "I love you, Logan."

"I love you, too, sweetheart."

Then he kissed her, softly, slowly, sealing the vow they'd made at that moment, and those vows Hannah believed were yet to come.

"I guess this means brunch is off."

She broke the kiss to find Gina standing in the middle of the sidewalk, gawking. "I suppose we'll have to postpone until next year."

Gina shrugged. "That's probably for the best. Frank's been complaining of a cold all morning and Trey's teething. I'd feel guilty if I left him with three kids, and even more guilty if I spoiled this wonderful little reunion. However, it does pain me to break a long-standing tradition."

"Tell you what, Gina," Logan said as he kept his arms around Hannah. "If you'll let me take my lady to lunch, I'll give you and your husband a night on the town, my treat. We'll even keep the kids."

Gina's eyes went as wide as saucers. "How about tonight? That would so cure Frank of what ails him."

He returned his attention back to Hannah. "Works for me, if it works for you."

With one exception. "Sure, as long as we have a few hours alone before we're left in charge of the troops."

"It's a deal," Gina said as she backed up a few steps. "Have a good lunch, and have some of that wild monkey sex for dessert, too."

As soon as her friend left the immediate premises, Hannah gave Logan another quick kiss. "You're mighty brave, taking on three kids."

He responded with a grin. "Hey, I've got to get into practice for when we have our three. Or maybe four."

Sweet, welcome music to Hannah's ears. "Don't get ahead of yourself, buster. You'll have to marry me first, Logan Whittaker, my repressed plumber."

"You know, Hannah Armstrong, my maid-in-waiting, I just might do that sooner than you think."

The past six weeks had whirled by in a flurry of changes. She'd sold the house, moved into the Big Blue for the sake of her minor child, spent every day with Logan, and even a few nights alone with him, thanks to Marlene's generosity. Aside from that, the saintly woman hadn't even flinched when Cassie had begun to call her Grandma.

Best of all, Hannah had learned that morning she'd been awarded the high school biology teaching job and would begin in the fall. Things couldn't be going any better, and tonight she and Logan planned to celebrate with a night on the town and a hotel stay in Denver. But she'd better hurry up with the preparations, otherwise Logan might leave without her.

On that thought, she inserted the diamond earrings he'd given her two weeks ago on the one-month anniversary of their meeting. Admittedly, and ridiculously, she'd secretly hoped for jewelry that fit on her left ring finger, but she had no doubt that would eventually come. She had no doubts whatsoever about their future.

After a quick dab of lipstick and a mirror check to make sure the white satin dress was properly fitted, Hannah grabbed her clutch in one hand and slipped the overnight bag's strap over one bare shoulder. She then rushed out of the bedroom and down the hall of the wing she shared with Marlene.

She was somewhat winded when she reached the staircase, and her breath deserted her completely when she saw Logan standing at the bottom landing. He'd donned a black tuxedo with a silver tie, and he was actually wearing Italian loafers, not the usual Western boots.

She couldn't help but smile as she floated down the stairs and took his extended hand when she reached the bottom. "Okay, what did you do with my cowboy lawyer?"

"According to your daughter, tonight I'm supposed to be a prince. This is as close as I could get because I refuse to wear those damn tights and a codpiece."

She reached up and kissed his neck. "I'd buy tickets to see you in tights."

He sent her a champion scowl. "Save your money 'cause it ain't happenin'."

"That's too bad."

He grinned. "You like bad, especially when it comes to me."

Oh, yeah. "I won't argue with that."

He crooked his arm for her to take. "Are you ready, Ms. Armstrong?"

"I am, Prince Logan. Take me away."

Instead of heading toward the front door, Logan guided Hannah down the corridor and into the great room, where an unexpected crowd had gathered. A crowd consisting of Marlene wearing a beautiful white chiffon dress, Chance dressed in a navy shirt and dark jeans, Cassie decked out in her pink princess gown, complete with pretty coat and feather boa, and of all people, senior law partner, Walter Drake, who had debonair down pat. Hannah had to wonder if they were going to pile all these people into a car caravan and head to Denver together.

"Did you plan a party without me knowing?" she asked when Logan positioned her next to the floor-to-ceiling stone fireplace.

"That's somewhat accurate," Logan said. "And you're the guest of honor."

A frenzy of applause rang out, accompanied by a few ear-piercing whistles, compliments of Chance. Her half brother had become very special to her, and he'd proven to be a stellar uncle to Cassie, evidenced by the fact he'd picked up his niece and held her in his arms.

"First, thank you all for being here," Logan began, sounding every bit the attorney, with a little Texas accent thrown in. "But before we get to the celebration, I have something important to ask a very special lady."

Surely he wasn't going to... Hannah held her breath so long she thought her chest might explode, until Logan said, "Cassie, come here."

While Logan took a seat on the raised heart, Chance lowered Cassie to the ground. She ran over as fast as her little pink patent leather shoes allowed. She then came to a sliding stop, plopped herself down in Logan's lap and draped her tiny arms around his neck.

"Darlin'," Logan began, "you know I love your mama, and I love you, right?"

She nodded emphatically, causing her red ringlets to bounce. "Uh-huh."

"And you know that I'm never going to try to take your daddy's place."

"My Heaven daddy."

"That's right. But I sure would like to be your daddy here on earth, if that's okay."

"I'd like you to be my earth daddy, too," Cassie said.

Hannah placed a hand over her mouth to stifle a sob when she saw the look of sheer love in both Cassie's and Logan's eyes.

Logan kissed her daughter's forehead before setting her back on her feet. "Now I have to ask your mom a few questions."

Cassie responded with a grin. "You betcha." She then looked up at Hannah, who could barely see due to the moisture clouding her eyes. "I told you so, Mama. Logan is your prince."

Cassie ran back to her uncle while Logan came to his feet. He moved right in front of Hannah, his gaze unwavering. "Sweetheart, I want to wake up with you every morning and go to bed with you every night. I want to find a good balance between work and family. I don't want to replace Cassie's real dad, but I want to be the best father I can be to her. And I want, God willing, for your face to be the last one I see before I'm gone from this earth. Therefore, if you'll have me, Hannah Armstrong, I want more than anything for you to be my wife."

The room had grown so silent, Hannah would swear everyone could hear her pounding heart. This was no time for smart remarks. For questions or doubts. This precious request Logan had made only required one answer. "Yes, I will be your wife."

Following a kiss, and more applause, Logan pulled a black velvet box from his inner pocket and opened it to a brilliant, emerald-cut diamond ring flanked by more diamonds. "This should seal the deal," he said as he removed it from the holder, pocketed the box again, then placed it on her left finger.

Hannah held it up to the light. "Heavens, Logan Whittaker, this could rival the Rocky Mountains. I might have to wear a sling to hold it up."

Logan leaned over and whispered, "Always the smart-ass, and I love it. I love you."

She sent him a wily grin. "I love you, too, and I really and truly love the ring."

The pop of the cork signaled the party had begun as Marlene started doling out champagne to everyone of legal age. When Cassie asked, "Can I have some?" Logan and Hannah barked out, "No!" simultaneously.

She turned to Logan and smiled. "You're going to come in handy when she turns sixteen and the boys come calling."

"She's not going to date until she's twenty-one," he said in a gruff tone.

"And I'm the Princess of Romania," she replied, although tonight she did feel like a princess. A happy, beloved princess, thanks to her unpredictable prince.

Following a few toasts, many congratulations and a lot of hugs and kisses, Logan finally escorted Hannah out the door and into the awaiting black limousine, just one more surprise in her husband-to-be's repertoire. Then again, everything about her relationship with Logan had been one gigantic surprise.

After they were seated side by side, and the partition dividing the front and back of the car had been raised, Logan kissed her with all the passion they'd come to know in each other's arms.

"How did you enjoy that proposal?" he asked once they'd come up for air.

"It was okay. I really hoped you would have dressed like a plumber and presented the ring on a wrench."

He grinned. "Would you have worn a maid's uniform?"

"Sure. And I'd even pack a feather duster."

The levity seemed to subside when Logan's expression turned serious. "I've set up a trust fund in Cassie's name, in case you want to tell your former in-laws thanks, but no thanks."

"I'd be glad to tell them to take their trust fund and control and go to Hades. And if I did, frankly I don't think they'd care. But if they do decide they want to see her again, it wouldn't be fair to keep her from them." The same way she'd been kept from her father.

"We'll deal with it when and if the time comes. Together." Logan pulled an open bottle of champagne from the onboard ice bucket, then filled the two available glasses. "To our future and our family."

Hannah tipped her crystal flute against his. "And to weddings. Which reminds me, when are we going to do it?"

He laid his free hand on her thigh. "The seat back here is pretty big, so I say let's do it now."

Spoken like a man who'd spent a lot of time with a wise-cracker. She gave him an elbow in the side for good measure. "I meant, as if you didn't know, when are we going to get married?"

He faked a disappointed look that melted into an endearing smile. "I'm thinking maybe on July Fourth."

That allowed Hannah very little time to plan. But since this would be both their second marriages, it wouldn't require anything elaborate. "You know something? People will speculate I'm pregnant if we have the ceremony that soon."

He nuzzled her neck and blew softly in her ear. "Let's just give them all something to talk about."

Lovely. More rumors, as if the Lassiter family hadn't had enough of that lately. Oh, well. It certainly kept things interesting. So did Logan's talented mouth. "Then July Fourth it is. We can even have fireworks."

He winked. "Fireworks on Independence Day for my beautiful independent woman works well for me."

An independent woman and single mom, and a one-time secret heiress, who'd had the good fortune to fall in love with a man who had given her an incredible sense of freedom.

Now, as Hannah gazed at her gorgeous new fiancé, this onetime secret heiress was more than ready for the lifetime celebration to begin. Starting now.

* * * * *

EXPECTING THE CEO'S CHILD

YVONNE LINDSAY

To my dear friend Rose-Marie, who has known me since we were both teenagers—thank you for always being my friend and an especial thank you for calling florists in Wyoming for me!
J I owe you, Smithy!

One

Jenna puzzled over the complex wreath design a family had requested for their grandmother's funeral the coming Wednesday. She just about had it nailed; all she needed to confirm with the wholesale suppliers was that she'd be able to get the right shade of lilacs that had been the grandmother's favorite.

The sound of the door buzzer alerted her to a customer out front. She listened to see if her new Saturday part-time assistant would attend to the client, but the subsequent ding of the counter bell told her that Millie was likely in the cool room out back, or, unfortunately more likely, outside on the phone to her boyfriend again.

Making a mental note to discuss with the girl the importance of actually *working* during work hours, Jenna pushed herself up from her desk, pasted a smile on her face and walked out into the showroom. Only to feel the smile freeze in place as she recognized Dylan Lassiter, in all his decadent glory, standing with his back to her, his attention apparently captured by the ready-made bouquets she kept in the refrigerated unit along one wall.

Her reaction was instantaneous; heat, desire and shock flooded her in turn. The last time she'd seen him had been in the coat closet where they'd impulsively sought refuge—to release the sexual energy that had ignited so dangerously and suddenly between them. They'd struck sparks off one another so bright and so fierce it had almost been a relief when he'd returned to his base in Los Angeles. Almost.

Jenna fought the urge to place a hand protectively across her belly—to hide the evidence of that uncharacteristic and spontaneous act. She'd known from the day her pregnancy was confirmed that she'd have to tell him at some stage. She hadn't planned for it to be right now. At first she'd been a little piqued that he'd made no effort to contact her since that one incredible encounter. She had half understood he'd been too busy to call her in the aftermath of his father's sudden death during Dylan's sister's wedding rehearsal dinner. But afterward? When everything had begun to settle down again?

She gave herself a mental shake. No, she'd successfully convinced herself that she didn't need or want the complication of a relationship. Especially not now and especially not with someone as high profile as Dylan Lassiter. Not after all the years of work she'd put into rebuilding her reputation. She'd made a conscious choice to put off contacting him, too, and despite the slight wound to her feminine ego that he'd obviously done the same, she would just have to get over it because she sure as heck had plenty else to keep her mind occupied now.

"Can I help you?" she said, feigning a lack of recognition right up until the moment he turned around and impaled her with those cerulean-blue eyes of his.

Air fled from her lungs and her throat closed up. A perfectly tailored blue-gray suit emphasized the width of his shoulders, while his white shirt and pale blue tie emphasized the California tan that warmed his skin. Her mouth dried. It was a crime against nature that any man could look so beautiful and so masculine at the same time.

A hank of softly curling hair fell across his high forehead, making her hand itch to smooth it back, then trace the stubbled line of his jaw. She clenched her fingers into a tight fist, embedding her nails in her palms as she reminded herself exactly where such an action would inevitably lead.

He was like a drug to her. An instant high that, once taken, created a craving like no other. She'd spent the past two and a half months in a state of disbelief at her actions. She, who'd strived to be so careful—to keep her nose clean and to fly under the radar—was now carrying the child of a man she'd met the day it was conceived. A man she'd barely known, yet knew so much about. Certainly enough not to have succumbed the way she had.

It had literally been a one-night *stand,* she reminded herself cynically. The coat closet hadn't allowed for anything else. But as close as the confines had been, her body still remembered every second of how he'd made her feel—and it reacted in kind again.

"Jenna," Dylan said with a slow nod of his head, his gaze not moving from her face for so much as a second.

"Dylan," she replied, taking a deep breath and feigning surprise. "What brings you back to Cheyenne?"

The instant she said the words she silently groaned. The opening. Of course he was here for that. The local chamber of commerce—heck, the whole town—was abuzz with the news. She'd tried to ignore anything Lassiter-related for weeks now, but there was no ignoring the man in front of her.

The father of her unborn child.

A noise from the back of the store made both of them

turn around. Oh, thank God. Millie had finally deigned to show up and do her job.

"Ah," Jenna said, fighting to hide her relief. "Here's Millie. She'll be able to assist you with any requirements you might have. Millie, this is Mr. Lassiter, he's opening the Lassiter Grill in town. Please make sure you give him our best service."

She sent Dylan a distracted smile and turned to go, only to feel him snag her wrist with warm strong fingers. Fingers that had done unmentionably wicked things to her and whose touch now sent a spiral of need to clench deep inside her.

"Not so fast," Dylan said, spinning her gently back to face him again. "As capable as I'm sure Millie is," he continued, flashing a smile that had the impressionable teen virtually melting on the spot, "I'd prefer to deal with you directly."

"I'm sure you would," Jenna answered as quellingly as she could. "But Millie is available to help you with your inquiry. I am not."

Her heart rate skipped up a beat as a hint of annoyance dulled his eyes.

"Scared, Jenna?"

His low tones were laced with challenge. Jenna stiffened her spine.

"Not at all, just very busy."

"Not too busy, I'm sure, to catch up with an old *friend.*"

Hot color stained her cheeks. They weren't anything near approaching friends. She barely knew him any better now than she had the day they'd met—the day they were so drawn to one another that flirtation had turned to touching, and touching had turned to impassioned, frenzied lovemaking in the nearest available private space.

A butterfly whisper of movement rippled across her lower belly, shocking her into gasping aloud. Of course—the moment she'd been awaiting for weeks, her baby's first perceptible motion, would have to happen with its father standing right here in front of her.

Dylan's fingers tightened on her wrist. "Are you okay?"

"I'm fine," she said hurriedly. "Just very busy."

"Then I'll only take a few minutes of your time." He gave her a searching look. "Your office?"

Her body wilted in defeat. "Through here."

He released her wrist and she felt the cool air of the showroom swirl around her sensitized skin, as if her body instantly mourned the loss of contact, his touch. She found herself rubbing at the spot where he'd held her, as if she could somehow rub away the invisible imprint he'd left upon her.

Stop being ridiculous, she growled silently. *He was nothing to you before, aside from an out of character dalliance, and he's nothing to you now.* Logically she knew she couldn't avoid him forever. Despite the fact he was based in L.A., with the new restaurant opening here in town they were bound to cross paths again sometime. It might as well be now.

The tiny fluttering sensation rippled through her belly again, reminding her that there was a great deal more to consider than just her own feelings about seeing Dylan Lassiter. Thankfully, he hadn't noticed that her petite frame carried a new softness about it now. That her figure, rather than being taut and flat, was gently rounded as the baby's presence had suddenly become more visible at thirteen weeks.

She hadn't shared news of her pregnancy with anyone yet, and had no plans to start right now. Instead, she'd sought to hide it by changing from her usual style of figure-hugging attire to longer, more flowing lines.

As they entered the tiny office she used for administration, she gestured to the chair opposite her desk and sank, gratefully, into her own on the other side. Instead of taking the seat offered to him, Dylan sat on the edge of her desk. She couldn't help but notice the way the fine wool of his trousers skimmed his long powerful thighs, or how the fabric now stretched across his groin.

Her mouth suddenly felt parched and she turned to reach for the water jug and glasses that she kept on a credenza behind her desk.

"Water?" she offered with a croak.

"No, I'm fine, thank you."

She hastily splashed a measure of clear liquid into a glass for herself and lifted it to her lips, relishing the cooling and hydrating sensation as the drink slid over her tongue. After putting the glass down on the desk, she pulled a pad toward her and picked up a pen.

"So," she said, looking up at him. "What is it you want?"

He reached out and took the pen from her hand, laying it very deliberately down on the notepad. "I thought we could talk. You know, reminisce about old times."

Heat pooled at the apex of her thighs and she pushed her chair back from her desk. Anything to increase the distance between them.

"Look, you said a few minutes, and frankly, that's all I had. Your time's up. If there's nothing business related you need to discuss...?" She hesitated a moment, her temper snapping now at the humor reflected in his eyes. "Then you'll have to excuse me so I can attend to my work."

Dylan's sinfully sensuous lips curved into a half smile.

"You're different, Jenna. I can't quite put my finger on it, but I'll figure it out."

She fought back a groan. The man was all about detail. She knew that intimately. If she didn't get him out of here soon he was bound to notice exactly what it was that was different about her. She wasn't ready for that, not right now, anyway. She needed more time.

Before she could respond, he continued, "I want you to do the flowers for the opening. Wildflowers, grasses, rustic—that kind of thing. Can you do it?"

"I'll get my staff on to preparing some samples for you on Monday. I take it you'll be around?"

His smile widened. "Oh, yes, I'll be around. And your staff won't be handling this for me. You will."

"My staff are well trained and efficient—"

"But they're not you—and I *want* you."

His words hung in the air between them. She could feel them as if he'd actually reached out and touched her.

"You can't have me," she whispered.

"Can't I? Hmm, that's a darn shame," he said. "Because then I'd have to take my business elsewhere."

His words, so gently spoken, sent a spear of ice straight through her. It would take only a day for the news that she'd turned his business away to get through town. Less than that again before more people would follow his cue and take their business to other florists, as well. She'd fought long and hard to get a reputation as the leading florist in town and she wasn't going to lose it just like that.

She bit the inside of her cheek as she swiftly considered her options. Well, option. She really had no other choice but to take his business. Refusing it, with the associated fallout when word got around that she'd turned down a Lassiter—well, it didn't bear thinking about. However, the benefits would roll in pretty quickly when it was known that she'd done the flowers for the opening. There was nothing some of the better-heeled members of Cheyenne society loved more than following a trend set by the Lassiter family.

"I may be able to carve out a little time," she hedged, not wanting him to see how easily he'd forced her to capitulate. "Do you have particular designs in mind?"

"Tell you what. Why don't we discuss this further over dinner tonight."

"I'm sorry, I have plans for tonight." Plans that included a long soak with her feet in a tub filled with warm water and Epsom salts, followed by a home pedicure while she could still bend down and reach her toes. "Perhaps you could give me your contact number for while you're here. I'll call you when I'm free."

He gave her a narrow-eyed glance, then lazily got to his feet, reached into his back pocket for his wallet and slid out a card. She went to take it, but he didn't immediately let it go. Instead, he tugged it closer to his body, thereby tugging her a little closer, too.

"You'll call me?"

"Of course. We're closed tomorrow, but I'll check my schedule on Monday and call you then."

"I'll look forward to it," he said with a lazy wink and released the card.

She followed him from the office into the showroom. Even though she'd worked here since she was a teenager, she was still attuned to the sweet, luscious fragrance of the blooms she had on display. The various layers of scent filled the air with a strong feminine presence. A complete contrast to the powerful masculinity that was Dylan Lassiter.

Jenna held the front door to the store open for him.

"Thanks for stopping by," she said as he stepped past her and onto the sidewalk.

Just as he did, a large delivery truck passed on the street. The subsequent whoosh of warm air hit her full on, the gust plastering her short-sleeved tunic against her body. Dylan didn't miss a trick. His eyes drifted over the new fullness of her breasts, then lower, to where her waist had thickened, and to the gentle roundness of her tummy. He stared at her for what felt like an aeon before his eyes flicked upward to her face.

What she saw reflected back at her had the ability to nail her feet to the ground, right where she stood. She'd read about his convivial side, his laissez-faire attitude to life and his ability to continually land on his feet even as he eschewed traditional choices. Conversely, it was widely known that he was a perfectionist in the kitchen, which took a keen mind and grim determination.

The expression that he presented to her belonged to a different man entirely. This was the face of the CEO of the Lassiter Grill Corporation, not the playboy, not the one-time lover. No, this was the face of a man who had a question and, she thought with a shiver, would do whatever it took to get his answer.

"Looks like we have a bit more than just flowers to discuss. I think we'd best be having that dinner mighty soon, don't you?"

He turned on the heel of his hand-tooled boot and strode toward a dark SUV parked a few spaces down the street. She couldn't help but watch the lithe way his body moved. Jenna closed her eyes for a second but still his image burned there as if imprinted on her retinas. And she knew, without a shadow of a doubt, that her time for keeping this baby a secret had well and truly passed.

Two

Dylan swung his SUV into the traffic and fought to control the anger that roiled inside him like a building head of thunderclouds.

She was pregnant. No wonder she'd been as skittish as one of Sage's newborn foals when he'd arrived. He was probably the last person on earth she either expected, or wanted, to see.

His baby? The timing would be about right—unless she was the type of woman who indulged in casual assignations with just about any man she met. The thought made his stomach pitch uneasily. He needed to know for sure if their encounter had resulted in pregnancy. God, pregnancy. A kid of his own. And with her.

It wasn't hard to recall how his eye had been drawn to her that cool March Friday. He'd wanted her, right there, right then.

He remembered his first sight of her as she flitted about like some exotic bird, her attention solely on the flower arrangements she'd designed for his sister, Angelica's, wedding rehearsal dinner—a dinner that had ended before it began when his adoptive father, J.D., had collapsed with a fatal heart attack—for a wedding that had been called off, permanently now it seemed.

The building had been full of people doing what they did best, but Jenna stood out among them all in her jewel bright colors. An effervescent energy simply vibrated off her. Their initial banter had been fun and she'd given as good as she got. But the real craziness had started the moment he caught her hand in his and pulled her into an alcove where he kissed her, so he could see for himself if she tasted as intoxicating as he'd imagined.

She'd spun out of his arms the instant he'd loosened his hold on her but the imprint of her slight frame against his body had stayed with him through the course of the next hour, until he'd known that one kiss was definitely not enough. Satisfied the catering team in the kitchen knew what they were doing, he'd hunted Jenna down as she'd applied the finishing touches to the floral design she'd created for the entrance to the Cheyenne Depot—a historic railroad station that had been converted into a popular reception hall. Hunted her down and entrapped her in his arms for what he'd planned to be just one more kiss.

One more kiss had turned into a frenzy of need and they'd found their way into the coat closet at the front of the building. In its dark recesses, they'd discovered just what level of delight they could bring each other to.

He'd never been the kind of guy who waited for anything to come to him. No, he always went out and got it. And he'd certainly gone out and gotten her—both of them swept along on a tide of attraction that still left him breathless whenever he thought about it. He'd had casual encounters before, but this had been so very different. But then his father had died and his world had changed.

By the time the formalities here in Cheyenne had been taken care of, he'd had to race back to L.A. to continue his duties as CEO of the Lassiter Grill Corporation. Hassling Angelica for the contact details of the florist she'd used for that night—a night from which repercussions continued to cause his sister pain—had seemed a cruel and unnecessary thing to do. Besides, he'd had enough on his plate with work. Now, it seemed, he had a great deal more.

His inattention to the road forced him to jam on his brakes when the traffic ahead slowed suddenly. He swore softly. Two hours. He'd give her two hours to call him about dinner—max. If she hadn't phoned by then, he'd sure as heck be calling her.

In the end it was fifty-eight minutes exactly before his cell phone began vibrating in his pocket. He took it out, a smile curving his lips as he saw the name of her store come up on the screen.

"I was thinking we could make it tonight," he said without preamble. "My place, seven o'clock."

"Y-your place?"

He rattled off the address. "You know where it is?"

"Sure. I'll find it," she answered, her voice a little breathless.

"Maybe I ought to pick you up. Don't want you changing your mind at the last minute."

"I won't, I promise. I'll see you at seven."

She hung up before he could say another thing. His mouth firmed into a grim line as he slid his phone back into his pocket. It was a rare thing indeed to find a woman of so few words. Even when they'd first met they'd been bigger on action than conversation.

That was certainly going to change. He had a list of questions as long as his arm and he wasn't letting her go until she'd answered every last one.

One thing was certain. If she was carrying his child, he was going to be a part of that baby's life. Losing his own parents when he was young, then being raised by his aunt Ellie and her husband, J. D. Lassiter, Dylan knew just how important family was. He'd been too young to remember his mom and dad properly, too young to mourn more than the sense of security he'd taken for granted from birth. After his parents died, however, that all changed, until Aunt Ellie and J.D. stepped in and ensured that he, his brother, Sage, and sister, Angelica, never wanted for a thing. Even after Ellie Lassiter passed away, her sister-in-law, Marlene, had become a surrogate mom to them. It had been family that had gotten them through.

Now, with J.D. gone, too, the whole concept of family was even more important to him than ever. His brother thought he was nuts putting so much store by it. At constant loggerheads with J.D. and determined to make his own place in the world, Sage had always insisted that the only family he needed was Dylan. As close as they were, Dylan had always wanted more. And, if Jenna Montgomery's baby was his, it looked like he might be getting it.

Jenna reluctantly got ready to go out to Dylan's place. He was a complication she would rather ignore right now, but clearly, he wasn't about to let that happen. She quickly showered, then took her time rubbing scented moisturizer into her skin. So what if she had just shaved her legs— they needed it. She certainly hadn't done it for *his* benefit.

Nor had she applied the makeup she barely ever wore anymore for him, either. She was doing this all for herself. Pure and simple. If it made her feel good, feel stronger, then she was doing it. The same principle applied to the clothes she'd chosen to wear tonight. The royal purple stretch lace dress flattered her figure, even with the additional curves that now showed. It empowered her, as did the black spike-heeled pumps she teetered on.

She paused for a moment to assess herself in the mirror. Too much? Her eyes scanned from her dark brown hair, worn loose and flat-ironed dead straight, to her shiny patent leather shoes. She swiveled sideways. This was a total contrast to the kind of thing she'd worn in recent weeks. And, yes, it was definitely too much—which was why she wasn't going to change a thing.

She grabbed her purse from the bed and told herself she was not nervous about this meeting. That's all it was. A meeting. She'd tell Dylan what she'd been planning to tell him all along, and that would be that.

She wouldn't be swayed by the depth of his blue eyes, or the careless fall of his hair, which always looked as if he'd just tumbled from bed. She knew he was handsome; she'd fallen prey to that so easily. She also knew he was successful and intelligent and had a charm that could melt a polar ice cap. But she'd be immune to all that now, too. At least she hoped she would be.

She'd had weeks to think about this. Weeks in which to decide that while Dylan should know about his baby, she was most definitely bringing it up on her own. She knew full well what not to do when raising a child. Her own parents had been the prime example of that. No, her baby would want for nothing. He or she would grow up secure in the knowledge of Jenna's love and protection.

A man like Dylan Lassiter, with his cavalier lifestyle, a girl for every day of the week, every week of the year, not to mention his celebrity status, which ensured he traveled constantly, did not fit into the picture at all. She'd taken a walk on that wild side of his and yes, she had enjoyed every precious second. But life, real life, had to be lived in a far more stable and measured way. She owned her own home and had a business that was doing well.... With a few economies she could and would do this all on her own.

With those thoughts to arm her, she locked up and

walked out to her car. Checking the map one more time, she headed north to the address he'd given her, on the outskirts of town.

Doubts began to assail Jenna as she pulled in between the massive gated pillars, each adorned with a wrought-iron, stylized *L,* at the entrance to the driveway. The drive itself had to be several football fields long. She knew the family was wealthy, but seriously, who did this? Who kept a property this immense when they spent only about two months of every year living here? The Lassiters, that's who. It was a stark and somewhat intimidating reminder of the differences between herself and Dylan, and it struck a nervous chime deep inside her.

What if he used his money and his position to make things difficult for her? She had no idea what he was really like, although she remembered, without the slightest hesitation, how he'd felt and how he'd tasted. He was forbidden fruit. The kind of man every woman, no matter her age, turned her head to watch go past. The kind of man every woman deserved to savor—as Jenna had—at least once in her lifetime. But he wasn't a forever kind of guy. She'd been thankful he hadn't contacted her after their…their…*tryst,* she reminded herself again. She definitely wasn't looking for the roller coaster ride or the intrusive media publicity a relationship with him would offer.

Almost everything she knew about Dylan Lassiter she'd gleaned from social media and word of mouth around town—of which there was plenty. He'd basically gone wherever whim had taken him, spurning the opportunities and advantages afforded him by his adoptive father, and refusing to go into the family business or even attend college. Jenna sighed. What would it have been like, she wondered, to be able to be so carefree? She knew he'd traveled widely, eventually training in Europe as a chef and then coming back to L.A. and building a solid name for his skills, together with a certain celebrity notoriety at the same time. His life, to her, just seemed so...*indulgent*.

Her upbringing had been as different from Dylan's as a bridal bouquet was from a sizzling steak platter. And from her perspective, while there was plenty about Dylan Lassiter to recommend him to anyone who liked to run fast and loose, there was very little to recommend him as father material.

That said, this baby was *their* creation. Dylan had rights—and she had no plans to stand in the way of those. But she also wanted her child to grow up secure, in one place, with a stable and loving parent. Not used in a tug-of-war between parents, as she had been. Not dragged from pillar to post as her father moved from country to country, then state to state in pursuit of some unattainable happily-ever-after. And certainly not implicated by her father's fraudulent schemes or left abandoned at the age of fifteen because her sole surviving parent was doing time in jail.

No, Jenna's baby was going to have everything she hadn't.

She gently applied the brake and her car came to a stop outside the impressive portico. She rested a hand on the slight mound of her belly, determined not to be totally overwhelmed by the obvious wealth on display before her. This baby had rights, too, and yes, he or she was entitled to be a part of what stood before Jenna. But right now she was the baby's only advocate, and she knew what was best for him or her. And she'd fight to her very last breath to ensure her child got exactly that.

She grabbed her bag and got out of the car. The front

door opened as she walked toward it, and Dylan stood on the threshold. Jenna's heart did that little double skip, just as it had the very first time she saw him. It was hard to remain objective when the man stood before her. He'd tamed his hair slightly, giving him a more refined look, and he'd changed his suit for a pale blue cotton shirt that made his eyes seem even bluer than before.

"You found the place okay?" he asked unnecessarily as she ascended the wide steps.

"Hard to miss it, don't you think?" she replied, not even bothering to keep the note of acerbity from her tone.

She didn't want him to think even for a minute that he had the upper hand in this meeting. He inclined his head slightly, as if acknowledging she'd scored a valid point.

"Come on in," he invited, opening the door wide. "You must be ready to put your feet up after working all day. Can I get you something to drink?"

"Just mineral water, if you have it, thanks."

She hadn't drunk alcohol since she'd known she might be pregnant. In fact, there were a lot of things she didn't eat or drink as a result of the changes happening deep inside her body.

"Sure, take a seat," he said, gesturing to the large and comfortable-looking furniture that dominated the living room off the main entrance. "I'll be right back."

He was as good as his word. She'd barely settled herself against the butter-soft leather of a sofa big enough to sleep on before he was back with two drinks. An ice-cold beer for himself and a tall glass of sparkling water for her.

"Thank you," she said stiffly, taking the glass from his hand and studiously avoiding making eye contact.

But she couldn't avoid the slight brush of fingers, nor could she ignore the zing of awareness that speared through her at that faint touch. She rapidly lifted the glass to her lips to mask her reaction. The bubbles leaping from the water's surface tickled her nose, further irritating her. She swallowed carefully and put the glass on the coaster on the table in front of her.

Dylan sprawled in the seat opposite, his large, rangy frame filling the chair. His gaze never left her face and an increasingly uncomfortable silence stretched out between them. Jenna cleared her throat nervously. Obviously, she was going to have to start this conversation.

"I—I wanted to say how sorry I was about your father's passing."

"Thank you."

"He was much respected and I'm sure you must miss him very much," she persisted.

"I do," Dylan acknowledged, then took a long draw of his beer.

Damn him, he wasn't making this easy for her. But then again, what had she expected?

"He'd have been proud of the new restaurant opening here in town," she continued valiantly.

"That he would."

"And you? You must be pleased with everything being on time."

"I am."

A muscle tugged at the edge of his mouth, pulling his lips into a half smile that was as cynical as it was appealing. Jenna suddenly had the overwhelming sense that she shouldn't have come here. That perhaps she should have waited a day or two before calling him. Hard on its heels came the contradictory but certain knowledge that she definitely should have been in touch with him long before now.

Was this how a mouse felt, she wondered, just before a cat pounced? Did it feel helpless, confused and fright-ened, with nowhere to look but straight into a maw of dread?

She watched, mesmerized, as Dylan leaned forward and carefully put his beer on the table. He rested his elbows on his knees, those sinfully dexterous hands of his loosely clasped between them. Warmth unfurled from her core like a slowly opening bud, and she forced her eyes to lift upward, to meet the challenge in his.

She fought to suppress a shudder when she saw the determination that reflected back at her. She reached for her water and took another sip, shocked to discover that her hand shook ever so slightly. She dug deep for the last ounce of courage she possessed. Since he was determined to make this so awkward, she'd find some inane way to carry the conversation even if it killed her.

"Thank you for asking me to dinner tonight. It's not every day I'm catered to by a European-trained celebrity chef."

She was surprised to hear Dylan sigh, as if he was disappointed in something. In her?

"Jenna, stop dancing around the issue and cut to the chase. Are you pregnant with my baby?"

Three

Dylan cursed inwardly. He'd been determined to be charming. He could do charming with his eyes closed and both hands behind his back. So why, then, had he so ham-fistedly screwed up what he'd planned to be a relaxing evening of fact-finding with a woman he'd been fiercely attracted to from the second he'd first laid eyes on her?

It was too late now. The words were out and he couldn't drag them back no matter how much he wanted to. He huffed out a breath of frustration. Jenna looked about as stunned by his question as he was at actually blurting it out that way. Damage control. He desperately needed to go into damage control mode, but try as he might, he couldn't think of the words to say. What he wanted was the answer. An answer that only Jenna Montgomery could provide.

Beneath his gaze she appeared to shrink a little into the voluminous furniture. She was already a dainty thing—her small body perfectly formed—but right now she was dwarfed by her surroundings and, no doubt, daunted by the conversation they were about to have.

Dylan knew he should try and put her at ease, but the second she'd alighted from her car he had felt the shields she'd erected between them. It had aroused a side of him he hadn't displayed in years, made him deliberately uncooperative as she'd tried to observe the niceties of polite conversation. It had driven him to ask the question that had been plaguing him since that gust of wind off the road had revealed changes in her slender form that were too obvious to someone who knew that form as intimately, even if fleetingly, as he had.

"Well?" he prompted.

"Yes," she said in a strangled whisper.

Dylan didn't know what to say. Inside he felt as if he'd just scored a touchdown at the Super Bowl, but he also had this weird feeling of detachment, as if he was looking in on some other guy's life. As if what she'd just said wasn't real—didn't involve him. But he was involved, very much so. Or at least he *would* be, whether she liked it or not.

"Were you going to tell me sometime, or did you just hope that I'd never know?"

As much as he fought to keep the hard note of anger from his voice, he could feel it lacing every word. It left a bitter taste in his mouth and he struggled to pull himself under control. He didn't want to antagonize her or scare her away, and it wasn't as if he'd made an effort to get in touch with her again before today. This was way too important, and at the crux of it all an innocent child's future depended on the outcome of tonight.

"I meant to tell you, and I was going to—in my own time. I've been busy and I had a bit of a struggle coming to terms with it myself. Getting my head around how I'm going to cope."

Jenna's voice shook, but even though she was upset, he sensed the shields she'd erected earlier growing even thicker, her defense even stronger.

"And you didn't think I should have known about this earlier?"

"What difference would it have made?"

Her words shocked him. What difference? Did she think that knowing he was going to be a father made no discernible difference to his life, to how he felt about *everything?* Hell, he'd lost his own father only a couple months ago. Didn't she think he at least deserved a light in the darkness of mourning? Something to get him through the responsibility of having to get up every day and keep putting one foot in front of the other, all because so many other people depended on him to not only do exactly that, but to do it brilliantly—even when he wanted to wallow in grief?

"Trust me." He fought to keep his tone even. "It would have made a difference. When did you know?"

"About three weeks after we—" Her voice broke off and she appeared to gather up her courage before she spoke again. "I began to suspect I might be pregnant, and waited another week before going to my doctor."

Dylan sucked in a breath between his teeth. So, by his reckoning, she'd had confirmation that their encounter had resulted in conception for plenty of time. She could have shared the news—no matter how busy she was.

Damn it, he'd used a condom; they should have been safe. But nothing was 100 percent effective, except maybe abstinence. And there was one thing that was guaranteed, when it came to Jenna: abstinence was the last thing on Dylan's mind.

Even now, as quietly irate as he was right this second, she still had a power over him. His skin felt too tight for his body, as if he was itching to burst out and lose himself in her. His flesh stirred to life even as the idea took flight. Desire uncoiled from the pit of his belly and sent snaking tendrils in a heated path throughout him.

No one had had that power over him before. Ever.

Yet this diminutive woman had once driven him to a sexual frenzy that had tipped over into sheer madness. She still could.

A ringing sound penetrated Dylan's consciousness, a much needed reminder of the here and now and the fact that Jenna sat opposite him, quite a different woman from the one he'd so quickly but thoroughly made love to two and a half months ago.

"I'll be right back," he said, surreptitiously adjusting himself as he rose from the seat. "I need to check on something in the kitchen."

After a quick examination of the beef bourguignonne simmering on the stovetop, and checking that the rice in the cooker was fluffy and ready, he grunted with satisfaction. They would continue this discussion at the table, where, hopefully, he'd find his manners again and stand a better chance of hiding the effect she had on him.

He returned to the living room and painted a smile on his face.

"Dinner's ready. Would you like to come through to the kitchen? I thought we could eat in there, if you're comfortable with that."

"Since I usually eat standing up at the store or off a tray on my lap when I'm home, just sitting at a table sounds lovely."

She stood and smoothed her clothes, her hand lingering on the tiny bump that revealed a child of his now existed. It hit Dylan like a fist to the chest. His child. Someone of his blood. Everything else in his life right now faded into the background as that knowledge took precedence. Now there was another generation to think about, to protect and to teach.

The thought filled him with a new sense of purpose, of hope. The past five years had been challenging, the past couple of months even more so. But this baby was a new beginning. A reason for Dylan to ground himself in what was good, and to put some much needed balance back in his life, balance that was sadly lacking. This baby, his son or daughter, was a lifeline out of a spiral of work and hard play that had threatened to consume him. One way or another he would be a part of his child's world— every single day if he could, although that would take some engineering with him based in L.A. and Jenna here in Cheyenne. Whatever the logistics, he was prepared to work this situation out. He just needed to be certain that Jenna felt the same way.

She crossed the room to where he stood, and he put his hand at the small of her back and guided her through to the kitchen. He felt her stiffen slightly beneath his touch, and heard her breath hitch just a little. Knowing she wasn't as unaffected by him as she pretended went a long way toward making him feel better about the semi-erection he was constantly battling to keep in control.

He seated her at the square wooden table in the kitchen and gestured to the vase containing a handful of wild-flowers he'd found on his four-acre property when he'd gone to walk off some steam this afternoon.

"They could probably have done with your touch," he said as he turned to the oven to take warmed plates out and lay them on the table.

"They look fine just the way they are," Jenna commented.

But as if she couldn't resist, he saw her reach out and tweak a few stems. Before he knew it, the bouquet looked a hundred times better.

"How do you do that?" he asked, bringing the Dutch oven filled with the deliciously fragrant beef across from the stove.

"Do what?"

"Make a jumble of weeds look so good."

She shrugged. "It's a knack I picked up, I guess."

"What made you decide to work with flowers?"

"I didn't, really." She sighed. "They kind of picked me."

"Not a family business, then?" he probed, curious to discover just how she had ended up under Mrs. Connell's roof.

Jenna gave a rueful laugh. "No, not a family business at all, although once I started working at the store it felt like home to me."

There was a wistful note in her voice, one he wanted to explore further, but found himself reluctant to. There was time enough to find out all her secrets, he told himself.

He spooned rice from the cooker onto the warmed plates, and put them on the table.

"This looks great," Jenna commented, leaning forward to inhale deeply. "And smells even better. To be honest, I think your skills with food far outweigh mine with flowers. I can barely reheat a TV dinner without burning something."

Dylan feigned horror. "Wash your mouth out. TV dinners? You're going to have to do much better than that for the baby."

He reached for a ladle and spooned a generous portion of the beef onto her plate before serving himself. When she didn't immediately pick up her fork, he sat back and looked at her. Her lips had firmed into a mutinous line and there was a frown of annoyance on her forehead.

"What did I say?"

"I didn't come here to be told what to do. Maybe it's better if I go."

She pushed back her chair a little, but before she could go any farther he reached out and grabbed her hand.

"Okay, truce. I will try not to tell you what to eat, but you have to admit, for me it comes with the territory. It's what I do. It's in my nature to want to feed people well."

It was also in his nature to want to lift her from her chair, march her to the nearest accommodatingly soft surface and relive some of the passion they'd shared. She looked down at where his fingers were curled around her wrist, and he slowly eased his grip and let her go.

"As long as we're clear on that," she muttered, scooting her chair closer to the table again and lifting her fork.

She scooped up a mouthful and brought it to her lips. His brain ceased to function as she closed her eyes and moaned in pleasure. Other body parts had no such difficulty.

"That's so good," she said, opening her eyes again.

For a second Dylan allowed himself to be lost in their chocolate-brown depths. Just a second. Then he forced himself to look away and apply himself to his own meal.

"Thanks, I aim to please," he said with a nonchalance he was far from feeling.

It didn't seem to matter what he did or what he said, or even how she reacted to any of it—he was drawn to her on a level he'd never experienced before. Sure, that could play to his advantage, but he had the sneaking suspicion that Jenna Montgomery was a great deal more hardheaded than her feminine presence at his table suggested.

"Home grown?" she asked, spearing some beef and popping it into her mouth.

For a second he was distracted by her lips closing around the fork, then the enticing half smile they curved into as she tasted and chewed.

"Yeah, from the Big Blue. Nothing but the best."

"Your cousin runs it, doesn't he? Chance Lassiter?"

"And very well, too. It's in his blood."

And therein lay the rub. While he and Sage had been raised Lassiters, they weren't Lassiter by birth. Not like Chance, not like their sister, Angelica. It was one of the reasons why this baby meant so much more to Dylan than he had ever imagined. This child was a part of his legacy, his mark on the world. It was all very well gaining fame and fortune for doing something you excelled at and loved, but raising a child and setting him or her on a path for life—nothing compared to that.

"Have you thought about what you're going to do when the baby is born?" he asked, deliberately changing the subject.

"Do?"

"About work."

"I'll manage. I figure that in the early stages I should be able to keep the baby at work with me."

He nodded, turning the idea over in his mind. "Yes, sure—initially. I think that would be a good idea."

"I'm sorry?"

He looked at her in puzzlement. But his confusion didn't last long.

"What you think should matter to me, why, exactly?"

He let his fork clatter onto his plate. "Well, it is my baby, too. I have some say in what happens to him or her."

Even though he'd tried to keep his voice neutral, some of his frustration must have leaked through.

"Dylan, as far as I'm concerned, while you have rights to be a part of this baby's life, it doesn't mean you have a say in how I bring it up."

"Oh? And how do you see that working? Just let me jet in every now and then, have a visit and then jet out again?"

"Pretty much. After all, you live most of the time in L.A., or wherever else in the world you're flying off to—not here where the baby and I will be. Obviously, I won't stand in your way when you want to see him or her, though, as long as it's clear I'm the one raising the child."

That was not how things were going to happen. Dylan's hands curled into fists on the table and took in a deep, steadying breath. "That's good of you," he said, as evenly as he could. "Although I have another suggestion, one that I find far more palatable, and which will be better for all of us."

She looked at him in surprise. "Oh? What's that?"

"That we get married and raise the baby together."

To his chagrin she laughed. Not just laughed but snorted and snuffled with it as if she couldn't contain her mirth.

"It's not so impossible to think of, is it?" he demanded.

"Impossible? It's ridiculous, Dylan. We barely know one another."

He nodded in agreement. "True. That's something easily rectified."

All humor fled from her face. "You're serious, aren't you?"

"Never more so."

"No. It would never work. Not in a million years."

"Why not? We already know we're..." he paused a moment for effect, his eyes skimming her face, her throat and lower "...compatible."

"Great sex isn't the sole basis for a compatible marriage," she protested.

"It's a start," he said, his voice deepening.

Hot color danced in her cheeks—due to anger or something else? he wondered. Something like desire, perhaps?

"Not for me it isn't. Look, can we agree to disagree on

the subject of marriage? I've already said I won't stand in your way when it comes to seeing the child. Can we leave it at that for now?"

"Sure, for now. But, Jenna, one thing you will learn about me is that I never give up. Especially not on something this important."

Four

Jenna's heart hammered a steady drumbeat in her chest. He looked deadly serious. This wasn't how she had imagined their meal together going, not at all. She certainly hadn't imagined that he'd spring an offer of marriage on her like that.

Sure, there was probably a list as long as her arm of women who would jump at the opportunity. But she wasn't like that. And she'd meant it when she'd said his life was in L.A. and not here, because it *was*. While it was true that he'd been in Wyoming more often lately, it was only because of the new Grill opening in town. Once that was up and running he'd be straight back to the West Coast. Back to his high life and being featured in the celebrity news with his beautiful women.

No, marriage to Dylan Lassiter didn't even bear thinking of, she decided as she forced herself to take another bite of the melt-in-your-mouth perfection of the meal he'd prepared. He might be spending more time in the boardroom these days, she mused, but he hadn't lost his knack in the kitchen.

Maybe it would be worth marrying him just to have meals like this every day, she thought flippantly. An image of him barefoot and in the kitchen, wearing an apron and not much else, hovered in her mind, sending a pull of longing through her.

No, get a grip on yourself, she chided silently. She'd never settled for anything less than perfection when it came to a relationship. It was why she so rarely dated. That was why her behavior with Dylan back in March was such an aberration.

Once people began to notice her pregnancy, she had no doubt there'd be a whole ton of questions asked. Uncomfortable questions. Her hard-fought-for privacy would be invaded—her reputation open for all of Cheyenne to discuss. It shouldn't bother her, but it did. She knew what it was like to be the focus of unwanted attention, and she'd worked hard to stay out of the public eye ever since.

"I'm glad you acknowledge that our child is important. I happen to agree, which is why I'm not going to rush into anything or make any decisions today," she finally stated.

"You're important, too, Jenna," he answered softly.

For a second she felt a swelling in her chest—a glimmer of something ephemeral, an intangible dream emerging on the periphery of her thoughts. Then reality intruded. She shook her head.

"Don't lie to me, Dylan. We both know that since March neither of us has made any attempt to contact or see one another, until today. In fact, if you didn't have the restaurant opening coming up, we probably wouldn't even be here right now."

"I don't know about you, but I've thought about that evening a lot."

Jenna couldn't stop the warm tingling sensation that spread from the pit of her belly at his words.

"Don't!" she blurted.

"Don't what? Don't admit that we were blisteringly good together? Tell me you haven't thought about us, about what we did—and haven't wanted to try again. Even just to see if it wasn't some kind of weird fluke."

"I—"

Her throat closed up, blocked by a swell of need so fierce it overwhelmed her. She forced herself to erase the visual image that now burned in the back of her mind. An image he'd put there without so much as a speck of effort because it was always there, always waiting to be brought out into the light and examined, relived. She squirmed on her seat, suddenly uncomfortable, aching. For him. For more.

"Fine," she muttered curtly. "We were good together, but that's no basis for a future. We are two totally different people. Our lives barely intersect."

"That's not to say that they couldn't. Don't you want to just try it?"

He looked so earnest, sitting there opposite her at the table. It would be all too easy to give in, but she'd worked too hard for too damn long to even consider giving up her hard-won freedom, not to mention her hard-earned respect from the community.

She herself had been the product of a hurried marriage, one that hadn't worked on any level and had led to hardship and unhappiness for all concerned. She would not inflict that on her baby. No matter how enticing that baby's father was. No matter how much she wanted him.

What did he know of marriage, of commitment? Their own liaison was a perfect example of the impulsive life he led. See something? Want it? Have it, then just walk away without a backward glance. She couldn't risk that he'd do that with their child, let alone her. Not now, not ever.

"No," she said firmly. "I don't. Please don't push me on this issue, Dylan."

"Okay," he acceded.

She felt her shoulders relax.

"For today," he amended.

And the tension was right back again. He cracked a smile and she was struck again by his male beauty. There was not a thing about him, physically at least, that didn't set her body on fire. As to his morals, well, that was something else entirely. But her behavior didn't reflect so well on her, either, she reminded herself.

"Don't look so serious, Jenna. We'll declare a truce for this evening, all right?"

His voice was coaxing, warm. And almost her very undoing.

"Truce, then," she agreed, and applied herself again to her meal.

It truly was too good to ignore and, much as she hated to admit it, he was right that she should be eating better. Weariness had been quite an issue for her, and while prenatal vitamins and supplements were helping, nothing really substituted for a healthy diet and plenty of rest.

"More?" Dylan asked when her plate was empty.

"I'm stuffed," she said, leaning back in her chair with a smile on her face. "That was excellent, thank you."

"Just part of the package," he said with a smile. "So, are you too stuffed to think about dessert? Can I tempt you with some raspberry and white chocolate cheesecake?"

"Tempt me? Are you kidding? Of course I want dessert."

When he took the dish from the refrigerator she almost dissolved into a puddle of delight.

"You made that, too?" she asked as he sliced a piece for her. She reached out and nabbed a white chocolate curl from off the top, laughing as he went to slap her hand away and missed.

"Not me personally this time. It's one of the desserts

we're trialing for the steak house," he said, sliding her plate toward her. "I picked it up this afternoon."

She spooned up a taste and then another.

"Good?" Dylan asked.

"Divine. Don't talk to me, you're messing with my concentration."

He laughed aloud and the sound traveled straight to her heart and gave it a fierce tug. *Oh, yeah, it was all too easy to think you could fall in love with a man like Dylan Lassiter,* she told herself. He was the whole package. Not just tall, dark and handsome, but wealthy, entertaining to be with and bloody good in bed. Well, in a coat closet, anyway. And then there was the near orgasmic cooking.

Don't go there, she warned herself. But it was too late. Arousal spread through her like a wildfire. Licking and teasing at her until she felt her breasts grow full and achy, her nipples tightening and becoming almost unbearably sensitive against the sheer fabric of her bra. She knew the very second Dylan's line of vision moved, the precise moment he became aware of her reaction.

"Remind me to feed you cheesecake more often," he said, his voice slightly choked. "I'm going to make coffee. Can I offer you some, or a cup of something else, maybe?"

"Hot tea, please," Jenna answered, fighting to get her wayward hormones back under control.

Dylan stood and turned away from the table, but not before she noticed he wasn't exactly unaffected himself. So it seemed the crazy attraction between them showed no sign of abating. What on earth was she going to do about it?

Nothing. Abso-freaking-lutely nothing at all. They'd get through the rest of this evening. They might even discuss the baby a little more. But they were not going to do a single thing about this undeniable magnetism between them. After all, look where it had led them the last time.

Dylan ground fresh coffee beans and measured them into his coffeemaker, taking his time over the task. This was getting ridiculous. Why couldn't she see just how suited they were to one another? Why wouldn't anyone want to take that further? Her physical attraction to him was painstakingly obvious. Not that he needed any help in that department, but it was a natural trigger for his own.

There was a lot to be said for being a caveman, he thought as he switched on the electric kettle and heated the water for her tea. He'd never before felt so inclined to drag a woman by her hair into his lair and keep her there—making love to her until she no longer wanted to leave. He gave himself a mental shake. No, that image was completely unacceptable. He liked his women willing. He'd never used force or coercion before and he wouldn't start now—no matter how tempting Ms. Jenna Montgomery made the idea seem. Somehow, he had to make her see that they'd be good together. Good enough for marriage and raising a kid.

He heard the scrape of her spoon on the plate as she finished her cheesecake, and he returned to the table with their hot drinks on a tray.

"Shall we take these back through to the living room?" he suggested.

"Sure."

She got up to follow him and his eyes drifted again to her belly, to where his baby lay safely nestled. It roused something feral in him. Something he'd never experienced before today. Something he knew, deep in his heart, would never go away. He knew it was possible to love another person's child—knew it from firsthand experience, from *being* that child, from being loved. For some reason, though, knowing it was his son or daughter she carried made Dylan feel as if he could give a certain superhero a decent run for his money in the leaping tall buildings department.

He also knew he'd do anything, lay down his life if necessary, to provide the best for his kid.

Jenna returned to her seat on the sofa and Dylan sat next to her, a sense of satisfaction spreading inside when she didn't scoot away from him.

"When's the baby due?" he asked, after taking a sip of his coffee.

"First week in December, all going well."

"A baby by Christmas," he mused aloud, struck by how much his life could change in a year.

"Life will be different, that's for sure."

"So what have you planned so far?"

Suddenly he needed to know everything she'd already done, and what she wanted to do for the rest of her pregnancy. This should involve him.

"Well, I've started getting a few things for the spare room in my house, you know, to turn it into a nursery. I found a bassinet at a yard sale last weekend. I'm going to reline it and get a collapsible stand. That way I'll be able to use it in my office at the store as well as at home, until the baby gets a little bigger."

Dylan suppressed the shudder that threatened to run through him at the thought that his child would have secondhand anything. Did that make him a snob? Probably. He and his brother had shared things as they grew up, and there'd been nothing wrong with that. It didn't stop him from wanting to race out to the nearest store and buy all new equipment for his child, though.

Jenna, sensitive already, obviously picked up on his thoughts. "What's wrong? You think our baby is too good for a secondhand bassinet?"

"Actually," he started, thinking he needed to tread very carefully, "I was thinking more along the lines of what I could do to help out financially."

If she was scouring yard sales, maybe she was a bit stretched when it came to money. She had the store, but also had her own home. Financing both took a lot of hard work and determination. And dollars and cents.

"I can manage, you know," she said defensively.

"The point is you don't have to *manage*," he said. "I meant what I said when I told you I'm going to be a part of this baby's life, and I don't just mean the occasional visit. I'm happy to support you both."

She looked as if she was about to bristle and reject his words, but then she slumped a little, as though a load had been lifted from her slender shoulders.

"Thank you." She sighed softly. "It won't be necessary, but I do appreciate the offer."

"Hey," he said, taking one of her hands in his and mentally comparing how small and dainty it felt in his much larger palm. It roused a fierce sense of protection inside him. One he knew would be smacked straight into next week if he showed her even an inkling of how she made him feel. "We got into this together, and that's how it's going to stay."

She looked up at him, her dark eyes awash with moisture. "Do you think we can do that? Stay friends through this?"

"Of course we can."

"It's not going to be easy."

"Nothing worthwhile ever is," he commented.

At the same time he promised himself that no matter

what, she would not be doing this on her own. And one way or another, he'd get her to change her mind about marrying him. Now that he had her back in his life, he didn't want to let her go again. There was a damn fine reason why he hadn't been able to shake her image from his thoughts every single day. Now he had every incentive to find out exactly what that reason was.

Five

By the time Jenna rose to leave, weariness pulled at every muscle in her body. She was grateful tomorrow was Sunday. A blessed day of rest, with time to weigh up everything that had happened since Dylan Lassiter had walked back into her life. Maybe she'd get to work in the garden for a while, too—she always found that restful. Or even a lazy stroll around the Cheyenne Botanic Gardens might be nice.

"It's late," she said, stifling a yawn. "I'd better get home. Thank you for tonight. I mean that."

"You're welcome," Dylan replied, getting to his feet and putting his hand at the small of her back again.

Despite her exhaustion, her body responded instantly. It would be so easy to give in. To turn toward him, press her body against his large hard frame and sink into the attraction between them. To allow him back behind the barriers she'd erected when the reality of their encounter had hit home. Instead, she put one foot in front of the other and headed for the door.

"Are you okay to drive?" he asked, a small frown of concern causing parallel lines to form between his brows. "I don't mind dropping you home. I can always bring your car to you tomorrow."

"No, I'll be all right. Thank you."

"You know, independence is fine and all that, but accepting help every now and then is okay, too."

"I know, and when I need help, I'll ask for it," she answered firmly.

She could feel the heat rolling gently from his body, bringing with it the leather and spicy wood scent of his cologne. It made her want to do something crazy, like nibble on the hard line of his jaw, or bury her nose in the hollow at the base of his throat. Man, she really needed to get out of here before she acted on those irrational thoughts.

"Thanks again for tonight," she said.

"You're welcome. We still have plenty more to discuss. Okay if I get in touch?"

She hesitated, wishing she could say no, and knowing she needed to say yes. Given the way he tugged at her, emotionally and mentally, she knew it wasn't going to be easy sharing a baby with him. Jenna settled for a quick nod and all but fled down the stairs. But he was right at her side, so that when she got to her car it was his hand that opened the door for her. He leaned down once she was settled inside.

"Red fluffy dice?" he asked with a chuckle when he saw the things dangling from the rearview mirror of her ever-so-practical station wagon.

"I have dreams of owning a red convertible one day. *Had* dreams," she corrected.

With the baby on the way, that was one dream that would have to be shelved for a while. Maybe even forever.

"Classic or new?" Dylan persisted.

"Classic, of course."

He gave her a wink. "That's my girl."

She felt an almost ridiculous sense of pride in his obvious approval, and forced herself to quash it. It didn't matter whether he approved of her dreams or not. They weren't going to happen, not now. She was doing her best to hold everything else together. Luxury items were exactly that: luxury. An extravagance that was definitely not in her current budget.

"Well, good night," she said, staring pointedly at his hand on the door.

To her surprise he leaned down and reached for her chin, turning her head to face him, before capturing her lips in an all too short, entirely too sweet kiss.

"Good night. Drive safe," he instructed as he swung her door closed.

Her hands were shaking as she started the car and then placed them on the wheel. As she drove around the turning loop to head down the driveway, she sought refuge in anger. He'd done it on purpose, just to prove his point about compatibility. The thing was, she *knew* they were compatible sexually. Now they had to be compatible as parents. Seemed to her they'd definitely missed a few steps along the way, and now there was no going back.

His proposal of marriage was preposterous. She sneaked a glance in her rearview mirror at the two-story house, fully lit up from the outside and looking as unattainable as she knew a long-term relationship with a man like Dylan Lassiter was, too. Jenna forced her eyes forward, to focus on the road ahead, and her future. One where she'd have to fight to keep Dylan Lassiter on the periphery if she hoped to keep her sanity.

By the time she rolled her car into her garage and hit the remote to make the door close behind her, she felt no better. Seeing Dylan again had just put her well-ordered world into turmoil. She'd had enough chaos to last a lifetime. It was why, when she'd been placed with Margaret Connell after her father was jailed, she'd put her head down and worked her butt off to fit in and to do things right. Mrs. Connell's firm but steady presence had been a rock to a fifteen-year-old teetering on the rails of a very unsteady life.

Mrs. Connell had not only provided a home for her, she'd provided a compass—one Jenna could live by for the rest of her life. The woman had also provided a sense of accountability, paying Jenna a wage for the hours she spent cleaning up in the florist shop after school and learning how to put together basic bouquets for people who came in off the street and wanted something quick and simple.

By the time Jenna had finished high school, she'd known exactly what she wanted to do. She'd put herself through business school, spending every spare hour she wasn't studying working in the flower store, which she'd eventually bought and made her own. Mrs. Connell was now enjoying a well-earned retirement in Palm Springs, secure in the knowledge that all her hard work, both with Jenna and the business, hadn't been in vain.

Jenna calculated the time difference between here and Palm Springs. It probably still wasn't too late to call Mrs. Connell, and she so desperately needed the guidance of someone else right now. Someone older and wiser. Someone stronger than she was. But that would mean disclosing how she'd gotten herself into this situation. Telling someone else about behavior that she wasn't terribly proud of. The last thing Jenna wanted to hear in her mentor's voice was disappointment.

She climbed out of her car, went inside the house and got ready for bed. For all that Dylan had said about wanting to be a part of everything, she'd never felt so alone in her life, nor so confused.

Would he be so keen, she wondered, if he knew exactly who she was and what her life had been like? It was hardly the stuff of Disney movies. Her father had come home from work one day when she was nine, to find Jenna alone after school—her mother having abandoned them to sail, from New Zealand and her family, with the outgoing tide and pursue her dream of being a singer on a cruise ship. He'd pulled up stakes by the time Jenna was ten, and taken her to his native U.S.A., where he'd told her again and again that they'd strike it lucky any time, and that happily-ever-after was just around the corner for them both.

Unfortunately, his idea of luck had been inextricably linked to fleecing older, vulnerable women of their wealth, and using his looks and charm to get away with it. Until one day he'd gone a step too far.

Jenna pushed the memory to the back of her mind, where it belonged. She'd learned the hard way what it meant to be an unwitting public figure, and how cruel the media could be. Given the Lassiter family profile, any relationship between her and Dylan would be bound to garner attention—attention she didn't want or need. For her own sake, and that of her unborn baby, she would do whatever it took to keep a low profile.

She slid between the 800-thread-count bed linens she'd happily picked up in a clearance sale, and smoothed her feet and legs over the silky soft surface. She might not be in his league financially, but she didn't do so badly. She could provide for her baby, who certainly wouldn't want for anything. So what if some of their possessions were a little care-worn or threadbare or—Jenna grimaced in the dark, remembering Dylan's reaction—secondhand. She would manage, and her private life would remain that way: private.

* * *

Dylan whistled cheerfully as he drove away from the classic car dealer, relishing the sensation of the wind ruffling his hair. The thrum of the V8 engine under the shiny red hood before him set up an answering beat in his blood. Today was a perfect day for a picnic and he had just the partner in mind to share it.

After swinging by the Grill to make sure everything was running smoothly, he put together some food and drink, checked the GPS on his phone and headed toward Jenna's address, which he'd happily plucked from a phone book. He was curious to see where she lived— where she'd planned to raise their baby. *Planned* being in the past tense, because now that he was on the scene, he didn't intend for them to live apart. All he needed to do was convince Jenna.

When he turned into her driveway he had to admit he was surprised at where she lived: it was a new neighborhood, the streets lined with modern homes. Skateboards, bikes and balls littered the front yards. He could see why she'd be comfortable here. Even though he hadn't seen anyone yet, there was a sense of community and projected longevity about the area.

He saw curtains in windows on either side of her house twitch as he turned off the ignition and sat a moment in the car. A smile played at his lips. Neighborhood watch, no doubt. It was good to know Jenna had people looking out for her when he wouldn't be.

Dylan got out of the car. He couldn't wait to see her face. He strode up the path that led to the front door and pressed the doorbell. Nothing. He waited a minute and tried again.

"You looking for someone?" A woman's voice came

from over the well-trimmed hedge on one side of Jenna's property.

"Yes, ma'am," he answered with a smile that wiped the distrustful look off her face in an instant. "Is Jenna home?"

The woman blushed prettily. "She's gardening out back. Just follow the path around the side of the house and you'll find her."

"Thank you."

Clearly, he'd passed muster. He jangled the car keys in his hand as he made his way around to the rear of the house. It only took a minute to find her. She knelt by a raised bed of roses, pulling vigorously at the weeds and dumping them in a bucket beside her.

"That looks suspiciously like hard work. Need a break?"

Jenna jumped at his voice and looked up, using the back of her hand to push a few loose strands of hair from her eyes.

"No, thank you. This job isn't going to do itself."

"Why don't you get someone else in to help?"

"Because first, I don't have money to throw around like that, and second, I enjoy it."

His eyes swept across her face, taking in the smear of dirt on her flushed cheek and the dark shadows that were painted beneath her eyes.

"If you tell me what to do, will you let me help for a while so I can take you out to play after we're done?"

She looked startled for a minute. "Seriously?"

"Yeah, of course I'm serious."

She pursed her lips a second, making him wish he could taste them again. Last night's chaste kiss had done nothing but ignite a desire for more.

"You don't really want to garden, do you."

It was a statement, not a question. He shrugged. "I'd be lying if I said I did. But I'll do what's necessary to achieve my objective."

Jenna narrowed her eyes. "And your objective is...?"

"Taking you out to lunch."

"I'm not dressed for lunch."

"That's okay, I prepared a picnic."

A wistful expression replaced the wariness in her eyes. "A picnic? I've never been on one of those."

He couldn't hide his shock. "Never?"

She shook her head.

"Then let me be the one to remedy that for you." He stepped closer and took her hand in his, stripping off her gardening glove before doing the same with the other hand. "The weeds will still be here when we get back."

"Unfortunately."

"Then worry about them later. Come with me," he coaxed. "Now."

For a second she chewed at her lower lip, her gaze fixed on her hand still held in his.

"Shouldn't you be at work? The grand opening's not all that far away now, is it?"

"No, it's not. I've already been by the Grill today. Everything's under control. Besides, I'm the boss—when I say I need a bit of time out, I take it. So, are you coming?"

"Okay. But let me freshen up first."

"No problem. I'll meet you out front."

As much as he was itching to step inside her small home, to see what things she'd chosen to surround herself with, he sensed he'd pushed enough for one day. That she'd agreed to come out on the picnic with him was a coup in itself, and he'd take that victory before reaching for the next one.

"Give me ten minutes, then," she said, already walking toward the screened back door.

"No problem. Take all the time you need."

The door slammed behind her and he took a moment to look around the garden. Here and there were splashes of color, interspersed among some midsize trees. It was a good backyard, as backyards went. But it wasn't where his kid would grow up playing. Kids needed space—and he'd be providing it. Eventually.

Inside Jenna quickly changed from her tattered and dirty gardening gear into a T-shirt and jeans. To her surprise, she couldn't fasten the top button on her jeans, which was something she'd been able to manage, barely, last week. That was one thing pregnancy definitely guaranteed—change, and plenty of it.

She washed her face and smoothed on some tinted moisturizer. It would probably be too much to apply her usual makeup, but she wasn't going out with Dylan without feeling at least a little in control. She attempted a quick brush of her hair, but it was impossible to smooth the tangles that a sleepless night had wrought, so instead she carelessly swept it up and secured it with a few pins, then tied a scarf around her head.

Surveying the results in the mirror, she allowed herself a grin of approval. Her T-shirt was long and loose-fitting, her bra made of sturdier material than last night's. She'd be fine.

It took only a few seconds to lock up and head out the front door, but the instant her feet hit the porch she came to an abrupt halt. There, in her driveway, sat the car that had featured in all her fantasies. It was as if Dylan had reached into her mind and extracted the information himself, she thought, as she surveyed the fire-engine-red Cadillac convertible with whitewall tires and the top down. It was her dream car—right down to the red fluffy dice, twins to her own, hanging in front.

Dylan straightened from where he leaned against the passenger door, and flashed her a smile.

"You like it?"

Jenna forced herself to walk toward him, still locked in a state of disbelief.

"I love it. What...? How...?" She shook her head. "Did you hire it for the day or something?"

"No," he said. "After you mentioned it last night I thought I'd look around online. I saw it this morning and bought it."

"You *bought* it? Just like that?"

He lifted the keys and dangled them in front of her face. "You want to drive?"

"Do I!" She snatched the set from his hand and tossed her bag in the back before racing around to the driver's side. She threw herself into the seat and ran her hands over the steering wheel and the dash. "I can't believe it. You really bought this today?"

Dylan seated himself next to her with another one of those smiles that made her insides melt. "Sure did. Shall we give her a run? I was thinking we could head out to the Crystal Lake Reservoir, find a nice spot and have our picnic."

It was at least a forty-minute drive to get there. She'd love every second of it.

"Let's get going then," she said, smiling back at him.

He stared at her, the smile on his face changing, his expression becoming more serious. He lifted a hand and touched her cheek with one finger.

"You're so beautiful, you know that?"

Jenna didn't know what to say. Her stomach clenched

in reaction to his touch, to his softly spoken words. She wanted to refute it, but at the same time wanted to hold those words in a safe place in the corner of her heart, forever.

Dylan let his hand drop, breaking the spell. "C'mon," he said, "let's get this show on the road."

The engine's powerful roar when it turned over sent a shiver of happiness up her spine.

"I still can't believe you bought this," she said as she backed out the drive and onto the street. "That's just so impulsive."

"Why shouldn't I?" He shrugged. "I bought it for you."

Six

Dylan watched as her expression turned from one of sheer glee to one of horror. She jammed on the brakes, throwing him slightly forward.

"Whoa, there. Easy on the brakes, sweetheart."

"Tell me you didn't do that."

"Didn't do what?"

"Buy me this car."

"If I did, I'd be lying."

"I can't accept it." She shook her head vehemently. "That's just crazy."

"It is what it is."

But he was walking on thin air. She was out of the car—leaving the engine still running, the driver's door open—and standing on the sidewalk, her arms wrapped around herself in protection as if warding off some terrible pain.

Dylan shot out of the car and closed in on her, but she put up her hands, halting him in his tracks. What had he done? He could see her shaking from here.

"What is it? What's wrong?"

"You're trying to buy me, aren't you?" Her voice quavered and her face was pale. "Trying to make me do what you want."

"Jenna, the car's a gift."

"Some bloody gift!" she snapped, her eyes now burning as she looked at him squarely. "I know what a car like that is worth. You don't just buy one in the morning and give it away by the afternoon."

"Jenna, I'm hardly a poor man. I want to see you have nice things."

"Why?"

He was confused. *"Why?"*

"Yes, why? Why me? Why now? As I said last night, we hardly know each other. We had sex *once*. We're having a baby. That's it. That's all there is to us, and now you're buying me a Cadillac?"

"Maybe I'm buying it just because I can. Maybe I need to prove to you that I can provide for you, that you don't need to do all this on your own, that you don't need to keep pushing me away. Yes, we're having a baby—*together*. I know we're doing this all back to front, but I want to get to know the mother of my kid. I want to see if we can be a couple."

Jenna's eyes flicked away from his, but not before he saw the sheen of tears reflected there. Before he could close the distance between them, the first drop spilled off a lash and tracked down her cheek. She lifted a hand and furiously scrubbed it, and those that followed, away.

"I don't want the car," she said adamantly, through clenched teeth. "I will not be bought."

"Fine. I'll take it back tomorrow. But can't we just enjoy today? Take it for a spin. Enjoy it while we can?"

He tentatively put his arms around her, pulling her closer. She lifted her chin and blinked away the moisture in her eyes. She was one tough chick, that was for sure.

"Just for today?" she asked, her voice tight.

"Sure, if that's what you want."

"So it's not mine anymore?"

"Nope."

He felt a pang of regret that he'd have to say goodbye to the big red beast, but if that's what it took to begin to win her trust, then that's what he'd do. Jenna looked past him at the car and he could see the longing in her gaze. Even though she wanted it, she would still refuse it. Her moral ground remained solid, even in the face of a desire so hungry she was almost salivating with it.

"Jen?" he said, noticing that he wasn't the only one with eyes on her right now. In fact, not only were curtains twitching, but there were faces appearing at windows, too.

"What?"

"I don't want to rush you, but shall we go? We're providing a bit of a show here."

"Oh, God," she groaned. Her lips firmed and she drew in a breath. "Fine, let's go then. But you can drive."

He didn't argue. Instead he guided her around to the passenger side of the car and helped her into her seat before closing the door and heading to the driver's side.

"You okay?" he said, reaching across the car to squeeze her hand.

"I'm fine. Just go, will you?"

"Whatever the lady wants."

The trip to the reservoir was accomplished in silence. Dylan kept throwing surreptitious looks at Jenna during the journey and was relieved to note the tension in her body had begun to ease as they headed out of Cheyenne. As they wound along the route that led to the reservoir he kept an eye out for a place with a vantage point overlooking the lake. He gave a grunt of satisfaction when he found just the spot, and brought the car to a stop beneath some trees.

Through a gap between the trunks, the lake gleamed like highly polished mirrored glass, reflecting the surrounding rock formations and flora in a perfect echo of their surroundings.

Dylan got out of the car and opened the trunk, unloading a large rubber-backed blanket and a picnic hamper. He passed the blanket to Jenna.

"Here, find us a spot. I'll bring the food and drinks."

She took it without a word and headed a little closer to the water. When he joined her she'd spread it out in a sunny spot in a small clearing.

"I...I'm sorry. For before," she said in a stilted tone. "I'm sure my reaction probably appeared over the top to you."

"A little, but that's okay. No apology needed."

"No," she said vehemently. "You were trying to be nice and I threw it back at you. I just..."

She averted her gaze out over the water, as if searching for something to draw strength from to help her get her words out. Dylan waited quietly, watching the internal battle reflected on her face.

"I just don't like it when people think they can buy someone else with things, or when other people accept them."

Dylan scratched his jaw as he played her words over in his mind. Sounded as if there was a story behind that statement. Would he ever hear it from her? He hoped so.

"Fair comment," he answered, putting the hamper and the small drinks cooler down at the edge of the blanket. "And duly noted for future reference."

"You're mad at me, aren't you?"

"Not mad. Disappointed, maybe, that you don't feel you can accept the car from me, but hey, I'm a big boy now. I'll get over it."

And, he added silently, *I'll find a way through that wall of yours, one day.*

He opened the cooler and handed Jenna a bottle of mineral water before snagging one for himself.

"Italian?" she asked, looking at the label. "Is there anything you do normally?"

"Define *normally.*"

She chewed on her lower lip a moment before speaking. "Well, inexpensively, then."

"Why should I?"

"Because one day you might wish you had, for one. What if the bottom drops out of steak houses and the Lassiter Grill Corporation goes down with it?"

Dylan shook his head, a smile playing around his mouth. "It'll never happen. People like food, especially good food. Plus, they're more conscious these days of how their food is raised. The cattle on the Big Blue are free range and grass fed. Only nature's goodness. The beef served in the Grills is the best in the country, probably the world, and I ensure our staff and our dishes live up to that promise."

"You're very confident."

He paused a moment, thinking about it. "Yeah, I guess so. I haven't always been this way. Being raised by J.D. made a big difference, though. It took a while, but we got there."

"You lost your parents quite young, didn't you?"

"Sage was six and I was four. I don't remember too much about them, but Sage—" Dylan sighed "—he took it real hard. Kind of put himself in opposition to anything J.D. said or suggested from day one."

"I always wished I had a brother or sister," Jenna said wistfully, taking a sip of her water.

He found his gaze caught by her actions, riveted by the movement of her slender throat as she swallowed.

"Only child?"

"Only and lonely," she said lightly, but even so, he heard the truth behind her words.

"Where did you grow up?"

"All over. I was born in New Zealand and grew up there before my mom and dad broke up."

"New Zealand, huh? I thought you had a bit of an accent."

"Hardly," she snorted. "When we heard my mom had died, Dad packed us up and brought us back here to the States. Any accent soon got teased out of me at school."

"Back to the States?"

"My father's American. We traveled a bit and eventually I got to settle here in Cheyenne. The rest, as they say, is history."

Painful history by the sound of things. What she didn't say spoke louder than what she did. Dylan turned to the hamper in a bid to break the somber mood that had settled over them. He reached past the cooling pads he'd packed around the food and lifted out a couple covered containers. He popped the lids off, revealing in one, sandwiches made with freshly baked whole grain bread, and in the other, a selection of sliced fruit.

"I can promise you I prepared these myself and that I carefully studied what you can and can't eat in pregnancy," he said, putting the dishes down between them on the blanket.

Jenna picked up a sandwich and studied the filling. "You mean you washed and dried the lettuce in here yourself?"

"With my own fair hands," he assured her with a grin. "But don't tell any of my kitchen staff that or they'll expect me to do everything myself."

They ate in companionable silence and Dylan quietly cleared up when they were done.

"Tell me why you've never been on a picnic before," he suggested, interrupting her contemplation of the lake's beauty.

She remained silent for a while, and so still he began to wonder if she'd even heard him.

"I guess I just never had the opportunity before," she eventually said, but he could tell she was leaving plenty out of that trite little answer. "It's nice, though. Thank you."

He'd have to be satisfied with that, he told himself, and filled in the gap in conversation that followed with his own tales of the times he and Sage had raided their aunt's kitchen to take a picnic outdoors. He loved it when he made Jenna laugh. It lifted the shadows from her eyes and showed a different side to her than the one that constantly met him head-on and tried to thwart his every attempt to spoil her.

It wasn't much later that Jenna lay down in the sunshine and closed her eyes. She was asleep in seconds. The day's temperature was still pretty mild, but the wind had a bite in it, so Dylan got his sweater from the trunk of the car and gently put it over her as she slept.

He stretched out beside her, wishing they had the kind of relationship where he could pull her into his arms, curl around her body and keep her warm with his heat alone.

All in good time, he assured himself. All in good time.

Jenna woke with a shiver as a shadow passed over the sun. She opened her eyes to see a cloud sailing overhead. She realized that she had something covering her and lifted it to see what it was. Dylan's sweater? When had he done that? A warm sensation filled her at his consideration.

For a minute or two she just lay there, absorbing the

sounds of the insects and birds, and relishing the peaceful surroundings, before she became aware of a deep steady breathing that came from close by. She turned her head and saw Dylan lying on his back beside her. Well, that answered one question, she thought. He didn't snore. His arms were bent up under his head and even in sleep the latent strength of his biceps were obvious. She observed the steady rise and fall of his chest. His T-shirt had risen above the waistband of his jeans, exposing just a hint of his lower belly.

At the sight of his bare flesh a tingle washed through her, and her fingertips itched to reach out—to touch and trace that line of flesh with the faint smattering of dark hair. She didn't dare give in to the temptation, though. Things were already incendiary between them. They didn't need any further complications and right now, to her, a relationship with Dylan was a complication she'd rather avoid.

She looked past him to the Caddy, sitting in all its shiny glory under the trees.

What kind of man did that? she asked herself. Who on earth bought a classic car on a whim for someone he barely knew from Adam, just because she said it was a dream of hers? The thought triggered a memory of the day her dad had come to pick her up from junior high. They were living in Seattle at the time and he'd rolled up in a brand-new 5-series BMW, looking like a cat that got the cream.

Soon after, she'd met the reason behind the car. His latest conquest had bought it for him when he'd admired it one day as they'd passed a dealership. It was payment, he'd said flippantly, for services rendered. Jenna hadn't fully understood, at the time, just what he'd meant by that. Just as she'd never understood, until she got older, why all the women he dated had at least ten, sometimes more, years on him. Or why he was always turning up with expensive things. Even back then it had made her uncomfortable. It hadn't seemed right, especially when her dad never appeared to hold down a real job. But her father had just laughed off her concerns when she got brave enough to broach them.

He'd never stayed with anyone for long. All of a sudden she'd wake one morning and they'd be on the move again. Sometimes clear across the country in pursuit of his next happily-ever-after. She'd had no idea that even while he was dating one woman, he was casually grooming up to five others via the internet. Nor did she know that when they'd moved to Laramie when she was fifteen, and she'd shaved her head as part of a school-run fund-raiser for one of their cancer-stricken teachers, that her father would use that picture to create a whole new set of lies to fleece his victims with.

Lies that eventually saw him hauled off to jail for fraud and caused her to be placed here in Cheyenne with Margaret Connell. Jenna squeezed her eyes shut. She didn't want to think about that time—about the gross invasion of her life by the media, the reporters who'd accused her of being complicit in her father's schemes. She'd been just a kid, with nowhere and no one else to turn to. When child services had taken her, she'd wondered if she was going to end up in prison, too. After all, she had no one else. Her mother was dead. They'd learned she'd died less than a year after she'd left them, choking on her meal aboard ship. And there'd been no other family to come in and pick up Jenna's fractured life.

Mrs. Connell had been a much-needed anchor and a comfort. For the first time in her life Jenna had been able to stay in one place for more than what felt like five minutes. It hadn't broken her reticence about making friends, though. Even now she found it a struggle to get close to anyone. She'd learned growing up that it was better that way, better than having to say heart-wrenching goodbyes every time her life turned topsy-turvy again.

She studied Dylan's strong features. Even in sleep he looked capable, secure in his world. What would it be like to take a chance on him? To just go with the flow and let him take control of her and the baby's worlds?

Even as she considered it, the idea soured in her mind. And what about when he lost interest and moved on? she asked herself. As her father had moved on so many times? As Dylan himself had moved on from various publicly touted relationships in his life? She wouldn't do that to her child, or to herself. They were both worth so much more than that.

Self-worth. It was a hard lesson to learn, but it was one Margaret Connell had reinforced every day Jenna had lived under her roof. It was why Jenna could never accept anything that was a facsimile of a real life, or a real love. She'd been there already and she still bore those scars. Probably always would.

Dylan's eyes flicked open and he turned his head to look at her. "Nice sleep?" he asked with a teasing smile.

"Mmm, it was lovely. Thank you for this. It was a great idea."

"Even though we had to do it in that?" He nodded over toward the Cadillac.

"Yes." She heaved a mock long-suffering sigh. "Even though we had to do it in that."

He rolled onto his side, facing her. "You certain you don't want it? You're allowed to change your mind, y'know."

"No, thank you. I don't want it. Besides, there's no anchor point for an approved child restraint," she said soberly, reminded anew of how much her life, her dreams, would change in a few short months' time.

"Good point. Maybe I'll keep it for date nights."

Jenna felt her entire body revolt at the statement. Here she was contemplating approved child restraints for *their* baby, and he was busily planning his next night out with some woman.

"*Our* date nights," he specified with a wicked grin that told her he knew exactly what she'd been thinking.

"We won't be having any of those," she said in an attempt to suppress his humor, especially since it was humor at her expense.

"I think it would be good for our kid to see our common interests don't just revolve around him or her. I've seen too many couples lose sight of what they feel for one another when they're crazy busy with their kids and with work. They lose themselves, and worse, they lose each other."

His words, spoken so simply, ignited a yearning inside her that made her heart ache. He made it sound so simple. But she knew to the soles of her feet that life just wasn't like that.

"You're forgetting one thing," she murmured. "We aren't a couple."

He leaned a little closer. "We could be."

And with that, he inched a tiny bit nearer and closed his lips on hers.

Seven

The second their lips touched, Dylan knew it was a mistake. If only because they were in a public place and there was no way he could take this all the way. Not here, not right now—even though his body demanded he do so. He should have waited until they were behind closed doors. Someplace where they could relish their privacy and take the time to explore one another fully. Enjoy one another without fear of discovery.

It didn't mean he couldn't make the most of the moment, though, and he slid his hand under Jenna's head, cradling her gently as he sipped at the nectar of her mouth. Her lips were soft and warm, pliant beneath his. A rush of need burst through what was left of his brain, urging him to coax, to plunder, to take this so much further than a kiss. But he held back.

He wanted her, there was no denying it. But he was prepared to take this slowly—as painful as that would be—if that was what he had to do to convince her he was serious.

Jenna's hands lifted up to bracket his face, and he took that as permission to use his mouth to tease her some more—to open her up and taste her, their tongues meshing, their teeth bumping. How he wished he could see all of her, and touch and taste every inch.

She was pregnant with his child and he'd never seen her naked. Just the idea of it made his nerves burn with raging heat, and urged him to go further. But still he held back, eventually forcing himself to ease away, to create at least a hand span of distance between them. It wasn't enough. There could be an entire continent between them and it wouldn't deaden how he felt about her. How much he wanted her.

"Think about it," he said, rolling away and standing up.

"Think about what?" she asked, looking up at him with a dazed expression in her eyes.

He fought back a smile. Maybe that's all he'd have to do to convince her they should get married. Kiss her senseless until she simply said yes.

He offered her a hand and helped her to her feet, then picked up and folded the blanket, slinging it over one arm. "Us. Together. You know—a couple."

She started to shake her head, but he reached up and gently took her chin between his fingers.

"Think about it, Jenna. At least give me a chance to prove to you how good we could be together. Not just as lovers, although I know that will take us off the Richter scale—again. But as a couple." His hand dropped to the slight mound of her belly. "As a family."

Before she could respond, he grabbed the cooler and turned and walked to the car. He didn't want to see rejection in her eyes. Not when he'd realized, even as he spoke, just how much he wanted this. He'd lost his parents when he was only four, Aunt Ellie—his adoptive mother—only three years after that. He was luckier than most. He'd had four parents in his lifetime, five when he counted Marlene as well, and each one had left an imprint of devotion. An imprint so indelible it had made him promise himself that, when he eventually had a family, he would be a part of his children's lives. They would know the security of parents who loved them unreservedly. He'd had that, and he would walk over flaming gas ranges if necessary, to make sure his kid had it, too.

Jenna appeared beside him, handing him the now empty hamper as he stowed the cooler and blanket in the trunk.

"Will you at least consider it?" he asked, closing the trunk with a solid thud.

She looked up at him, vulnerability reflecting starkly at him from those dark brown eyes of hers. "Okay."

One small word and yet it had the power to change everything about the life he lived, about the choices he'd made. It should be daunting and yet it made him feel excited on a level he hadn't anticipated. Made him almost feel a sense of relief that he could, maybe, stop searching for that one ephemeral thing that he'd always felt was missing from a life rich in so much already. The thing he'd sought in travel and women and had yet to find. He shoved his hands in his jeans pockets to hold himself back, to stop himself from giving in to the impulse to grab her and twirl her around with a whoop of satisfaction.

"Thank you."

The drive back to her home was completed in silence but it was a comfortable one. With one hand on the wheel, he'd reached across and tangled his fingers in hers for most of the journey. It wasn't something he'd ever stopped to consider before with anyone else but, right now, he felt as if the connection between Jenna and him had solidified just that bit more. And it felt strangely right. By the time he dropped her off and saw her into her house he was already formulating plans for tomorrow. Plans that most definitely featured Jenna Montgomery.

Monday morning, the smell of fresh paint and new carpet filled Dylan's nose the moment he strode in through the front door to check on progress at the restaurant and was pleased to see the delivery of the new furniture was well under way. He stopped a second to inhale the newness, the potential that awaited. The excitement that had thrummed quietly inside of him built to new levels. It was happening. He'd felt excited about each of the previous three Lassiter Grills to date but this one was even more special to him than the others.

Hard on the heels of his excitement came a thrust of regret that J.D. couldn't be here to see their dreams become a reality. It was still hard to accept that his larger-than-life, hard-as-nails father figure was really gone. At moments like this, it was that much worse.

God, but he missed that man. And as much as he grieved for J.D. with a still-raw ache, he owed it to the old man to make sure that everything about this new restaurant would match, if not eclipse, their existing venues. That meant keeping up his hands-on approach to business and proving that J.D.'s faith in making him CEO of the Lassiter Grill Corporation was well founded.

With a nod of approval, he walked past the massive polished wood bar to the double doors that led into the kitchen. As much as he loved the front of the restaurant, this was the hub of what made the Lassiter Grills great. This was where he belonged, amongst the stainless steel countertops and the sizzle and steam and noisy organized chaos of cooking. The last of the equipment had been installed a week ago and his team had spent the past week trialing the signature dishes that would be specific to the Cheyenne steak house, along with the much loved menu that made the Lassiter Grills so popular in L.A., Las Vegas and Chicago.

It was ironic, Dylan thought as he surveyed the hand-picked team, that he'd spent the better part of his adult years running away from responsibility and family commitment and yet in the past five years he'd embraced every aspect of both of those things. Clearly, he was ready to settle down.

The very idea would have sent a chill through him not so long ago but over the past few months, well, it had tickled at the back of his mind over and over again. Maybe it was losing J.D. so suddenly that had made him begin to question his own mortality and his own expectations of life. Or maybe he was finally, at the age of thirty-five, mature enough to accept there was more to life than the hedonistic whirlwind that had been his world to date. It was a sobering thought.

Satisfied that his staff had it all under control, he drove over to Jenna's store. He pushed the door open and stepped in, his nostrils flaring at the totally different scents in the air, compared to those back at the Grill. As before, there was no one in the front of the store, but he could hear off-key humming coming from out back. The humming came closer and he saw Jenna walking through, carrying an armload of bright fresh daisies. She'd pulled her hair into a ponytail today, lifting it high off her face and exposing her cheekbones and the perfectly shaped shells of her ears. He imagined taking one of those sweet lobes between his teeth and his body stirred in instant response.

"Oh, I didn't hear you come in," she said, placing the flowers on the main counter.

"No problem. I haven't been waiting long."

He studied her carefully. She looked tired, a little pale.

As if she'd had about as much trouble getting to sleep last night as he had. He couldn't help himself; he lifted a hand and skimmed the back of his fingers across her cheek.

"You okay? You're not overdoing things, are you?"

She pulled away from his touch. "I'm fine, Dylan. Trust me, I won't do anything to harm this baby. I may not have planned for it, but now that it's a reality, there's nothing I want more in my life."

There was a fierce undertone to her voice that convinced him she was telling the truth. It didn't stop him worrying, especially when she bent to shift a large container filled with water to another spot on the floor.

"Here," he said, brushing her aside. "Let me do that for you. I thought you had staff to help you."

Jenna stood back, a quizzical expression on her face. "I do, but they're part-time. I open and close the store each day."

"Then let me do the heavy stuff today."

"No problem, but I'll be back to doing it again tomorrow. Unless you plan on being here for me every morning to help me rearrange everything in the store?

"If that's what it takes," he said as he straightened. "Or I could arrange that you had someone here first and last thing to do this if you'd rather."

She shook her head, a rueful smile pulling at those kissable lips of hers. "I'd prefer to do it myself."

"Hey, can you blame me for wanting to take care of you? You're carrying precious cargo there."

A wistful expression settled on her face. "Yeah, I am, aren't I? But I still have a job to do. Now, I guess you're here to see what I've worked out for the flowers for the opening? I've sketched a few ideas and also thought I'd put something together quickly with what I had out back."

She grabbed a square of burlap and some twine, and

wrapped them around a plastic-lined cardboard base. She then moved around the store, selecting stems of greenery and laying them on the counter next to the daisies. Before his eyes, she used the assortment of items to create a vision of beauty.

"Hmm, needs some berries, too, I think," she muttered, more to herself than anything. A second or two later she turned the arrangement around to face him. "There, what do you think?"

He eyed the compilation of color and texture and decided he liked it very much. She had a genuine talent for this. There was nothing generic about what she'd created. She'd taken his minimal instructions and put together what he'd wanted without his fully understanding it himself.

"That's great. So these would be for the tables?"

She nodded. "And then I'd do something bigger, maybe in a crate propped on some hay bales, in the foyer. What do you think?"

"I think you're an artist."

She gave a little shrug. "I have a knack, I guess."

"Don't sell yourself short, Jenna." Dylan cast his eye over the arrangement again. "I'm thinking, though, that the colors need to be bolder. These might disappear in the decor. Why don't you come back with me to the restaurant for lunch? You can get a better feel of what I mean."

"You're going to feed me again? Three times in three days? This is getting to be a habit."

"We need live subjects to try the menu, and some of our waitstaff need the experience, too," he explained, even though it was more a case of now that he'd seen her again, he didn't want to let her out of his sight. "You'd be doing me a favor."

He didn't fool her for a second, that much was obvious

from the smile that spread across her face. "A favor, huh? Well, since one of my workers is due in shortly, I think I'd be able to slip away for an hour for lunch."

"Just an hour?"

"I do have a business to run. Besides, won't it be better for your team to get used to working with customers who are in a hurry?"

"Good point," he acceded, even though he wished he could just whisk her away for the afternoon and keep her to himself.

"I'll come at one, okay? I have some orders I need to put together for our delivery guy and—" she glanced at her wristwatch "—I need to get to work on them now if they're to be ready on time."

"That's great. I'll be waiting."

Jenna watched him leave, surprised at herself for agreeing to lunch today. Despite all her tossing and turning last night, and her resolve to try and keep things purely business between them, it appeared she wanted to see him again more than she'd realized. True, this visit was under the guise of checking the decor of the restaurant, but the prospect of spending more time with him, even if only an hour, made her bubble inside, as if the blood in her veins was carbonated.

Valerie, her assistant, came in through the front door.

"Wow, tell me the guy just leaving wasn't an apparition."

"Oh, no." Jenna smiled. "He's quite real."

"Just my luck to be running late today, or I could've served him."

Jenna looked at her long-married friend, a mother of four, and raised a brow. "Seriously?"

"Well, a girl's entitled to her dreams, isn't she? He

looks vaguely familiar. What did he want? Please tell me he wasn't ordering flowers for his girlfriend."

"That was Dylan Lassiter," Jenna said with a laugh, "and he's ordering flowers, through us, for the latest Lassiter Grill opening."

"He is? Wow, that's got to be good for business. You think they'll keep us as a regular florist? It'd be a fabulous lift for our profile."

"I haven't discussed future work with him, but we have a good start. Which reminds me, if I don't get my work out of the way this morning, I won't be able to make it to the restaurant for our next meeting at one."

"I could always go for you," Valerie suggested with a wink.

"I'm sure you could," Jenna said, still laughing, and imagining Dylan's face if she took Valerie up on her offer. But an unexpected surge of possessiveness filled her. She didn't want anyone handling Dylan's requests but herself. Dragging her thoughts together, she briskly continued, "C'mon, help me with these orders before Bill gets here for pickup."

The balance of the morning flew by. While she worked, Jenna considered the ramifications of having a regular corporate account with the Lassiter Grill. The exposure for her business would be great, there was no denying it. She made a mental note to raise the subject with Dylan, and went to get ready for their lunch date.

She was running late by the time she arrived at the restaurant but luckily found a parking space just around the corner.

Dylan was waiting by the front door as she jogged up the sidewalk.

"I was beginning to think you'd stood me up," he said, opening the door for her and guiding her inside.

"Just a busy morning, that's all."

"We have company for lunch. My brother, Sage, is joining us, together with his fiancée, Colleen."

Jenna immediately felt at a disadvantage. "Oh, I wish you'd said so. I'm not dressed for company."

Dylan turned his gaze to her and she felt him assess her from top to toe. "You look mighty fine from where I'm standing."

Heat bloomed in her chest and flooded all the way up to her cheeks. Great, now she'd look like a little red fire engine when introduced to his family.

"I mean it, Dylan," she said awkwardly.

"So do I. Seriously, you have nothing to worry about. They're my family and they'll love you any way you're dressed."

He grabbed her hand and led her inside. Her eyes darted around the dining room, taking in the design features that were such an integral part of the pictures she'd seen of each Lassiter Grill. While the building had a stone exterior, the interior walls were log lined. Her eyes roamed over the high ceilings, hung with massive iron fans, and down to the wooden plank floors. A huge floor-to-ceiling stone fireplace held a place of dominance in the center of the restaurant. What they'd sacrificed in space they'd more than made up in character. She loved the ranch-style atmosphere. It was realistic without being over the top. An idea popped into her head.

"I've been thinking about the opening and about how you'll dress the tables for the night," she began.

"Uh-huh?"

"What do you think of burlap table runners on white linen?"

He paused a moment, considering. "That sounds like a good idea. D'you have pictures of what you're thinking?"

She nodded.

"Good, we can talk about them after lunch. C'mon over and meet my brother."

Her nerves assailed her and she tugged at Dylan's hand, making him stop and turn to face her.

"Do they know?"

"Know?"

"About us, about the baby."

"Not yet. Do you want to tell them?"

She shook her head vehemently. It was enough that Dylan knew, but she wasn't ready to share the news with others.

"Okay, but they're going to find out sooner or later," he warned.

"Just not yet, okay?"

They crossed to the table where the couple were seated. Sage rose to his feet as they approached. Slightly taller than his brother, with medium brown hair sprinkled with a touch of gray at the temples, he looked like a man used to being in control. He also didn't seem like the type you could hide anything from for long, and the way his gaze dropped to her hand clasped in Dylan's larger one, and then back to his brother's face, told her he saw a great deal more than what lay on the surface. She pulled free of Dylan's grip as a frisson of unease wended its way down her spine. She so wasn't ready for this.

"Jenna, this is my brother, Sage, and his fiancée, Colleen. Sage, Colleen, this is Jenna Montgomery."

"Pleased to meet you," Jenna said, taking the bull by the horns and stepping forward with her hand outstretched. "Dylan's asked my firm to do the flowers for the opening. I hope you don't mind my crashing your lunch, but he wanted me to see the restaurant before we confirmed a color palette."

She knew, as soon as the words left her mouth, that she'd overcompensated. As if sensing her discomfort, Colleen rose from her chair with a welcoming smile and shook Jenna's hand.

"I'm pleased to meet you. Didn't you do the flowers for—"

"Angelica's rehearsal dinner, yes," Dylan interrupted, his swift interjection earning him a curious glance from his brother.

"I was going to say for a friend of mine's dinner party a couple of weeks ago," Colleen corrected smoothly, still holding Jenna's hand. "She was thrilled with what you did. I know you'll do a great job for Dylan."

Jenna began to feel herself relax as Colleen took over the conversation. It didn't mean that Sage stopped his perusal of her, but she allowed his fiancée to distract her as they turned the discussion to the pair's upcoming wedding and what the best flowers and style of bouquet might be. Across the square table, Dylan and his brother bent their heads together in deep discussion. Despite the differences in their coloring, their eyes were very much the same and the shape of their jaw and their mannerisms spoke of their strong familial connection.

Dylan looked up and flashed Jenna a smile before shifting his attention back to his brother, and she felt herself relax a little more. Colleen was very easy to talk to, and by the time they'd ordered off the menus and awaited their meals, Jenna found herself beginning to enjoy the other couple's company. Sage, while appearing a little standoffish at first, was clearly very much in love with his fiancée, and Jenna had to quell a pang of envy.

What would it have been like to meet Dylan and let a relationship with him progress the way most normal couples started? She shoved the thought aside for the piece of mental candy floss it was. She couldn't afford to indulge in thoughts of what might have been. She had been dealt large doses of reality in her lifetime, and coping with those, while keeping her wits about her, was paramount.

When their orders came Jenna applied herself vigorously to her serving of smoked baby back ribs with fries and grilled corn on the cob, which certainly beat a hasty sandwich grabbed in between customers at her shop. It felt strange being the only diners in a restaurant, waited on so industriously by the staff there, although the other three seemed to take it in stride. Jenna took her cue from Dylan and tried to act as if she was used to this kind of thing.

About thirty minutes later, when Sage made his apologies and rose to leave the table, Jenna decided she should do the same.

"No, wait for me here while I see Sage and Colleen out," Dylan insisted. "We still have those colors to discuss, as well as the table dressing you mentioned."

She nodded and turned her attention to the glass of mineral water Dylan had ordered for her. The water reminded her she needed to find the restroom. She got up and moved to the front of the restaurant, but before she could reach the facilities she overheard Sage talking to his brother.

"She's pregnant, Dylan. I hope you know what you're doing."

"I know she's pregnant. It's my baby."

"It's what?" Sage couldn't hide the shock in his voice.

"It's my baby and I'm going to marry her."

"Don't be a fool, man. It's not like you were even dating. You don't *know* her or anything about her. You don't even know for sure if the baby's yours—it could be anyone's. Shouldn't you at least wait until it's born, so you can do a paternity test?"

The sour taste of fear filled Jenna's mouth. This was exactly what she'd hoped to avoid. She didn't need Sage's censure or his implications. Yes, she had behaved like a tramp that Friday evening back in March. But so had Dylan. It was unfair that there was always one set of rules for guys and then another for women. The fact remained that they were dealing with the outcome of their dalliance, but the last thing she wanted was for it to become common knowledge. Not when she'd worked so hard, for so long, to wash away the taint of her father's behavior from her life.

She was where she was and who she was despite her upbringing. And, dammit, she would make a great mother even if juggling her business and motherhood would be a challenge. Jenna knew, to her cost, that life wasn't about easy solutions. It was about making the right choices and working hard to hold on to them.

"I don't like your insinuation, brother. Be very careful what you say about Jenna. I plan to marry her and I will raise my kid with her."

Dylan's tone brooked no argument and Jenna's spirits lifted to hear him defend her.

"Look, I didn't mean to offend you, but let's be realistic about this. At least have her investigated. If you won't, I will."

Ice cold sensation spilled through her veins. Investigation? It wouldn't take much to unearth her past, a past she'd fought hard to put behind her. Dylan's voice was raised when he answered his brother.

"I am being realistic about this, Sage. You know what family means to me. You know what *you* mean to me. I am not walking away from my son or daughter, and I'm not walking away from Jenna."

She held her breath through the tense silence that developed between the brothers, but she couldn't help but shift slightly. She really needed to pee. Her movement must have made some sound, because Dylan turned his head, his eyes spearing her where she stood.

"Um, I was just looking for the restrooms?" she said, horribly uncomfortable that she'd been caught standing there, eavesdropping.

"Through there," he said, pointing.

She scurried in the direction he'd indicated. After she relieved herself, she washed her hands under cold water, and then assessed her reflection in the mirror. She'd faced condemnation before and survived. It wasn't pretty, but she'd do it again if she had to. She dried her hands and returned to the restaurant. Dylan stood waiting for her.

"I'm sorry you had to hear that."

"It's okay. It's only what everyone will think, anyway." She brushed it off, but a note of how she was feeling must have crept into her voice.

"Jenna, I—"

"Look, let's just leave it, okay? Thank you for lunch. Now that I've been here I think I'll have a better idea about what you'll need for the floral designs, and I agree, bold and strong colors will be best." She flicked a look at her wristwatch. "I need to get back to the store."

"What about the other matters we were going to discuss?" he asked, searching her eyes. But she found herself unwilling to meet his.

"I'll email you."

"That sounds suspiciously like a brush-off." He cupped her shoulders with his big strong hands, the warmth of them swiftly penetrating the thin knit jacket and silk blouse she wore. "I'm not giving up on us, Jenna."

"Dylan, there is no *us*."

"I refuse to accept that," he said succinctly. "And one thing you need to know about me is that when something or someone is important to me, I never give up. You are important to me, Jenna Montgomery. Don't doubt it for a second."

When had anyone ever said anything like that to her before and meant it? She'd tried these past few days to keep Dylan at a distance, emotionally at least, but those few words wedged a tiny crack in the shell that had formed around her heart and began to split it apart. And when he lowered his face to hers, and caught her lips with his own, she felt herself reaching up to meet him halfway, as needy as a flower seeking rain on a drought-parched prairie. Wanting his promises, wanting his attention as she'd never wanted anything from anyone before.

Eight

Two days later Dylan paced the confines of his L.A. office. He was restless. Something had shifted inside him last Monday at the new restaurant. From the second he'd seen Sage take in Jenna's presence at his side and come to the correct conclusion about her pregnancy, he'd known he would defend her to anyone for any reason. For all time.

During his training in France he'd heard people refer to a *coup de foudre*—love at first sight—and he'd eschewed it for the fantastical notion it was. But thinking about that split second when he'd first noticed Jenna back in March, it was the only way to describe how he'd felt and behaved that night. It certainly described how he felt now. His family would just have to struggle to understand. Hell, even he struggled to get a grip on just how much one woman could turn his world upside down.

Since he'd walked back into her world five days ago, his every thought had been consumed by her, his every action taken with her in mind. Now, instead of focusing on the business and meetings to discuss the commencement of their planned East Coast expansion that had called him back to L.A., he was resenting the fact that it had taken him away from Cheyenne—away from Jenna.

He'd called her last night, but he'd sensed a reserve in her again, as if overhearing Sage's words had somehow erected an invisible wall thwarting the tentative connection they'd been building on. If only Dylan hadn't been forced to let her leave on Monday. If only he'd been able to pursue that kiss they'd shared at the restaurant just a little further. Instead, she'd all but fled from him and he'd had to let her go, his cell phone ringing in his pocket even as he watched her flee.

It was as if she was too scared to trust him, too scared to allow him into her life. But there was more to it than that. So many more layers to Jenna Montgomery that his hands itched to peel away. He'd have to bide his time, though, at least until Saturday, when he was due back in Cheyenne.

Dylan came to a halt at his office window and looked down over the sprawling metropolis that was Los Angeles. This had been his home, his city, for the past five years, and he'd fit in here. After training and cooking in restaurants in continental Europe and the United Kingdom, he'd been ready to come back to the States, ready to take on his next role in his career. But with J.D.'s death he'd been forced to take stock, to reevaluate his belief system and what was important in his life.

Right now, he missed Cheyenne. More to the point, he missed a certain woman who lived there. The perfect solution would be to take her and simply transplant her here into his life, his world. But even he knew that wouldn't be fair to her. She had a life in Cheyenne, a business and a home. Until he'd shown up in her store, she'd had everything worked out quite perfectly, Dylan had no doubt.

He forced his mind back to work, back to the task at hand. He'd get through these days because he had to, and because, ultimately, doing so would let him return to where he most wanted to be right now.

His phone chirping in his breast pocket was a welcome interruption to the frustration of his thoughts.

"Lassiter," he answered, without checking the caller I.D.

"Hey, Dylan, it's Chance. How are you?"

"I'm good, thanks, and you? How're things at the Big Blue?" Dylan smiled as he spoke. A call from his cousin was always a welcome break from everything else.

"I'm thinking of putting a barbecue together for Saturday. Think you could handle someone else's cooking for a change?"

Dylan laughed out loud. "Sure. For you, anything."

"Great. I was also thinking you might have a certain someone you'd like to bring along with you?"

"You been talking to Sage?"

"I might have."

Dylan could hear the smirk that was undoubtedly on his cousin's face.

"Chance—" he said, a grim note of warning in his voice.

"Hey, I promise I'll be on my best behavior, truly. I just want to meet her."

"And if she doesn't want to come?"

"I guess I can probably feed you, anyway," Chance drawled teasingly as if doing so would be a great hardship.

"That's big of you."

"But I'm sure, with your charm and skills, you'll manage to get her to come along."

"I'll let you know. What time do you want us?"

"Let's make it early. Hannah is visiting with her little girl, Cassie. She's the cutest tyke."

Since the discovery that Chance had a half sister—his father's secret daughter—the family had been getting to know one another, with great results. Now Hannah was engaged to Logan Whittaker, the lawyer who had been responsible for finding her when the contents of J.D.'s will had become known, and their family continued to expand. It was a good thing, Dylan thought privately.

"You getting ready to settle down, cuz?" It was Dylan's turn to tease now.

"Not likely," Chance replied, "but it's hard not to love her. She's a good kid. Anyway, come around six."

Dylan did a little mental calculation. By the time Jenna closed shop on Saturday and he picked her up, they could just about make it.

"We might be a little late," he said, "but we'll be there."

"Great, I'll let Mom know. She loves having family over. The more the merrier, right?"

Right, Dylan thought grimly as he disconnected the call. Now all he had to do was convince Jenna she wanted to meet more of his family, when all they probably wanted to do was subject her to the third degree. Damn Sage and his flapping mouth. Still, when push came to shove, his family was the backbone of who he was today, and Dylan wanted Jenna to see that, to be a part of it and to want their baby to be a part of it also. This gave her a perfect opportunity to see just what his family's lives were like.

Dylan had never been happier to leave L.A. and take the flight that brought him back to Cheyenne. As he pulled up in his SUV outside Jenna's house, he saw her at the front door before he could even get out of the car. He'd toyed with bringing the Caddy—he hadn't quite been able to bring himself to part with it just yet—but he knew it would probably make her uncomfortable. Besides, with the temperatures tonight set to drop to around fifty degrees, they'd probably welcome the climate control in the SUV instead.

He got out from behind the wheel and walked around to open her door for her, his eyes drinking in her appearance. He hadn't seen her for four days, but it felt like four weeks. Was it his imagination or was her tummy just that tiny bit rounder, her breasts that much fuller? Everything inside him tightened up a notch.

"Hi," she said, ducking her head as if she was a little shy.

"Hi back," he replied, bending his head to kiss her on the cheek. She blushed a pale pink when he did. He loved that he could do that to her, unnerve her like that. "I missed you."

She flicked her gaze up toward him and he saw her bite her lip, an action that sent heat rushing to his groin.

"I missed you, too."

She sounded puzzled by the fact and it made him quirk his lips in a smile. Dylan handed her into her seat and closed the door, suppressing the urge to punch the air and give a primal whoop of satisfaction. Progress. At last he was making progress.

He filled the time during their thirty-mile drive out to the Big Blue with what he'd been doing in L.A.

"So your sister lives in the house in L.A., too?"

"Yeah. Dad bought the property about twenty years ago and Angelica has really made it her own. She has a knack for decorating, for making a place feel like a home." He sighed inwardly. "It's always good to see her, but she's been pretty angry since Dad died. Things are strained between all of us."

"Angry?"

"Yeah." Dylan suddenly wished he hadn't brought the

subject up, but it probably deserved airing. "Dad was pretty old-fashioned, but I always thought he was fair. What he did to her when he left a controlling share in Lassiter Media to her fiancé, rather than to her, was a slap in the face. It's really upset her, especially since she'd basically been the one running Lassiter Media up until J.D.'s heart attack."

"Wow, I can see why she'd be upset. Is that why the wedding got called off?"

Dylan nodded. It still made him sick to his stomach. "Lassiter Media was Angelica's life, and now she's left wondering if the whole reason Evan asked her to marry him was so he could gain control of the company. Not exactly the basis for a good start to marriage."

Jenna was quiet for the rest of the journey, until Dylan reached across the center console and laced his fingers through hers.

"You okay?" he asked, flicking her a glance.

"Just a bit nervous."

"Don't be. Chance is a great guy."

"Who else will be there?"

"His mom, Marlene—she'll love you, don't worry. And his half sister, Hannah, is visiting with her daughter, Cassie. And look, we're nearly there."

He pulled in through the gates to what had, in his mind, always been home. After his parents died, J.D. and Ellie had brought him and Sage here to the ranch. Originally, the main house had been far more modest, but as the Big Blue had become more successful, it was replaced by the two-story wood-and-metal structure they were now approaching. Wraparound porches with hand-hewn wooden railings graced both levels.

"Wow, this is quite a place," Jenna commented, sitting up a little straighter in her seat. "You and Sage grew up here?"

"Lucky, huh? Just think, all this land and these big wide-open spaces for two little boys to burn their energy off in. I had a great childhood."

It occurred to Dylan that she hadn't talked much about her own upbringing. Aside from knowing she was born in New Zealand and had, for the most part, grown up in the U.S., he still had a lot to find out about her.

They got out of the car and walked up to the entrance. Dylan pushed open the front door and guided Jenna inside, yelling out a "hello" as he did so. Footsteps sounded in the hall and an older woman came forward.

"Dylan! Great to see you!" She enveloped him in a huge hug.

"Aunt Marlene, I'd like you to meet Miss Jenna Montgomery. Jenna, this is my aunt, Marlene Lassiter."

"Mrs. Lassiter, I'm pleased to meet you."

"Oh, go on now, we don't stand on ceremony here. Call me Marlene and I'm going to call you Jenna. Head on through. I've still got a few things to see to in the kitchen. Hannah and Cassie are outside on the patio and Chance is fiddling with the grill, as if he thinks he knows what he's doing."

"No Logan today?" Dylan asked.

Marlene shook her head. "No, he called me to apologize and say he'd been called out of town for legal work for some high-profile corporate client but just between you and me I think he's ducked away to avoid the wedding planning." She finished with a wink and a sparkle in her eyes that took the sting out of her words. "So, go on outside. They're waiting for you."

Jenna appeared to hold a little tighter to Dylan's hand. He guessed it was a bit overwhelming when you came here the first time. He looked around the house he'd grown up in. Maybe the second time, too. Out on the patio she seemed to relax a bit more. The expansive gardens stretched out before them.

"Is that a pond?" Jenna asked.

"It's a saltwater pool designed to look like a pond. When Sage and I were younger we used to swing from a rope tied to a branch on that tree there—" he gestured to the limb in question "—and drop into the deep end."

"Wow, you really had it all, didn't you?" she said, almost to herself.

A little girl bounced toward them, her bright red hair hanging in disordered ringlets around her pretty face and her green eyes sparkling with mischief.

"You're my uncle Dylan, aren't you? But Mama says you're more like a cousin something-removed. What's that?"

"Cassie! Let Dylan and his guest say hello to the rest of us first, before you start bothering them," a woman's voice called from the patio.

Dylan watched as Chance's half sister, Hannah, rose from her seat and came over to greet them.

"Hi again," she said to him before turning to Jenna. "I'm Hannah Armstrong."

"Jenna Montgomery," she said. "Is that your daughter? She's adorable."

Hannah beamed with pride. "Yes, that's my little treasure. She's quite the character. Here, you leave Jenna with me and go and see what Chance is doing over by the grill."

Dylan gave Jenna a glance to see if she was comfortable with that. She inclined her head slightly.

"Sure, I'll be fine," she said, but he could see by the pallor of her cheeks that she was still a little nervous, as if, given the right provocation, she'd turn and run like hell back to Cheyenne.

"I'll say hi and then I'll be right back."

"It's okay," Hannah assured him in her gentle voice. "I won't bite."

Jenna let Hannah draw her over to where she'd been sitting a moment ago, and they relaxed in the late afternoon sun.

"I'm gonna help Grandma with the horse derves," Cassie announced importantly, before skipping back inside the house.

"Wow, she's full of energy, isn't she?" Jenna commented, her lips still pulled into a smile over the little girl's mispronunciation of *hors d'oeuvres.*

"Sure is. Has been like that from the day she was born. Never a dull moment with her around, and I wouldn't have it any other way."

There was a steely vein of pride running through Hannah's voice. One that made Jenna press her hand on her lower belly. Yes, that's how she felt, too. As scary and unknown as what lay before her was, she wouldn't have it any other way, either.

"It's so beautiful here," she remarked, looking around again, trying to take it all in.

"I know. When I first saw the place it totally blew me away."

"You didn't grow up here?"

"No, I'm from Boulder, Colorado. But I'm getting married next month and Cheyenne will be our permanent home after that. In the meantime, Cassie and I are staying here. She's loving having an uncle she can twist around her little finger, not to mention a Grandma who just adores her."

Jenna tried to put all that information together, but something was still out of sync in her mind. "Marlene's not your mom?"

"It's complicated. Chance and I share a dad," Hannah explained with a wistful smile. "But they've all been so welcoming since we found out about one another. Especially Marlene, which was so much more than I could have hoped for."

"They seem very tight-knit," Jenna observed, watching Dylan and Chance laughing together over something one of them had said.

"But inclusive at the same time. Don't worry." Hannah patted Jenna's hand. "I wondered what I'd be letting myself in for, but they made me welcome from the start. You'll fit right in."

Would she? Her heart yearned for stability; she'd created as much as she could herself by working hard and buying her own home. She was almost fanatical about establishing roots, about grounding herself in familiarity and routine after her younger years filled with instability. From what she saw here, the Lassiters were clearly just as invested in permanence.

"Here you are, ladies. Some icy cold lemonade for you, honey," Marlene said to Jenna as she returned, putting a tray with a couple of frosted pitchers and some fresh glasses on the table in front of her. "And margaritas for us."

Jenna felt uncomfortable. So they knew already that she was pregnant. She murmured her thanks and watched Cassie carry a tray with inch-high edges to Chase and Dylan.

"Used to be a time she'd serve me first," Hannah commented with a rueful smile. "But now it's all about her uncle."

"She might have him wrapped around her pinky," Marlene observed, "but it's mutual. It's good to have a child around here again. It's been too long since those boys were growing up."

The older woman turned to face Jenna, a warm glow lighting her hazel eyes. "How are you keeping with the baby, Jenna? Well, I hope?"

Jenna's upset that news of her pregnancy had preceded her must have been evident on her face.

"Oh, I'm sorry, hon. Is it supposed to be a secret? Chance told me and I just thought the whole family knew."

Jenna hastened to reassure her hostess. "No, really, it's okay. I'm just not used to people knowing just yet." She smiled to soften her words. "As to how I've been? I've been pretty lucky. A little nausea in the early stages but my main problem has been tiredness."

"You're in your second trimester now, aren't you?" Marlene asked. When she nodded, the other woman said, "You should notice you're feeling better again soon. This is where you get to experience all the fun of a pregnancy, without the sickness or the aches and pains. Is your family looking forward to the baby's arrival?"

Jenna squirmed a little. She was totally unused to someone being so inquisitive, though friendly. "I don't have any family locally," she settled on saying— unwilling to admit to anyone here that her father was doing time at the state penitentiary in Rawlins.

"Oh, you poor girl," Marlene clucked sympathetically. "Never mind. If you'll let us, we'd be glad to help you out. If you have any questions, anything at all, you just ask away."

"Thank you." Jenna blinked back the burn of tears at the kindness of Marlene's unexpected offer. Her eyes hazed over again and she lifted a hand to wipe at the moisture that began to spill.

"Don't you worry, honey," Marlene said softly as she handed Jenna a crisply laundered, lace-edged handkerchief. "We'll take good care of you."

Jenna wiped her eyes and fought to get her ridiculous emotions under control. She was a virtual stranger to these people. Yet because of one impulsive accident, they were prepared to open their hearts to her. She'd been so closed up, so reluctant to let anyone in, that she felt slightly off-kilter at the prospect of even thinking of accepting help and support. She didn't deserve this. Didn't deserve their trust or their generosity.

Even so, the idea of it dangled before her like a tantalizing, yet forbidden, fruit.

Nine

Dylan looked over to where the women were talking. Something tightened in his chest when he saw Jenna's expression and recognized the distress on her face. He went to step toward her, but was arrested by Chance's hand on his shoulder.

"Don't," his cousin said.

"She's upset. She needs me."

"Mom will look after her. Trust me. She'll have everything under control."

Dylan watched as Jenna recovered her usual poise. And as the women seemed to grow closer and enjoy one another's company, their laughter floated toward him on the light evening breeze.

"Do you want some more horse derves, Uncle Dylan?" Cassie asked from beside him, shifting her weight from one leg to the other.

"No, thank you," he replied, squatting down to her level. "But thank you for taking such great care of us. How about you offer some of those to the ladies?"

"Okay!" the little girl said brightly.

He watched as she strutted importantly to the table where the women sat. A sense of wonder stirred deep inside him. Would his kid be a boy or a girl? Would it one day be right here, playing on this patio like he had?

"So when did you knock her up?" Chance's voice interrupted his reverie.

Dylan's hackles rose. He didn't care for his cousin's turn of phrase. "I don't think that's any of your business."

"Of course it is. Sage thinks it isn't yours—that she's maybe pulling a fast one on you."

"Sage should keep his thoughts to himself," Dylan growled. "It's mine. And so is she."

His cousin nodded, clearly satisfied with that response. "You going to be a hands-on dad?"

"Every chance I get," Dylan replied emphatically.

Chance looked pensive. "I often wonder what life would have been like to have grown up with my own dad around longer, y'know?" His father had died when Chance was eight years old. He, too, knew what it was like to grow up without his natural father.

"Yeah. It's why I'm going to be there for my kid, through thick and thin."

"And Jenna? How does she feel about that?"

Dylan took a swig of his beer and rolled the brew over his tongue for a moment before swallowing. "She's coming around to the idea," he said with a grin.

Chance gave him a punch on the arm. "Thatta boy. Besides, with all you can offer, why would she refuse?"

"That's the thing. She doesn't seem to want what I can offer. She's fierce about her independence, and from what I can tell, she's worked hard for it. I just need to convince her that it's okay to share the load."

"Well, good luck with that. I'd rather rope a steer in a bad mood than try and convince a woman of anything."

"Good point," Dylan concurred, before gesturing to the platter of raw steak waiting to be cooked. "Hey, you going to do anything with those or are you waiting for them to cook themselves?"

The seriousness of their discussion broken, they turned to the matter of cooking the meat. But a niggling thought remained at the back of Dylan's mind. What if Jenna wouldn't let him in? What if she wouldn't share the load? What then? He knew he could use his power and his money to get what he wanted, but the very idea soured his stomach. No, he wanted her to come to him willingly and wholeheartedly. Not because she had to, not because she was being coerced. But because she wanted to as much as he wanted her.

It was late when he drove Jenna home. Dylan had fully expected her to want to leave soon after they'd enjoyed their meal, but it seemed that the longer she spent with his family, the more she wanted to stay. It made him begin to hope that she could see herself being a part of his own close circle. Part of his life.

"Thank you for taking me tonight. I really enjoyed it," she said softly.

"It was my pleasure. I'm glad you came."

"They're all so lovely. And Cassie's so sweet. I loved how she crawled into your lap after dinner and just fell asleep there."

He'd loved it, too. Had welcomed the little girl's trust in him. It had been a precious gift, and he'd missed the weight of her little body when Hannah had eventually lifted her and carted her off to bed. It made him yearn even more to be a father, to cradle a child of his own in his arms.

"Kids are special. No doubt about it."

Dylan drove onto Jenna's driveway and got out to walk her to her front door. He waited on the porch as she fitted her key in the lock, the breeze bringing a teasing hint of her fragrance toward him. Roses. She always carried

that sweet scent on her. It suited her. The flower was so
beautiful yet could be prickly at the same time.

She pushed the door open and hesitated a second or
two. He saw her shoulders lift and then drop, as if she'd
drawn in a deep breath.

"Jenna? You okay?"

She turned to face him. "Do you…?"

She bit her bottom lip, the action having the exact
same effect on him as it had the other day. Fire licked
along his veins as he waited for her to finish her sentence.

"Do you want to come in for a nightcap?"

Hell, yeah, a little voice all but screamed at the back
of his mind. He didn't want tonight to end. She'd soft-
ened, somehow. Her defenses seemed lower than before.
He pushed the screaming voice aside. He needed to tread
softly. He certainly didn't want to scare her or damage the
tentative closeness that had grown between them tonight.

"One more drink and I'll be over the limit to drive,"
he said quietly—asking her the important question without putting it into so many words. He'd go if that's what
she wanted. He wouldn't be happy about it. But he'd go.

Jenna took a step closer to him and placed her hand
on his chest. "Then perhaps you should stay."

His breath caught in his lungs. Could she feel his
heart all but leap from his chest at her words? "Perhaps I
should," he managed to reply, and hooked an arm around
her waist.

They headed in together. He let her go as she walked
around her sitting room, flicking on the occasional light.

"I'm not even sure what I have in the way of spirits,
but I'm bound to have some wine. Would that be—?"

Her voice broke off as he caught her hand and drew
her to him.

"I don't really want a drink, Jenna," he said, his voice a low rumble.

"You don't?"

"No, I just want you."

"Oh."

It was all she got time to say before he kissed her. The taste of her lips almost blew his head off and ignited the slow-burning embers within him to flaming, ravenous heat. His kiss was hungry, demanding, and to his delight she met his need with corresponding passion. Her hands slid upward, from his chest to his neck, then cupped the back of his head, not letting him break the kiss.

"Bedroom," he demanded against her mouth, not wanting to remove his lips from hers for even a second.

She pointed down the hallway. "At the end, on the right."

He scooped one arm behind her knees and the other behind her back and lifted her, holding her body against his. She snaked an arm around his shoulders and caressed his cheek with her free hand, as if she was as reluctant to break their connection, their kiss, as he. He covered the short distance down the hall and pushed the door open with his foot. Her bedroom was small, with minimal decoration. Simple in its design. A plainly covered bed took up most of the space, a solid plank of blond wood serving as a headboard.

Dylan let Jenna slide to her feet.

"I want to see you this time," he growled, moving away from her for the brief second it took to switch on the bedside lamp.

He turned back to her and reached to lift her loose-fitting tunic from her body. His mouth dried at the sight he revealed, his untaken breath burning in his chest. Her skin was smooth, with the lightest touch of summer in its tone. He let his gaze track down her throat, across her shoulders and to her breasts, which spilled from the lacy cups of her bra.

"I told you you were beautiful. I was wrong," he said, his voice thick with emotion. "You're so much more than that."

His hand reached out to trace a faint blue vein on her breast, and he heard her sharply indrawn breath. He followed the line to where it disappeared beneath the pale blue scalloped edge of her bra.

"I'm going to kiss you there," he promised, lifting his eyes to hers—his stomach clenching at the heat he saw burning back at him. "But first, I'm going to see all of you."

He took his time removing her sandals and slim-fitted capris until she had only her bra and panties left. Fine tremors quivered through her body as he let his hands drift up her arms to her shoulders. Her skin was so soft, and sweetly fragrant, and he trailed fine kisses along her shoulder and then up the side of her neck.

"Let me get the bed ready," she said as he nibbled on her earlobe, just as he'd imagined doing a few short days ago.

"It looks pretty damn ready to me," he said when she pulled away with a small laugh.

Still, he was happy to use the time she took turning down the comforter and tugging back the sheets to shuck off his clothing—something he managed with record speed. His erection strained at the cotton of his boxer briefs and he rubbed his hand down his aching flesh. Soon, he promised himself, soon. But first there were more important things to attend to. Such as examining the woman in front of him from head to foot. Getting to know what made her breathless with desire. Making her scream with pleasure such as she'd never experienced before.

Jenna lay down on the bed and held out a hand to him. He took it, stretching out next to her and marveling at how perfectly formed she was. He traced the curve of her collarbone again—such a delicate line—and followed his touch with the tip of his tongue. She rewarded him with a sigh of pleasure so he did it again, his tongue lingering in the hollow just at the base of her throat. Her pulse leaped against him, as avid and hungry as his own.

Dylan continued his voyage of discovery, his fingertips tingling as they met the swell of her breasts. He swept over their shape before letting his hand travel to her shoulders, slipping first one, then the other bra strap down, and reaching beneath her to unsnap the clasp.

"Should I be worried that you did that so easily?" Jenna teased, but then her voice ended on a gasp as he traced the pale blue line of her vein to where it collided with the dark pink distended nipple.

"Never," he said, before using the tip of his tongue to meet that pink tip.

She shuddered beneath him. "Do that again, please?"

"Your wish is my command," he promised, and did as she asked.

Her moan of delight drove a fierce spear of lust straight to his groin, but he forced himself to ignore it. To dwell instead on her pleasure, on her. He took his time with the rest of her body, lingering over her breasts, her ribs, her belly button, and then moving down to the small firm swell of her belly.

His hand hovered there and he willed the connection between them to go beyond skin, beyond sensation. His baby. His woman. His life. He pressed a kiss against her skin, his hands now skimming her panties, tracing the outside edge of the fabric where they met the top of her thighs. Her legs trembled at his touch, her pelvis thrusting upward toward him. He cupped her, marveling at the heat and dampness that collected at her core.

"Dylan, please!"

He pressed his palm against her, felt her shudder against him.

"You're teasing me. It's not fair," she cried, her voice a strangled sound.

"All's fair," he said easing her panties down her legs and punctuating his next words with firm kisses on her thighs, then the junction where they met. "In." Kiss. "Love." Kiss. "And." Kiss. "War."

His mouth found her center and he saw her hands knot into fists on the sheets as his tongue flicked against her glistening sex. The scent of her was driving him crazy. A delicious blend of rose and musk.

He couldn't stand it a second longer. He had to have her, be inside her, be one with her. He shoved his briefs down and settled between her legs, feeling her jolt as he nudged the blunt tip of his erection at her entrance. She lifted her hips in welcome and he slowly let himself be absorbed by the tight warm heat of her body. Slowly, so slowly, until he was buried in her. Until he was exactly where he needed to be.

His hips flexed and she met his movement with her own, her inner muscles holding and releasing him in time with their actions. Her irises darkened to near black, clouded with the fog of her desire. He tried to make it last, to make it even more special, but when her body began to pulse around his, when her eyes slid closed and she released a keening cry as her body shuddered toward its peak, he lost control—his hips pumping until he, too, reached his climax.

Lost in the power of wonder and emotion that swept over him, Dylan let his body take him on the ride as he crested wave after wave of pleasure. His entire frame shook with the force of what he'd just undergone—with the perfection of how it had felt. He rolled to one side and gathered Jenna against him, waiting for his heartbeat to return to anything approximating normal.

It was a long time before he could speak.

"I think we just proved our first time wasn't an aberration," he said with a huff of breath. He felt her chuckle ripple through her.

"Yes, I think we did."

He could hear the humor in her voice, humor mixed with a languid satisfaction that made him feel even better, knowing he'd contributed to her well-being. Everything was right in this moment. Perfect. He knew he'd never tire of this. Of the feeling of her in his arms, of the curve of her sweet bottom beneath his hand. Of this sense of connection he'd never shared with another woman.

He wanted this—forever, with her. It took all his self-restraint not to press her again to agree to marriage. To agree to committing to one another forever.

Deep down he knew she still had reservations. Understandable, given the short length of time they'd actually known one another. But they had the rest of their lives to discover all those finer points that kept a relationship interesting. What they shared was a gift beyond compare. He should know—he'd sought perfection wherever he went in whatever he did.

Jenna Montgomery was that perfection for him. He just needed to convince her of that fact.

Ten

Jenna could hear Dylan's heart racing beneath her ear, and her lips curved into a smile. He might be the CEO of the Lassiter Grill Corporation, he might be a world-renowned chef and playboy, but underneath it all he was still just a man. A pretty damn fine one, that was for sure. And, right now, he was hers.

Her man forever? She was beginning to believe it could be true. She'd loved spending time with him and his family this evening. Could she find the courage to reach out from behind her safe fortress and grasp what he offered? Only time would tell.

Dylan's fingers traced a lazy trail from her hip to her shoulders and back again, his touch setting off tiny shivers beneath her skin. She stretched beneath his touch, like a cat, almost purring.

"Tell me what you like," he asked softly. "This?" He firmed his touch. "Or this?"

"Hmm, let me take about the next twenty minutes or so to get back to you on that," she replied.

He laughed and the sound filled her heart with happiness.

"Twenty minutes? That's quite a commitment."

"It might be," she said, realizing that if she really wanted this—really wanted *him*—she needed to take the bull by the horns and open up to him.

But whenever he started talking about commitment it still struck a knell of fear inside her. He knew virtually nothing about her but the face she presented to him right here, right now. The person she was today was a far cry from the person she'd been eleven years ago.

Pretty much everything about Dylan and his life was an open book. Yes, he'd had sorrow in his life with the death of his parents and then his adoptive mother, and more recently, J.D. But with each loss, he'd had the advantage of family, of someone else willing to step up to the plate and fill that yearning hole in his life.

With the loss of his parents it had been J.D. and his wife, Ellie. With the death of Ellie, Jenna had learned tonight, Marlene had stepped into the breach to provide mothering to Dylan and his brother. What had Jenna ever had growing up, except a will for survival? That will had gotten her through her parents' arguments, their one-up-manship and then her mother's desertion.

It had gotten her through the news that her father was taking her to America, away from everything and everyone she'd ever known or allowed herself to anchor to.

Did she dare anchor herself to Dylan?

"You're thinking so hard I can just about hear the cogs turning in your brain," Dylan said teasingly. "Wanna share?"

She began to say no, but then realized that this was a perfect opportunity to give him some of her truths. What he did with it would define what happened between them in the future.

"I was just thinking about how different our lives were, growing up."

"How so?"

"You had such stability, such strength behind your

family. It's like everyone has a place and they fit there, y'know?"

"Uh-huh. It's not always a bed of roses but we get along pretty well."

"Pretty well?" she said, tweaking one of his nipples with a pinch that made him yelp.

"Okay, very well. But we work at it."

"That's part of what I mean," she said, smoothing her hand over his chest to soothe his injured flesh. "You do work at it, together. I guess I've never had that sense of community within a family. From what I know, my parents were both only children, and their parents died before I was born. It should have made them closer to one another, but instead it always felt like they were tearing each other apart."

"Doesn't sound comfortable, for them or for you."

"No, it wasn't. It was confusing, unstable. I never knew from one day to the next if they'd be happy and loving or morose and picking a fight. When my mother left us, I almost felt a sense of relief, y'know? But by the same token I was distraught because she didn't take me, too. Dad said she felt like we were holding her back."

Dylan sighed. "That was unfair of him for saying it and, if it was true, of her for feeling it. You can't do that to a kid. Your job as a parent is to nurture, to support and love your children. Yes, that means putting your own needs last a lot of the time, but I reckon there's a time and a place for everything and everyone, and when your kids are young it's *their* time, *their* place."

Jenna closed her eyes as a swell of something rich and true buoyed up inside her. His words were so simple, yet they rang with such a deep certainty about what was right and wrong. Tenets she held dear to her own heart.

"Well, obviously they didn't feel that way."

"Do you stay in touch with your dad now?" Dylan asked.

Jenna shook her head. She didn't want to tell Dylan that her father would be locked up behind bars for at least another two years. He'd probably have been out on parole by now if the prison staff hadn't discovered he'd begun grooming wealthy widows for future cons during his computer time inside.

"No. We lead totally separate lives. To be honest, I don't want anything to do with him," she said emphatically.

"Will you tell him about the baby?"

"No. I don't want him anywhere near us."

"Family is family, Jen," Dylan said, still stroking her skin, his actions soothing the anger that had risen in her as they discussed her dad. "I wouldn't be where I am now without mine."

She laughed, but it was a bitter sound. "Nor would I. But I've learned the hard way that just because someone is family doesn't mean they have your best interests at heart. My foster mum gave me more care and stability than my parents ever did. Thanks to her, I've learned to do very well on my own and I like it that way. I work hard, and what I have is my own. Okay, so I can't provide luxuries like saltwater ponds with swinging ropes, or private jets and silver spoons. But I can provide what counts—stability and constancy in a loving home. I've set down roots here. I finally belong somewhere and I'll protect that, and my baby's right to that, with every last breath in my body if I have to."

Dylan was silent for a while, but then he spoke. "And do you see any room for me in that life of yours?"

She rolled on top of him, her legs tangling with his

and her hands on either side of his face as she rose up to kiss him.

"That depends," she said, pulling away so they were inches apart.

"On what?"

"On whether you plan to keep telling me what to do, or whether you want to be an equal partner in what happens in our baby's life."

Tiny twin frown lines appeared between his brows as he looked into her eyes. "I can do partnership," he said carefully. "But I'd rather do marriage."

This time, when he said it, it didn't send quite the same shaft of anxiety through her. Instead, she felt a sense of curiosity—a need to take his suggestion and examine it more closely instead of rejecting it out of hand.

"I'll think about it," she said, hardly believing it herself as the words fell from her lips.

"Thank you," he answered simply.

His strong, warm arms closed around her and she caught his lips again, letting herself and her fears go in his touch until once more they were lost in each other.

The air had grown cool around them and Dylan shifted to drag the covers up over their naked forms. Jenna had fallen asleep almost immediately after the second time they'd made love, but he'd continue to lie there turning over her words.

Her family had hurt her, had made her doubt and fear closeness. Chipping away at her barriers would take time and care. And love? Yes, and love. Love and dependability. Those had been the backbone of his upbringing. He wanted those attributes to be the backbone of his kid's upbringing, too, and to do that he needed to woo Jenna with those promises. He'd known all along that courting her would be a challenge. They'd done everything from back to front, for a start. But he'd get there, he decided as he finally drifted off to sleep. What he and Jenna had between them was far too important. Failure was not an option.

In the morning Dylan eased himself from the bed-sheets without disturbing her. Dragging on his jeans, he padded through to her kitchen to see what he could rustle up for breakfast. He eyed her appliances with interest. Everything was new and in near pristine condition. Either she was a fanatical housekeeper or she didn't do a great deal of cooking in here. From what she'd said about TV dinners, he suspected it was the latter.

He opened her fridge and confirmed that she didn't do a great deal of cooking. His brow furrowed as he considered his options. A quick check of the vegetable drawer revealed a red pepper that was just about past its best by date, and some fresh mushrooms. He made a sound of satisfaction. Further rummaging in the kitchen uncovered potatoes and onions in matching earthenware containers.

So, with these items combined with the eggs in the fridge, he could do a Spanish omelet with red pepper and a side of fried mushrooms. His mouth was already watering at the thought. But when it came to slicing the potatoes, he eyed Jenna's knives in despair and wished he was in his own kitchen with his quality steel blades honed to perfection. Still, he'd made do with worse, he thought, testing the blunt edge.

He fried the potato and onions together in a pan while he went to work slicing mushrooms and beating the eggs. By the time he was ready to turn the halved omelet onto two warmed plates he heard a sound in the hall.

"Good morning," he said as Jenna stumbled into the kitchen, wrapped in a fluffy long bathrobe.

She looked as though she'd forced herself awake. Her hair was mussed and her eyes had a sleepy look about them that almost made him abandon their breakfast and take her straight back to bed to wake her up properly.

"Good morning," she said as she went over to the fridge and grabbed a bottle of water and screwed off the cap. "Something smells good. Are you feeding me again?"

"Spanish omelet. You hungry?"

She groaned. "Hungry? I'm always hungry lately."

"Then," he said, scooping up the sliced mushrooms he'd fried in a little butter, and sharing them between their plates, "you'd better wrap yourself around this."

She gave him a puzzled look. "You did this?"

He waggled his fingers in front of her. "With my own fair hands."

"Did I actually have the ingredients or have you been out?"

He laughed. "You had everything here. I haven't left you for a moment."

Nor did he plan to for the rest of this weekend, or any of the time he had free until the official opening of the Grill next week.

"Hmm," she said, quickly setting the small table she had in the dining area and transferring their plates onto the table. "Maybe you should give me some lessons."

His mouth quirked in a smile. Lessons? Oh, yeah, he'd love to do that. His mind filled with the possibilities, starting with Jenna wearing an apron...and nothing else.

"Sure. Shall we start today?"

"I was kidding, but if you're serious..."

"I never kid about food."

"Okay, today would be fine."

"Good, I'll take you back to my place. We'll have more to work with there."

She returned his smile and he felt as though the sun had just risen again. "Thank you, I'd like that."

Dylan heard his phone beep. "Excuse me a second," he said, sliding it from his pocket and checking the display.

It was a message from Felicity Sinclair, Lassiter Media's queen of PR, confirming her arrival in Cheyenne tomorrow morning. He tapped in a quick acknowledgment and turned his attention back to Jenna.

"Sorry, work," he said by way of explanation.

"Do you always work on weekends?"

He shrugged. "When it's necessary. With the Grill opening next week everything has become more time sensitive. That was just a text from our PR executive. She's flying in tomorrow. I'll bring her by your store and introduce you."

"That'd be nice. Hopefully, she can make sure that Connell's Floral Design's logo is featured prominently in your advertising," she said with a cheeky smile.

Jenna leaned forward as she scooped up a mouthful of omelet, her action making her robe gape open enough to give him a glimpse of one pink-tipped breast. Any thoughts of work and the people associated with it flew from his mind as he allowed his gaze to drift over her. She continued eating, oblivious to his perusal, until her plate was empty and she lifted her attention to him—and realized just what had caught his attention.

Her eyes darkened, as they had last night, and her cheeks became tinged with pink.

"Not hungry?" she asked, her voice a little husky.

"Starving," he replied, putting his fork down and pushing his plate away.

He eased from his chair, dropping to his knees and

sliding one hand inside her robe to cup her breast. Her nipple instantly tightened against his palm.

"Ah, now I see why you're feeding me so well," Jenna said, drawing in a deep breath. "You want to keep my energy levels up."

"Among other things," he drawled, letting his thumb graze back and forth over the taut nub that just begged him to take it in his mouth.

Never a man to ignore his instincts, Dylan did just that. Jenna's fingers tunneled through his hair, holding him to her as he nibbled and sucked her flesh.

"Well, it's a good thing I've eaten then," Jenna managed to say before he pushed aside her robe and lavished her other breast with equal attention. "Because I have a feeling I'm going to need the extra calories."

"Them and more," he murmured against her skin.

They didn't get out to his place until well after lunchtime and by then they were both famished again, for each other and for more sustenance. How they even made it into his high-tech kitchen bemused him, when all he wanted to do was take Jenna to the dizzying heights they'd shared, over and over again.

Instead, he supervised her as she put together a simple lunch for them both. Jenna surveyed the assembled ingredients on the island in the center of the kitchen.

"You always buy this extensively from the grocery store?" she commented as she tore up some romaine lettuce and threw it into a bowl.

"When I'm in the mood for Greek salad, yeah. What's wrong? Didn't your family ever cook?"

As soon as the words were out of his mouth he wished them back again. He already knew talking about her family created an invisible barrier between them, one he'd unwittingly put back in place.

"I can remember baking cookies with my mom once or twice when I was little, but aside from that, nothing really. Dad was big on takeout, or eating out. He often wasn't home for meals anyway, so I just learned to make do."

It was what she didn't say that struck him. How old had she been when she'd been left to fend for herself come mealtimes? Dylan moved around the granite-topped island and slid his arms around her waist, pulling her gently back against him.

"I'm sorry," he said, pressing a kiss against the back of her neck. "I didn't mean to bring that up."

"It is what it is," she said, studiously concentrating on slicing the red onion and then the red and green bell peppers she'd laid out in a row on the countertop in front of her.

"Here, do you want me to do that?" he offered, wanting to do anything to change the subject and shift her focus to something else.

"Actually, no. I'm enjoying this. I never thought I would, but it's true."

She flung him a smile over her shoulder and kept chopping and slicing until the bowl was filled with the earlier ingredients, together with tomatoes, olives and cucumber. Her hand hesitated over the feta cheese.

"It's okay," Dylan said. "I checked. It's made from pasteurized milk."

"Are you sure?"

"Hey, leave it out if you want to. It's not a food crime." To save her the hassle, he swept the packet up and put it back in the fridge, substituting it for a sliced cooked chicken breast. "Use this instead. There's no reason why we can't play around with tradition."

"Thanks," she said. "I'm sorry, I just don't want to do anything that will potentially harm the baby. He or she is all I have."

She placed one hand on her belly and Dylan could see the love in her face. He put his hand over hers. "You have me now, too. I want you to remember that, because I'm not going anywhere, Jenna. Not unless you're coming with me."

Eleven

She wanted to believe him. With all her heart she wanted it to be true. But she'd heard such platitudes from her father's mouth all the years she'd spent with him. He'd used them with her and also with his many lady friends. He'd always made it sound so sincere, as if the words truly came from his heart, but they'd come from a place far more closely associated with his wallet.

"Seeing is believing," Jenna said, trying to keep her words light. But she knew they'd struck to Dylan's core.

"You don't believe me?"

He reached to take the knife from her and turned her to face him. His hands framed her face and forced her to maintain eye contact with him.

"I didn't say that, exactly," she hedged, knowing to the depth of her soul that she wanted to be certain of him, to be able to trust what he said without looking for an ulterior motive.

Still, aside from the baby, and obviously the incredible sexual chemistry they shared, what else was there? A marriage took so much more than those two things. Her parents had been the perfect example of that. A marriage needed commitment, togetherness and mutual minds. What motive could he have to want to be with her? It wasn't as if she had something he needed. He had it all and then some.

"Jenna, I meant what I said. Yes, I know we haven't known each other all that long and, yes, we've gone at this all the wrong way. If I could, I'd turn back the clock and take the time to woo you, to prove that you can rely on me. Something brought us together, I firmly believe that. And we're meant to be, Jenna."

"I wish it could be that easy." She sighed.

"It can be. If you just let it."

"I'm trying, Dylan, honestly I am. I…I want to trust you."

"Then that's progress. I'll take it. We're halfway there, right? C'mon, let's get this salad finished and I'll show you around the house."

The next morning Jenna was happily reflecting on her day with Dylan when Valerie knocked on her office door and popped her head in.

"You have visitors. Mr. Drop-Dead-Gorgeous and a woman who looks as if she walked straight off Rodeo Drive. They make a nice couple," Valerie said, closing the office door behind her as she returned to the showroom.

A couple? Jenna didn't think so, not after the very thorough loving Dylan had given her yesterday. But even so, she felt a twinge of jealousy and insecurity. This PR chick, whoever she was, was certainly more suited to Dylan's world than Jenna ever could be. And she'd lay odds that she didn't have any dark or shameful secrets lurking in her past, either. Insecurity made Jenna uncomfortable as she rose from her desk and checked her appearance in the mirror that hung on the back of her office door.

Well, there wasn't a hair out of place and her makeup hadn't disappeared since she'd lightly applied it this morning. There was nothing else to do but go out and face them.

Her heart skipped a double beat when she thought about seeing Dylan. He'd been so attentive yesterday and had made her feel so incredibly special. She wished she was the kind of person who could simply embrace that and not constantly read between the lines of everything he said and did for an ulterior motive.

There was another knock at her office door.

"Jenna?"

It was Dylan. She pasted a smile on her face and reached for the handle. She felt her heart thump as she saw him. He was all sartorial corporate elegance today, dressed in a charcoal-gray suit, white shirt and striped tie. Her eyes skimmed past him to the tall, slim, golden-haired woman who was examining some pink holly-hocks. No wonder Valerie thought they made a cute couple. With the woman's tailored suit and high heels—Louboutin by the looks of them—she and Dylan looked as if they'd stepped out of the pages of *Forbes Magazine.* Jenna tugged at the loose-fitting tunic she'd teamed with a pair of stretch pants this morning, and wished her wardrobe had extended to something a little sharper for this meeting.

"Good morning," she said as brightly as she could.

Dylan didn't waste a second. He surprised her by swooping down and planting his lips on hers. Jenna put her hand on his chest to steady herself as her blood instantly turned molten. Two seconds in his presence and she was already starry-eyed. Man, she was so gone.

"Now it's a good morning," he said with a smile that crinkled his eyes at the corners. He linked her arm through his and drew her to his side. "Come over and meet Fee."

As he mentioned the other woman's name, she lifted her head and smiled in Jenna's direction. She took a few steps toward them, her hand outstretched in greeting.

"Hi, I'm Felicity Sinclair, but call me Fee," she said warmly. "Are these your designs? They're fantastic," she said, gesturing to some of the more artistic pieces the store had on display.

"Yes, mine and Valerie's," Jenna said, feeling a little more charitable toward the newcomer.

"You'd be very popular back home. I wish we had someone like you doing the flowers for our offices and functions. Dylan tells me you've got everything under control for Saturday's opening?"

"Yes, would you like to see a mock-up of the table settings?"

The next twenty minutes passed swiftly as Jenna went over her plans for the floral displays at the restaurant. By the time they left she felt a whole lot more confident in herself and her ability to hold her own with women like Fee Sinclair.

Dylan whispered in her ear as they were leaving, "Ready for another cooking lesson tonight? I was thinking of something along the lines of dessert, maybe with chocolate sauce?"

Fire lit inside Jenna, flooding her limbs and making them instantly feel heavy and lethargic. Her cheeks flamed in turn, earning her a considering glance from Valerie.

"Sure, your place or mine?" she asked, keeping her voice low.

"How about your place. It's closer to here for you in case we oversleep in the morning."

She nodded, not trusting herself to speak. He kissed her again, taking her in a hard and swift embrace that promised everything, but left her hanging in a daze of sensual awareness that clouded her already foggy mind.

"See you after work," he said, ushering Fee from the store.

After the front door had closed, Valerie zoomed straight to her side.

"And just when were you going to let me in on the secret?" she demanded, waggling a playful finger in Jenna's direction.

"Secret?"

"You and Mr. Drop-Dead-Gorgeous. You never told me you were an item."

Jenna smiled. "An item?"

"Sweetie, I saw the way he looked at you." She fanned herself theatrically. "And the way he kissed you? Well, suffice to say it had my hormones racing, and it wasn't even me he was kissing!"

"We're friends, Valerie. Good friends," she amended.

"He's your baby's daddy, isn't he?"

Jenna felt her cheeks drain of color. Aside from Dylan, and obviously his family, no one else was supposed to know yet that she was pregnant.

"I've had four kids of my own, remember. I know the signs. Look, I can understand you wanting to keep it quiet, especially with him being a Lassiter and all," Valerie continued. "I just wanted to say, good on you, girl. You work so hard, it's about time you had a bit of play. If there's one thing life has taught me, it's to grab what's offered and make the most of every darn second. You never know what's around the corner."

Valerie's words continued to ring in Jenna's ears as she forced herself to focus on her work for the day. Was she being a fool for trying to play it safe with Dylan? For not jumping, boots and all, into a future together? She didn't doubt he'd take care of her, but did she want to be taken care of? She'd fought to be independent, to be able to stand on her own two feet. Did he accept her as an equal? She weighed the thoughts in her mind, along with the realization that she was learning to trust him, to accept who he was. Could she take that final step and agree to marry him?

"So, what did you think?" Dylan asked as he drove Fee back toward the restaurant.

"Of the designs or of Ms. Montgomery?" she asked with a twinkle in her eye.

"Both. Either. Hell, I don't care." Dylan laughed. "By the way, I'd like you to see that her store gets linked to the Grill in the advertising push over the next few days."

Fee raised her eyebrows but took out her planner and made some notes. "Sure, no problem. The floral work is going to be fantastic—a perfect complement to the opening and the restaurant in general. About Jenna—she seemed familiar to me for some reason. I can't figure out where from. I'm not sure if it's her face or her name."

"She did the flowers for Angelica's rehearsal dinner. Maybe that's where you remember her from," Dylan said offhandedly.

"No, I don't think it's that. Not to worry, it'll come to me soon enough."

At the restaurant Dylan found it difficult to remain focused. All he wanted to do was race back to Jenna's store and sneak her home. Fee kept him occupied for the better part of the day, though, walking him through a couple of interviews she'd scheduled for tomorrow, among other things, and by the time he left the restaurant he was itching to get to Jenna's.

He'd barely thrown the car into Park when the front

door opened and she stood on the porch, waiting for him. He couldn't hold back the smile of satisfaction that wreathed his face. So, she'd missed him today as much as he'd missed her. That was definitely a step in the right direction. He snagged the bag of groceries he'd picked up on the way over, and raced up the path, sweeping her into his arms and delivering a kiss that he hoped showed how much he'd looked forward to seeing her again.

When he set her back down she looked a little starry-eyed, but a stab of concern pierced him when he saw how pale she was.

"C'mon, let's get you inside and off your feet. You look as if you've been overdoing things today."

He shepherded her through to her living room and sat her down on the long sofa, making her laugh when he picked up her feet and swiveled her around so she was fully reclined.

"Dylan, don't. It's not necessary. I just had a full day, that's all."

"And now you can relax. I'm here."

He said the words with a quiet authority he didn't really feel. In fact, with Jenna, he was never too sure just how close he was to overstepping the mark. He wanted to take care of her, to lift her problems from her slender shoulders and onto his broader ones. Especially when he saw her looking like this.

Despite her protests, he noted that she didn't make an effort to move off the couch, so he took the groceries through to the kitchen and poured her a glass of water, bringing it back immediately.

"Did you get off your feet at all today?" he asked, sitting at the end of the sofa and picking up one of her feet in his strong hands.

He began to massage her arches, and smiled when she groaned in delight.

"Oh, that feels good," she said, effectively dodging his question. "I'm thinking of keeping you on if you can promise you'll do this for me every day after work."

"You only have to say the word and I'm yours," he answered.

"The word?"

"Yes. And in case you've forgotten, that would be a yes to the will-you-marry-me question."

He deliberately kept his tone light.

"Okay, duly noted, and I consider myself fully informed," she teased with a tired smile.

Dylan picked up her other foot and began to massage it, as well, watching as she let her eyelids drift closed. When he stopped she didn't even move, so he gently placed her foot back down on the sofa and rose to go and prepare their evening meal. It worried him that she was so tired. Was that normal? He needed to do some research or talk to a doctor or someone. Maybe Marlene could help, or Hannah. He made a mental note to call the ranch in the morning, and then eyed the ingredients he'd bought for dessert before deciding to put them away for another time.

He worked quickly and efficiently in Jenna's kitchen, combining ingredients to form the spinach and pesto stuffing for the plump, free-range chicken breasts he'd purchased. He placed them in a shallow glass casserole dish, on top of quartered red potatoes that he'd tossed in olive oil. Then he smothered the breasts with the leftover stuffing before placing the lid on the dish and sliding it into the oven.

Just as he turned back from the oven, Jenna's home phone began to ring. He cursed the noise it made and dived for the handset on the kitchen countertop, hoping he'd get it before the sound woke Jenna.

"Hello?"

"Um, hello. Have I dialed the right number? Is this Jenna Montgomery's house?"

Dylan recognized Valerie's voice from the store.

"Yes, it's Dylan Lassiter here. Jenna's resting."

"Oh, good. I was just calling to see if she's okay. She took a dizzy turn in the shop today, and while I tried to encourage her to head home early, she flat out refused. Tell her that I've arranged for someone to keep an eye on the kids for me, so I'll open up for her tomorrow, would you? She can come in a bit later."

Dylan promised to pass the message on and placed the phone back on its station. A dizzy spell? No wonder she'd been looking pale. Clearly, she was overdoing things. His gut twisted in frustration. He was in no position to tell her what to do, but every cell in his body urged him to take charge and to make it clear that her health, and that of her unborn baby, should take greater precedence over her work.

But he was beginning to understand what her work meant to her. Without the support of family, she'd grown up missing the markers of encouragement and success that most other kids enjoyed. He thought about what he'd had growing up, and how he'd had the luxury of traveling and finding his niche in the world. How he'd taken all that for granted.

There were still huge gaps in what he knew about Jenna's past, not least of which being how she'd gone from living with her father to living here in Cheyenne with Margaret Connell. Dylan could only hope that eventually she'd trust him enough to tell him everything, to help him know her that much better so he could prove to her that spending the rest of her life with him was the best thing she could do for them all.

"Was that the phone?"

Damn, the call had disturbed her. By his reckoning she'd had only about twenty minutes or so of sleep, and judging by the darkness that underscored her eyes, she needed a whole lot more than that.

"Yeah, it was Valerie. She phoned to check up on you and to say she'd open for you tomorrow."

"She doesn't need to do that. I'm perfectly capable of opening the store myself. She has four kids to juggle in the morning," Jenna protested. "It's why she starts later."

"Clearly, she's juggled them so she can help you out. Why didn't you tell me you weren't feeling well today?" he asked, coming back into the sitting room and parking himself on the sofa again.

He lifted her legs and positioned her feet in his lap. Jenna got a defensive look on her face.

"I felt fine. I'd been bending down and when I stood up I just got a little bit dizzy. That's all."

"Have you felt dizzy before?"

"No, never. Seriously, I'm fine. Please don't fuss."

"Maybe I want to fuss over you," he countered. "Maybe I think you need a little fussing in your life."

She gave him a reluctant smile. "Oh, you do, do you?"

"Tell me, when was the last time anyone paid attention to you, real attention of the spoiling variety?"

Her grin grew wider. "I think that would have been last night, in bed, when you—"

"That's not what I mean, and you know it. Jenna, sometimes it's okay to let someone into your life, to let them share the load. I want that someone to be me."

Her face grew serious again and for a while she was silent. When she spoke, her voice trembled ever so slightly. "I want that to be you, too. I just—"

He leaned over her and placed a finger on her lips. "No, don't justify anything. I'll take what you said and I'll hold on to that for now, okay? Remember, I'm not going anywhere. I'm right here for you, whether you think you need me or not."

Twelve

Jenna stretched against the sheets in Dylan's bed, relishing the decadent luxury of the high thread count cotton against her bare skin. Last night they'd been out to the Big Blue for a family dinner, where the Lassiters had celebrated Hannah's engagement to Logan Whittaker. Again she'd been struck by the genuine love and warmth shared within the family. Love and warmth that had included her.

The siren call of being a part of all of that, the whole family thing, was growing louder in her mind, especially when combined with Dylan's attentiveness to her since Monday. He'd remained true to his word and shared her load; to be more accurate, it felt as if he'd shouldered the whole thing. Jenna still found it hard to accept gracefully, but she was learning. God, how she was learning. He'd delivered breakfast in bed each morning before driving her to work, his argument being that he didn't want her to suffer a dizzy spell while driving. And he'd collected her at the end of each day, to return to his or her home for dinner and to sleep.

And sleep they had. He hadn't made love to her since last weekend, insisting instead that she rest, and somehow, cradled securely in his arms each night, she'd slept better than she ever had before. She'd been unable to argue in the face of his logic, and had promised to follow up with her doctor if she felt the slightest bit dizzy again.

It was a novelty being so thoroughly spoiled. She couldn't remember a time in her life when she'd ever felt so pampered.

Or so loved.

He might not actually say it in so many words, but with every meal, every gesture, Dylan was using his attentiveness and care to prove that he'd meant what he said about wanting to be there for her in everything. Maybe they really could make this work, she thought, stroking the small mound of her belly through the sheets. Maybe they really could be a family.

She looked up as Dylan appeared in the doorway to the bedroom. He looked so sexy in just a pair of drawstring pajama bottoms slung low on his hips. His jaw was unshaved and his hair disheveled, and she had never wanted a man more in her life than she wanted him right now.

"How are you feeling this morning?" he asked, putting the tray with her breakfast on a bedside table and sitting down on the bed next to her to kiss her good morning.

"Fantastic," she answered with a smile. She raised a hand to trace the muscles of his chest, letting her fingers drift low over his ridged abdomen until they teased at the waistband of his pants. "In fact, any better and I think I'd be dangerous."

"Dangerous, huh?" He smiled in return.

She nodded. "I think I should show you how dangerous. Actions always speak louder than words, don't you think?"

Jenna rose up onto her knees, letting the sheet fall away from her body and exposing her nakedness to his hungry gaze. The look on his face empowered her. He made her feel so beautiful, so sexy, so very much in love. The realization should have hit her like a blow, she thought, but it felt right to admit it. To play around with the idea in her mind and to accept that with Dylan she could let go of the rigid control she'd developed to direct her life.

She pushed him back down on the bed, tugging at the drawstring of his pants and pushing the fabric aside to expose him to her gaze, to her fingers, to her lips. Then she showed him, slowly and lovingly, just how much he'd come to mean to her—imbuing every caress, every stroke of her tongue, with all that she felt and all that she wanted for the future. Their future.

Afterward, as they lay side by side, spent, their heart rates slowly returning to normal, Jenna looked across at the man who'd inveigled his way behind her defenses and come to mean so very much to her.

"Yes," she said simply.

Dylan's eyes narrowed and he looked at her intently, rolling onto his side. "Yes? Is that what I think it means?"

She nodded, suddenly shy and a little bit scared. This was letting go of her last vestige of control. But it would be okay, wouldn't it? With Dylan?

He reached for her hand and linked his fingers through hers before drawing them to his lips and kissing her knuckles.

"Thank you," he said with a reverence that brought tears to her eyes.

"Do you think your family will be okay with it? I mean, we haven't known each other all that long."

"They'll be more than fine, don't you worry. I'd like to announce it soon, though. No more secrets. What about at the opening the day after tomorrow? Everyone who matters to us will be there. Okay?"

No more secrets. Yet she still held one very close to her

chest. One that might change the way he thought about her forever. What the hell should she do? Tell him, and hope like mad that it wouldn't make any difference? Or keep it hidden away where it would hopefully never see the light of day ever again? It was impossible to know, but at least she didn't have to make a decision right now. After all, hadn't she just made the biggest decision in her life by accepting Dylan's proposal?

There was a time and a place for everything, and right now was not the time for the past. Right now was all about the future.

She slowly nodded. "Okay."

"Then I'd like you to wear this."

He slid open a bedside drawer and removed a pale blue ring box. Jenna's heart raced in her chest. Was that what she thought it was? Dylan slowly lifted the lid and showed the contents to her. A giant solitaire diamond, set high on a band embedded with smaller diamonds, winked at her in the morning light.

"Dylan, are you sure?"

He lifted the ring from its cushion and reached for her left hand, sliding the ring firmly onto her finger.

"I've never been more sure of anything in my life."

Dylan glanced around the restaurant. It looked, in a word, *perfect*. Jenna and her weekend girl, Millie, had delivered the table centerpieces, and they'd just left after putting together the massive tiered floral design in the foyer. Jenna had come up with an idea to use three up-ended logs of different lengths, and cunningly secured them so they wouldn't fall over. Her colorful floral displays cascaded over the logs in a tumble of nature's beauty.

It had given him a new appreciation for her talent as a

floral designer, and made him realize there was so much more to her than simply her ability to tweak a few wild-flowers in a vase and make them look appealing. An ember of excitement burned deep inside him. He couldn't wait to announce to all the world tonight that she was his, that they were to be a family.

Today really was turning into the culmination of so many years of hard work, so many of his dreams. God, he missed J.D. and wished the old man could have been here to witness it all. He'd been at Dylan's side for the opening of each of their previous Grills. Dylan had to hope J.D. was here with him in spirit today. He would have been so proud.

"Dylan?"

Sage's voice interrupted him, dragging his attention back to the here and now. Dylan turned with a welcoming smile, surprised to see Sage here. But the serious expression on his brother's face wiped his smile clean away.

"Problem?" he asked.

"Mind if I talk to you for a minute?"

"Sure, fire away."

"In private?"

Dylan looked around at the hive of activity that buzzed about them. Waitstaff scurried back and forth, checking that the tables were all set to perfection and that every glass glistened. Through the serving window a similar hum of commotion came from the kitchen. If they wanted privacy, they'd need to go into his office.

Once they were inside, Sage made a point of closing the door behind him.

"What is it?" Dylan asked, getting the distinct feeling that he wasn't going to like what he had to say.

"Look, I don't quite know how to begin this."

"How about at the beginning," he prompted.

Sage's expression was stony. He drew in a deep breath before speaking. "I got that report back."

"Report?"

"The investigation into Jenna."

Dylan's blood hit boiling point in an instant. "You had no right—!"

"I had every right, as it turns out," Sage interrupted. He shook the contents of a large envelope onto Dylan's desk.

"What's all this?" he demanded, even as his eyes skimmed the words on one of the sheets that had fanned out.

Thief of Hearts! a headline proclaimed. The story went on to detail the trail of heartbroken victims a scam artist had left in his wake across the length and breadth of the country. Dylan continued to skim the article until his eyes jolted to a halt on a name: James Montgomery.

"Just because this guy shares her surname doesn't mean there's any connection," Dylan said, even though he had the distinct impression he was now grasping at straws.

Jenna had said she didn't see her father anymore. No wonder, if he'd been caught, tried and incarcerated for perpetuating such calculated crimes against innocent and vulnerable women.

"Keep reading. You ought to know," Sage said.

A knock sounded at the door and Fee popped her head inside.

"Am I interrupting?"

"No," Sage said before Dylan could answer. "Come in. You need to know this in case there's any fallout tonight."

"Know what?" she asked, coming into the room and closing the door.

"It seems my little brother's girlfriend is not who she appears to be."

"You don't know that," Dylan argued.

"Don't be so quick to judge me, Dylan. There's one thing I do know. That baby she's carrying *is* most likely yours. My investigator couldn't turn up any dirt on her in all the time she's lived in Cheyenne. Which begs the question, why did she suddenly latch on to you? Did she plan to get pregnant all along?"

"You bast—!"

Dylan lurched closer to his brother, only to have Fee step in between them. She looked from one man to the other.

"Guys, this isn't going to get physical, is it? I'd rather not be forced to explain black eyes at the opening tonight."

Her words compelled Dylan to relax the fists he hadn't even realized he'd made.

"You overstepped the mark, Sage," he growled.

"Can you blame me for wanting to look out for you? Read the articles then make up your own mind."

Through the fury that clouded his thinking, his brother's concern for him filtered through.

"Fine," he agreed, his jaw clenched tight.

"I'll leave you to it. Fee, you might need to read those, too." As Dylan began to protest, Sage overrode him again. "If my guy could discover this information, bear in mind others could, too. People who might want to cause trouble."

After Sage turned and left, Fee let out an audible breath.

"Wow, that was intense. What's it all about?"

Dylan swallowed back the bitter taste that had risen in his throat. "Some information he has on Jenna."

"Jenna? Really? Should we…?" Her voice trailed off as if she wasn't sure if going any further would be stepping on his toes.

Dylan sighed. "Yeah, we should. Here," he thrust half the papers in her direction. "Read."

Dylan finished reading the article he'd already started, feeling a sense of anger rising against Jenna's father for his callous behavior toward the women involved. Many of them were widows, women who'd lost their husbands and had sought male companionship, even love, only to find their bank accounts emptied and a pile of debt left in his wake when Jenna's dad left them. Imagine if something like that had happened to his aunt Marlene? Anger welled inside Dylan like a boiling cauldron.

He resolutely picked up the next article. Daughter In On It? questioned the headline. A photo of Jenna, much younger than she was now and with her head shaven beneath a tight headscarf, dominated the page. Even though she couldn't have been older than fourteen or fifteen, her beauty was easily apparent—perhaps even more so as she'd had no hair, so that the picture highlighted her large brown eyes and sweet smile.

Dylan's anger burned into a glowing mass of molten rock as the facts were grimly detailed. Jenna's father, the so-called Thief of Hearts, had used this photo of her and created an online fund-raising profile, saying she was dying of cancer and that they'd needed funds for her treatment. Dylan could barely believe what was there in stark black-and-white. While it was never proved that Jenna was a willing accomplice, questions still remained as to the depth of her involvement in that specific scam, as well as what had happened to all the money her father had conned out of his targets.

The article further revealed that as a minor, under the

care of the state when her father was sent down, Jenna would be put into foster care. That certainly explained how she had arrived in Cheyenne and ended up under Margaret Connell's roof—even though Mrs. Connell had never been known to foster anyone before then. Dylan reached for the printed single page report that summarized the investigator's findings. It went into interesting details about her financials. She'd attended the University of Wyoming without incurring any student loans and she'd also used a large cash deposit when buying her own home. A business loan had helped her buy the florist business. On their own, he could understand and accept each point, but the report raised far more questions than it answered. Like, where had Jenna gotten the money to attend university and buy her house?

Dylan reread the paragraph of the second article that talked about the sum of money that had been donated toward Jenna's "treatment." It was a hefty sum, reflective of the good will that had been shown by their community, and then abused and stomped on by her father. Apparently, the fund had been augmented by a six-figure donation from the woman Jenna's father had been known to be seeing at the time. Somehow, though, before the full investigation into her father's behavior, all that money had been withdrawn from the account set up in Jenna's name, and no amount of investigation had been able to reveal what had happened to it.

By the time he and Fee had finished reading the papers, a worried frown creased the PR manager's brow.

"Do you want to can the Q&A this evening?" she asked. "It might be best."

"It would be a complete break in our usual format. Wouldn't it raise even more questions if we do that?"

Fee pursed her lips. "You're probably right. I guess

we'll just have to hope that we can steer off any awkward questions, though I have to admit, I'm worried. As Sage said, if he could get this information, so can anyone."

Again that sense of being duped hammered at the back of Dylan's mind. It was information he'd have discovered himself if he'd been more diligent. If he hadn't been so swift to see only what he'd wanted to see.

"Let's just deal with it if it arises. Jenna's involvement in her father's scams was conjecture only."

Even as he said it, he felt his own doubts rise in his throat to choke him. Fee worried at her bottom lip with her teeth as she scanned the papers one more time.

"Are you sure that's how you want to handle it? In fact, are you sure you even still want Jenna there tonight?"

No, he wasn't. What he wanted was answers from Jenna. Answers he should have had from her before now. The fact she'd hidden all this from him hurt at a level he didn't want to discuss right now.

"Again, that would probably raise more questions than if she wasn't there. So, yes, I'm sure," he said firmly.

"Okay, then. I'll see you tonight."

Fee rose and left the office. He'd go to Jenna right now, he decided. He had to talk to her, to ask her for the truth behind this whole story. Determined to have this out with her face-to-face, he started to rise from his chair.

A loud crash sounded out in the kitchen, and within seconds a rapid knocking started at his door.

"Chef! Chef! We have a problem!"

Dylan groaned out loud, knowing that whatever was happening outside was far more urgent than talking to Jenna right now. He had more than a problem, he thought, as he shot from his office and into the kitchen to deal with the latest crisis. He had potentially opened up his whole family to someone who could be an accomplished scammer. One to whom he'd be inextricably connected for the rest of his life through their child. One who'd inveigled her way into his heart so securely that even entertaining the suspicion that she'd been a willing accomplice in her father's scheme caused a physical pain in his chest.

Sage had cautioned him about racing into this full-on, and Dylan hadn't listened. Had he been thoroughly duped? Had her playing hard to get all been part of her act? He didn't want to believe it could be true, but a devil of rationality perched on his shoulder told him he needed to consider all his options before taking this any further. As far as he knew Jenna had lived an exemplary life here in Cheyenne. Finishing high school, attending college, working hard and buying a home and a business. On the surface, it all looked so perfect. Too perfect maybe?

"Chef! We need you."

The shout spurred him into action. Right now, the kitchen was his priority; unfortunately, just when it looked as if his life was jumping out of the frying pan and into the fire. Deep down, though, Dylan couldn't help feeling a sense of betrayal. The other night, when she'd finally accepted his proposal, they'd agreed—no more secrets. And if this wasn't a breach of that agreement, he didn't know what was.

Thirteen

Jenna stepped from the car Dylan had sent for her, her gown falling around her in a delicate swirl of fiery-orange. The halter neck and empire waistline drew attention away from her bump, although she doubted she'd be able to continue to hide it for much longer. She thumbed the diamond ring on her finger with a small smile. Once their engagement was public knowledge it would be okay to let the news of their baby leak out.

She ducked her head shyly as some of the assembled media took her photo as she walked toward the front door.

"Name please, miss?" the stylishly suited young man at the door asked, before referring to his clipboard and ushering her through when she'd told him.

Dylan was part of a receiving line in the entrance. She drank in the sight of him in a dark pinstripe suit that looked as if it had been tailored specifically for him.

He was hers. The idea filled her with a sense of completion she could hardly dare believe. She really was the luckiest woman on earth. After all she'd been through, he'd become her light in the darkness. Her true north.

He looked up and she beamed at him, covering the carpeted distance between them as quickly and gracefully as her high heels would allow.

"Dylan, this looks amazing!" she breathed as she reached his side and lifted her face for his kiss.

She was surprised when his lips just grazed her cheek, but put it down to the swell of people pressing behind her as they came through the main entrance.

"I won't take up your time," she said quickly. "I'll leave you to your duties."

"No, wait just a second." Dylan caught her by the hand and turned to the man beside him.

"Evan, could you look after Jenna for me? Just until I can get free, okay?"

"Sure, absolutely no problem whatsoever."

"Jenna," Dylan continued, "this is Evan McCain, CEO of Lassiter Media. He's come in from L.A. for this evening. You'll be in good hands."

Jenna had recognized the ex-fiancé of Dylan's sister, Angelica, the minute she'd walked in the door, and said as much.

"It's good to see you again, Evan. I'm glad you could make it," she added.

"I wouldn't have missed it for the world." He smiled, his hazel eyes crinkling at the corners. "So, shall we go and see what the waitstaff are serving on those ridiculously large trays they're carrying around? I don't know about you, but I'm starving."

He offered her his arm and Jenna took it with a smile. She glanced back at Dylan, who was watching her with that little frown between his brows.

"I'll be fine. Just looking forward to when you're free," she said with a small wave.

He gave her a nod and turned his attention to the next newcomers in the line, welcoming the mayor and his wife with his accomplished smile and polite patter. As Evan led her away toward the dining room, Jenna couldn't help but feel that something was amiss. Aside from getting the message, through Fee Sinclair, that he'd be sending a car for her instead of picking her up himself today, she'd not had a single call from him. That in itself had been unusual.

Still, she silently reasoned, he was under a lot of pressure for tonight. In her call, Fee had mentioned the accident one of his staff had suffered in the kitchen earlier today, and Jenna knew he'd stepped into the breach. Did that explain the undercurrent of tension she'd felt? She hoped that was all it was, and that once he knew everything was running smoothly for tonight he could relax.

There was a loud murmur of activity at the entrance and Jenna turned her head in time to see Angelica Lassiter arrive, accompanied by a striking man. Tall, with dark brown hair and eyes that appeared to miss nothing, he looked incredibly handsome and yet had an air of ruthlessness about him that set her on edge. On his arm, Angelica looked absolutely stunning. Her shoulder-length hair was swept up into an elegant chignon that exposed the delicate line of her neck.

Jenna could feel Evan's tension as he watched his ex-fiancée's entrance. "Him? Of all the people she could have come with, she chose him?" he muttered.

"Who is he? I don't think I've seen him around here before," Jenna said, allowing Evan to turn her away from the newcomers and toward a waitress carrying a tray of canapés.

"No, you wouldn't have. No disrespect to you, but you don't move in Jack Reed's exalted circles."

Jenna couldn't help but recognize the bitterness in his voice. Evan continued, "He's from L.A., and has a hard-earned reputation as a corporate raider—all of which makes me wonder why he's even here. Unless Angelica did this to deliberately annoy me."

Jenna's first instinct was to refute what Evan had said.

She'd met Angelica again at Hannah and Logan's engagement dinner, and Dylan's sister had been gracious and charming. She certainly hadn't struck Jenna as malicious, even though there was clearly some undercurrent between Evan and Angelica's date. But then a tiny voice reminded her of something Dylan had said several days ago, about how upset Angelica had been when her father had cut her out of Lassiter Media in his will, leaving the controlling share to Evan.

"Well," Jenna said quietly, "I guess whatever the reason, the best thing for now is to make do with my company and show her that you don't mind who she's shown up with."

"Make do? Having your company is far better than making do," he said with a charming smile that lit up his face. "I apologize if I made it sound any other way."

Jenna laughed, the sound drawing the attention of the newcomers—in particular Angelica, whose set expression and sharp-eyed glare at Evan showed she was about as happy seeing him here as he was in seeing Jack Reed at her side. A swell of people moved between them, breaking the moment, and Jenna felt a wave of relief sweep through her.

Evan led her through the room, circulating among the gathering guests. The crowd consisted of Lassiters and members of the local chamber of commerce, interspersed with a few celebrities and a smattering of media. Jenna received many compliments on her floral displays and, from the number of business cards she was given and was asked for, would be rushed off her feet with work in the coming weeks. Things were really looking up, she thought, as everyone was invited to take their seats.

Evan showed Jenna to a seat at a table near the large stone fireplace in the center of the restaurant. The placeholder next to hers showed Dylan would be seated on her right, and Evan slid into the chair at her left. It took some time for the room to settle into quiet and for everyone to be seated. The lighting dimmed until only a podium near the front was well lit. She smiled through the gloom as Marlene and her date, Walter Drake, whom Jenna had also met at Hannah and Logan's engagement dinner, sat down opposite her.

Dylan took the floor, introducing his new Lassiter Grill team with pride. Jenna squirmed with excitement. Any minute now he'd be closing up the official business and inviting her to join him to share their news—their happiness—with everyone assembled. It felt odd, after so many years of keeping her head down and struggling to remain unnoticed, to be looking forward to being the center of attention. But as she watched the man she loved with all her heart standing there in front of everyone, she knew she could do anything in this world as long as he was by her side.

She thumbed the engagement ring he'd given her two days ago, and felt a swell of love build inside. She'd never been happier than she was right at this moment.

Dylan wound up the formal section of the evening, thanking everyone for being there, and asked if there were any questions from the floor. He smoothly fielded a number of questions relating to the restaurant before the tone began to swing toward a more personal note.

"Dylan, you've been spending a lot of time in Cheyenne lately. Aside from the restaurant, is there something or some*one* else responsible for that?" one of the female reporters asked with a sugary sweet tone.

Dylan nodded his head. "I've been seeing someone, yes, that's true."

The same reporter asked, "Are you going to tell us who that someone is?"

Fee, standing slightly to one side of Dylan, whispered something in his ear. He nodded and addressed the reporter.

"Jenna Montgomery. Many of you will know her already. She's responsible for the stunning floral designs here tonight."

A prickle of unease crept across Jenna's skin. That was it? Nothing about their engagement? She thought tonight was when he'd wanted to make the announcement. To shout it, loud and proud, that they were getting married and having a family together.

A different voice, a man's this time, rang out.

"Is it true that Jenna Montgomery is pregnant with your child?"

How on earth had some journalist heard about the baby?

Dylan kept his composure. "That is true," he answered smoothly as if the news was of no consequence.

The same man persisted. "Are you and your family aware that the woman carrying your baby is the same Jenna Montgomery who faked terminal cancer to help her father swindle nearly a quarter million dollars from a fund set up in her name eleven years ago?" the reporter persisted.

The room exploded in an uproar. Jenna felt the world tilt and a sensation like icy cold water ran through her veins. Through the haze of terror in her mind she heard Dylan's voice asking for calm. As the room once more fell quiet, Jenna found herself—like pretty much everyone else there—hanging on a thread waiting to find out what he would say.

"Yes, I am aware of Jenna's past and of the unproved

charges against her." He paused and whispered something to Fee, who went immediately across the room to two men standing to the side in dark suits. Together with them, she walked toward the reporter who had asked the questions. Dylan turned his attention back to the assembly as the reporter was quietly ushered from the restaurant. "Now, if there are no more questions, let's enjoy dinner."

An eerie silence filled the room like a vacuum as all eyes turned to Jenna. Across the table, Marlene looked at her in concern, a question in her eyes that Jenna had no wish to answer right here and now—or ever, if it could have come to that. She wanted nothing more than to run, and glanced around the room for the nearest exit, feeling like a cornered creature with nowhere to hide. Beside Marlene, Sage Lassiter's eyes bored into her as if he could see right through her to the woman he'd thought she was all along.

Her gaze flittered past them all, frantic to find a compassionate face, but everyone simply looked at her in a blend of shock or accusation. Here she was, a viper in their midst. Someone they'd accepted, welcomed—someone they really shouldn't trust.

Eventually, she looked at Dylan, silently begging him to believe in her. To *know* that she had been an innocent party in all that had happened. She should have told him long before. Her silence now made her appear complicit. Finally, his eyes met hers and she felt every last glimmer of hope for a future together fade into nothing. In his gaze she saw no trace of the teasing lover who'd shared her nights, nor the conscientious and caring soul who'd paid such devoted attention to her this past week. No longer was he the man who'd determinedly suggested marriage and then cajoled her into love—into believing in a time ahead where they could be happy together, be *parents* together.

A shudder rippled through her body, numbness taking her over until it was a struggle to draw in a deep enough breath. This was her worst nightmare. Her darkest, most shameful secret had been exposed to everyone here. People she admired and had come to trust. People who had come to trust her. Now that trust was crushed to smithereens, her hard-won reputation scattered to the corners of the county. She'd truly thought she'd managed to put all that behind her, but now, well, nothing could ever be the same again.

Dylan's eyes flicked from hers to someone else nearby, and seconds later she heard Felicity Sinclair's voice in her ear.

"Come, let me take you home. This can't be good for you or for the baby," she said in her capable, no-nonsense manner.

"Th-thank you," Jenna said gratefully, rising to her feet as Dylan continued to field a melee of questions from the media who'd been asked to cover the opening.

Fee guided her past the beautifully dressed tables—tables Jenna had helped decorate herself, in excited preparation for tonight—and the accusatory stares of the people gathered here punctured her as though each one was a spear of loathing. She couldn't believe how her world had turned on a dime, from one filled with joy and expectations to one where the future once again appeared bleak and lonely.

It seemed like forever, but eventually they were at the front of the restaurant and out the main doors. Fee ushered her immediately into a waiting car. Jenna didn't even stop to wonder how the woman had arranged for the driver to be there so quickly. Instead, she sagged against the seat, locked in a cocoon of loss, as Fee slid into the seat beside her and instructed the man to take them to Jenna's home.

Fee's hand slipped into hers. "Take a deep breath, Jenna. And another. Okay? Leave it to Dylan. He'll take care of everything."

How could he take care of everything? Why would he even want to? Jenna squeezed her eyes shut, but his image still burned there, especially the look on his face just before Fee had led her from the restaurant. The numbness that encased her slowly began to recede—replaced instead by a tearing pain deep inside her chest.

"It's going to be okay," Fee soothed. "You're out of there now."

Sure, they were out of there, but nothing was ever going to be okay again. Jenna had seen the questions in Dylan's eyes, the hurt and mistrust that had replaced the warmth and the love she'd already grown accustomed to seeing in him. Inside she began to mourn what they would never be able to share again.

She should have known better than to hope, known better than to reach out and take what he'd offered her so tantalizingly. She thought about all she'd undoubtedly lost. His trust, their future, his family. She would miss it all. Would she ever be able to look at him again and not see the accusation in his eyes? The knowledge that, of all the things she'd shared with him, that piece of her past was the one she should have shared first?

A discreet buzz came from Fee's delicate evening bag and she slid out her phone.

"Yes, we're on our way to her house."

Jenna could make out a muffled male voice at the other end.

"She's okay, for now. I'll stay with her until you can

come, just to be sure." Fee popped her phone back into her bag. "Dylan will be over as soon as he can get away."

Jenna nodded, but knew it wouldn't make any difference. What they'd had would be gone now. A man like him—a family like theirs—didn't need the notoriety that being with someone like her would bring. She'd known that all along, and yet she'd foolishly dared to dream it could be different.

Now, she knew, it would never be.

Fourteen

Dylan parked at the curb outside Jenna's house, leaving the driveway clear for the limousine that remained parked in the drive. He nodded to the driver as he walked past and up to the front door.

Fee opened it before he could knock.

"How is she?" he asked, his voice tight.

"She went to lie down as soon as we got here. Do you want me to head back to the Grill now?"

"If you don't mind. I guess you've probably already worked out a strategy to cope with any fallout over tonight?"

Fee smiled. "Of course. Leave it to me. This will blow over, you know. It won't affect the Lassiter Grill Corporation. If anything, the notoriety might even be good for you."

It might not affect the company, but it certainly affected everything else that was important to him, he thought as he escorted Fee out to the limousine. He watched as it drove away, and then turned and went back inside Jenna's compact home.

She was standing in the living room when he got inside. He was shocked to see how her dark eyes stood out in her eerily pale face. She hadn't changed from the gown she'd been wearing tonight, and it looked crumpled. His eyes drifted over her graceful shoulders, over the fullness of her breasts and lower, to where his baby nestled inside her. His gut twisted.

"Are you all right?" he asked, concern for her and the baby uppermost in his mind.

"A bit upset," she said, her hand fluttering to her belly. She gave a humorless laugh. "Actually, a lot upset."

He wasn't surprised. It had been a shock for him, too. First of all to discover that secret in her past, and then to have it laid out in front of everyone at the opening tonight.

Why had she kept it hidden from him? She could have told him at any time over the past few days, especially once she'd agreed to plan a future together. Did she honestly think that if she was an innocent party, he'd have felt any differently about her? Hell, she'd been so young she *had* to be innocent. Even if she'd participated in the scam, surely she would have been compelled to do so by the one person who was supposed to have been taking care of her.

Unless the real answer was all too damning. In general, people didn't hide the truth—which left an alternative that Dylan found distinctly unpalatable.

"It is true?" he asked. Everything depended on her answer.

"What part, exactly?"

He bit back the frustration that threatened to overwhelm him. How could she be flip about this? How could she continue to avoid telling him what he needed to know?

"All of it? Any of it?" He bit out the questions.

"There is some truth to it," she said softly, ducking her head.

"So you were involved."

Something passed across her face, something he couldn't quite define.

"Yes," she said, lifting her chin and meeting his scrutiny. "I was involved, but not voluntarily. I didn't know what my father was doing."

Could he believe her? He wanted to, but all the evidence, especially her silence on this very matter, suggested he shouldn't.

And it still didn't answer the question why she hadn't told him.

"What about me?" he asked.

"What do you mean?"

"What am I to you?"

"Dylan!" She sped across the carpet to stand directly in front of him, placing a hand on his chest. "You know what you are to me. You're my lover, the man I want to marry. You're the father of my baby. The man I love."

It sounded so sincere, and yet there were still shadows in her eyes. Truths that couldn't be told because maybe they weren't truths, after all. The questions that had been tumbling around in his mind all day were as irrational now as they'd seemed when they'd first evolved in his brain. Yet they still spewed forth from his mouth before he could have time to weigh them properly.

"Did I come across to you as an easy mark? Is that what it was? Did you see me at the rehearsal dinner setup and target me then? Or maybe the idea came to you later, when you discovered you were pregnant. Was that it?"

He saw her flinch beneath his onslaught. Felt her pull her hand away from his chest, and in its place felt coldness invade that part of him where his heart had beat steadily for her.

"I can't believe you'd think that of me," she said, her eyes wide with horror.

"Seriously, Jenna? We agreed, only two nights ago, no more secrets. What am I supposed to think?"

She stiffened her shoulders. "I can't tell you what to think. Look, perhaps it would be in the best interests of everyone concerned, especially your family and the Lassiter brand, if we didn't see one another again. I won't stand in your way when it comes to access to the baby, I promise you that. It's what I expected to do from the first, anyway."

She took one step back, then another, her fingers frantically working off the engagement ring he'd chosen with all the love he carried for her in his heart. She dropped the ring onto the occasional table beside her.

"Take it," she said bluntly, determination overlaying the anguish that still reflected in her eyes. "Just take it. I don't want it anymore."

He looked at the ring sitting on the table—its beauty an empty symbol of all his hopes. He scooped it up and put it in his suit pocket and turned and walked away.

"Fine. Since you still can't be honest with me, I'll go," he said bitterly. But nothing was fine at all. At the door he hesitated and turned back to face her. "You know what the worst thing about all of this is?"

She stared back at him, mute.

"The worst thing is that you wouldn't trust me enough to tell me the truth. I love you, Jenna. I really thought you'd learned to love me in return. Last chance. Tell me the truth."

She shook her head, her arms wrapping around her body, her cheeks glistening with the tears that ran freely down her face. Every instinct in his body urged him to go to her, to take her in his arms and to tell her that they could still work this out. That everything would be okay.

"Please," she said, her voice thick and choked. "Let yourself out."

She wheeled on her feet and fled down the hallway toward her bedroom. A second later he heard the door slam in finality. Raw pain, the likes of which he'd never known before, clawed viciously through him. Somehow he managed to walk out the door and get to his SUV. He sat there in the dark, staring at her house for a full five minutes, before starting the car and driving away.

Anger bubbled up from beneath his agony. Why couldn't she just tell him? Why couldn't she share that part of her that had now effectively driven them apart? Dammit, she'd chosen doing what was right for his family—even the Lassiter brand—over sharing the truth with him. What about his feelings? Didn't she care about them? Didn't she care that she'd let them both down?

Somehow he drove back to the restaurant, where the opening night party was still in full swing. He slid in through the rear entrance, but Sage caught him when he was in his office, about to put Jenna's ring in the safe.

"You all right?" his brother asked.

"No, I'm not all right," he growled, one hand swinging open the safe's door while the other closed in a fist around the ring in his pocket. It cut into his palm and he welcomed the pain. It matched how he felt inside. He flung a glance at his brother. "So, are you going to gloat? Tell me you were right all along?"

Sage shook his head. "You didn't see her face when that reporter threw that question at you. She looked as if her entire world had blown up."

"Her fabricated world, you mean," Dylan said bitterly.

"No," Sage said firmly. "Her real world. Maybe I was too hasty in showing you that report. Maybe we should have delved a bit deeper first. I agree," he said in response to his brother's snort of disgust, "it was my idea. But, Dylan, you didn't see how tonight affected her. Give it a few days. Go back to her. Talk it out."

He shook his head. "Not going to happen. She doesn't want to see me anymore."

He pulled his fist from his pocket and uncurled his fingers from around the ring, exposing the glittering piece before hurling it into the back of the safe and slamming the door shut.

"I didn't mean to hurt you, Dylan. You deserved to know the truth. But think on this. If she really was what those articles say she is, she'd still be wearing that ring."

Dylan weighed his brother's words. "You're probably right," he said with a sigh. "But until she's prepared to be open with me, I can't see us working this thing out. Besides, she'll probably never forgive me for what I said."

"What exactly did you say?"

"I asked her if I was her latest mark. I couldn't help it. It just came out. I was so mad that she'd kept something so important from me. Nothing about her life adds up, Sage. Nothing. Not unless she really was a part of her father's scheme and has been happily living off those proceeds all this time."

He didn't want to believe his own words, but without proof, without Jenna's own testimony, how could he think anything different?

Jenna walked on aching legs to her office to tally up the day's receipts. So much for today's cashless society, she thought, as she extracted the float to go back into the cash register, and then counted the notes to go to the bank the next morning.

She'd been beyond worried that after the disaster of Lassiter Grill's opening night, her business would slowly dwindle and die off. Instead, the opposite had been true. She'd barely been able to keep up with demand, and had been forced to increase her orders from the wholesalers. She and Valerie had been swamped working on special orders, and the foot traffic coming in through the front door had doubled over the previous week.

"Why don't you let me finish that up," Valerie offered as she entered the office. "You look dead on your feet."

"No, I'm halfway there already," Jenna insisted, even as a wave of weariness swept through her.

It wasn't the first time this week she'd felt weak and slightly disoriented. Considering she'd barely been able to force herself from bed each morning, or to eat or drink properly, it really was no wonder. Logically, she knew she had to look after herself, to look after the baby. But just now everything to do with herself fell into the "too hard" basket. She was glad they were crazy busy. At least at work she could get lost in the oblivion of one order to fill after another.

Valerie sat in the chair opposite Jenna's desk and studied her. "Have you heard from him yet?"

"What? No, I haven't. And I don't expect to, either."

"Never?" Valerie sounded regretful.

"Never, at least not directly," Jenna responded. She could hear the flatness in her voice and tried to inject some life back into it. "It's better that way."

"I don't see how. You're still pregnant with his baby. That takes two."

"Valerie, please. This week's hard enough as it is," Jenna implored her friend. "Can you just let it go?"

Valerie studied her from across the table. "Not when you look the way you do. I'm sorry, but I care about you. In fact, no. I'm not sorry. I *care* about you, Jenna. I've watched you go all the way from sweeping floors to taking this business over from Margaret and getting us to where we are today. You're bright, you're clever—but most of all you're honest. I know people have been saying things about you, and yes, I remember the stories about your dad from back when. It's shameful what he did to you and it's shameful that it's coming back to haunt you. You're not the person they said you are. The past belongs right there, in the past. I believe in you, Jenna. I just wanted you to know that."

Jenna gave the other woman a weak smile. "Thank you. I appreciate it."

"But it's not enough, is it? You still love him."

Jenna felt the all too familiar burn of tears in her eyes. She resolutely blinked them back, again. "That doesn't matter. What matters is this little person in here." She patted her tummy and was rewarded with a ripple of movement.

"Honey, trust me, it matters. You're killing yourself over this."

Of course it mattered. It mattered enough that barely a minute went by without her thinking of Dylan. Without seeing again and again the pain she'd inflicted on him and the disappointment that had been etched on his face before he'd left her on Saturday night. She drew in a deep breath. It would get better, eventually. She had to hold on to that thought.

Valerie persisted. "I think you should see him. Talk this out some more."

"He's gone back to L.A. At least that's what I heard."

"So pick up a telephone."

"No, really. It's over, Valerie. If I can accept that, I think you should, too. In fact, I'd appreciate it if you didn't mention it again."

Never would be too soon, Jenna thought as Valerie reluctantly agreed to her request.

"At least come to my house tonight for dinner. You can put up your feet. I'll make sure the kids wait on you and I'll cook you up one of my famous chicken casseroles."

"It sounds lovely, but to be honest, I'm beat. I just want to go home and go to bed."

"And have something to eat," Valerie added.

"Yes, yes, and have something to eat." Jenna gathered up the cash and checks and handed Valerie the float to put back in the cash register. "I'll do the banking on my way in tomorrow. Will you be okay to open up?"

"Sure. With my eldest and her best friend happy to mind the younger kids for a few extra dollars while they're on summer vacation, life's a whole lot less chaotic for me in the mornings. Don't rush in."

"I'll be here just after nine, I hope. We have another big day ahead."

"Which is exactly why I don't think you should be rushing around," Valerie teased with a laugh.

"Okay, okay. Don't you have enough mothering to do with your kids?"

"Hey, once a mother, always a mother."

Valerie went to put the spare cash in the register and then walked out the back with Jenna. "You take care tonight," her friend said, then got in her car and drove away with a cheerful wave.

Jenna watched her go with a wistful smile on her face. She'd never stopped to think all that much about Valerie's life beyond what she saw on the surface—married for sixteen years, with four great kids. Jenna was hit with a near overwhelming sense of envy for the simplicity of Valerie's world. For the security within it. She tightened her grip on the steering wheel and breathed in deep. She could do this. She'd been on her own for a long time now and she didn't need anyone else.

But even as she thought it, Dylan's face swam into her thoughts and with it a feeling of loss so devastating it made her head swim. She leaned back on the headrest and dragged in one breath after another until the woozy sensation left her. Then she turned on the ignition and put her car into gear, easing it out of the parking lot and onto the street, heading home.

She'd get through this. She just had to.

Fifteen

She was dragging her feet from the moment she got up the next morning. It was as if no matter how much time she spent in bed, or resting, it was never quite enough. Jenna surveyed the miserable offerings of food she had left in her fridge. Nothing worth eating for breakfast, she realized. She'd pick something up at a drive-through on the way to the store. She filled her traveling cup with drinking water, picked up her bag and went through to her garage.

Just as she pressed the garage door opener a wave of vertigo hit, and she put out a hand to the doorjamb to steady herself. It took about a full minute to pass.

"Pull yourself together," Jenna chastised herself out loud, adjusting her bag on her shoulder and stepping toward her car. "You ate a decentish meal last night. You can survive until after the bank."

She took a sip of her water, then another. There, she was feeling better already, she told herself, and walked the short distance to her car.

Driving to the bank, she felt fine. She found a parking spot close by and then went inside to wait for a free teller. Despite the early hour, it was busy for a Thursday. She hadn't been waiting terribly long before she felt the earth tilt beneath her feet once more.

"Not again," she muttered under her breath.

"What's that, miss?" said the older man in the line ahead of her.

"Oh, nothing, sorry."

"Are you sure? You look a bit—"

That was all Jenna heard before the blackness came out of nowhere to swallow her whole. She never even felt it when she hit the floor, nor did she hear the concerned cries from the people around her.

"You look like crap, man," Dylan's second in charge, Noel, said as he came into his office on Friday morning.

"Why, thank you," he replied in a voice loaded with sarcasm.

Truth was, he knew he looked like crap. Felt it, too. Since leaving Cheyenne he'd felt as if something—or more precisely, someone—was calling him back. He'd tried to tell himself he'd done all he could, that he'd overseen the opening to the best of his ability and that he'd left things in his executive chef's and restaurant manager's capable hands. Hell, he wouldn't have hired them if they weren't up to the job in the first place. It was time to pour himself back into what his job called for here in L.A.

Even so, his mind kept turning over that last conversation with Jenna, and with it, all the questions that remained unanswered between them. He'd done some more research and discovered that her father, James, had quite the reputation with the ladies. Exactly when he'd started fleecing them for every penny had been unclear, but when a couple of widows had begun comparing notes about their new beau over a game of bridge at their country club one afternoon, they'd seen and heard enough from one another to realize they were dating the same man.

After pressure from their families, they'd been the ones to bring the original complaints to the police, instigating the investigation into James Montgomery's habits. An inquiry that had unearthed a string of similarly swindled lovers in his past. Women who'd been too embarrassed to bring their situation to the attention of their families, let alone the authorities.

It made Dylan furious to think of so many innocents being duped by the charmer. A man whose first priority should have been the care and raising of his daughter. Dylan didn't understand how anyone could be so remiss in his duty to his own flesh and blood.

Speaking of *his* flesh and blood, he wondered how Jenna was doing. She'd be sixteen weeks along by now. When had she been due next for a scan? He huffed out a sigh and forced himself to relax his hand around the Montblanc pen he was strangling to death over the papers he was supposed to sign, and which Noel was waiting so patiently for.

"Your EA asked me to bring these in to you," Noel said, putting some pink message slips on Dylan's desk.

His eye scanned the papers, but it wasn't until he picked up the Cheyenne area code on one that he sat up and took notice. It wasn't like Chance to call him here at the office; his cousin usually called him direct on his cell phone, Dylan thought as he flourished his pen across the necessary pages and then passed the stack of documents over the desk to Noel.

"Was there anything else you needed from me today?" he asked the younger guy.

"No, I'm pretty sure we're up to date with these," he said, flicking through the pages. "I'll call you if anything arises from them."

"Thanks." Dylan nodded absently. He checked his cell

phone as he picked up the office handset to dial home. Two missed calls from Chance—yesterday. Whatever it was, it had to be urgent. His cousin picked up on the second ring, his voice gruff.

"Chance Lassiter."

"Hey, just the man I wanted to speak to. How come you're not working?"

"I wish I wasn't working. I'm going through the ranch accounts before handing them over to the accountant. But that's beside the point. Where have you been, man? I've been trying to get hold of you since yesterday."

"I had my phone on Do Not Disturb and forgot to change it back. What's up?"

"Have you heard about Jenna?"

Dylan stiffened in his chair. "Heard about her? Why? What's happened?"

"She collapsed in the bank yesterday morning. They had to rush her to the hospital."

"She collapsed? Do you know why?"

Dammit, he shouldn't have left Cheyenne. He shouldn't have walked away from his responsibilities to his unborn baby or to its mother.

"Mom called the hospital as soon as she heard, but they wouldn't give her any information other than to say Jenna was stable."

Stable was good, wasn't it, he consoled himself. At least she wasn't in serious or critical condition. "Has anyone tried to contact Jenna directly?"

"Sure. But her cell must be turned off. A woman called Valerie answered at the store, but she was about as forthcoming as a clam when Mom asked after Jenna."

Dylan mentally calculated what he had to complete today to be able to get back home to Cheyenne. Home. When had L.A. stopped being home for him? he wondered briefly, and then realized it never really had been. Sure, it was where he lived, but it wasn't where he belonged. Right now he belonged back in Cheyenne.

"I'll be there as soon as I can. Thanks for the heads-up, Chance."

"I knew you'd want to know. Hey, man. You're going to sort this out, aren't you? The rest of us don't care what happened to her in the past, or what she was involved in. We do care about who she is now, and she's going to be the mother of one of a new generation of Lassiters. She's one of us, whether she wants to be or not."

"Yeah, I'm going to sort this out," Dylan said, ending the call. *Somehow.*

But it was as if the world conspired to prevent him from getting to Cheyenne, from getting to Jenna and finding out what was wrong with her. He was as gnarly as a wildcat with a thorn in its paw by the time he dumped his remaining work onto Noel and instructed him that if anything else urgent came up, he'd have to handle it himself. To the younger guy's credit, he didn't so much as blink.

Dylan's executive assistant filled him in on the booking details for the flight she'd just managed to squeeze him onto at short notice. It would mean a stop in Denver, but at least he'd arrive in Cheyenne before midnight tonight. He cursed the fact that the company jet was down for routine maintenance. While he waited at the airport, he called the hospital and asked to be put through to Jenna, but was surprised to be told she'd already been discharged. That meant she had to be home, right?

In the departure lounge he tried her home phone number, but there was no reply. He tried her cell—again, no reply. He looked at his watch; her store would just about be closing. He dialed the number, only to hear the final boarding call for his flight. A security guard gave him a strange look as Dylan muttered a string of curses before grabbing his briefcase and heading to the gate. He'd have to stow his impatience and his concerns until he got to Wyoming and could see her for himself.

A delay in Denver saw his flight into Cheyenne land well after midnight. Dylan was chafing at the bit to drive straight to Jenna's house, but logic and reason told him that would be stupid. If she was home, she'd be sound asleep by now. The morning would have to suffice.

Once he arrived at his house Dylan shrugged out of his suit jacket and tore off his tie. He poured himself a generous measure of aged Scotch and threw himself into one of the large chairs in the living room. Sleep was the furthest thing from his mind right now. From the moment he'd received the news about Jenna, his primary focus had been on getting here. He hadn't really stopped to think about what he'd do when he arrived. Sure, he wanted to see for himself that she and the baby were okay, and he most definitely wanted to know what had caused the collapse that had sent her to the hospital in the first place. But what then? What came after that?

He still had questions to which she was the only one who held the answers. It had hurt him deeply when he learned she'd been holding back and made him say things he never would have under normal circumstances. But then again, their circumstances had never been normal, exactly, had they? That said, he'd been upfront about his desire to want to take care of her from the beginning. To build a future for her and their baby. Seeing her again, after their first encounter, had proved to him that their attraction was definitely not the kind of thing that crossed a person's path more than once in a lifetime. In fact, for many people, it never entered their life at all. He'd believed, down deep in his soul, that she was the one for him. Had that changed?

Aside from his natural concern for her, how did he feel now? Had knowing what lay in her past changed his emotions when it came to Jenna Montgomery? He took a sip of his whiskey and rolled the liquid around on his tongue before swallowing it. The answer to his question took a long time coming. No, he didn't love her any less. Sure, he was stung that she hadn't told him, but it didn't change how he felt about her at his core. He'd accused her of not trusting him with the full story about her past, but wasn't he just as bad not trusting her when she had told him she hadn't been knowingly involved in the cancer scam? Had he been so hurt by her withholding the truth that he hadn't even wanted to listen—had somehow wanted to punish her for that secret and therefore hadn't been prepared to believe her?

This past week had been hell without her. Without hearing the sound of her voice, the husky timbre of her laughter, the delicious hitch in her breathing when he kissed her intimately.

Could he imagine life without her? Hell, no, he couldn't. Every night since the opening he'd tried to see how his future would evolve without Jenna being an intrinsic part of it, and it had been a dark and harrowing place. He wanted her. More than that, he loved her with a passion so great he knew he could never settle for anyone else but her. Ever.

Which left him in a difficult position. He'd known from the start that their relationship was fragile, that it needed careful tending to bring it to its fullest and most exciting best. Had he crushed that tender seedling when he'd asked her if she'd thought him to be an easy mark? Could they revive the bond between them? She'd looked so battered, so bruised. He'd been so locked in his own anger and disbelief at what he'd perceived as disloyalty, not to mention dishonesty. He still wanted to know the truth, the full truth this time. They couldn't move forward until everything had been laid bare between them.

What was it she'd said, exactly? That she couldn't believe he'd think that of her. Somewhere along the line he'd earned her confidence, which was a far cry from where they'd been that day he'd swanned into Connell's Floral Design and back into her life. And, with a single comment, he'd destroyed it. But trust was a two way street. If she couldn't be 100 percent honest with him, too, then they didn't stand a chance.

He had his work cut out for him if he wanted to get her to open up to him fully, that was for sure. But he was driven to succeed in this, to surpass his success in everything else he'd wanted in his life to date. She'd said she wouldn't stand in his way with the baby, but he wasn't satisfied with that. He wanted them both.

What Chance had said resonated with Dylan. Whatever she'd done or been involved with in the past wasn't who she was now. Why should it matter? She was the mother of his baby. She was the woman who held his heart. That was all that counted. The rest, well, he'd deal with it one way or another, provided she'd let him. The morning couldn't come soon enough.

It was only ten o'clock and already Jenna was exhausted. Millie hadn't shown this morning, too hungover, if the garbled text message she'd sent had been anything to go by. Had Jenna ever been like that? she wondered. No, of course not. She'd been too busy trying to be invisible, yet invaluable at the same time.

A call to Valerie, to see if she could come in, even if

only for a couple of hours, had revealed that during the night she'd fallen victim to an apparently short-lived, but virulent, stomach virus that was ripping through their household. There was no way she'd come in and risk infecting Jenna, even if she could tear herself away from the bathroom right now.

Jenna had assured her tearful friend that she'd cope— after all, they'd completed most of the work for today's wedding client yesterday and by working back about three hours last night—but her head swam a little and she leaned against the counter, taking a swig of her water bottle and reaching for the salty snack the doctor had told her to introduce into her diet. She certainly didn't want a repeat of what had happened the day before last, and especially not at a time when she was on her own at the store. She'd had three bouquets to finish for the wedding today—now thankfully completed. With no Millie and with Valerie laid low with that stomach virus, it was all up to Jenna to handle those last-minute things, the things she'd counted on Millie helping her with so she wouldn't overdo it, she thought with a grimace. Not to mention walk-ins.

She heard the buzzer out front in the store. Ah, good, hopefully that'd be her wedding people in to pick up their table arrangements and the bouquets and boutonnieres. She forced a smile onto her face as she left the workroom.

Her smile faded the instant she saw who'd arrived.

"What are you doing here?" Dylan demanded. His face was a taut mask of control but she could see fire glinting in his eyes.

Jenna took a step back. "Where did you expect me to be? And what business is it of yours, anyway?"

"It's my business because that's my baby you're carrying. I went around to your place this morning, expecting to find you there, but you weren't."

"Well, obviously," she said drily, even as her heart rate picked up several beats at seeing him again.

"Why aren't you at home, resting?"

Oh, so he'd heard. She sighed.

"I just fainted, that's all." Jenna reached toward some roses she had on special in a tubular vase next to the cash register, and tore away a few damaged petals.

"Why? Have you been looking after yourself?"

"You're not my mother," she snapped. "I'm perfectly capable—"

"Don't give me that, Jenna," he growled. "I've seen inside your refrigerator. I know you don't cook for squat. Why were you hospitalized?"

"My blood pressure's a little low, that's all. I have to be careful not to let myself get dehydrated, and they recommended I up my salt intake. So you see, there's nothing to worry about."

"And the fall? You didn't hurt yourself?"

"No, and the baby's fine, too. Seriously, Dylan. I'm okay." Someone else came in through the front door. Ah, the father of the bride to pick up the flowers. "I'm also very busy, so if you'll excuse me?"

He didn't leave. Not through her discussion with her customer, nor when it came to helping the guy load the flowers into his van. Dylan even had the temerity to insist she stay in the store and sit down while he helped instead. She was seething by the time he came back inside.

"I don't need babying and I don't appreciate you coming in here telling me how to do my job."

"You're working far too hard. Aren't you supposed to have help here today? Where's Millie?"

"She couldn't make it, and...oh, there's a customer."

He waited while Jenna dealt with the woman. Then helped the client out to her car with the flowers she'd ordered.

"What do you mean, Millie couldn't make it?" he asked the second he and Jenna were alone again. "Don't you have backup?"

"Well, yes, sometimes Valerie will come for an extra day, but she's sick and she's already been doing most of the heavy stuff for me since my little incident."

"Little incident?"

Jenna could see he wasn't impressed by the terminology.

"Look, I fainted at the bank. The staff called an ambulance because that's their procedure. I was checked into the emergency department, and kept overnight for observation. I was rehydrated and then released in the morning with a set of instructions that I promise I've been following." *Mostly.*

It was as if he could hear her thoughts.

"Not completely, if I know you. What are your plans for lunch today?"

"I was just going to grab a sandwich—"

"How, when you can't leave the store unattended? How are you supposed to have a decent break if you don't have an assistant?"

"Well, I didn't know that she wouldn't be here until I got in this morning, did I?"

"Are you expecting any more customers today?"

"There are always a few walk-ins on a Saturday, but I have no more orders to fill."

"Good, then you won't mind me doing this."

He strode out back and she heard him locking the back door.

"What are you doing?" she asked.

"Get your bag."

"I won't do any such thing!"

"Fine. I'll do it myself." He shot through to her office and came out with her handbag slung over his shoulder. She'd have laughed at the sight he presented if she hadn't seen the look of absolute determination on his face.

"Dylan…" she started, but her words trailed away when he swept her up in his arms and carried her out the front door, hesitating only a second to turn the sign around to Closed. The door banged shut behind them.

"Key," he demanded, and she reached into her bag for her set, and while he still held her in his arms, turned the lock.

A group of people began to gather on the sidewalk.

"Hey, look at that! Isn't that Dylan Lassiter?"

"Yeah. Go, Dylan!"

To her chagrin, he flung them a beaming smile and began to walk toward his SUV, parked a few spaces down the street. As he went, the crowd grew larger, and began to applaud and cheer. Someone raced up to open the passenger door for him and another cheer rose into the air as he gently slid Jenna onto the passenger seat, before reaching around her to secure her seat belt.

Jenna was certain her cheeks were flaming. Dylan closed her door and marched resolutely around to the driver's side.

As he got into the car she flung him a murderous glance.

"This is kidnapping, you know."

"I know," he responded succinctly, right before he reached out to cup the back of her head and draw her to him.

Sixteen

His lips closed on hers with familiarity and yet with a sense of newness and wonder that tantalized and terrified her in equal proportions. On the sidewalk, the crowd went wild. Dylan broke away and reached for the ignition. For a second Jenna thought to protest once more, but the set of his jaw convinced her any argument would fall on deaf ears. She'd have to wait until he got her to wherever they were going.

It didn't take long to figure out. She recognized the route out to his home immediately.

"Dylan—" she started.

"Don't mess with me, Jenna. We'll talk when we're home."

He said it with such strength and distinctness it echoed in her mind. His home was in L.A. now, but from his tone it sounded as though he'd chosen the word quite deliberately. As if he meant to stay here. Her heart leaped in her chest even as her stomach dropped. The prospect of seeing him more often would be both torture and an illicit pleasure at the same time. She'd told him all along that she'd give him free access to their baby, so did this mean he meant to make his visits more frequent? Another more frightening thought occurred to her. Did he mean to get permanent custody? He had the funds at his disposal, and the family support.

She shoved the idea from her mind as quickly as it had bloomed there. He'd never once spoken along those lines. Why would he start now? Her thoughts flew back to last Saturday night at the opening—to the exact moment she'd felt her world come inexorably apart, like a dandelion destroyed in a powerful gust of wind. She simply couldn't go through all that again.

When they arrived at the house, he surprised her by parking in the garage rather than out front. She was even more surprised to see the red Cadillac gleaming under the overhead lights in the four-bay garage.

"You kept it?"

"I couldn't let it go," he answered simply as he lifted her from her seat and into his arms again. "A bit like you, really," he added cryptically.

He carried her inside to the casual family room off the massive kitchen, and put her down on a long L-shaped couch in the corner.

"Stay," he commanded, then wheeled around to the kitchen and went straight to the fridge, where he started pulling things out. In no time, he'd made a couple sandwiches on what smelled like freshly baked bread. He came back over to her and put a plate on her lap. "Eat."

She looked at him in annoyance, tempted to tell him where to stick his sandwich. But her mouth watered at the sight of it and she knew she needed to eat. Heck, she wanted to eat this layered concoction filled with freshness and flavor.

Once she'd finished, he took her plate, poured a glass of mineral water and handed it to her.

"Yeah, yeah, I know. Drink," she said, her voice dripping with sarcasm. This dictatorial side of Dylan was already starting to get old. "I am capable of taking care of myself, you know."

He just looked at her, his derision clear in those blue eyes that seemed to be able to stare straight through her. She couldn't hold his gaze. She might be capable of taking care of herself, but being capable and actually doing it had been two very different things.

"Things are going to change, Jenna," Dylan said, once she'd drained her glass and he'd taken it from her. "You are too important to me to leave either your health or the baby's to chance. You could have really hurt yourself in that fall, and what if it happens again?"

"It won't. I'm more aware of how I'm feeling now, and despite what you might think, I plan to take better care of myself." *It's just that everything else in the past two days has gotten in the way,* she added silently.

"Planning isn't good enough. You need more help if you're going to look after yourself properly."

"I know," she admitted. It was something she'd thought about a great deal this morning. One other person could make all the difference.

"So you'll hire more staff at the store."

Jenna's mind raced over the logistics of employing another full-time staff member—with wages, insurance and paperwork—and how that would upset her careful budget.

"At my expense—I insist on it," Dylan continued.

"Oh, no," she resisted firmly. What if he then decided to try to call all the shots when it came to her business? "Besides, it's not that easy to find a good florist. They don't just grow on trees, you know." The ridiculousness of that statement struck her at about the same time it struck him, and they both laughed. The sound lightened the mood, clearing the air as if by magic. Jenna let her barriers down. It *would* be great to hire another florist, someone who was innovative with design, yet didn't mind throwing together the traditional bouquets and arrangements that remained the backbone of her business.

"I'll look into it," she acceded.

"Thank you. I appreciate that you won't just get some walk-in off the street, and that in a business the size of yours, finding the right person might take some time. Can you get a temp until you find the right one? Do they even have temps for this kind of work?"

"I'll find out on Monday."

"I could do that for you," he offered.

"I said I'll do it and I will." She didn't want to relinquish an ounce of control to him if she could help it. This was her business and while, yes, he had a very valid point about her needing help, she would be the one looking for that help. Not him. Besides, didn't he have enough on his plate already? Jenna swung her feet to the floor and started to get up from the chair.

"Right, now that we have that sorted out, perhaps you could take me back to work."

"No."

Dylan stared back at her, his feet planted firmly on the floor and his arms crossed in front of him as if he was some kind of human barrier.

"Dylan, please. You've fed me, again. I've rested. Now I really need to get back."

"We need to talk."

"We've talked," she pointed out. "And I've agreed to get more help at the store. I thought—hoped—that would settle your concerns."

"On that score, yes. But there's a whole lot we didn't discuss last weekend that needs to come out in the open."

Jenna felt a fist close around her heart. So, they were back to her father. Would she never be free of his crimes?

Dylan reached out and took her hands in his. "I reacted

badly last Saturday. It hurt more than I wanted to admit when I learned you'd withheld stuff from me and in turn I hurt you back. I'm sorry for that. But I need to know everything. If you can be honest with me, Jenna, I believe we can work things out. Don't you want to at least try?"

She studied his beautiful face for a long time. He looked tired, with lines of strain around his eyes and those parallel creases between his brows that told her he was still worried, deep down. Could she do it? Could she share her shame with him and come out on the other side intact? There was only one way to find out.

"Okay," she said softly, dipping her head.

He let go of one hand to tip her chin back up again.

"Don't hide from me, Jenna. Don't ever hide."

Tears filled her eyes, but she blinked them back and drew strength instead from the reassurance in his voice.

"At first it was okay when Dad packed us up and brought us here to the States. We settled in Austin, Texas, where he was originally from. He met a lady, fell in love, but when it ended he just packed us up again, and off we went, somewhere else."

"It must have been hard, shifting around like that," Dylan sympathized.

"It was. I'd just get settled somewhere and the same thing would happen all over again." Jenna sighed. "I retreated into myself more and more, made friends less and less. His girlfriends started getting older and wealthier, and he started receiving more extravagant and expensive gifts from them. I would, too, because he always introduced them to me—maybe having me there in the background gave him some degree of respectability. They were usually nice to me, some more than others.

"One of them in particular, Lisa Fieldman, was especially lovely and she lasted the longest of all his girlfriends. There was a stage when I began to wonder—to even hope—they'd get married. That I'd have a mom again. She used to say she'd always wished for a daughter and that we'd do together very nicely.

"Lisa always had time for me and showed an interest in whatever I was doing. She even got my dad to come along to a school recital I was in when he'd never been to one before. I can still remember the big wink she gave me when I saw them in the audience. Lisa gave me a stock portfolio for my thirteenth birthday. She told me it would be something to fall back on—my 'rainy day fund.' I had no idea what that was and promptly forgot about it. I vaguely remember Dad trying to cajole her for control of it straightaway but she was adamant its management remain in the hands of her investment advisers. That was probably when Dad realized that she could see right through him. Despite that, I'm pretty sure she loved him, faults and all, but she wasn't a complete fool and kept a pretty tight rein on her finances. Of course, by the time the penny dropped for Dad and he realized he couldn't get any more out of Lisa, we moved on. It just about broke my heart. I'm pretty sure it broke hers."

Jenna paused a moment to swipe at her eyes.

"Your dad sounds like a real piece of work."

Jenna gave him a wry smile. "You have no idea. Anyway, I'd forgotten about the portfolio until I turned eighteen and some lawyer tracked me down to say it was mine to do with what I wanted. I couldn't believe it. Suddenly, I had funds that if I managed them carefully, could see me set up for life. I cashed in enough so I could get my degree without a student loan, and I kept working weekends at the store to meet my other expenses. I eventually sold off the balance a couple of years ago and used it toward buying my house."

She felt Dylan shift at her side and she gave him a piercing look. "You thought I'd somehow used the money my father swindled to buy my house, didn't you?"

He had the grace to appear shamefaced. "It was starting to look that way. The sums just didn't add up."

She nodded. "Yeah, I guess you're right. Anyway, I was able to use the house as collateral to borrow the money I needed to buy out Margaret when she was ready to retire. The repayments make things tight, but as long as I can keep afloat I'll get there in the end. The business will be all mine."

"That security is important to you," Dylan commented. "Owning your own home, your own business. Being answerable only to yourself."

Jenna nodded. "It became everything to me. It's the antithesis of what my life had been like up until my father was put in jail and I was sent here to Cheyenne to live."

"You were in Laramie when your father was investigated, weren't you? How did you end up here?"

Jenna rubbed at the mound of her belly absently. "Dad's arrest was national news and Lisa heard about it. Despite Dad ditching her the way he did and all that he'd put her through, she was still fond of me. Turned out she had a recently widowed college friend who lived here. That was Margaret. Lisa contacted her about taking me on. It was only supposed to be until I was eighteen, when I was theoretically supposed to be cut loose, but we got on well. I worked hard and she appreciated that. Plus, I also loved working with her and with flowers. We ended up being a natural fit. I have so much to be grateful to Lisa for, but I'm particularly grateful to her for using her influence to convince the authorities to send me to Margaret.

"Being here was a gift that I certainly wasn't going to

throw away. It gave me a chance to start over in a town where people barely knew of me. I hated every second of the publicity that surrounded my father's arrest. It was even worse when the media began to point a finger at me, saying I'd been complicit in his behavior. If I was guilty of anything, it was of ignorance. Maybe by the time I was fifteen I should have been asking questions about how he made so much money when he never appeared to work, but my head was filled with school and teenage stuff, so it never occurred to me to question any of it.

"One of my teachers got sick with cancer and the student council came up with the idea of a sponsored head shave to raise money to help her family out while she had treatment. When my dad saw me he was horrified at first. But then he took some pictures of me while I was visiting my teacher in the hospital. Without my knowledge or consent, he used those pictures to create a fake profile online, and used his imagination for the rest. It didn't take long for investigators to clear me of any involvement, but mud sticks and for me it stuck hard."

She thought back to that time when she'd been too afraid to leave the house and face the media assembled outside. Her father, then out on bail and awaiting the case to be brought before court, had simply taken it all in his stride, even laughing and joking with the reporters when he'd gone out. But for Jenna, who was still growing her hair back, every moment at school had become a trial by her peers, each day more unpleasant than the last.

"When Margaret placed me in school here I just did what I'd always done. Kept my head down and focused on my grades. By the time I attended the University of Wyoming people had begun to forget. Sure, I crossed paths with a couple of the kids I'd gone to school with in

Laramie, but time has a really good way of blurring the edges of people's memory."

Jenna studied Dylan's face again, and was grateful he'd listened without passing judgment. When given the chance, she'd grabbed the opportunity to forge a new life for herself, with both hands holding on tight. Sure, in hindsight she could see that her father had always believed he'd tried to do his best by her. That he'd obtained all those things under false pretenses was his cross to bear, not hers. Jenna knew that now. It didn't mean that she forgave him for it, but it was who he was.

"As to the money he raised, I have no idea where it is. He managed to hide it somewhere. No doubt he'll use it to seed his lifestyle when he gets out and the instant he does I hope the police will be back onto him. I'm sorry I didn't tell you all this before," she said softly. "I should never have accepted your proposal without doing so, but I guess a part of me was scared that you'd believe the worst of me when you knew."

"And then I did, didn't I?" he said ruefully. "Or at least it probably looked that way to you, huh?"

"In part. You have such a wonderful family, Dylan. I sullied them and your opening night at the Grill by bringing my life's ugliness into it."

"No, don't say that. What you went through made you who you are now. And we love you for it. All of us."

She searched his eyes to see if he was telling her what she thought, and hoped, he was saying. Sharing her past with him had made her feel lighter inside, as if it was no longer her burden to carry alone.

"Yes, Jenna. I do love you. I shouldn't have walked away from you last weekend. I was so angry and so hurt when I learned you'd kept such an important piece of yourself from me. I shouldn't have reacted the way I did.

You needed strength and support from me, and I didn't give it to you. But if you'll let me try again, that's what I'm offering you now.

"Everything, Jenna. My heart, my soul, my life. Knowing what you went through in your past just makes me want to create a better future with you, one for all three of us," he affirmed, placing his hand on her belly. "So I'm going to ask you again. Jenna Montgomery, will you marry me?"

Seventeen

Dylan's heart beat double time as he waited for her answer. He wanted this, her, the baby, more than anything he'd ever wanted his whole life. His happiness and his future hung now on Jenna's reply.

When it came, her simple *yes* was the most magical word he'd ever heard.

"I promise to make sure you never regret it," he vowed as he leaned forward and took her lips in a kiss that transcended every previous contact they'd ever had before. Nothing stood between them now. Their lives and their love were laid bare to one another.

"I know I never will, Dylan. You offer me so much, it makes me wonder what I offer you in return," she said uneasily as they broke apart.

"Everything," he said, and it was heartfelt. "I thought it was just a fluke, the way you made me feel the first day I met you, but you never left my thoughts. Through J.D. dying, through Angelica's wedding being called off... even when I was working hard on the Cheyenne Grill's opening, you were always there."

Dylan shifted on the couch so he could pull her into his lap, one arm wrapped around her while his other hand rested on the mound that resulted from their first meeting.

"I couldn't stop thinking about you, either," Jenna

admitted with a rueful smile. "It was…quite uncomfortable at times. I knew you were back in Cheyenne on and off, while the restaurant was being built. I guess I was a bit like a crazy teenager with a crush, hoping I'd get a glimpse of you. Your world, your background, is so different to mine. I convinced myself that you were unattainable for me, that our lives were too far apart and that I was happy not to hear from you or get in touch with you myself. But then I discovered I was pregnant, and it made me reassess everything. Made me wonder if you'd even be interested. After all, it's not like we got to know each other before we—"

"Shh," he said, pressing a short kiss to her lips. "So we didn't do things the conventional way. That doesn't mean we can't be as old-fashioned as we like, if we want to be, for the rest of our lives. Let's not wait to get married. I want us to be together, as husband and wife, as soon as we can."

"But what about where we're going to live? I—"

"I've been thinking about that. I have a strong team at my back. I can afford to work from here in Cheyenne, at least until the baby's born. After that, we can decide what we're going to do next, although I'd like to think I can make the move home permanent. I'd like to see our baby raised here, closer to my family's roots. So, what do you say? How does next Saturday sound?"

"Are you sure? That's a lot of organizing in a short period of time."

"We can do it, if we want to. I have contacts in the catering business," he said with a cheeky grin, "and I know someone who has a real way with flowers. If you're okay with it, I'd like to keep it small and invite family and close friends only. What do you think?"

She nodded. "That sounds perfect. Do you think we

could get married out at the Big Blue? It's an important part of your past and your family. I think it would be so special to be married there, where you grew up."

"I think that would be perfect," he said, kissing her again. "And I'm sure Chance and Marlene would be thrilled. So, shall we do it? I'll get the license on Monday and we can be married by the end of the week."

"I can't believe it's true, that it's really happening."

"Believe it, Jenna. Believe me. You are all I've ever wanted, you and our baby. I had some wonderful examples of love growing up. First my parents, and then J.D. and Ellie. Losing Aunt Ellie crushed J.D. He never stopped loving her until he drew his last breath.

"Even as a kid, I knew I wanted to know that kind of love with another person. I'm thirty-five years old, Jenna, I was beginning to think that kind of love wasn't out there for me, and God only knows I looked. I never expected to find it, to find you, right here under my nose in Cheyenne. And now that I have you, I'm never going to let you go."

"I'm going to hold you to that, Dylan Lassiter. Every day for the rest of your life," she promised, her eyes burning fiercely with her love.

"I can't wait."

It was a dazzling afternoon out at the Big Blue. As Dylan had expected, Marlene had taken the initiative and organized the wedding with the flair and efficiency he'd always known her to have. Strange how he'd thought he'd be wildly excited about today; instead, he was filled with a deep sense of rightness and calm. Everything he'd ever done to this point in time had led to this moment, this day, where he would declare his love for Jenna in front of their nearest and dearest.

He looked out the window of the second floor of the house and down toward the garden, where a hastily erected bower of flowers on the patio marked the spot where he and Jenna would become husband and wife very soon. A handful of waitstaff from the Grill circulated among the small gathering with trays of drinks and hors d'oeuvres, and he knew his executive chef had taken over Marlene's expansive kitchen to create a wedding supper that would rival anything he'd ever done before.

A knock sounded at the guest room door and his sister stepped inside. A smile wreathed Angelica's beautiful face, but he could see the concern in her eyes.

"Hey," she said, moving across the room to give him a quick hug.

"Hey, yourself," he answered. "I'm glad you could make it."

"Well, it was rather short notice, Dylan. Seriously," she teased, "a girl needs time to plan for these things."

"I figured if the bride could be ready in a week, our family and friends could, too."

"Good point," she said, stepping back and assessing him thoroughly. She flicked a tiny piece of lint off the lapel of his suit. "Speaking of which, this wedding is all rather sudden, don't you think? To be honest with you, I can't believe you're actually going through with it. Are you absolutely sure you're doing the right thing? It's no small step you're taking."

"I've never been more certain of anything in my life."

"Dylan, you don't have to marry her to be a father. You know that, don't you?" she pressed. "We hardly know anything about her."

"I know all that I need to know for now. I look forward to spending the rest of my life discovering the rest. As to not having to marry her—Angelica, I want to. I want her to be my wife more than I've wanted anything else in the world. It's a destination that I know, deep in here—" he thumped his chest "—we would have come to anyway. Having the baby, well, that just speeds it along."

"What if things go wrong?" she persisted. "Even when you think you know a person…"

Angelica's voice trailed off, leaving her bitterness and anger toward her ex-fiancé to hang in the air between them. Another knock at the door interrupted what Dylan was going to say, and Sage came into the room.

"You scrub up pretty well," he teased his younger brother.

"You don't look so bad yourself," Dylan replied, taking comfort in the usual banter.

"I never expected you'd beat me down the aisle," Sage commented lightly. But then his face grew more serious. "It's not too late to change your mind."

"Not you, too," Dylan groaned. "Look, guys, I appreciate the concern, but I know I'm doing the right thing. She's going to be one of us now. I'd like you to respect that. Can I have your promise you won't say anything about it again, please?"

Angelica and Sage each agreed, and the conversation turned to other matters.

Sage spoke first, directing his attention to their sister. "Since the three of us are together, I wanted to discuss the rumors that you're moving forward with contesting J.D.'s will."

"You're not still going ahead with that, are you?" Dylan asked.

"Of course I am," Angelica said with a stubborn look that the brothers knew all too well. She might have all her mother's beauty and grace, but deep down inside she was

J.D.'s daughter through and through. "As I recall, Sage, you were originally the one to suggest it."

His eyes reflected his frustration with her. "Yeah, but I also realized early on, and advised you, that continuing with the idea would prevent J.D.'s other wishes for inheritance from happening. Did you really want to see Marlene unable to live here? Or for any of the other bequests to be frozen while you battled this out? I thought you understood that it was more important to observe J.D.'s wishes in the end than to persist in something that's only going to cause bigger and bigger problems."

"Oh, sure." Angelica laughed, but the sound was insincere. "Nothing like the good ol' boys backslapping and agreeing to hush the little woman on her ideas, right? We all know Lassiter Media should have been mine. I did all the hard work. I picked up and carried on when Dad started to pull back from the day-to-day operations. Me! It's my baby and I want it back."

Dylan interrupted before things could get any more heated. Sage was right, but he could see where Angelica was coming from, even if he believed she was wrong. "I would have thought you'd want what's right for Lassiter Media. We all know that while we didn't agree with everything J.D. did, he was a brilliant businessman. He made his decision. Think of the wider picture, Angelica, if you even can anymore. You've become so dogged about this that your behavior is damaging the company. Is that what you want?"

She sighed and her shoulders sagged beneath the couture gown she wore. "No, it isn't what I want at all, but I have to fight for what's right. For what's *mine.*"

Dylan put an arm around her. "We're going to have to

keep agreeing to disagree on this, Ange. This obsession isn't good for you, isn't good for any of us."

"That's easy for you to say," she retorted. "You got what you wanted."

"And I'd walk away from it all today if I knew that was what was best for the corporation."

The air was thick with the conflict until Angelica shook her head. "Let's not talk about this today, okay? We're here to celebrate you getting married."

The men grunted their assent, but Dylan knew the subject would not be forgotten. It was far too important to simply try and sweep under the rug. But for now, they could pretend there was nothing contentious simmering between them. He looked out the window once more, noting that the white folding chairs on the patio were filling with guests.

"Let's go do this," he said with a smile at his siblings.

Downstairs there was a hum of excitement in the air, yet it did little to ruffle the calm that wrapped around Dylan like a cloak. He'd spent every day in the past week looking forward to this moment, and finally it was here. Everything was coming right in his world, and he only hoped his sister could one day be as happy as he was.

Dylan took his place under the floral bower and smiled at the celebrant they'd booked to conduct the ceremony. Then he turned and looked down the aisle at the eager faces of the people he loved most in the world. All except for one, and she'd be coming from the house any moment now.

Jenna had elected to walk alone toward him, stating that she'd stood on her own two feet for so many years, she didn't need anyone to give her away. She was coming to this marriage freely and wholeheartedly. In response,

Dylan had elected not to have a best man, although they'd asked Sage and Valerie to be their official witnesses.

After a flurry of activity at the doors leading onto the patio, Marlene appeared with Cassie, who was dressed in mint-green organza and carried a basket of petals. Marlene flung Dylan a smile and gave him a thumbs-up. Until then, he hadn't realized he'd begun to feel nervous. No, it wasn't nerves, exactly, it was more anticipation. He couldn't help it; a big smile spread across his face.

Marlene took her seat and the music began. Cassie skipped her way down the aisle, throwing handfuls of petals on the ground, in the air and toward anyone who looked her way. Everyone was quietly laughing by the time she took her seat beside her mother.

And then silence fell upon them all as Jenna stood framed in the doorway. Dylan's breath caught in his chest as his eyes drank in the sight of her. Dressed in a simple white gown, with a broad satin sash under her breasts that lovingly contoured her slightly swollen belly, she looked radiantly beautiful. Her dark hair was swept up on her head, with tendrils drifting loose to caress the sides of her face and throat, and the diamond drop earrings he'd given her last night sparkled in the late afternoon sunlight. If he could have frozen this one moment in time forever, he would have. She was perfection, and she was about to be his.

Their gazes met and held as she began to walk slowly toward him, a smile on her face and her love for him beaming from her eyes. Then, finally, she was at his side, where she belonged for the rest of their lives.

The celebrant began to speak, and Dylan and Jenna made their responses, pledging their vows to one another. And Dylan knew, without a doubt in his heart, that he now had the family of his own he'd always wanted.

And as they turned to the assembly of guests as husband and wife, he looked at everyone's loving faces and knew this was the family he, Jenna and their baby deserved.

* * * * *

JOIN US ON SOCIAL MEDIA!

Stay up to date with our latest releases, author news and gossip, special offers and discounts, and all the behind-the-scenes action from Mills & Boon...

 millsandboon

 millsandboonuk

 millsandboon

It might just be true love...